CABLE...GETTING EVEN

Jeffery A. Pitts

Moonshine Cove Publishing, LLC

Abbeville, South Carolina U.S.A.

First Moonshine Cove Edition February 2022

ISBN: 9781952439261

Library of Congress LCCN: 2022901545

© Copyright 2022 by Jeffrey A. Pitts

Cover illustration and design by Stacia Leigh at www.espialdesign.com. "Upper Missouri Wild and Scenic River, Montana" photograph by mypubliclands on Foter.com/CC BY

Edited by Chase Nottingham; interior design by Moonshine Cove staff.

A RANCHER WHO IS NEAR SUICIDE FROM A TERRIBLE TRAGEDY AT THE HANDS OF A MOTORCYCLE GANG FINDS HIS SOLACE IN HELPING ANOTHER RANCHER SAVE THEIR SPREAD, BUT THIS BRINGS THE WRATH OF THE SAME GANG DOWN ON THEM ALL.

Guzzling alcohol as a way out of this world and into the next, but needing money to finish the job, Cable accepts employment at a dude ranch near the hole in the woods where he stays. What he doesn't expect is that the owners— mother and daughter Caroline and Annie—give him a reason to live and a brute of a horse to break. Yet to continue living means he must finally take responsibility for his violent reaction after losing the two people in the world he loves the most. Cable is eventually forced to confront the gang once again, except now they're on his home turf and he now has help.

What People are Saying about CABLE

CABLE is the guy I want in my corner! Driven, knowledgeable, strong, and fearless. His knowledge of weapons is phenomenal and his accuracy with guns is key to his being able to protect his loved ones and forge ahead in his life when others would not be able to carry on.—*Sally Clark, Retired Human Resource Manager*

A story of a young man who finally faced his past so he could return from where he was running from–home. Jeffrey A Pitts has become one of my favorite authors over the past couple years. His words illustrate the pages in such a way that I feel like I'm watching the story unfold firsthand and he has a special gift to write characters with both truth and complexity. Like all his books, I found myself to be emotionally invested in Cable after just a few pages. I rarely find an author who has the ability to create characters with such depth that I care for them like friends. Do yourself a favor and go on Cable's journey!—*Michael Johnson, Washington State DOC Officer*

i

This was my first book written by Jeffrey A Pitts, and I didn't know what to expect. I greatly enjoyed the characters and their transformation throughout the story. The book had me laughing and crying, and I didn't want it to end.—*Sandra Brenner, avid reader*

Jeffrey A Pitts has done it again with another great story. Characters that draw you in and hold your attention. "Cable" has you going in one direction at first then shifts you in a new one by developing the main character in a completely different way, very multi-dimensional. It was an enjoyable read. Once I started reading, I had to keep going. Thanks, Jeffrey, for another weekend lost in an amazing story!—*Carey V. Lasley, D.D.S., Olympia, WA*

Read and review a western novel? Not since Louis L'Amour. Yet, I must confess: that which I began reluctantly, I could not put it down. What a portrayal of the human element. From Colorado to Montana, I shared the challenges of people I met along the way. Jeffrey A Pitts is indeed a talented storyteller as well as a student of human nature. His protagonist is not Jack Reacher, a super hero, but rather simply someone life broke...and was put back together through the magic of an author who knows how to blend reality with a damn fine tale. Absolutely a worthwhile read.—*Kathy Simonis, English/LA instructor: White Pass High School WA - Riverside High School, OR*

About the Author

Jeffrey A Pitts grew up on farms in Oregon and Washington, and spent most of his time in whatever backcountry he could reach on horseback or afoot. Now, this dedicated storyteller's characters walk in the same tracks. Seldom does he utilize a wilderness setting he hasn't hiked, camped, fished, or hunted. Jeff loads, tests, and maintains important ballistic data of his own ammunition, because the harvest of wild game is a way of life to him, not a hobby.

After graduating from high school, Jeff worked as a carpenter, log home builder, logger, and heavy equipment operator. Fascinated by the roughest wilderness areas the US has to offer, he's spent much of his life exploring the wildest country possible, sometimes living off the land as he traveled. From the Goat Rocks Wilderness of Washington state, the Bob Marshall of Montana, to the Frank Church River of No Return Wilderness of Idaho, he's hiked thousands of miles on and off trails.

After the loss of a special German shorthair pointer, he filled the void with wirehair pointers and adds dogs into much of his writings.

An avid powerlifter, Jeff enjoys the big loads of squatting, benching, and deadlifting. He is married to Jodi, his childhood sweetheart, they have two children, Tyrel and Terin, son-in-law Dave and three grandchildren, Noah, Hayden, and Kody.

A lifelong reader, he began writing stories when they could no longer be contained in his head and spilled over onto paper and computer screens.

Jeff derives pleasure from a slow rural life, enjoying friends and family, crafting his stories, growing a garden, and living off the grid in the Pacific Northwest with wife, a German wirehair, and a flock of chickens

www.jeffreyapitts.com

Acknowledgment

To my brother, not my twin, but the next best thing. My brother, my partner in crime, my friend.

CABLE

Chapter I

Ammunition or booze? A difficult choice with only a few pennies over thirteen dollars in the palm of my dirty hand. A box of cartridges for my revolver cost around seven bucks. Surely a cheap fifth of vodka would go for less than six. I wasn't a consumer of high-end alcohol in my condition. Any bottle would do, and I felt myself in a tremendous pinch with no way out.

Eighteen miles lay between the town I took empty glass and aluminum containers to earn a few bucks and where I stayed. I wished like hell more people tossed trash from their car windows. I was pretty sure I'd canvassed most of both sides of the narrow highway while traveling the distance on foot. Hungry, exhausted, with little funds to fill an empty belly and likewise vacant cylinders of my revolver. I needed to swing by the hardware shop first. After, armed again I'd require a steady hand to anchor a rabbit or other game I could put the sneak on.

Forgot the goddamned liquor store lay between me and my planned goal. I fingered the money in my pocket as I passed and thought about needs versus wants. Somehow, I found myself looking at booze prices and noticed the sale. Five-fifty for a vodka I'd never heard of, but each container held a fifth. All I needed. I avoided the look of pity from the cashier as she rang up two. At least I got change. One plastic bottle went into my knapsack, the other I twisted the top from the moment I stepped outside. Two long swallows were followed by the burn, offering the scorch I desired in my throat and stomach. It clawed and twisted my guts—pain I was required to face each day. No doubt it slowly killed me, but I didn't have the courage to do it any other way. I deserved my torture.

* * *

I woke to voices and a hand on my shoulder. "He's snoring, so I guess he isn't dead, Mom." Even with my mind clouded with drink, I could hear the disgust in a female's tone.

More ladylike words came from above. "We don't have cell service here. Should we drive for help?"

"Dunno." The reply changed from disgusted to angry. "We can leave the drunk here for all I care and call nine-one-one after we get home."

Rolling over, I pushed out a palm. "Lemme...lemme leave me...burp...alone." I opened my lids to expose bleary eyes to a wavering silhouette. "I can...take care of...of...m'self." Didn't need no goddamned do-gooders sticking their noses into my business.

"Says he doesn't need our help, Mom." I closed my eyes to dust created by jeans beaten with a hand or hat.

"He won't die if we leave, will he?"

"What do you think, cowboy? Plan on croaking if we leave you in this spot you've earned?" The younger woman's tone exposed a granite edge. It surprised me I didn't hear her spit.

I forced myself to my knees where I swayed like a tall tree in a strong gust. The world whirred around me forcing the use of a hand for a brace. What I could see of the horizon continued its crazy tilt. I fell to my side and lay still. "Only if I'm lucky," I whispered to myself. If the gods favored me, I'd stumble in front of a cross-country truck, except I'd feel for the poor bastard driving.

"Can you stand if I get under a shoulder?" Which was worse, matronly pity or more girlish disgust? I couldn't make up my mind. I lay quietly thinking about it until a boot impacted my ass. "Well?" the latter demanded.

Although I couldn't focus on her, she helped me from the ditch and up to her pickup. It wasn't unexpected when she dropped the tailgate and rolled me into the bed with a stick. I stunk and knew it. The truck jerked—the sound of whining tires and cool wind were too much.

I woke the second time in a pile of hay. Damned if I wasn't in a haymow still wearing my knapsack. Forcing myself to a seated position,

I took in my surroundings. No doubt the barn was old, also tall and cavernous with a pair of yawning doors on the far end. A set of tire tracks made sense. The driver simply backed in and rolled me out. I didn't blame her a bit. Probably didn't touch me with the exception of her boot.

Although my bladder was full, the feeling of a wet crotch and leg alerted me to having pissed myself at some point. I stood and stumbled to a wall, leaning against it while I did my business again in the dirt—this time outside my jeans. Squatting and falling to my butt on the loose hay after I finished, I struggled out of my pack. The devil must've kept a sharp eye on me. My second bottle of hooch still resided intact within my knapsack. Better yet, the haul I made from behind the Mexican restaurant was still bagged. Dumpster diving kept me alive more than once. I'd filled a sack with anything I could find—half eaten enchiladas, tacos, burritos, and containers of refried beans were a favorite.

The food didn't look appetizing, but it didn't smell bad. Even if it did, I'd still eat it. Only things I tried to stay away from was chicken still on the bone and fish. A half-eaten burrito was enough to fill me, but it threatened to come up from a stomach made queasy by the previously downed bottle of booze. The rest of my haul got put away for another day or two of meals. Perhaps by then I could shoot something substantial enough to stick to my bones. Then I remembered. Not enough money was left for .22 Long Rifles after I drank my earnings. The reason for scouring the ditches and bushes along the road was to return with a box of cartridges.

"Looks like you lived. Need a ride home?" I didn't jump in surprise at the voice so close, although I didn't hear my benefactor come through a side door.

I got my first good look at her. She appeared to be in her thirties with prematurely graying hair—a bit younger than her surly voice indicated. "Where am I?"

"About fifteen miles from town...same direction you were walking."

"The dude ranch?"

Her lips compressed and eyes narrowed. "Want the ride or not?"

11

I knew right where I was, often skirting the edges when I walked past the place and sometimes fished the creek crossing their property. "No thanks." I struggled to my feet and tucked my future meals away before swinging my pack into place and tightening the straps. "I don't live far."

The danger in her voice was clear. "Excuse me? We're next to the last owners of land on this stretch of road, and you ain't them."

"Yup." I brushed past—or would've if she didn't recoil to avoid my stench. "Appreciate the ride, ma'am."

First thing I noticed outside was the rising sun. It was clear I'd slept the night away. I might want to consider hay for my regular bed. My head swam, letting me know I was still drunk. Not so much so I couldn't hoof it another three miles home. Three and a half if I counted her damned driveway to reach the main road again. The women's place lay quite a distance from the little-used thoroughfare.

My once planned short-term home now made permanent awaited my arrival. It was tough to see from the lake and impossible to detect from the trail leading past. I left the path to intersect with the water after a quarter-mile. There, along the edge, was an enormous cedar stump from a tree felled a century before. What remained rose almost fifteen feet with springboard holes left in the trunk. The base sprawled outward like a spider, and I accidently located an opening while fishing for my supper. Over the years, animals dug beneath the old growth cedar and formed a cave of sorts. It didn't take me long between bouts of drunkenness to fashion comfortable quarters. In what was once a living tree's heart, I could stand without hitting my head. I figured it to be about ten feet across with plenty of room for storage.

No one located my grotto during my absence. First thing I did was check to make sure my Ruger Single-Six revolver was still hidden. Opening the side gate, I counted the four remaining cartridges again. Without more after drinking my cash, each would have to be husbanded against wants rather than needs. A grouse is what I wanted— I needed a large snowshoe rabbit or towhead whitetail.

With the days warming as spring was well under way, my place stayed cool inside the second-growth pine timber. I'd worked at the opening throughout winter, lining the edges with stone and covering it with part of a blanket I found along the road. My site was in pretty good shape after almost a year, and at six miles long and three wide, the lake was large enough to keep me in fish. I'd thought about a garden, except I didn't figure anything would grow under the forest canopy. Instead, dumpsters behind the restaurants in town kept me going when I couldn't find or afford food until the time came to man-up and take my leave of this world.

The Mexican fare lasted three days. It grew hair toward the end. Then, I self-medicated with the last of my final bottle of liquor to chase away dark thoughts. Oh, sweet oblivion, how I love you. If only I could afford rotgut booze by the case. I'd eventually shit my liver out and be done. My hollow stump would be the perfect resting place.

I roused from my stupor with an astonishing appetite. Nothing remained of my stores, making the only choice clear. Enough line remained on my reel, and a half dozen bare hooks were in my dwindling box of gear. I stumbled from my lair to piss first and look for bait second. A spring trickling from beneath a jumble of downed boles slaked my thirst, although I wished it were vodka or whiskey instead. Cold, clear water merely extended my life.

Disgusting insects big enough to frighten me were found under chunks of bark and wood. I thought most might bite rather than allow a hook to be driven through their external skeletons. Then, a gentle toss to deep water before hunkering down to wait. The morning breeze felt good until I felt a rumble within my stomach. Tossing the rod aside, I fumbled at my clothing too late. Before I could lower my drawers, I'd crapped my pants. There was nothing I could do about the drizzling shits but wait it out. The combination of alcohol and food gone bad didn't set well in my intestines. The smell overpowered even my rank body odor.

I'll admit I wept like a baby. Obviously, rock bottom was deeper than I could've imagined. I lost my balance and fell to my rear feeling the warm squish of fecal matter on my ass and legs before rolling into a fetal position and bawling like I did when Mom died.

My torpor eventually passed. Not much a man—if I could still consider myself one—could do when nothing of his life remained. Something pulled my pole into the water, leaving the reel and butt hooked on a root. Otherwise I might've regained senses to lost fishing gear. I set the hook already swallowed and dragged a nice rainbow from somewhere deep onto dry land. Shucking my clothes after killing and laying the fish aside, I shivered and waded into cold water with my dirty and soiled garments.

My body disgusted me. A concave stomach below protruding ribs led to jutting hipbones. What wasn't filthy was white as a fish's belly. I scrubbed at my ass and legs with the shirt before cleaning my garb by rubbing it together underwater. Shuddering my way back to shore, I squeegeed the remaining water away with my hands. With only my thick coat still dry, I pulled it around my shoulders and left most of my wardrobe dripping from tree limbs.

The heavy trout got me through two days. I cooked it in a pan covered by nettle tops and leaves. An early spring made the herbaceous plant pop from the ground overnight. I cooked it as a vegetable, along with boiling it into a tea.

Energy eluded me without enough protein intake, but for some reason God prolonged my days among the living. Certain my time was finally here, I enjoyed a last few days in my sleeping bag watching waves lap ashore. The day was bright and warm, causing me to lift the blanket covering my entry. Steps outside crunched on the gravel shore, and I reached for my revolver. Cocking it as the noise grew closer, I hoped it wasn't a lion or bear to make the end of my life painful. Dying wasn't what I feared—I dreaded suffering at the end.

Instead, a young whitetail doe walked into the open. Less than twenty feet away, I didn't hesitate to line the sights on the base of her ear and squeeze the trigger. The forty grain twenty-two caliber bullet entered her brain and ended her life. Wasn't until her spasms stilled before I realized my error. Without thought on my part, man's natural will to survive overrode my hope to die. I set the revolver aside and cursed my stupidity. So close, yet now I found myself forced to go through it again, because I refused to take the life of an animal and let it go to waste.

If nothing else, I kept my gun clean and knife sharp. Neither took any effort and helped fill my time. Hanging the poor animal was far more difficult than the evisceration process and skinning. After the hide got stretched and tacked inside my grotto, I cut away one side of the loin. It got salted and peppered before wrapped in a saved piece of foil found in a dumpster. While it roasted on a wire grate over the fire, I sliced away smaller pieces missed when removing the big chunk. These went into my pan for a quick stir and fry. My taste buds went wild while I savored each bite—allowing the juices to flow over my palate before swallowing the meat. Dwindling energy increased with each bite. Organ meat—heart, liver, and kidneys—would provide much-needed nutrients such as iron, vitamin B12, and folate.

Three days filled with protein provided enough enthusiasm for another hike to town. Three remaining cartridges haunted my dreams. Once they were gone, I would have no way to secure meat other than my fishing pole. Sometimes I went four or five days without a bite.

Sight of the highway made me sigh and square my shoulders. A couple pounds of cooked venison should see me through to town, but I dreaded the walk and exhaustion from carrying saleable refuse.

Three miles to the dude ranch netted two cans and one bottle. It's possible I scoured the road too well before. Already tired, I set my pack aside and made a seat against a wooden post. I gnawed through half my lunch before a growing clatter made me set it aside. A pickup barreled toward where I waited. For a moment it didn't look as if it could make the corner from asphalt to driveway. I damned near rolled aside before it skidded to a stop. A familiar female voice called out as the passenger window lowered. "You again?"

Getting to my feet with the meat between my teeth, I swung my knapsack around my shoulders. "Just resting," I said before crossing the ditch to walk the highway.

I barely went fifty feet before hearing the whine of reverse and the bark of tires on the road. The woman idled next to me as I hoofed it away—didn't want to be arrested for vagrancy. "You drunk?" she asked. I didn't bother to respond. She could suck a lemon as far as I was concerned. "I don't have time for this, asshole. Answer the question. Are you drunk?"

Rarely did I meet others eyes any longer when I engaged in conversation. I found it impossible to hide my rage coming from suppressed anguish, but this gal asked for it. I met her anger with my fury. "None of your business, you goddamn battle-axe," I fumed aloud.

Guess my response wasn't what she was looking for. Giving her truck a little gas, she sped to turn it and block my passage before jumping out. "I asked a simple question. A drunk can't help me. Yes or no, are you sloshed?" Not sure if it was my filthy clothes or stench, but she changed her mind before almost poking me in the chest with a finger.

My lips pulled back from teeth in desperate need of a toothbrush. "No. Now get the hell out of my way."

Her attitude changed in an instant. "You stink too bad to ride in front. Crawl into the back. I got a stuck foal needing pulled."

"What?"

She stared after slamming her door. "Are you deaf as well as dumb? I have a mare about to die if she can't finish giving birth. I need help pulling it." The damned woman finally made sense. Tossing my bag in first, I made myself comfortable in the bed of her truck.

I admired the ranch with eyes unclouded by drink as we raced toward the big barn. Her place would look better if they fixed a few of the wood fences where planks were rotting. Mowing along the drive would make it appear nicer yet. Although an impressive spread, it seemed rundown.

Her stop was enough to roll me forward against the cab. "Jesus Christ, lady," I said, stopping when an older woman stepped from behind the big slider.

She looked from me to the driver with a bemused expression. "The vagabond, Annie?"

"We can't pull it alone, Mom. Take at least three of us even if I can find the come-a-long. Filthy bastard was sleeping along the driveway."

No way was I taking her shit. "I'm out of here." Using the rear tire as a step, I went over the side of the bed.

The older lady stopped me. "Hold it, son. Twenty bucks and a sandwich if you'll lend your help."

I stopped and turned to find the woman waiting. "Fifty," I grumbled.

She grinned. "Thirty and two sandwiches."

"Forty and three, and they'd better be thick."

"Done. Can we try to save our mare's life now?"

Damned if we didn't. The horse lay on her side in the stall with a leg protruding from the birth canal. Seemed the little fellow wasn't ready. "You're right, Mom. It's a breach birth," the younger woman whispered.

"She's been up and down three times I've seen, honey. Hard labor has gone almost an hour now." Both women kept their voices low.

Wasn't my first dance. I'd seen it before and braced my feet against the mare's hindquarters and pulled with every fiber of muscle remaining to me. He was a slick little bastard. I lost my hold a half-dozen times before something gave, and he slipped out when I was least ready. A hand tugged at my collar. "Easy, and be very quiet," the voice whispered. "We need to tiptoe from here and leave 'em alone."

I followed Annie and her mother outside. Emotion threatened as I considered the miracle I'd witnessed and was a part of. "Time for us to uphold our part of the bargain," the elder of the two said. "Give us a couple minutes, and we'll be back with your money and food."

Annie gave her mom a head start before turning on me. "Wait here and don't steal anything, you hear?"

I'd never stolen a thing in my life. The more I considered her words, the madder I got. She made it to the house about the time I was kicking up dust on their driveway. I might be good-for-nothing and filthy, but I wasn't a thief.

I traveled a good half-mile on the asphalt toward town before the clatter caught me again. It slowed and kept pace. "I'm not letting you get away without holding up our end of the bargain," the matriarch called. I didn't slow or answer. To hell with them. I stepped from the asphalt and turned my back to avoid the hard wind of an oncoming gravel truck only to find the pickup stopped, too. "I'm not sure what my daughter said, but I apologize for her. Won't you let me make it right?"

"She called me a thief," I shouted. "A thief. I've never stolen a damn thing in my life."

The woman showed me the thickest sandwich I'd seen in a long time. "Roast beef, cheese, and lettuce," she said. "Got three right here."

Hunger and fatigue wore me down. I crossed the road to snatch the meal from her hand. Didn't care about the money—something in my stomach made better sense. Too big for a Ziplock bag, I peeled cellophane away and tore into the best meal I'd enjoyed in a year. Homemade sourdough piled thick with meat—my taste buds delighted at the heady flavor of horseradish.

I didn't care if she watched me devour it. "Hungry one, aren't you?" I didn't answer and licked my dirty fingers and slipped the plastic into my pocket. Might come in useful. "I can offer a ride if you're heading to town. It's time to finish the chores Annie planned when I called." She got a curt nod before I tossed my pack in the bed. "Sit up front with me. You'll find I'm not as crotchety as my daughter."

I glared and said, "I reek."

She smiled and nodded. "I know. Nothing a little soap can't take care of."

We drove a mile in silence before she went and ruined it. "My name's Caroline...my daughter's Annie."

I thought about my answer first. "Cable." I said. First time anyone looked past the dirt and stink to ask since I lost my way.

"Nice name," she said. "One I haven't heard before. Anywhere in particular you'd like me to drop you?"

"Grocery." I eyed the two remaining sandwiches before deciding against eating more. Already my stomach rebelled against the rich meal. In fact, I hoped like hell I could keep it down. Be a damned shame to waste it.

She stopped at the store before handing me the money—a twenty, ten, five, three ones, and eight quarters. More cash than I'd seen in months. Caroline didn't release it until she got my attention. "Stop by if you need work. We don't have much, but we'll do the best we can. At least a meal or two and a few dollars in your pocket."

I nodded while she made sure I caught the change. "Yes, ma'am." I couldn't imagine taking her up on the offer. Too easy to get caught up in proper living again, although being exposed to her daughter might be enough to make me check out.

I strolled the aisles in search of things to get me by. A big box of potato flakes would store well, so I bought two. Apples caught my eye, and a pair went into my cart. Canned mixed vegetables were on sale, and I bought four at fifty cents each. Bread cost too much, but a bag of carrots couldn't be avoided. Everything I enjoyed was out of my price range, although eighteen eggs didn't break the bank.

Twenty-six and change remained in my pocket when I left. The hardware store beckoned with their stock of ammunition, but I stopped on the way to look in a window of liquor displayed. They ran a sale again, but I squared my shoulders and walked away. Twenty-twos were far more important, and I found some at fourteen bucks in bulk for three hundred twenty-five rounds, coming to a few pennies over fifteen dollars including tax.

Eleven dollars left got me two more bottles of hooch—rum in this case—before my windfall of forty dollars dwindled to nickels and dimes. Planning to wait until I left town before cracking open the first, I cursed aloud when a familiar clatter slowed. Caroline rolled to keep pace with my steps. "Need a ride home?" she called. "We're going the same direction."

I accepted and hugged my pack and its contents on the drive. The acrid bite of rotgut filled my thoughts—the burning prospect making my mouth water. Knowing it resided inside was enough to help me wait.

Caroline passed her drive. "How much farther?" she asked.

"Anywhere. Stop anywhere. I'll walk."

"Taking you all the way is the least I can do to make up for my daughter."

I halted her not far from where I normally left the roadway and entered the forest. I pointed. "Here."

She rolled to a stop. "Where? I don't know of a house in this area."

I slid out and slung the straps of my knapsack around my shoulders. "Doesn't matter," I said. "I don't have a regular home."

* * *

The sandwiches last four days. I'd planned to stretch them two, but I passed out after downing three-quarters of the rum soon after reaching my stump. The deer meat still smelled good from where it hung inside high above my open smudge. The smoke did a good job of curing the venison. I figured about thirty pounds remained.

Nice to wake from my stupor after the rum ran out to find food still waiting. The final beef sandwich smelled a little, but not enough to dissuade me from downing it. At least mice didn't find their way into my stores while I systematically worked to destroy my liver. The dead of winter was worst when the hungry bastards searched for any tidbit they could sniff out. Tough to keep them away while awake—they ran rampant while I slept overnight or was feeling the effects of alcohol.

The sun overhead grew warmer each day. Although I got the shakes from not enough booze, my belly was full. Probably didn't put on needed weight, but pangs of hunger were kept at bay through my small windfall and resulting stores. The eggs went too fast. I loved the blasted things and stretched them almost two weeks. Although I'd grown used to one meal each day, not much tasted better than mashed potatoes with a trout and an egg. If only my courage were stronger, I could dispense with food.

My gun got a thorough scrubbing. I removed the cylinder for cleaning followed by the bore. I loved the revolver, a collectable Ruger Single-Six with a seven-and-a-half-inch barrel. Mom bought it unfired before I was born, and it got handed down to me when she passed. She'd bought and paid a gunsmith to fit a .22 Magnum cylinder to it. While it lay stored in my few belongings, I couldn't afford the more expensive and powerful rounds. The .22 long rifles did yeomen work instead. From grouse and rabbits to headshot deer, I dispatched game with ease unless my hand shook. It carried naturally in front of my hip when I hunted, snugged within a custom leather holster my dad ordered. Afterward, I filled the six-gun with five rounds—load one, skip one, load four more before cocking and lowering the hammer. By my figures, my replenished stash of cartridges would last longer than I would have need.

The small inlet where my stump stood was shielded from the lake by timber and brush. While the body of water was expansive with a significant amount of shoreline, I stayed hidden from view whenever I could, because I didn't want a nosy fisherman or official to come looking. Numerous species of fish could be caught from where I holed up. Small game, however, required me to spend significant time afoot searching for their sign and whereabouts. Hours better spent elsewhere—such as sleeping or gathering wood. I knew the basics of setting a snare, yet putting the theory into practice proved difficult. After a year of trying, I still hadn't mastered the trick. Instead, I hunted them and anything else I could find with my revolver. I did better than could be expected—my sleeping bag lay on a pile of roughly-tanned rabbit pelts and two deer skins.

A combination of warmer weather, the memory of four sandwiches and the need for rotgut drove me from the woods. Other than a single trout, I'd not eaten in three days. My hands shook with a palsy not allowing me to hunt. Should another towhead have passed my door, I couldn't have made the shot. Time to swallow my pride.

Chapter II

No sense in hoping Annie wasn't home. She was or wasn't. No was no—
"get the hell out of here!" was the likely answer. I stopped to catch my
breath at the start of their drive and to again question my plan. There
weren't enough calories in me to stave off weakness.

Caroline was the first person I saw as she disappeared into the barn.
Hoping the elder of the two woke on the right side of the bed, I
followed. She pushed a wheelbarrow toward a stall I remembered well.
A nicker greeted her as she parked the cart to one side and reached a
hand between the planks. A horsehead came over top and nuzzled the
woman's hair. "Hi, Momma. Mind if I move you and Stranger to
another stall?" The woman drew a carrot from a coat pocket and
offered it before glancing in my direction. "Oh!" She blinked and
stepped back. "Can I help you?"

I stopped twenty feet away. "You mentioned you might have an odd
job or two."

"Huh?" She stared hard for a moment before I saw recognition.
"Cable, isn't it?"

"Yes, ma'am. I helped you pull a foal a week or so ago."

She laughed. "Your calendar must work different from mine. Been a
month...maybe five weeks."

"You're probably right. About work—?"

"Ever clean a stall?"

I nodded. "Yes, ma'am."

She didn't seem surprised and pointed. "There's the wheelbarrow
and shovel. You'll find a ramp on the south wall. Run the load of
manure up and dump it outside. We'll spread it on a field with the
tractor later. Don't be stingy replacing the straw. I want my mare and
colt to be comfortable."

I started after she led them out. Rather than find something else to do, Caroline made herself comfortable on a bale of hay. Not one to be afraid of blisters, I leaned into my shovel and got to work.

It'd been a longtime since I labored with my hands. I stopped twice to catch my breath and on the second break, noticed my observer had disappeared. Weak and shaking, I rested while pulling the corners and along the concrete stub-wall to remove caked droppings. Caroline appeared about halfway through the job with a sandwich and glass of milk on a platter. "Looks like you could use this."

The sight of the food caused me to lick my lips and swallow. "Thanks." I sat on the floor against the stall planking and savored the first bite. Tuna on homemade sourdough with cheese sliced thick and crunchy lettuce. My taste buds went wild at the flavor. It was all I could do not to make short work of the meal. I stretched it—a small bite of sandwich followed by a swallow of milk.

"When's the last time you ate?"

I'd forgotten about Caroline while I searched for any fallen crumbs on the front of my filthy shirt. I shrugged and combed a straggly beard with dirty fingers. "Couple days ago, I think."

My admission didn't faze her. "I'll be back when you're finished."

A bale of straw was barely spread when she appeared with another sandwich. She handed it over while passing me to give my work a thorough inspection. I sat to enjoy my second meal in the same hour. I wasn't used to so much food. "Not bad," she praised. "You've worked with livestock. Been around horses?"

I took a bite and bobbed my head, taking time to chew and swallow before answering. "Yes, ma'am."

She raised an eyebrow. "Been accused of talking too much?"

I reckoned it was supposed to be a joke, but I didn't see the humor and ignored her. I guess she gave up on getting a response and moved the mare and foal to the clean pen while I finished eating. A little horseradish remained on my thumb, and I licked it from the grimy digit.

Feet stopping a yard away caused me to look up. "How much work are you asking for?" Caroline asked.

I shrugged and let my eyes wander. While the horse barn was tidy, it needed cleaned and spruced up. "What do you got?"

"We have twenty-four stalls...twelve per side. It's almost time to gather the herd and prepare 'em for the season. We need to wash and brush twenty-eight mares and geldings after calling the farrier. You up for the job?"

"Cleaning pens?" I wasn't sure how much she planned for me.

She nodded. "Oughta take you a few days."

Increased energy levels helped me finish the next two enclosures. I went through them in a reasonable amount of time, including sweeping the floor before replacing the straw. Only water and a mop could have cleaned them better. I estimated a couple tons of hay and straw remained in the lofts and wasn't stingy laying wheat stubble down. I wondered if they owned a high-pressure sprayer. Probably not—while the ranch appeared clean, there was a rundown feeling about it.

I was resting after finishing the fifth when Caroline appeared with her big platter again. It'd been a long day for a drunk unused to hard physical labor. She set it on the nearest bale to inspect my work. While her back was turned, I looked at what she brought. A small steak and two baked potatoes—each cut in half and covered in gravy, a bowl of beans, and two rolls. "You aren't afraid of work," she said after finishing. "Best they've been cleaned in years. You've definitely earned supper."

My belly was in hog-heaven. The meal was all I could eat, and I worried it might come up while I forced down the last of the beans. A couple deep burps made sure there was room to finish the milk. I stood and brushed my clothes free of straw. "I'll be back in the morning."

I got eleven more cleaned the following day. First four on the backend hadn't been touched by a flat shovel in years. Caroline wasn't outside, and I saw no signs of life when I passed the house on the way to the barn. Two tough ones were done before the elder woman

24

appeared with a plate. "Caught me before I expected you," she said. "Hope you don't mind...I brought a stack of hotcakes, eggs, and bacon."

My shovel got set aside while I took care not to show my palms while accepting the meal. More of my hands were covered by blisters than not. "Appreciate it," I said.

She sat to watch me eat. "I know everyone in the area, but you don't fit. Aren't from around here, are you?" Nobody needed to know my business. I gave a curt shake of my head and kept my attention focused on eating. "Henry and I bought this place over forty years ago. Almost four sections of hillside, bottomland, and timber. We raised three kids here, losing one in the lake on his thirteenth birthday, his sister to a stupid bee sting, and my husband didn't survive his heart attack. Annie's all I got, so running our ranch is now left to two women."

I considered carefully before answering with a half-truth. "Place looks good."

She snorted. "Looks worse each season. We can't handle day-to-day operations and upkeep, too. Annie's tough and hard-working, but not even she can do everything."

Curiosity got the better of me. "Haven't seen her. She gone?"

Caroline didn't hesitate in answering. "She's meeting with a group to get the bank off our backs."

Her comment made sense. The mother/daughter team likely didn't bring in enough money to cover expenditures. I felt bad understanding why she used small denominations and change when she paid me for services rendered. They likely didn't have readily available cash. Probably lived off credit during the offseason. No wonder much-needed repairs were overlooked.

Annie returned sometime after I walked home with a full belly and a sandwich in my pocket. My back ached, and muscles I'd forgotten made me want to moan in agony. With six stalls to go, I slept from the moment I returned to my tree stump home until summer birds heralded the next gray morning. Forcing myself to the lake's edge, I knelt to wash my face and care for blistered palms. Not much I could do but keep them clean—or at least cleaner.

The damned witch caught me after finishing the second stall while spreading straw. She took a decade off my life when she came up from behind. I wished I could've suffered the same heart attack killing her father. "What're you doing here?" Venom dripped from her tongue. "Drag your filthy, stinking, bony ass back to whatever rock you crawled from beneath."

I wasn't going to argue with the woman. Besides, I'd eaten more than I needed. "Yes, ma'am."

She followed me through the barn and outside, spewing her vitriol with each step. I damned near ran into Caroline when turning the corner. It took her a micro-second before understanding, and she put up a hand to stop me. "Anastasia Compton, I won't have you speak to anyone the way you've been berating this poor man. You've embarrassed me and your father, let alone our ranch and what we stand for. You'll go to the house this instant and clean the kitchen. Do you understand me, young woman?" While Caroline's voice didn't raise, her daughter shrank with each word.

"Yes, Momma."

I didn't move when Annie passed me. She didn't even react to my stench. Her mom and I watched until she disappeared into the house. Caroline sighed and handed me the plate she'd brought. Fried potatoes, eggs, toast from the homemade bread, and steak looking suspiciously like it'd been warmed from last night. She pointed to a folded chair inside the barn and opened it for me. "Sit," she said. "Take your time eating."

Christ, it was good, and I told her. "You should consider opening a restaurant."

"I cook enough for the dudes we get each summer and early fall." She hesitated for a moment, so I directed my attention to the meal balanced on my lap. "I'd like to apologize for my daughter's behavior. She was raised better than what you've been exposed to.

Annie's...well...she's dealt with heartbreak of the worst kind. Forgive her if you can find it in you."

She didn't speak again until I finished my breakfast and stood. "I reckon, ma'am. Don't have it in me to hold grudges. Thanks for the meals you've provided. Maybe I'll see you on the road between here and town." Wasn't a reason to stick around, and I left by a side entrance.

Damned if the old gal didn't follow me outside. "Did you finish the stalls? Are you leaving?" Caroline asked.

I stopped to face her. "Four left. Should be easy for you."

"Don't leave because of my daughter. Please."

"I know when I'm not wanted and refuse to put myself between a parent and her girl." Time for me to make myself scarce before the banshee made her appearance again.

"Pay no attention to her, Cable. Please, don't make an old woman beg. I need you...we need you to help get this place ready. If I've learned anything over the past two years, this place requires the strong hand of a man."

I'd made a mistake. Rather than get paid in cash so I could end a half-finished job with booze, I'd gotten fed without a way to drink myself to death. Perhaps it was time to see if the Ruger was my way out, but first to finish what I promised. "I'll get 'em."

I didn't take long to complete the last stalls which were used most and cleaned, but I noticed the top plank on most pens were chewed the way horses tend to do when bored or out of habit. I doubted any suffered a nutritional deficiency. I'd exposed a healthy stack of lumber stored in the loft—hidden under bales of straw. A quick search of the tack room yielded a tape measure, hammer, nails, and a handsaw.

Starting with the worst stalls, I knocked the top railing off and used it as a template—barely holding together in the middle. The job to saw the replacement, fit it, and nail it into place was but a few minutes. I'd finished those in the worst condition when Caroline came to check on the banging. She stopped next to me with a surprised look. "Oh," she said with a hand over her mouth. "Cable, they're beautiful. It's hard to remember a time when our pens looked so good."

"Finished the stalls early and wanted to give you an honest day of work." I peered out the window to gauge the time of day. "I should have 'em done before I leave."

The last few went quicker than I supposed. Many of the gate hinges and latches loosened over the years, and I took time to tighten the screws and give each a squirt of oil. I was putting things away when Caroline appeared again with her tray filled with supper. Pot roast, mashed potatoes and gravy, and cooked carrots. I finished quickly—eager to leave Annie and the ranch in my rearview mirror—except Caroline asked me to show her my repairs. My bragging took a bit, but her joy in finding how easy each gate swung and latched sucked me in.

A present awaited me at the end of their driveway when I left for my stump. A bag with a large note attached and addressed to me. I opened it to find the motherlode—a fifth of 190 proof Everclear grain spirits. If I couldn't finish the job with such a powerful alcohol, the afterlife wasn't yet ready for me.

The first swallow burned from taste buds to belly and made my eyes water. I stopped to gag and cough, clearing my throat for what was to come. Another pull on the jug was every bit as bad, but already the alcohol started working its way through my veins. Wouldn't take long if I was man enough.

I made it a couple hundred yards before falling to the seat of my pants. My guts churning, eyesight hazy, and the world spinning, I stayed where I was along the road. The alcohol gave me the bravery I needed. A hard pull on the jug—opening my throat as best I could—I gasped and repeated it. The landscape around me grayed as my eyesight failed. Never relinquishing my grip on the neck, I forced myself to swallow more.

Tipping to my side didn't hurt, although I was vaguely aware it should. The powerful liquor coursed through my veins, providing the poisoning I desired. Pulling the bottle to my mouth a last time, I was surprised to find my hand empty. The end I longed for neared, and my breathing slowed because there was no need.

Time ceased to exist as I waited, wishing I could finish the grain alcohol. Something far off moved, and I caught sight of them in the distance, coming closer with each step. Both seemed sad where I expected joy at our reunion. My arms held wide, I hoped they would run into them, but they stopped out of reach. "Jess..." I slurred. "I miss you, Jess..." I wanted to hold them, but they backed away, staying out of reach. "Dan...Danny?"

Something struck me. Hard. The apparitions fled as I battled to stay with them. "Open your eyes, Cable," a loud voice ordered. "You're not dying on my watch." Fingers pried my lids apart, but I couldn't see. Perhaps I wouldn't return to my earthly plane. *Wait, Jess. Wait. I'm coming.* As if reading my mind, she appeared from behind a curtain before backing away with Danny and shaking her head.

"They're on their way, Momma." God, just hand me the bottle. If I never heard Annie's voice again, I'd be happy man. A dead one, but happy.

The return comment was grim. "You'd better hope they get here in time, girl. This man doesn't have long."

"I'm sorry, I'm sorry, I'm sorry," Annie said.

I needed the bottle. If the voices made sense, I needed more booze in my system. So close, so very close, yet I couldn't move a muscle to reach and finish the job. Mist swirled where Jess and Danny departed. I couldn't forget their sadness.

Hands rolled me to my side. My palm fell to the ground hitting the bottle. My fingers clenched at the neck in an effort to suckle at the teat of sweet oblivion. "No, you don't, bastard." A strong grip twisted it from mine without effort. My final chance at rejoining loved ones gone, I wept for all I lost.

* * *

I most likely provided the female deputy sheriff with a different account than Annie or Caroline, perhaps both. The deputy seemed to believe Annie supplied me with the alcohol—an account I vigorously contradicted. Instead, I admitted to stealing it while using their bathroom. A three-day stay in the hospital after getting my stomach pumped and a tube inserted to keep me breathing went a long way in me deciding no charges need be filed. I was no different than millions of other drunks.

An IV drip and six meals over seventy-two hours helped me regain some strength, but the trek back to my stump hide-a-way wasn't a hike I looked forward to. I enjoyed the opportunity for a long shower before I left, first I'd gotten in almost eighteen months. Without a nickel in my pockets, I couldn't even purchase a bar of soap to keep up on my neglected hygiene. Instead, I kept a sandwich bag coming with a meal and squirted it full of hand soap from the bathroom. My wet washcloth got dropped in a pocket of my coat. With my body and hair clean, I hated to slide into the filthy jacket.

Although I protested, my nurse insisted she push me outside in a wheelchair after my formal discharge. We got to the lobby and almost ran over Caroline carrying a bag and hurrying in my direction. "Cable!" You look different."

I ran a hand through my hair, pushing it out of my eyes. Most of it fell back. "Amazing what a little soap and hot water can accomplish."

"I'm sorry I'm late. I went through Henry's things and brought a change of clothes for you. He was much heavier toward the last, but they're..." Her eyes darted to the filthy rags I wore. "...they should fit," she finished.

I sure as hell didn't need charity. Another bottle of Everclear was as far as I'd go. She got a lazy hand waved in her direction. "Thanks, I'm good."

She followed us outside. The nurse disappeared after making sure I felt well enough to stand on my own. I bet she didn't appreciate the stench of my threadbare rags any more than I did. Caroline tried to push the ones she brought into my arms. "A bit worn and dated, but they're quality clothing."

The soap stored in my pocket made me nervous. I sure as hell didn't want it to rupture. "Make you a deal," I said. "Give me a ride, and I'll consider your offer."

Caroline did better than a ride. Turns out she came prepared. Still before noon, I'd only eaten breakfast. On the seat between us were two egg salad sandwiches. She pushed them nearer to me and pointed to a travel mug in the cupholder. "Not sure if you like coffee, but it should still be hot."

She was right, and it was. I sighed after a sip, my taste buds having forgotten the robust flavor. I nursed it and made the sandwiches last until reaching their place. Caroline slowed as if to turn up her drive. "Let me out here," I said. "I can walk home."

She braked to a stop. "You were discharged from a hospital less than thirty minutes ago. Let us take care of you until you're a hundred percent again."

"No, thank you. The farther I can stay from your daughter the better. Unless she's got another bottle of hooch."

Her jaw dropped. "You barely survived, and you're ready to drink more? Are you out of your mind?"

I opened the door and struggled to unfasten the seatbelt. "My problems are none of your business, lady."

She continued to stare. "You're not talking about a problem, Cable. You've expressed a death wish."

"Like I said..." My tone was less than friendly after finally getting loose of the harness. "It's none of your business."

Caroline finally nodded. "You're right. It's not, but grant an old woman a last wish and let me drive you the rest of the way."

I entered the woods as quick as I could when she stopped the second time, so she couldn't ask more of me. After reaching my stump and find nothing bothered my things, I changed into the duds she sent. A nice pair of jeans were in the bag with an undershirt and a long-sleeved checkered flannel. Caroline didn't forget underwear nor socks. Still reasonably clean from my earlier shower, I sighed my pleasure after changing.

I didn't blame Annie for providing me the means for my demise. I guessed she thought it a prank and didn't consider the possible outcome. While I wouldn't hold it against her, neither did I want her as an employer or even casual acquaintance.

My time in the hospital and hike to my home left me exhausted. I rinsed my cup in the clear spring and dipped it full. Drinking until all thirst was slaked, I retired to my sleeping bag after shaking it free of possible bugs. Resting inside my stump, I found sleep much more peaceful.

I woke sometime after dark, my bladder screaming at me. With the moon offering enough illumination, I sighed in relief after my stream started. My eyes darted toward the water when I heard the slap of a jumping fish. The sound reminded me to toss a line with two baited hooks for a possible breakfast. A small chunk of venison stuck to a bone tossed aside was enough. I cast and secured the pole against a fish dragging it in. My head barely hit the pillow before I fell into another deep slumber.

The sun was well over the horizon when my eyes opened. I'd been dreaming about better days and of the two faces I longed to join. So real were they I wept after coming to my senses. Needing to rejoin them, I fought to sleep again without success.

A check of my fishing rig netted me a fish I couldn't identify and another I knew as a lake trout. It wasn't easy to wind in six pounds of fresh meat. Building a smudge in my firepit and laying both butterflied fish on the grate I'd found, I sat back to nurse a cup of water and watch them cook. What I couldn't eat would keep a couple days after curing due to all the smoke they absorbed.

Depression struck hard after I finished eating. There wasn't much to do but drink more water before losing myself in the sleeping bag. My stomach filled, I hoped to return to dreams of the past. My lost opportunity weighed heavily.

Two days got filled with little more than eating and dozing. I reckoned the hospital didn't provide quality nighttime rest judging by how much time I put in my bag. I figure I was awake four hours in forty-eight. Perhaps it was my body healing itself. All was for naught—I'd find a way out sooner than later.

I noticed the offering the third morning after returning from the hospital when I rolled to my side and looked out the doorway. Something wrapped in a towel lay a few feet from the opening of my stump. Reaching under a dirty shirt, I drew the Ruger from its leather scabbard. Someone located my lair. Throwing back the top of my fiber-filled bag, I crouched and peered from within my once-safe confines.

No sign was left behind, nor could I make out anyone skulking nearby. With my gun in one hand, I used a stick to pull back the cloth and reveal what was beneath. Looked like a foil-covered platter. Laying a hand on it told me whatever was inside was warm. I unwrapped it and stared. Chunked fried potatoes, scrambled eggs, a thick ham steak, and four buns. No doubt who left it behind—I clearly recognized the flower pattern on a plastic platter.

Caroline. Somehow, the old woman—who shouldn't be wandering the woods—tracked me. She must have cooked and left their ranch early to leave her offering. After locating me without my knowledge, she returned with much needed food. It creeped me out to realize someone looked in at me at least twice while I slumbered.

The food still warm, I squatted at the water's edge and ate with my fingers. A long time passed since needing a fork. Probably appeared like a wildman—taking a bite, then glancing around again before stuffing in the next. I moved to a log after finishing and burped. Noticing my paws were becoming grimy, I retrieved the hospital soap and washed my hands and rinsed my face.

What to do about being located? The problem weighed on my mind. If it came down to it, I hated to vacate the comfort of my stump. It took me a long time to make it the way I wanted. The floor was flat with every stone tossed outside, along with plenty of room to stretch out, sit, or even stand. Smoke got diffused as it worked its way upward and out fissures. My firepit was about two feet across and level enough for my grate. I even stayed comfortable inside with winter snow and heavy wind. Wood was stacked high on the far side—I brought an armload back with me each time I went out whether a blaze burned or not.

I left the towel folded neatly with the plate on top where I found them. The foil got saved inside my grotto. It came in handy when cooking almost anything. With my energy levels on the uptick, I took the time to search for my dinner. My .22 holstered and a few extra cartridges in my pocket, I traveled the shoreline from inside the timber searching for anything I could eat to carry in a plastic mesh bag made for potatoes in my pocket.

My return to camp was triumphant. I'd found a patch of morel mushrooms. Not just a few, but enough to keep me fed for a week if I was careful. I'd filled my bag to bulging with the delicious fungi. Adequate salt and pepper remained in my stores. I'd wash, salt, and wrap the delicate morsels in the foil and let them steam above the fire. Looking forward to my meal, I entered my camping area and stopped dead in my tracks. *"You!"*

Annie stood from where she sat on my log near the water. "I'm sorry. I'm so, so sorry," she cried and buried her face in her hands.

I pointed at the way back to the road after she stopped sobbing. "Get the hell out of here and don't come back. Forget where you found me."

She shook her head. "We need you. Mom made me see we both need you."

"Funny, but I don't need you or your shitty attitude. Find someone else to make their life miserable."

Her jaw tightened, and I reckoned I found a weakness. "I said I'm sorry. I should have never put the bottle where you'd find it."

I sneered. "You don't get it, do you? I'm happy about the bottle. In fact, leave another and don't come back." This time I would drain the jug in a few minutes on an empty belly to get the job done right.

Annie stared. "You got some sort of death wish?"

"Leave me alone." I squatted at the lake edge to rinse a double handful of my dinner, making sure dirt, pine needles, and bugs got washed from the delicate meat.

She didn't offer even brief respite. "Mom and I don't have money to spare, but we can put you up and provide three squares per day. We have customers coming next week and can't afford to hire a handyman."

I ducked inside my stump for salt, foil, and the fire. Ignoring Annie, I drained, seasoned, and carefully wrapped a couple pounds of morels. Embers smoldered, and I stirred them before breaking twigs to build a blaze. A glance outside let me know my intruding visitor wasn't going anywhere. Ten minutes, and I leaned to place my meal over a bed of coals. They wouldn't take long to cook. My mouth watered in anticipation.

Annie leaned against my home after I took a seat outside. Too nice of a day to eat in. She watched while I opened the foil and steam boiled out. "Looks good." I ignored her to fish out a piece with a sharpened stick. It burned my tongue but tasted better than any gourmet cook could produce. Perhaps hunger was the secret sauce. "You'll be out of the elements with a full stomach," she said.

It took until the sun was low on the horizon before she folded her cards. I think she was about to say something until I turned my back and left her outside. I lit the stub of a candle and set it on a carved shelf before dropping my curtain into place and blocking her out. There wasn't much light, but it afforded enough to crawl into my bag. I'd gotten my belly full of a certain raven-haired woman I wanted nothing to do with.

Chapter III

Suspicious noises outside my stump woke me. Nothing loud, just enough to get my attention. Light flickered around my cloth door dancing in a delicate breeze. Time to piss, eat a morel breakfast, then return to bed unless something edible was within range. Holding the revolver in my right hand and a long stick in the other, I moved the entry cover and prepared to cock and shoot. Instead, both Annie and Caroline waited outside of my tree trunk. I groaned and tossed the stick aside to block them out. "We brought breakfast for you," Caroline called.

"Go away. Both of you."

It seemed they weren't ready to give up. "You need us as much as we need you," she said. "We'd like you to know that we've got a place set aside if you're interested. Breakfast, lunch, and supper every day. We'll have to wait to see how much we can afford after the season ends, but I promise to make it worth your while."

"Go away."

"I'm leaving the food. Be sure to eat before it gets colder." I could barely hear their steps as they disappeared.

A big plate of biscuits and gravy wrapped in a thick towel awaited me, along with another of sausage patties and eggs. A thermos was left next to it. I wasn't going to waste good food, but it was time to consider moving on.

I savored each sip of coffee—the single item I omitted purchasing—not finishing the final cup until a couple hours later. Checking the jar inside my stump, I counted two dollars seventy-three cents. Not enough to purchase even a pound. My mouth watered when thinking of the many gourmet roasts I once enjoyed.

Caroline was surprised to see me in the afternoon, but I'm not sure about Annie. Leaving most of my gear stored inside the stump but my pack and a handful of personal items, I reached their ranch before supper. Caroline opened the door after I knocked. "Cable! We're so glad you came. Please, come inside." Annie appeared from another room at her mother's exclamation.

Instead of entering, I made my stand on the porch and offered her thermos and plate back. The foil was folded and left for emergencies inside my former home, which got carefully camouflaged. "Point me to my bunk and make a list of jobs you want done." I planned to help them, but no one said I needed to be friendly. Perhaps a strict attitude would keep the harpy at bay.

My new boss stepped outside onto the oversized covered and screened veranda containing a dozen small picnic tables. She seemed willing to go along. "Certainly. Come with me." Caroline enjoyed good posture for her age and chosen career. Tall and slender with salt and pepper hair reaching past her shoulders, one need only a glance to see Annie's future. I stayed even with her to walk behind their machine shed housing two tractors and other machinery I couldn't quite make out. She stopped at the door of an older Airstream camp trailer in back. "I wish it were bigger, but we'd like you to stay here. The cabins are for guests without the amenities you'll enjoy." I followed her inside and appreciated the quality surrounding me. It consisted of a small couch, basic kitchen with dining table, and a queen-sized bed I could close off from the rest with a fabric slider. I opened a door, expecting storage only to see a toilet, sink, and shower. "Everything works. You've got hot water, and the bathroom is connected to our septic."

I pointed. "The refrigerator?"

"It's already cold with a little freezer inside." She pointed to the ceiling. "Air conditioning works, too. The trailer is connected to its own circuit."

She left me to make myself at home and find a place for my meager belongings. My carefully packed hospital soap was left stored in my stump. A nightstand drawer next to the bed was big enough to house my holstered revolver and box of cartridges. I read a tag inside the door, and although the camper was listed at twenty-one feet, it was plenty big for me.

With the bathroom fully stocked and a stack of fluffy towels, I couldn't wait to shower. Searching through storage hoping for a razor, I was not only successful but found electric clippers, too. I couldn't stand what I saw each time I looked in the mirror. Wild and greasy hair reaching my shoulders combined with a beard touching my second shirt button needed to go.

My whiskers were shorn first. It shocked me to see the amount of gray within the growing pile. Too much for a mere thirty-two years of life. Rather than go cleanshaven, I shortened my beard to a quarter inch and moved to my scalp with a half-inch guide. It got the same treatment—leaving me appalled at the snow sprinkled above my ears. My natural color once a dark brown, I guessed forty percent was prematurely white.

My shower was long, hot, and soapy after spending quality time enjoying the toilet. I scrubbed my head and body with a wash cloth until my skin grew raw. A loud knock sounded when I stopped the water. "Cable? I'm leaving a pile of clothes inside," Caroline called. "You're welcome to use what you want and fits. Bring back anything you don't. We'll serve supper in an hour, so don't forget your dirty clothes."

Caroline's husband Henry must have been tall and fairly thin at one point. Four pairs of jeans still fit loose, but were long enough for my legs. At six-two, I was used to secondhand trousers too short. Clip-on suspenders held my britches up, and the thick, stout belt was long enough to go around me twice. I'd measure later and use a hole punch I'd seen in the tack room to make it fit.

Gotta admit I cleaned up reasonably well. My cheeks were drawn and eyes sunken, but the new duds covered a thin body well. I didn't recognize the happy and mischievous man I once knew looking back in the mirror. This facsimile was humorless, brooding, and stony-faced. Brown eyes were haunted by wretched secrets—of terrible things witnessed, and brutalities dealt out.

Work boots a size too big were left off while I tested the mattress. Firm without sag, I appreciated a clean case on a comfortable pillow. I closed my eyes for a moment, only to be woken by a loud clanging. Likely the same triangle dinner bell I noticed on the ranch house veranda. Tugging on and lacing new-to-me boots, I hustled to supper with my soiled clothing bagged.

An outside table was getting loaded with food. Caroline made one and Annie took two trips in and out after I came around the machine shed. The former saw me first and startled. "Oh, my! Cable?" she asked.

Annie turned at her mother's exclamation. "Holy shit!"

"You spruce up good," Caroline said. I didn't answer and turned my attention to the table. Meatloaf, baked potatoes, beans, and buns looked good and smelled better. "Got tea, milk, or water," she informed.

"Milk, please."

My bosses sat across from me. "Don't be shy," Caroline said. "Dig in and get all you want."

I took her at her word and covered thick slabs of baked meat and two potatoes with gravy. Nor did I slow shoveling food in until my belly applied the brakes to unseemly gluttony. Setting my fork aside, I emptied my glass, buttered a fourth bun and spread strawberry preserves on both halves. "What's on tomorrow's agenda?"

"Can you ride?" Annie asked.

I stared hard lest she think me a pushover and shrugged. I considered her an asshole and didn't care if she knew. "A little," my inflection cold.

"Breakfast at six and our butts in the saddle before seven. Got two farriers coming the day after tomorrow and twenty-eight horses need corralled." Her smile wasn't pretty. "Think you can hold up your end?"

"I'll do what I can."

Waking at five when the provided alarm went off, I was gratified at how well I slept. The bed was more comfortable than I hoped. No sense in taking a shower. The day would be dirty and dusty. Besides, I used to prefer going to bed clean. It was also nice to do my business on a toilet again.

I caught Caroline and Annie putting grub on the table. More potatoes. Made sense—I'd seen their garden plot, and the majority of it was spuds, beans, and greens. An inexpensive yet filling method to keep their clientele happy. Earlier, a rooster alerted me to a nearby chicken coop, and a hog pen wouldn't be a shock. The mother/daughter duo were good at cutting costs.

Annie was inside when Caroline saw me. "Good morning. Sleep well?"

"Yes, ma'am."

Hotcakes, eggs, and homemade hash browns filled my empty stomach. My bosses ignored me after I made it obvious I wasn't there to talk. Instead, they discussed upcoming bookings and how to make sure the ranch was ready for a first wave of clients. After finishing, I waited for them to get done while I drank coffee. Annie finally pushed away from the table. "Got two horses corralled. Jezebel is mine...you can ride Buster."

Caroline quit stacking dishes and stared. "Oh, Annie. Not that brute."

Her daughter shrugged and fought a tight smile. "Only one I could catch, Mother."

Buster was a big damned appaloosa. Mostly white with a dozen dark spots on his rump and sides, I figured he went seventeen hands if not taller. Jezebel was a quarter horse, standing fifteen. I followed Annie inside the tack room where she waved a careless hand. "Choose a saddle. If it's not comfortable, find another one the next time."

A worn western with a sixteen-inch seat looked good. A rope strap already held a lariat, and I followed Annie with a bridle and blanket in one hand, the other holding a saddle over my shoulder. Buster looked half-wild, rolling his eyes and blowing. Either Annie made plans to do me in again or at least embarrass me half to death.

Jezebel waited quietly and accepted her bit without a problem. The tall appaloosa took me around the corral several times before I cut him off to avoid using a rope if it wasn't needed. I saw no sense in starting out with an angry or fearful mount. He tolerated the bit—even allowing me to adjust the bridle. When he side-stepped the blanket, I stopped to speak softly. Stroking his muzzle and neck, his eye-rolling slowed while listening to my low, quiet, and even tone. It seemed Buster grew more relaxed the longer I spoke.

He required more petting and kind words before I mounted. Stroking his forehead and throat first, I let him know we needed to be friends. He skittered away when my foot went into the stirrup, but I mounted smoothly and swiftly. I was in my seat and ready when he felt obligated to pitch. His bucks were halfhearted, but with a horse as big as Buster and as weak as I was, it wasn't easy staying in place. His head jerked when Annie mounted and turned to face us. I leaned forward to pat his neck. "Easy, boy. You help me, and I'll help you. Let's get through this with minimal fuss." He seemed to enjoy my hand, so I continued stroking.

Our day was long and exhausting, but I held up my end without complaint. We rounded up twenty-six of the twenty-eight after giving up on a pair taking it in their heads to disappear over a far ridge. Annie made it plain they were my responsibility to locate and drive in while the farriers worked. I enjoyed the roundup—none of it what I considered difficult. Most horses knew what to expect and turned for the barn once they understood our seriousness. Annie held the gate while I pushed the last few in. "Take care of your horse. Get a feed bag on him while you brush his coat. He'll be your mount for tomorrow, so make sure you're back to have his feet inspected and shoes either tightened or replaced." She checked her wristwatch. "Supper in ninety minutes."

Annie barely spoke a dozen words before we returned, and mine were less than half of hers. Although physically attractive, the woman's blatant hatred for the world made her ugly. Her mouth twisted with contempt anytime she glanced in my direction. Fine with me. I wasn't particularly enamored with her.

Buster enjoyed his brushing while munching on oats. It gave me time to work harder at building a relationship with the tall horse. I spoke quietly while I worked at cleaning him of caked sweat, dust, and debris. My efforts would sooth his skin and give me a chance to search for sores or wounds. I found a scrape inside a rear leg and packed it with Bag Balm. Trust would build a crucial bond between us. He was tired and no longer rolled his eyes when I worked around him.

A long shower washed away dust after I shook my clothes free of pine needles. I dressed to eat in the same clothes I'd wear tomorrow. Caroline made it clear I was to bring my dirty duds to be washed each evening.

Thick porkchops, fried potatoes, and a Greek salad filled me to overflowing. I'd soon put weight on again if they continued to give me regular meals. "Need you to round up the quarter horse and Arabian first thing," Annie said. Her tone was far more pleasant when around her mom. "Farriers said they'd be here by eight but figure seven. They're always early."

"Do your best, Cable," Caroline said. "I can pack a lunch if you'd prefer."

"Yes, ma'am. I'll take you up on the offer."

Without Annie there to hurry us the following morning, I took far longer with Buster to keep on winning him over. I guess he wasn't convinced. The moment my butt hit the saddle, he didn't hesitate to make sure I was awake. With my lunch and thermos stowed safely in the saddlebags, we left the barn at a dead run when he finished bucking.

We headed east to where the escaping nags high-tailed. Low rolling hills could hide a thousand horses or cows. I understood about where the ranch boundaries were but didn't know exactly. Fences were natural barriers buoyed by limbs and debris to dissuade any but the most determined animal. Swinging south to higher ground, I hoped the pair could be observed from above. I'd left the ranch a few minutes after daylight. A glance at my watch reinforced I'd been searching four hours. A thick stand of timber below was my final opportunity to locate them before returning empty handed. I looked for a way down when movement farther east stopped me. Someone on horseback stood in the stirrups and waved a hat to get my attention.

We met on a flat ridge. The tall Tennessee walker nodded continuously as it performed a beautiful running walk for its female rider. "Are you on the hunt for a quarter horse and an Arabian?"

I grinned at the young woman. "Sure am. Seen 'em?"

"I watched them feeding about a half mile east around thirty minutes ago." She waved an arm in the general direction. "Couldn't have gone far."

"Thank you. I appreciate it."

"You one of the new guys Caroline Hagseth and Annie Compton hire each spring?"

I shrugged. "Not really. I'm helping spruce the place up a bit. I'll hit the road when they're on their feet."

"They can't be paying well. Word's out banks are avoiding them, and they're on their last gasp."

"Last gasp?" I frowned while considering how much Caroline loved her place.

The woman shook her head. "I apologize. Shouldn't gossip about other folks' problems. Need help pushing your stragglers west?"

A glance at my watch told me I'd better accept her offer. Didn't want the harpy to berate me worse than she already planned. "I'd appreciate it if you can spare the time."

The pair of geldings were obstinate and reasonably sure they didn't want to return home. It took us a fair amount of riding to change their minds. The moment they realized neither of us were going to quit, both lined out for the barn we could see in the distance. My companion halted, her walker high stepping in his eagerness to continue the chase. "You better take after 'em," she said, laughing as we watched them disappear. "They're going to beat you home." The girl turned her mount to face me, and I hoped I didn't show the shock I felt. A long scar started high on her cheek and extended to the corner of her mouth. It was a terrible blemish in otherwise attractive features. Thick chestnut locks extended from beneath her Stetson to halfway down her back.

I winked to avoid showing how startled I was. "Too late. The farriers are more than likely about to slap shoes on 'em."

She leaned in my direction. "Name's Leeann. Yours?"

I took her extended hand. "Cable." Buster didn't care to be so close to the walker and side-stepped away. "Looks like he's ready to go, too." I lifted a hand. "Thanks again, and I'll see you later."

It turned out my words were prophetic. The quarter horse and Arabian were hitched to a post long before I arrived. Half past noon wasn't bad in my opinion. Besides, the pair were the last ones in a long line. Two heavy trucks were parked nearby with four men measuring and shaping iron shoes to fit each horse. I led Buster into the barn after letting him drink before putting him in a stall and brushing the sweat and grime from his coat. I cleaned and reapplied Bag Balm on his scrape. He seemed to enjoy my one-sided conversation and turned once to see what was wrong when I stopped talking.

Caroline found me enjoying lunch with the gelding. He munched happily inside his feed bag, while I took my time with two egg salad sandwiches and coffee. "I saw you tear out of here this morning like your hair was on fire," she said.

"Buster was feeling his oats."

"I figured. You sit a saddle well. Annie complimented you by saying you know what you're doing."

I looked Caroline in the eye. "She set it up to get me hurt. Buster's no horse for a novice."

"Yet you rode him anyway. I can see you're no beginner."

"He could injure or kill someone if you aren't careful."

"Annie wouldn't have let you mount if she wasn't confident you could handle him," Caroline said. "I told her she was responsible for you."

"Your daughter's an asshole," I said flatly.

"The girl's too hard on you. I'm harder on her because of it. Cut her some slack if you can. Annie's in a lot of pain."

I finished the last bite of my lunch. "We've all got problems, lady. Me, you, her...everyone's got a cross to bear."

"Yeah...well..." Caroline frowned before coming to a decision. "Annie lost someone special to her." I didn't offer condolences, only a steady gaze. "Her husband was killed overseas not long ago. He was a computer specialist, but somehow a suicide bomber got inside their office. "They..." She stopped to gather herself for a moment and wiped a tear away. "They were married only eighteen months before Nelson was killed."

Her story put a human face to Annie's naked rage directed at the world and me in particular. I couldn't think of anything original to say. Instead, I cocked my head and nodded. "I'm sorry for you both." We could hear the ring of hammers on steel outside as the team of farriers worked their magic. I could trim a hoof, but to properly fit a shoe was beyond my meager skills.

"I didn't want an apology. Only for you to understand why my daughter turned into someone not even I recognize." Caroline stood from the haybale she used as a seat outside of the stall. "I'd like you to take a look at the cabins and see if they could do with a little paint. We've got a few cans stored in the machine shed. Just to warn you, our first paying customers will be here four days from today on Friday afternoon."

* * *

Painting was a skill I'd failed to master. Thankfully, plenty of tape, paper, and canvas made my work look better than it was. I touched up the trim and eaves, and put a new coat on the inside of them all. It was hard work from daylight until supper, but I finished none too soon. Caroline understood which ones wore the freshest paint and planned to keep her first tranche of dudes out. No sense in ruining wet or uncured work. A dozen or more hinges were either replaced or tightened, and all got oil. One doorknob needed disassembled and refitted before it latched correctly. Four of the cabins required new boards to rebuild rotten steps. I made do with what I could find in the barn, rather than cost Caroline money she couldn't afford.

I'd been warned—Doug and Julio arrived Friday morning. Each towed his own trailer. The former worked for Caroline over a decade, where this was Julio's third season. Both were in their late forties or early fifties and knew their way around the ranch. Caroline introduced us as I was cleaning up after painting. "Cable, I'd like you to meet Douglas Wanke and Julio Castrato. Cable's been doing odd jobs helping get the place ready for customers tonight."

They possessed impressive grips. Doug was taller than me, while Julio couldn't've been more than five-four. "Howdy," I said.

"Cable's not what I'd call an eager conversationalist," Caroline said. "Let him know if you find anything needing repaired. Gates, fences, or replacing fenceposts. He'll handle cleaning stalls, watering, brushing, and feeding the horses. Oh, keep the dudes away from Buster. Cable's handling him."

Doug seemed surprised. "The mean appy? I thought you were going to put him down or sell the damn animal. Hell, he 'bout broke me in half last season."

Caroline winked at me. "Yep, that's the one."

Julio'd been staring. "You look familiar, señor. Do I know you?"

The man probably watched me stumble through town blind drunk, but a haircut and shave made all the difference. I shook my head. "Nope."

Caroline served supper for the five of us about an hour before guests trickled in. Another meatloaf, a huge bowl of mashed potatoes, gravy, and more greens. Their garden was enormous, and I was learning the significance. Running their outfit on a shoestring budget, overhead was cut by everything they could raise. I soon understood the reason for the two-acre graveled parking. Cars, SUVs, and even pickups towing trailers arrived. Eight vehicles plus Doug's and Julio's rigs took up most of the room.

I considered it my job to avoid everyone. I rose at four to keep the barn clean and rotate horses. Most were kept in the corrals, but those ridden hardest were stabled for extra care. Caroline didn't mind if I rode Buster when my chores were finished. She figured he could either be sold or worked into her business if the gelding calmed.

Avoiding Annie was high on my priority list, and she ignored me whenever possible. Caroline, on the other hand, encouraged learning the country surrounding their ranch. I chose not to break my fast with the crew and customers for personal reasons. At first, she set aside a couple breakfast sandwiches for me and something for lunch, too. I either ate in the saddle, my silver-skinned abode, or while working. Meals were served family style, except my elder and kinder boss lady generally made an enormous plate for me to eat alone.

With lunch stowed in my saddlebags and the last buckle fastened, I led Buster outside the barn. "Let's make today a good one, okay, man? You promise not to buck me off, and I'll give you extra rations tonight." The appaloosa loved three things—the trail, his feedbag, and a desire to throw me.

Buster and I might've shared the first two, but the last item on his favorites and my own idea couldn't have been more diametrically opposed. My feet were barely in the stirrups and butt in the saddle when the damned horse exploded and sprang into the air like a cat. I wasn't getting points on form and gripped the cantle with my offhand. Unless he switched directions, rolled, or tried to scrape me off, no way could he dislodge me. He hopped around the barnyard until slipping in mud near the trough, his front hooves going out from under him. Although it happened fast, I felt the impending disaster and kicked my boots from the stirrups in time to land on my feet. Not releasing the reins, I grabbed the saddle horn and leaped astride again as he rose without missing a beat. Feeling the pesky rider again on his back, Buster lit off across the flatlands while I put my bootheels to his ribs with every step. I hoped he learned an important lesson. Breaking a hardheaded horse was difficult and not always successful.

We slowed to a canter and then an energetic walk as the hill became steeper. I wore my .22 on rides after nearly getting snakebit during a rest. Besides, I passed more than one coyote within handgun range. I patted my mount on the shoulder as he followed directions. "Good man." We approached an even steeper ridge, and I considered turning back. Buster grunted when I didn't haul him in and took the precipitous slope without slowing. The angle made me lean forward with my bellybutton on the horn and a hand wrapped in his mane. With no way of stopping safely, I gave him his head and let him choose the way.

Blowing and straining, Buster got us to better ground. I reined in, looking over new terrain with cautious eyes. We needed to locate a less treacherous avenue to descend when it came time to turn back. With my daily chores finished and not on Caroline's payroll other than room and board, I didn't mind spending time exploring.

Buster and I broke out of a thick stand of pine near the edge of a pinnacle. A saddled horse watched ears-up as we approached. A broad plateau stretched in front and to my left for a mile or more. A rider stepped around the animal and waved. I turned Buster toward them after I recognized Leeann. "You don't take the easy way, do you, Cable?" the young woman said. "There's a reason you won't find shod tracks on that ridge. Too damned steep for man or beast. Yet I watched you climb it for most of the last hour."

I swung down but kept a tight grip on the reins, leading my mount to where I could see better. As Leeann pointed out, the slope appeared far more menacing than I initially thought. "Ever tried it?" I asked.

"Heck, no!"

"It might surprise you. The worst parts are at the bottom and top. Between are plenty of game trails and openings."

"I see you're packing a hogleg this time. Snakes?"

"'Bout got struck a week ago when I almost parked my butt on a rattler. I was too interested in lunch than where I planned to sit."

"You're a better shot than anyone I know if you can hit a snake in the head," she said. "Unless you're using shotshells."

I shook my head. "Nope, don't have any. Probably should."

Dressed in a light blouse with long sleeves, worn jeans, and dusty cowgirl boots, Leeann was taller and far leaner than I initially thought. Standing only a few feet away while we peered over the edge, her crown reached above my shoulder. She seemed unaware of my gaze while she removed her Stetson and used a hand to push thick hair back. A stiff breeze blew upcanyon in late morning. "Have you been to the lake up above?" she asked and pointed to the main ridge.

"Huh uh. I'm new to this country."

"I can take you there, if you're interested," she said. "Good fishing because it's a fair distance from the nearest blacktop. It doesn't get many hikers, and is far too dangerous for Caroline's dudes."

Buster was ready to go the moment he felt my butt touch the saddle. If I wondered why Leeann wasn't alarmed to be alone on a mountain with a strange man, my question was answered when her horse turned. I could see a rifle protruding from a scabbard where she could easily grasp it. "Beautiful country," I said.

She waited until I came up beside her. "Gorgeous. Where'd you say you were from?"

I struggled to keep any surliness from my tone. "I didn't."

Rather than take offense, Leeann chuckled, clucked her tongue, and tickled her mount with spurs. Buster accepted the challenge of what he thought to be a race. I struggled to rein him in before we shot past. He went sideways in a spirited dance with his eyes flaring wide. Controlling the horse each day—combined with Caroline's cooking—built my strength rapidly. It was less than a month after I moved to the ranch, and my ribs were no longer showing. I thought about alcohol constantly, but my body wasn't reliant on intoxicants, leaving me without symptoms of withdrawal. If nothing else, I would help Caroline until the end of the season and use any money she paid me to purchase what I needed to move into the next realm.

Our ride was far longer than I envisioned. Leeann appeared sure and confident as she followed nondescript trails difficult to recognize. She halted after we crested a short ridge and waited for me before pointing at a deep blue body of water below. "There she is. I call her Leeann's Lake

Chapter IV

Caroline's voice from behind startled me, but I didn't let her see it when I turned. "What are you? Some sort of showoff or circus performer?" she demanded.

I'd finished brushing Buster while he munched a couple cups of oats from his feedbag. "Excuse me?"

"Annie, Doug, Julio, and I were having coffee on the veranda when you saddled Buster." She wasn't making sense, and I didn't hide my confusion." Caroline threw her hands out palms up. "I'm talking about the rodeo you put on before taking out of here like your hair was on fire."

She still didn't make sense. "I rode east and then north into the mountains," I said. "I thought you didn't mind if I worked on Buster's manners."

"I've never seen a bronc work harder to throw a rider than this morning. Nor have I watched a horse try to roll over one. You made handling him look like a walk in the park."

"It wasn't a big deal. Buster likes me to show him who's boss. Besides, he didn't try to roll on me. He slipped in mud next to the watering trough. He tried to right himself, so I stepped off to let him catch his balance and get his legs under him."

Caroline's snort was far from ladylike. "I've been around horses all my life. I know what I saw." She closed and locked the stall gate after me when I removed Buster's empty feedbag. "Pretty late, isn't it? I was getting worried." I took it as a good sign when she didn't mention the revolver on my hip. Her rules were explicit. No guns for any reason. I planned to use ignorance as my excuse if she complained. Perhaps the edict was for dudes only.

My way out of the mountains took longer than I anticipated. Figured I'd miss dinner, but knew half an egg salad sandwich remained in my refrigerator. "I've been busy exploring. What's on the agenda come morning?"

She frowned. "A window in number three is jammed. They've been good sports, but it stayed hot last night. Tonight won't be any better."

After I smoothed the stuck sash, Caroline offered up a dozen more tasks before I retired to my trailer looking forward to the luxury of a shower. Instead of a sandwich, a plate was in the refrigerator loaded with mashed potatoes covered in hamburger gravy. String beans, carrots, and a couple rolls were included. Even with my air conditioner running, I wasn't going to warm my meal and living space. After what I'd subjected myself to over the past year or longer, a cold supper still tasted good.

Chores kept me busy all next day. Two broken boards in one of the corrals needed replaced before guests noticed rot in the planks. A second stuck window, followed by loading, wheeling, and dumping manure into the spreader kept me on the move. Voices surprised me in the barn while I took a few minutes to rest and brush Buster's coat in his stall. "There's nothing more we can do, Mrs. Hagseth. It was the third time this year your payment was over ten days late. The bank's called your loan. You've got ninety days to pay the balance and late fees, or our institution will take possession and prepare it for auction."

"I went to school with your mother, Richard," Caroline said. "Bless her soul. What would Rhonda say if she were alive and knew you were working with Damien Slater to take my ranch? Hank and I built this place from the ground up, you know."

Whoever he was, Richard was polite. "I'm well aware of how hard you worked, Mrs. Hagseth. Your husband gave me my first job right here. I've helped unload hundreds of tons of alfalfa in the barn over the years. Hank was a good man."

"We're working to secure financing. Enough to repay the bank and for operating capital." Ah, now I knew why Annie was often absent and left wrangling the dudes to Doug and Julio.

The relief in what sounded like a young man's voice was clear. "I'm happy for you, ma'am. Between you and me? I hope you find a sponsor to get us out of this mess. Working for you and Mr. Hagseth made fond memories. I've recounted them to Kelli and our kids dozens of times."

Their voices faded as they left the barn. Who the hell was Damien Slater, and why did he want Hagseth Hills Guest Ranch? If Caroline's bank was a local branch she'd done business with for years, what was the real reason they suddenly pulled her loan? Community lending institutions were notorious for providing leeway to businesses behind on their payments for many months, even years. Even then, they would do their best to work with the debtor to restructure loans to the benefit of all. Granted, Caroline's ranch comprised of sixteen hundred acres with an impressive amount of prime bottomland worth an equally breathtaking price tag. I'd hate to see her ousted from a place I knew she loved.

* * *

I assumed Annie's return meant I would soon be on the receiving end of her wrath. I couldn't have been more wrong. Their battered Chevy rattled up the driveway while I backed the manure spreader with the John Deere. I kept it where horse dropping could be dumped from a ramp extending from inside the barn. Shoveling shit twice was a fool's game. After unhitching, I drove past the house to return the tractor to the machine shed. Annie's slumped shoulders as she slow-climbed the porch steps told me all I needed to know. Nor did she bother to shoot me a dirty look when I passed again. Horses coming in were in need of water, feed, and a brushing.

After finishing my last chores, I used the backdoor of the house to avoid dudes eating supper on the veranda. Caroline preferred I eat with them but left a plate on the counter. I wasn't trying to be sneaky, just quiet when I entered. My mouth watered at the sight of two enormous burritos covered in a sauce and a bowl of beans. "I don't know what to do, Mom," Annie said from another room. "I'm out of ideas. Haven't found a bank or other lending institution willing to help us. Can Slater have put out the word we're not to be touched?"

"Your guess is better than mine, honey," Caroline said. "What is, is, I guess. Slater can have the ranch if he wants it so badly. I feel terrible for you. Your dad and I built this place in the hope of leaving it to our children."

"A resort and golf courses," Annie said her tone filled with disgust. "They plan to bulldoze it all and cover it with hotels. They'll get our place for almost nothing and make millions."

I'd overheard enough. Although I didn't sneak in, I didn't make a sound on my way out. Their business was none of my concern, and Annie would skin me alive if she found me listening to their private affairs. I felt sorry for Caroline most of all. She's the one who put her life into the ranch.

The burritos were still hot inside and as good as I hoped. The spicy chipotle sauce raised my core temperature until I broke into a sweat. Even so, I finished it all and longed for a third. Already, my body responded to work combined with healthy portions of food. My ribs were no longer visible and lean muscle bulged my shirt and sleeves from cleaning stalls, shoveling, and wheeling manure. If not for the dead look in the eyes of the man staring back from the mirror, I almost recognized who I'd once been.

Buster behaved himself for three days. I reckoned it was too much for him, because he went wild on the fourth. My daily ride was late in coming after snaking a clogged toilet in the community bathrooms. My guesses were the damned horse got too much time to think and plan, or perhaps it was simply his excitement to hit the trail.

I'd switched to a western saddle with a seventeen-inch seat and a breast collar. Buster didn't mind steep country, and I needed the extra strap to keep the saddle from slipping back. I should have known he was feeling his oats when he pushed his belly out against the cinch. He got a knee to the gut as I pulled it tighter. He champed at the bit and rolled his eyes while waiting for me to get my lunch stowed. My butt no more than hit the saddle when his head went down and he lunged forward, kicking high with his hindquarters. "Goddamn it, Buster," I shouted as he crowhopped in circles. "Knock it off!" Rather than listen, his bucking intensified. A half-dozen dudes strolling past were quickly standing outside the corral watching the spectacle.

I strained to get his head up. A horse can't kick as high when the animal can't lower it. Rather than calm, he swapped ends in a concerted effort to dislodge me. The moment I saw we were aimed at the open gate, I put my heels hard to his ribs. Bolting through, Buster leaped a second fence rather than go around. How the twelve-hundred-pound animal cleared the top board with room to spare was a mystery to me. We landed hard enough to knock the wind from me as we tore across the pasture at top speed, my boots thumping his ribs with every step. The ornery animal could wear himself out with a sprint for all I cared, as long as we didn't find a gopher hole.

Most of my first sandwich was half gone when I heard steps above where I sat along the three-acre high country lakeshore. Buster searched for browse as best he could after I hobbled him until he nickered at company. I stood and brushed my butt off, shoving the last bite into my mouth. Leeann leaned back in her saddle to help the walker balance on his way down the steep hill. "Hey," she said after sliding to a stop. "Fancy meeting you here." The tall girl dismounted and left her ride ground tied.

"Hope you don't mind. It's peaceful."

"Nope, this's public ground."

I retrieved my second sandwich and raised my thermos. "Got a cup?" Leeann shook her head. "I'll split my sandwich with you."

"Sounds good," she said. "What kind?"

"You don't mind peanut butter and blackberry jam, do you?"

She didn't and took the smaller cut. "How do you like working for Caroline?"

"I enjoy it. She's a nice lady and a great cook. Five-star restaurants would clamor for her if they knew how good she is in the kitchen."

Her chuckle was low. "Eaten at a lot of five-star restaurants, have you?"

I gave a curt dip with my chin. "Enough."

"I should get a job with her wrangling dudes." She patted her stomach and moved her hand outward. "Probably fatten me to here."

"Where do you come from? It can't be far from Caroline's place."

Leeann pointed east. "Over that way. I live with my brother and his family."

"No husband or boyfriend?"

Her smile was always half grimace, but I'd grown used to the scar on her cheek. "No, men aren't interested after they get a load of me. It's best to spend my time riding."

"May I ask what happened?"

She shrugged. "Car wreck."

I nodded. "Oh." Her two-word explanation made sense.

"It's not what you're thinking," Leeann said. "No one hit me, and I didn't skid out of control in bad conditions. It was a single vehicle accident. I was driving blind drunk without wearing a seatbelt. Ran off the road and hit a utility pole. I've got more scars where you can't see them."

"I'm sorry."

"Me, too. I was a stupid girl drinking too much in college."

The way she took responsibility was refreshing. Anymore, it seemed most folks wanted someone else to shoulder their blame. "What's your brother do for a living?"

"Dee's in financing. He's fourteen years older than me. Owns a couple franchises, plus buys, sells, and rents commercial property. I thank God every day he doesn't mind taking care of his little sister."

"Dee sounds like a good guy."

Leeann nodded seriously. "He is. He really is."

"Is hiding from the world the answer to your problems?" My query made me cringe inside. I articulated her obvious shortcoming instead of facing my own difficulties.

"Of course, it isn't. I'll have to fend for myself one of these days...just not right now."

"How long ago was your accident?

"Four years. God, that sounds awful. It's hard to believe I've sponged off family for so long."

"Don't mean to keep prying, but what was your major?"

"I don't mind. My accident happened hallway through sophomore year before I declared one, and I didn't go back after I healed enough to leave the hospital." She lifted the same kerchief she wore around her neck each time we'd met, and I could see the scar on her throat. "Tracheotomy. I was unconscious for quite a long time."

Supper was finished before I returned to the ranch. Leeann eventually grew bored with my proclivity to stare at the lake and left me in peace. I missed the safety and anonymity of my stump and sounds of birds and lapping waves.

Prepared to go without an evening meal, I found a covered bowl in my refrigerator. At least two quarts of homemade chili with four thick buns and a cinnamon roll made for a filling supper. Rather than shower and hit the rack, I strolled behind the machine shed to where Caroline and Annie planted their garden. Two dozen hens complained in their coop as they jockeyed for position getting ready for the night. With Annie often absent and Caroline cooking alone, not enough time got spent weeding their plot. Only a few minutes of light remained, and I made good use of it by pulling grass around the pole beans. I got a good start on carrots, too. I needed to clean each row of vegetables more often if the owners planned for it to feed their customers throughout the season. Remaining lettuce and spinach rows were precariously short, but more replanted were forcing their way from the soil.

Voices surprised me as I neared the corner of the machine shed. I didn't recognize the male voice but grimaced at the female. "I don't date clients, Larry."

"Oh, c'mon," a man's suggestive voice made clear his interest in my elder boss's daughter. "I won't tell if you don't," he said. A rustle of clothing made it sound more serious than I first thought.

A body thunked against the wall about the time I decided to skulk off in a different direction. "Ow, you're hurting me," Annie said. "Knock it off."

A pair of White-Ox work gloves were tucked away in my back pocket. I certainly wasn't going to leave her to be manhandled no matter the level of my dislike, so I drew them on again and stepped around the corner. Although dark, enough glow came from a barn light in front to make out shapes. Braced with her shoulders against the shed to help push a man away, Annie was losing the battle against a far stronger antagonist. Only a moment was needed to see there was nothing playful going on before I reached the pair. Wrenching his shoulder back with my right hand, I struck with a straight left to the chin. He was unprepared and collapsed. Barely slowing to deliver the blow, I continued walking and made my escape. Annie could decide how to handle the matter.

* * *

Caroline was still inside her kitchen when I entered through the back. Usually eating with her guests by seven each morning, I wasn't expecting to see her. My plated breakfast and a brown paper sack were ready for me on the counter. She turned at the sound of my step. "Good morning, Cable. Hotcakes, eggs, and patty sausage. Should be plenty to fill you. Your lunch, too."

"Thanks." I got both meals and turned to go before stopping. "Ma'am, would you mind if I used your phone today?" A landline hung from the wall.

She saw where I was looking. "That old thing? It's only decoration, because I've been too lazy to throw it out. Our number was disconnected years ago." She fumbled in a pocket. "You're more than welcome to my cell."

I took her smart phone and wondered if I was doing the right thing. A computer might be a better idea. "Thanks. Shouldn't take but a minute. I'll leave it on the counter with my plate, okay?"

Caroline nodded while balancing a tall stack of 'cakes retrieved from the warming oven. "No problem."

My call was short but left me shaken by its intensity. The conversation lasted less than two minutes. Yet when I ended it there was no doubt my life was going to take a drastic turn again.

* * *

Annie made herself conspicuously absent. I'd figured to be fired and told to move on. Although it was dark the night before, I couldn't imagine her not recognizing me up close. Then again, I barely broke stride when belting the guy. The top board on the corral got busted by too many dudes sitting on it, giving me something constructive to do. I guessed they watched one too many cowboy movies. Only nine two-by-sixes eight feet long and another three at twelve feet remained in the barn after I finished repairs. The stack of boards I started with dwindled quickly with someone able to put them to good use.

With temperatures over ninety in the shade, and every living animal out of the sun, I took time to move into the barn and brush Buster. A guitar led a sing-along on the veranda, keeping visitors of all ages occupied. Julio couldn't read a lick of sheet music, but if he heard a song, he learned to pick it by ear. One or two female voices were incredible, while most were backup noise.

Buster nickered when I unlocked the gate to his stall and stepped inside. The damned horse could go from loving and rubbing his face on me to hating and bucking in the space of time it took to saddle him. With doors on either end of the barn thrown wide open, a breeze—albeit hot—whistled through. "When're you going to learn we're a team, horse?" His head was up while he stared at me. "There's no sense in trying to throw me every time I cinch a saddle to your back, you dumb animal." It wasn't true. The damned critter was one of the smarter ones I'd worked with over my lifetime. I was beginning to believe his hard-headedness was due to youth and excitement. I'd rather not crush his natural exuberance.

I eased my way around him, putting a hand on his butt to let him know when I crossed behind. I had an aversion to getting kicked inside a stall. Because of carelessness, a fellow caught a hoof on my mom's ranch while I was growing up, and the man was never the same. Caroline couldn't afford to have me or anyone else hurt.

Though supposedly equal owners, I considered the mom my boss and her daughter the ramrod. The former found me not long after I fitted Buster's bridle and left him tied outside his stall. She stood next to him when I came out of the tack room with my saddle. "Going somewhere?"

I shook my head. "Gotta put in time in the saddle if he's going to stay on your ranch. Otherwise, be a long spell before he's ready for anything but an experienced rider."

"Where were you last night after supper?" she asked.

I cocked my head and frowned. "It was lights out pretty early. Morning is always here before I know it. Why?"

Caroline wrinkled her nose. "One of my guests got a little handsy with Annie. He wasn't giving up until someone clobbered the guy. Annie was busy fighting him and didn't get a good look."

"Did you have a talk with the dude?"

"He was asked to leave first thing this morning. Worst of it was he brought his two boys as a birthday gift. They pulled out not long after first light."

I placed the blanket on Buster's back before tossing the saddle up. "Has a client attacked you or your daughter before?" I didn't show my face to Caroline while I tightened cinch and then the belly strap.

"No, although a few showed interest in me years ago. My husband put a quick end to it. This was Annie's first time. Likely the last, too."

I didn't let on I knew why. "Oh? How can you be so sure?"

She grimaced. "Might as well let you in on the secret. We're losing the ranch. Bank called the loan, and I can't pay the outstanding debt. We're out of business in six weeks and off the premises by Christmas."

"I'm sorry to hear it. Wish there was some way I could help."

"You have by working the place for an old woman when she needed it most. Annie appreciates it, too, although she'll never admit it."

Buster blew and turned his head to look at me after I dropped the stirrup into place. Bastard was already plotting against me. My boss

59

walked with us as I led him outside. "You're not old, Caroline. Travel or even get a job. There's a world waiting for you out there."

"We've put every dime we've made back into this place," she said. "It was supposed to go to Annie. She's the one who'll need to find a job. I've got no savings, so I'm planning to move into your stump."

Her declaration made me chuckle. "There isn't enough room for two. You're gonna have to find your own."

Maybe it was the heat or Buster wanted to impress his owner, but he barely hopped when I put a foot in the stirrup and threw my leg across, giving a half-hearted snort and hump of his back when he felt my butt in the saddle. I focused on keeping his head up rather than fight him across the barnyard. Tickling his ribs with my heels, I held him to a trot instead of his usual flat-out run. Time to work on manners.

* * *

Between parties leaving and more coming, I got opportunities to sand and put a couple coats of stain on the entryway sign above the drive arching across two massive pillars: HAGSETH HILLS GUEST RANCH. I stood away after I finished to admire my work. Spending time on a ladder propped in the bed of the Chevy didn't allow me to appreciate the fruits of my labor. A few mistakes were visible to me, but I doubted anyone else would notice. Caroline and Annie might have only a few weeks left, but all the investment they provided into a revamped sign was my labor. I'd found sandpaper and stain stored inside the machine shed.

Heavy frost in my hair and whiskers changed my appearance so much it startled me each time I looked in a mirror. Having spent my life clean-shaven, a growing beard was easy to maintain. Doug and Julio already wrangled away nearly two dozen dudes on horses I'd saddled, when an SUV barreled up the drive. With an empty veranda and a big lunch on the picnic table, I cursed to myself at more invaders. The impressive vehicle stopped at the edge of the barnyard where the lawn led up to the house. I knocked on the screen door and called, "Caroline? You've got company." Two men and a woman exited and stretched, looking around.

Annie was out first, followed by her mother. The three visitors obviously heard my voice and the squeaky spring. They spoke among themselves before coming our way. The closer they got, the more I pulled the brim of my borrowed Stetson low over my eyes and focused on my food. Anonymity was my friend. The trio stopped at the foot of the stairs. "Is one of you Caroline Hagseth?" the woman asked.

"I am," Caroline said. "How can I help you?"

"My name is Olivia Justice. We're here because it came to our attention you've been in search of a lender. Are the reports we've gotten accurate?"

"Yes, but how did you learn of us?"

I dobbed more hot sauce on my burrito while listening, peering from below the edge of my hat. Where I sat was on the far end of the porch where I couldn't make a beeline to my accommodations. I took a healthy slug of ice tea to get a better look. One of the men glanced in my direction when Ms. Justice brushed off Caroline's question. "A branch of the WCP Foundation is newly dedicated toward helping ailing businesses. We also provide capital needed to help you maintain operations. Have you already gotten funding, or are you interested in hearing our proposal?"

"We're still weighing our options, Ms. Justice," Annie said. "However, we're more than happy to listen to what your foundation has in mind."

Knowing their dire straits, I barely kept from rolling my eyes at Annie's remark. My employers were only weeks from losing their home, yet she was ready to play hardball. As long as it was fair, I guessed Caroline would jump at whatever they offered.

"May we sit and discuss options?" Ms. Justice asked.

Lunch finished, I stood with my empty plate and glass. "Here, let me take your dishes with me, Cable," Caroline said. "Would the rest of you like to come inside? We have tea, and I can make coffee if you'd like."

I stood to the side as the trio trooped up the stairs. Olivia Justice was closest to me when they passed, and she glanced up. I stood at least a foot taller than her. She offered a brief nod, catching a toe and stumbling on the top tread. I put a hand out to steady her, and she automatically grabbed it. She smiled her thanks before giving me a second look, her eyes flaring wide. What she saw or thought she did didn't matter to me, so I winked and left for the barn.

* * *

I got a significant portion of the center section of the stables swept and dumped into the manure spreader before the screen door sounded again. Peeking outside to gauge the excitement level of my boss ladies got me caught by the Justice woman. She shaded her eyes as she looked toward where I worked. My gaze narrowed as I tried to read minds when Caroline and Annie shook their visitors' hands. The trio stopped after reaching their SUV. I'm not sure what Ms. Justice said, but the two men peered in my direction. I withdrew inside rather than feed their curiosity. Another half the barn remained to be cleaned.

I took over when Doug and Julio returned with their wards in tow. After I put their saddles away, the animals were left tied so I could brush away sweat and matting before letting them out to roll in the corral. Part of my duty was to keep the watering trough filled, and each of the thirsty critters used it prior to ruining my hard work. No matter—a thorough currying was crucial for their overall health. Dust and dirt were also important for controlling small insects wanting to burrow into their flesh. A quick examination of each horse caused me to smear Bag Balm on six gouges and scrapes. Superficial injuries weren't uncommon on stock working for a living.

Annie's laughter was easy to pick out on the veranda when I skirted the house and entered the kitchen through the back. Caroline hummed while she loaded dinner to be moved outside. She heard the screen door close behind me. "Oh, good afternoon, Cable. Your plate and bowl are next to the microwave."

A juicy steak—she'd learned I preferred beef cooked medium rare—along with mashed potatoes and a green salad were next to a significant bowl of beans. I ducked my head. "Thank you, ma'am. After overhearing conversation earlier on the front porch, I hope you don't mind me asking if there's a chance of getting a loan to keep your ranch from vultures?"

Guarded optimism is the best way to describe her reaction. "They seem like nice people, but neither Annie nor me have heard of their foundation. Their offer was fair...far better than we could have hoped for. While they're running a credit check and getting our ranch appraised, we're looking into their institution. Annie's worried Slater could be behind this."

"Good idea. I hope it works out for you." My heart swelled to hear her hum again after I left with my meal. Hard-working people are the first ones victimized. I hoped Caroline's misfortunes were in the past.

Chapter V

Caroline was forced to expel a roomful of rowdies staying in cabin six. No alcohol was allowed on the ranch, and they not only drank but damaged the interior and kept other guests awake. Two of the quartet were remorseful, but my boss was forced to threaten the other pair with a visit by a deputy sheriff. Julio suffered a wrenched shoulder during a brief altercation, and Doug wore a black eye before our ruffians left. I watched from a safe distance with a softball bat close at hand. No way did I want punching a guest to become habit. Nor could I afford to be hauled off to the pokey and be fingerprinted. For one thing, bail money would be impossible to come by with $2.73 to my name.

I stayed out of the way when the assessor appeared. Although provided by the foundation, the woman was more than fair, and her numbers went in my bosses' favor, according to Caroline. I finished repairs to the cabin and added new paint a few days before she made her appearance. Caroline rigged it so the inspector arrived while we were between groups. Busy weeding the garden after breakfast until I heard the car door close, in no way did I want to get underfoot. This was an opportunity of a lifetime for Caroline and her daughter. I tossed a saddle on Buster and thanked the good Lord above when my mount didn't show off. Rather than ride for the lake, I pointed his head east to explore farther.

It was easy to see why Leeann chose to ride west toward Caroline's ranch. Terrain the other way flattened until only a few rises remained. Remembering she lived with her brother, I was curious about their home. Two hours of walking Buster brought me to a forest of tall pines mixed with firs. We wove between them to a high spot where I could see a place in the distance.

Where Caroline's home was an old ranch house and barn built in the early nineteen-hundreds, this spread was modern and expansive.

Two stories built over what I thought was a daylight basement sprawled to eight or ten thousand square feet. Three barns were equally large and impressive. It seemed Leeann's brother Dee did well for himself and his family. Rather than get closer and intrude, I turned my horse's nose south toward a creek I knew eventually fed into the lake where my stump waited for my final return. Sure I was well back onto the Hagseth ranch, I crossed tire tracks biting deep into the earth leading from the east. I filed the curious information away in the back of my mind.

Squatting next to the stream while Buster drank his fill, I could see fingerling trout darting about along with a crayfish visible beneath a submerged log. A turtle warmed itself in the hot sun on a flat rock along the shore. I automatically licked my lips and wondered if I could catch it. More than one of the small reptiles found itself in my stewpot suspended over a fire. I guessed the terrapin read my mind before lunging for the safety of water. Perhaps three feet deep along the edges and six feet across, he was as protected as he'd ever be around me.

I dawdled until early evening. Caroline waved me to the veranda after I got Buster watered, fed, curried, and put away. She, Annie, Doug, and Julio were sitting down to supper. "Why don't you eat with us tonight, Cable?" she said. "Let me get your plate."

With four of them sitting at one table, I made myself comfortable at another. "Pull a chair to the end," Doug said. "We can make room."

"I'm comfortable here, thanks." I tended to spread out when eating.

"We went simple today," Caroline said after returning with my supper in two hands. "Hamburgers, hotdogs, and baked beans."

My plate held two big burgers and a pair of hotdogs. She took an empty bowl and ladled it full from a pot of beans and brought it to me. They were drinking sun tea, and Caroline didn't ask before filling an extra glass. "Thank you."

I figured they must be running low on beef after a bite of burger. Much of it tasted like freezer-burned sausage. Hotdogs were the cheap $1.99 version found in almost any convenience store. Didn't matter to me. It all tasted good and filled my belly. "I noticed progress with Buster," Doug said. "Ain't seen him try to kill you lately."

Rather than answer, I stuffed my mouth full and grunted instead. I wasn't looking to make friends. I was helping out an old woman while waiting for a way to enter the next world. When I didn't answer, Doug turned his attention back their foursome. "She seemed impressed with the ranch when I showed it to her on Google Earth," Annie was saying. "If this outfit is legitimate, I think we stand a good chance of remaining in business."

"We may even hire more hands again. Keep you boys on permanent," Caroline said. "Put two or three more on the payroll and take on groups earlier next summer. How's a steady paycheck sound, Cable?"

I didn't look up from stuffing my face. "Don't figure I'll be around...but thanks."

Annie snorted. "Probably dead drunk in the ditch again." I hoped she was right—not only the drunk part.

The next bunch of dudes was larger than normal because of scheduling conflicts. I was hard-pressed to take care of the remuda after each daytrip. The only one not provided to the group was Buster—even Annie's quarter horse got a daily rider. One guest bragged of his prowess in the saddle and suggested he might like to try the appaloosa after he saw me lead Buster out one morning. Didn't take more than thirty seconds of me barely keeping my seat before the dude saw the light. We damned near busted a section of the corral and my leg when the crazy bastard swapped ends too close to the edge. I bit my lip and ignored the bloom of pain when an opening came. I put my heels to him, and we took it at a dead run. Three minutes later we were out of sight where I turned his head uphill. The knucklehead could wear himself out on steep slopes.

* * *

We got back early enough for me to do my job and still have time to eat a hot meal. Julio was already hanging saddles and bridles in the tack room. Each horse wore a halter and was tied to the corral. "I wasn't sure when you'd return, *señor*. The day was long and hot, and they needed water."

"Thanks, *amigo*, but I got this." I hated to see him struggle with a shoulder still bothering the hard-working man. Pain was obvious when he used it vigorously.

I passed the veranda where every table and place to sit was taken including porch steps. It didn't matter, my supper waited on the kitchen counter with a cellophane cover. The simple meal consisted of a thick porkchop with a hefty portion of mashed potatoes and gravy. A bowl with blackberry cobbler made my mouth water.

My meal went on the small table in my quarters while I used the bathroom and washed up. Something looked wrong in my bedroom when I stepped out wiping my hands, forearms, and face. Even though I left my place locked each day, a plain white sheet of folded paper was leaned against the equally light-colored pillow. When I lifted it away, the edge of a familiar case was visible beneath the head cushion. I opened the note and sat on the edge of my bed to read.

William,

I am both overwhelmed and relieved to find you survived. Dad and I hoped for the best but feared the worst. I understand why you haven't contacted us, and I've told no one after learning your whereabouts including Father. He remains optimistic you're alive when your body wasn't found.

Your life continues to be in danger. Take care and keep the faith. We'll find a way to bring you home.

With all my love,

Z

I could smell the familiar perfume when I kissed her single-letter signature. *Lalique de Lalique's* floral fragrance with a hint of vanilla was easy to recognize. I read the short missive over again—surprised by my sudden emotion. A door I thought nailed shut forever was reopened. Yet what did I expect after a stupid but essential phone call?

The aircraft aluminum hardcase was as heavy as I remembered. Entering the six-digit security code merely caused a pad to open. Pressing my thumb against it, three seconds passed before the locking mechanism disengaged. I unlatched it to find nothing changed—a sleek, powerful, and stainless Kimber 1911 Long Slide chambered in 10mm lay nestled within the padded confines. Spare magazines, a kydex holster, along with a single box of ammunition were also fitted within the custom case. I never expected to again see something which once provided so much pleasure. No doubt if I lifted a corner of the pad, the small compartment hidden behind was still filled with emergency cash and a debit card. A cellphone and charger tucked into a crevice made the hair on the back of my neck rise. Did I dare?

Supper was cooling. Locking the metal container with the letter inside, I left it at the bottom of a storage compartment beneath my bed. The meal was enough to fill a hungry man, and I tore into it with gusto. Even the empty bowl once filled with cobbler was licked clean when I finished. Retrieving a milk jug from my refrigerator, I poured a glass and washed my food down.

The evening meal continued on the veranda with Julio tuning his guitar. Singalongs were popular with some groups, but not with others. I almost smiled at his choice to open with, a ballad first sung by Marty Robbins, called "El Paso City." The fun and sad song told of a man flying over the southwest remembering another life he may have lived. I left my dishes and crossed back to my place just as a couple of women pulled their chairs closer to our Spanish crooner. After hanging on the last few sad notes of song, he immediately burst into another made famous by the same singer, "The Streets of Laredo." I almost laughed knowing he'd have some of the ladies in tears before he finished.

As usual, I retired to my camper with the air-conditioning on low and closed the shades. I locked the door before retrieving the hardcase from another lifetime. Opening it again, I stared at a gun I'd carried daily for three years and thought to never see again. While some might feel revulsion knowing its background, my memories were mostly of animals I'd harvested with it for the freezer. Whitetails, mule deer, bear, and small game all fell to its lethal bite. A powerhouse in the semi-automatic handgun world, it never failed to feed or eject. Even when compared to my trusty .22 Ruger passed down by my mother, it was the most accurate handgun I'd fired.

A check of the five magazines allowed me to see they were loaded. I pressed one into the handgun after assuring myself the chamber was empty. Gripping it as I did so many times before, I took careful aim at a spot on the wall. The sights lined up as if nothing changed in my life. I held it in both hands while powerful memories surged. Some of them were of triumph standing over game harvested for the table—others of midnight blazing structures and screaming and begging. I almost expected the grips to be stained crimson. Someone took very good care of my favorite weapon after I left it behind. Now in condition three, I locked away my old friend and reached for the phone. I held it as carefully as I would a sleeping viper, knowing the wrong move might cost me my life. Yet hadn't this been my goal? I was fascinated, but rather than anger it by switching it to charge, I set it down and retired for the evening.

My night was fitful and dream-filled. Little of what I could remember was pleasant when my eyes opened to a gray dawn. Instead, thoughts of a previous life made my guts churn. I sat up and swung my feet to the floor. If a bottle of Everclear grain alcohol would have been close, I would have drunk it all.

I washed my face and dressed for the day. After downing a big glass of water, I made my way to the garden to work and clear my head in the cool morning air. Breakfast wouldn't be ready for another hour, and I could get a bit of weeding in. Got the onions, carrots, beets, and beans finished when Caroline's voice interrupted my move into the corn. "Awful early for straining your low back, isn't it?"

Rather than show my surprise, I put knuckles against my spine and stretched. "Morning, ma'am," I said. "What can I help you pick?"

She checked the shortest row of onions first. "I need a couple of the biggest bulbs for breakfast. I'm mixing them with hash browns."

"There." I pointed at a spot two rows over where I'd noticed how big the Walla Walla sweets grew.

She tugged them from the ground and shook off most of the dirt. "Might as well tell you the good news. Annie and I got a call from the WCP Foundation last night. They've approved our loan! We'll meet here to sign papers Friday afternoon after our guests have left."

I smiled at her news. My face felt funny—it'd been a long time since I experienced happiness. "I'm glad. Pleased for both of you knowing your ranch stays in good hands."

Caroline shook her head in wonder. "So neat they heard about us and came here. It's why we were initially leery of their institution. We thought they were more oriented toward charities. I never considered they invested in business. Turns out we're their new department's first loan. Our lawyer looked into their background and suggested we jump at any fair offer."

Sprigs of grass caught my attention, and I chopped them into bits with my hoe. "You're okay with their proposal?"

Her tone was incredulous. "Okay? They charged almost no interest. Zero point five. How can a foundation stay in business with those terms?"

I shrugged. "Donations?"

"You're probably right." Caroline suddenly grinned. "Can't wait to hear about the look on Slater's face when he gets the news. Our monthly payments have been cut almost in half."

"Who is this Slater guy? Better yet, why does he want your place so bad he'd try to undercut your bank note?"

Caroline glanced at the house, and I knew she needed to hurry. "We have sixteen hundred acres of which less than a thousand is prime bottomland. From what I understand, he owns almost three thousand...nearly all of it choice acreage. His location is far better situated than ours. Your guess is as good as ours."

Her news made me frown at her disappearing backside. Was his reasoning simply because he could get it for pennies on the dollar? Greed was likely Slater's biggest motivator.

I continued hacking at weeds until the breakfast bell rang. Caroline and Annie would be setting out huge amounts of food in front. Thankfully, I found my plate on the counter heaped with hash browns under ladles of brown gravy, three eggs, a slab of ham better suited for an entire family, and four pieces of toast. Caroline certainly took good care of my burgeoning appetite.

Thirty minutes later, Julio strolled to where I leaned against the barn door, watching dudes of every age, size, and sex mounting their horses. "*Señor*? Everything, it is all okay?"

"Yeah, why wouldn't it be?"

"You always keep at work somewhere."

I nodded to a saddled horse left without a rider. "Got a missing guest?"

"*Sí*. A young woman left yesterday after we returned. She didn't ride with the group."

"Was there a problem?"

He thought a moment. "No, she told *Señora* Caroline there was an emergency at home. *Por qué?*

I shrugged because I wasn't sure enough of my Spanish to say I didn't know why. "One less horse to saddle."

The group left the ranch with Doug leading and Julio trailing with a packhorse loaded with their midday meal. The small roan didn't take well to getting left behind and fought to join the departing horses. I got the saddle off and hung in the tack room while giving our absent visitor thought. She—Julio affirmed it was a woman—left the same day the Kimber appeared in my trailer, somehow entering without a key and leaving soon thereafter. I could only assume she was a professional. The lock on my door could only be opened by me or Caroline.

Buster seemed ready for our daily explorations, nickering when I passed his stall leading the roan and energetic and excited when I returned. He champed the bit as I went over his head and behind his ears with the bridle, tightening the chin strap after I got it in place. I opened the gate and clucked my tongue. "C'mon, boy." He stomped when I left him to retrieve my saddle and blanket. In no time, I was leading the confused horse to my quarters. He was used to being mounted inside the breezeway or corral. I left him tied to the tongue of my trailer and hustled inside.

"Cable?" I heard my name called when I stepped out. Caroline stood shielding her eyes from the sun. The usual thermos tucked between her other arm and side, and the plastic lunchbox held out in the free hand. I turned my back quickly and slid the Kimber into a saddle bag.

"Yes, ma'am." I hurried to where she waited and accepted the containers. "Thank you. I appreciate such a big breakfast, too. Darned near put part of it away for supper tonight."

She frowned an instant before breaking into a smile. "Annie dished you. She always worries you're too thin." Caroline squeezed one of my shoulders. "You're beefing up nicely as far as I'm concerned."

Annie concerned about me? I damned near glanced around to see if pigs were flying or hell was freezing over. She'd never spoken a kind word to me since we met. I turned away, smiling to myself how Caroline was covering for her hateful daughter. We were oil and water, and my boss tried her best to sooth ruffled feathers on both sides. A question arose in my mind, and I stopped. "Ma'am? Julio mentioned we lost a dude yesterday? I only noticed because a horse was left over."

"Oh, yes, Teresa. A nice lady but couldn't stop looking at her phone. I guess she's one of those people who never quits working. Must've been busy...she stayed in the cabin she shared with three other ladies throughout the day."

"Can you describe her?"

Caroline frowned. "Around thirty and a little shorter than me, I think. Maybe five-five, and well proportioned. Brown hair cut just above her shoulders...a narrow nose with a diamond stud in her...left nostril."

While her description didn't sound familiar, the woman obviously knew what I looked like. She'd been at the ranch two days before catching the grounds empty. If I didn't know her, it meant she got paid for leaving the note and my gun behind. Obviously, Z understated her general warning to be careful.

Buster didn't fuss when I mounted, turning and trotting after I tickled his ribs with my heels. Perhaps he was learning and growing after all. The gelding was nobody's dummy. Rather, he was shrewd and sharp as a tack. Woe to his next rider if not experienced.

My plan was to explore the ridge behind and above Leeann's Lake. It appeared to run east and west, and I hoped to see if the timber opened into alpine country at higher elevations. Caroline's ranch lay at almost five-thousand feet above sea level. I guessed the lake was three-thousand feet higher and the ridgeline another two beyond. Without a map to read, it stood to reason the summit could well be over nine-thousand. Buster didn't hesitate when I turned his head toward the far steeper slope.

Larger timber dwindled as doghair pine crowded us. Soon, I was searching for anyway out of the mess. An opening appeared above us, and Buster lunged through a final barrier of jack pines. Five hundred feet higher, and we reached a plateau visible from my stump. My mount snorted and blew in his excitement, turning a circle as we surveyed my goal.

The lake where I lived was easy to pick out—with it the location of my secret hollowed bole. I dismounted and led my horse to where I could see better while stretching my legs. Caroline's house, barn, and outbuildings were visible, along with Leeann's brother's place. The road leading to town was barely a line disappearing into the distance. Buster demanded my attention by nosing my back, pushing me forward and off-balance. I chuckled. "Easy, man." Summer browse captured his attention, leading me to hobble him in belly-deep wild pasture.

Two egg salad sandwiches went down easy, followed by a bottle of water and two cups of coffee. It was good to be in the high country where I felt most at home. It'd be a fitting spot to meet my maker. No matter, loose ends requiring my full attention beckoned in the meantime.

Buster barely acknowledge me when I returned my thermos and empty lunch carrier to the saddlebags. Finding my Kimber, I belted the Kydex holster to my waist before admiring the gun. After making sure the chamber remained empty, I put the auto-loader back, gripped the butt, and drew slowly. Less than two years before, I could draw and put a round downrange in a fraction of a second. Repeating the actions, I found muscle memory returning quickly.

With the opportunity to see the mountainside from the summit down, I discovered a far better path to Leeann's Lake and then intersect Caroline's ranch. A trout surfaced as I passed the beautiful body of water, causing me to consider returning with a rod and can of worms.

I got back to the guest ranch after supper. My tardiness made me feel bad—Julio and Doug already finished my job and were retired to their trailers. Annie watched me ride in from where she sat on the veranda with a couple dudes. Our eyes met. It happened again after I finished with Buster and once more when I crossed the barnyard with my saddlebags. One of the dudes said something I couldn't make out, and Annie waved to get my attention. "Could I have a moment, Cable?"

It's a good thing even a gentle breeze didn't blow. I could've been knocked over with a feather. Tired from my long ride, all three watched as I limped my way to the steps and stopped at the top to relax against the bannister. "Ma'am."

For the first time since we'd met, I saw humor on Annie's face. "This's Mr. and Mrs. Godwin. They've watched you help out and work around the ranch." Annie struggled not to smile. "Said you're the first honest to God cowboy they've seen and wanted to meet you."

I shook his hand first followed by his wife's. "Nice to make your acquaintances."

He pulled a soft palm back. "I worked on my uncle's cattle ranch in Montana as a boy until a couple years after I finished college," he said. "Uncle John ran three thousand head of Angus and employed about a dozen hands. I forgot what they looked like on horseback until you rode through. Been working for Mrs. Hagseth long?"

I avoided Annie's obvious surprise. "No, sir. My capacity here is as a handyman. Let me know if you see something needing repaired."

Mr. Godwin glanced at his startled tablemate. "You're missing the boat, Mrs. Compton. Take it from me. This man knows his way around a horse, cattle, and a rope," he said. His eyes twinkled. "Wouldn't astonish me if you were handy with a six-shooter, too."

We all heard my stomach growl. "Nice meeting you folks," I said and turned to leave. "Be sure to come back as soon as you can and bring family and friends with you."

"Mom left dinner in your refrigerator, Cable," Annie called. "Thanks for your time."

She was right. A big chicken fried steak and potatoes coated with gravy waited for me. Four biscuits and a cinnamon roll, too. I'd miss Caroline's cooking and cheerfulness when the season ended.

* * *

Little rain fell over the summer after I came to live on the ranch. I'd felt moist air moving in and heard the first drops on my roof after getting comfortable in bed, following a cool shower. The phone in my hand beckoned after I'd charged it, but I found it impossible to switch on. What messages I might find could prove both frightening and heartbreaking. Some voices might threaten my very sanity. The drumming overhead grew loud and hard enough I eventually set the cell aside and switched off the light. Some things are better left until another time.

Mr. and Mrs. Godwin caught my eye the next morning and waved as they packed bags to their car. Buster got his daily currying and morning cup of oats while I worked. Their enthusiastic and wide grins made me smile and return their farewell. I switched my attention back to my horse but not before I noticed my interaction with the couple hadn't gone undetected. Both Caroline and Annie shook hands with guests before their departures and didn't miss my acknowledgement of the couple.

With barn stalls left filled for the day, my horse didn't mind staying inside. Knowing the worry of Annie and Caroline with the imminent arrival of the WCP Foundation representatives, I planned to remain indoors and away from prying eyes. I'd hoped to mow lawn and tidy the garden, but wet grass and passing rainstorms put an end to my intentions. The smell of summer rain was one of my favorites, and I planned to enjoy it through open windows and door of my trailer.

Olivia Justice led the team meeting with Caroline and Annie. I didn't recognize the other woman and man with her. Two males, more bodyguards than junior executives, accompanied her before. Their SUV was left parked where I could see it from my couch. All three stretched before disappearing in the direction of the farmhouse. I would feel much better when every "I" was dotted and "t" crossed. Until then, the ranch was exposed to Damien Slater's hostile takeover and self-serving plans.

I woke from a nap and acted before able to stop myself. I switched my phone on and watched in disbelief as both missed calls and texts downloaded. Names which could cause a descent into raging madness were overlooked as I scrolled through my contacts.

The one I searched for was at the very end of the alphabet. I texted a single word and three question marks. *Well???*

The return came almost immediately as if she waited for my missive. *Execution completed.*

TY, I replied.

It was our pleasure.

The afternoon grew late, but I saw the SUV remained. I got one more day of rest before the next batch of dudes arrived. Rather than interrupt ongoing negotiations, I elected to drink a glass of water and nap. If I were lucky, Caroline would call when supper was ready. If not, I could easily sleep until sunrise tomorrow.

Chapter VI

I woke to rapping and my name made tinny through an aluminum door. "Cable? Are you in there?"

"Yes, ma'am," I called. "Just a minute." I sat up and hurried from my bed to the curved side of the Airstream.

Caroline waited with a plate piled high with pizza slices when I opened. "Annie rang the bell. She said you were ignoring us, but I told her you might be sleeping when you didn't come." I yawned and accepted supper, expecting she'd leave. Instead, she didn't move and broke into a wide smile. It grew broader at my confusion. "It's official," she said. "The ranch stays ours."

"Caro..." I choked on her name. "I'm truly happy for you, Caroline. If I've learned one thing while helping out around here, no one works harder or deserves what you've built more than you."

She held her arms open, so I left the plate on the table and stepped outside. It'd been too long since I hugged another person. For a boss, she smelled good with kitchen odors overpowering any perfume. "I'm able to give you the fulltime position you so deserve," Caroline said after pushing back. "Douglas used to work here fulltime until money got tight, and now I can keep him on, too. We're going to offer the same deal to Julio. He's been a valuable asset."

I hesitated before shaking my head. "Don't expect to be around long after the season ends. Only need to make sure you're ready to go into the winter before I move on."

"Does your decision have anything to do with Annie and her attitude? I can assure you—"

I held up a hand and shook my head. "Your daughter has nothing to do with it. I've got...well...whatever future I have is elsewhere, ma'am."

Caroline's sad smile wasn't one I wanted to see again. "Make sure you have my number in case you change your mind. I'll wire money and a bus or plane ticket. The offer is good as long as I'm alive."

I bit my lip and kicked a rock I'd stepped on more than once. My excitement for her evaporated. My short future consisted of one thing, and I hoped to tie the loose end soon after their season finished. I finally met her eyes with my own defeated gaze. "Thanks, but I won't need anything for very long."

"Cable, you can't mean—" I left her outside and closed my curved door. "You better not mean what I think you do," she shouted.

Caroline stood outside and fumed for a minute before leaving. The pizza was good—I ate three pieces before wrapping the final four and stowing them in the fridge.

Not every group of dudes stayed five or seven days. The ranch also offered a three-night package. Rather than stick around the next morning, I lit out for the hills with Buster to miss midday orientation. My chores were finished, and I'd found a reel with fishing gear once belonging to Henry Hagseth in the machine shed. A length of monofilament, a half dozen hooks, along with a couple bobbers, and I pointed my horse's nose toward Leeann's Lake. Surely a big trout would love to nibble at some of the worms I dug from a pile of horse manure.

Buster nickered when we reached the steep drop-off to the water's edge. Movement caught my eye, and I saw Leeann's red walker through the timber. She grinned when we slid to a halt. "I haven't seen you in a month of Sundays," she said. "Kind of figured you moved on."

I dismounted. "Nope. I'm hanging around until I get Caroline squared away. Try to make sure they're ready for next season. Save them as much money as I can." There wouldn't be much to do. Most of the plank fences were rebuilt or in good shape, along with the barn's interior.

She cocked her head and frowned. "I thought they were losing the place?"

"Then, whoever buys it will appreciate the upkeep." I sure as hell wasn't going to blab about Caroline and Annie's good fortune. It was up to my bosses to say or the bank to let the information slip when the guest ranch note got paid.

Leeann watched as I loosened Buster's cinch and removed his bridle to allow him grazing freedom. Hobbles kept him from going far. I located a long branch to fashion into a fishing pole. "I brought lunch if you get skunked," she called after I made my first cast.

Her offer turned out prophetic when I got disgusted and stopped an hour later. Either I couldn't get my line out far enough, or I found fish turning up their noses at worms. A few jumped near the center but none close enough to excite me. I'd left the ranch without asking for a lunch and hoped to take Leeann up on her offer. She tossed me a bagged sub sandwich with a grin. "Roast beef, ham, and turkey. Lots of mayo and horseradish." I got a shrug after raising an eyebrow. "I couldn't decide what kind I wanted most."

It was good, and I wasn't shy telling her after I got the first bite down. "Tastes great. Thank you."

"I brought an extra cup in case you're interested in coffee."

"You knew I was going to be here?"

"Nope. I've made sure to carry an extra should we meet again."

I thanked her a second time. "Where've you been keeping yourself? Find a job?"

Leeann laughed. "I mentioned it to Dee. He isn't anymore ready for me to fly the coop than I am. As far as he's concerned, I should stay with him and Alexandra until I'm an old maid."

"Alexandra?"

"My sister-in-law."

It made sense. "How old are you?"

"Twenty-six. You?"

"Thirty-two."

She frowned and peered closer. "Awfully gray for someone so young."

Buster didn't give me a chance to ignore her comment when he pushed me with his nose from behind. Guess he needed my attention. Caroline was nice enough to loan me Henry's Stetson, and I twisted to face him only to lose the hat. The gelding swung it up and down by the brim as if fanning me. "Give it back, horse," I said and freed it from his teeth after I got a good hold. "Cripes. It's not even mine."

I inspected the damage from his teeth, plopped it on my head, and moved to the same log on which Leeann sat. She laughed hysterically at Buster's antics and my fight to get the loaner back. "Oh, if you could have seen your face!"

"Yeah, he's a funny guy." I kept a close eye on him as he short-stepped closer. It wasn't long until I felt hairy lips on my shoulder, and he nuzzled my cheek. "No sweet talking, mister."

"He likes you," Leeann said. "Is he the only horse you ride?"

"Yeah, he's a handful. Not one Caroline should let a dude on."

"I've noticed you're rather proficient in the saddle."

I hesitated before answering. Somehow when we were together, the young woman got me to talk more than I'd done in two years. "I grew up on a ranch. Pretty much raised on horseback from the time I could sit on one."

"What brings you to Colorado?"

How to explain my internal scars were far more debilitating than the ones on her cheek and throat? "Long story." I hoped my tone made it obvious I wasn't going to tell it.

The subject got changed, and we drank her coffee and shot the shit for another half hour while I watched fish jump out of range. Leeann was an easy woman to talk to. For one so self-conscious of her appearance, she laughed easily and spoke freely.

Time remaining in the afternoon waned, and I needed to get back to the ranch. There wouldn't be a formal supper, although Caroline would make sure her hired hands were well-fed. Leeann tightened her mount's cinch while I got Buster ready to go. She swung effortlessly into her saddle as I mounted, too. "Will I see you again, or are you moving on soon?" she asked.

I pointed Buster's nose at the steep hill and hung on. Leeann and her horse weren't far behind, and I waited until she caught me. "Hard to say. Got about three weeks left until the season wraps up. Then, I'll make sure the place is ready for next spring before I..." I licked my lips and used her term. "...I move on."

She guided the walker close and offered her hand. "In case we don't meet again, it was nice having a riding buddy this summer. Wish we could have done it more often."

I tried to memorize her face as we shook and couldn't imagine how she'd appear without the four-inch scar. "It was a great time, wasn't it?" She nodded. "I'll always remember you, Lee."

She laughed at the spontaneous nickname. "No one's called me that before. I think I like it!" I got a wave of her hat after she wheeled the walker to high-step home.

Caroline's veranda was filled with dudes when Buster and I trotted past. I dismounted near the livestock tank and allowed him to drink. After spending much of the day near the lake, he wasn't particularly thirsty. Leading him inside, I tied the horse outside his stall while I unsaddled. He looked forward to the curry brush and feedbag and wasn't shy to let me know.

The twenty- or twenty-five-mile round trip to Leeann's Lake was a long ride. Tired from traversing steep ground, I looked forward to eating, showering, and sleep. With morning came preparing and saddling the number of horses Doug or Julio indicated. I passed the veranda and cut behind to the kitchen. Caroline was loading her dishwasher when I knocked on the screen door. "Oh, hi, Cable. We saved supper." She motioned me in and pointed to the counter.

Two thick cheeseburgers, potato salad, and a bowl of beans made my mouth water. I nodded and loaded my hands. "Thank you."

She appeared worried. "Annie's gone the next few days. Can you help the boys make sure no one does anything stupid?"

Her cautiousness made me chuckle. "It's like herding cats. Never know when one might fall out of line to chase after a bird."

I opened the screen door with my butt when she stopped me. "We've got fourteen dudes for three nights. Shouldn't be a problem. There's only four wives or girlfriends, no children, and none obese."

She meant there was no reason to choose any of the largest or smallest horses. I thanked her for the information and hurried to my trailer. Washing before eating, I was leaving the bathroom when I heard my phone vibrate. I'd avoided looking at it again thus far, unwilling to allow myself to get tangled in events possibly giving me a reason to live.

It buzzed again after I sat. Stupidly, I retrieved it to place on the table next to my meal. A series of texts came in from Z throughout the afternoon.

Hiccup in the proceedings. Lawyers tackling it now.

Someone very interested is trying to tie us up in court.

Counsel predicts we'll prevail easily, but it'll cost. Your wishes?

I thought about my answer before responding. *All the way. Win no matter what.* I hoped it would be our final correspondence.

Her response came almost immediately. *Will do. I love you, LB. Take care and contact me when you can.*

I love you, too, Z. Except I wasn't going to text her again.

I ignored other unread texts and finished eating. My life was culminating in a final and unexpected act I hoped would define who I'd been. It certainly couldn't hurt in getting through the pearly gates. I'd never been a bad man—perhaps a little wild as a youth—but nothing worth regretting until my life was torn apart.

I woke to gray skies. It worried me, because Caroline started the process of digging her potatoes yesterday to box and put away for the winter. Already, she'd been feeding corn on the cob to her guests as it ripened. No sense in missing out on saving a buck until the loan went through, and money was in her account.

Sixteen horses were tied to hitching posts outside the corral when Doug and Julio appeared after breakfast. Only fourteen wore saddles since both men preferred to tend their own mounts. They'd give lessons for a couple hours before leading the bunch on their first group ride. It was time for me to clean stalls while they were empty. Caroline used my wheelbarrow in her garden, and I hustled to retrieve it.

The dudes were gathered around Doug as he handed out their itinerary. One of them turned his head to gaze directly at me when I passed. A well-cared for beard reaching his stomach caught my attention. Long facial hair always struck me as uncomfortable and difficult to care for. Before I trimmed mine, it not only stank but itched constantly. The man seemed to study me as I passed before quartering to Doug where I'd still be visible. His open scrutiny disturbed me, and I stopped inside the barn to peer between planks. Although he couldn't see where I stood hidden, the big man's attention stayed riveted on where I disappeared.

I got the barn cleaned and rolled the rest of Caroline's spuds from the ground before the group returned. She preferred to personally sack and store them in the barn and asked if I'd leave the job to her. With nothing to keep my hands busy, I used the push mower to work around the house. Doug and Julio rode in with their group as I used a trimmer to get the edges along the concrete walkway. Long Beard made sure we held eye contact as he trotted past. I didn't care for his smirk and turned my attention to the machine in my hands.

Annie showed up on the group's final day. The Chevy clattered up the drive and wheezed to a stop in the parking lot. I couldn't make out if she quietly seethed or was ambivalent. Wheeling loads of manure from barn to garden kept me busy. I planned to till it into harvested areas as the vegetables got pulled. Chicken manure would also be spread liberally, but only after the ground lay bare.

The season was grinding to an end. Dudes were milling as they said their goodbyes in the front yard. If I enjoyed learning one thing, it was how people arrived as strangers and many departed as friends. I nodded to a few who stepped in the way of my wheelbarrow as I pushed it to the garden in back. No sense in getting angry or blaming them for their carelessness. As I'd noticed from the beginning, the excitement level was higher on the day guests left than when they arrived. People chatted in small groups, and two of the ladies sat in the fresh-cut grass.

I knew exactly what message Long Beard conveyed when he stepped behind the pair of females. He waited for me to look and was staring intently when our gazes crossed. Drawing a hand as if a gun from the pocket of his Levi's, he aimed his index finger and acted as if he deliberately shot both in the backs of their heads. His arm gave the illusion of recoil as he pulled the trigger once, then again.

I was stunned by the obvious meaning, dropped the wheelbarrow handles, and sprinted to my trailer. I fumbled with the key before getting it in the lock and rushing inside. Opening my gun case seemed to take an eternity. I snatched the Kimber and ejected the magazine to assure myself it was full, then racked the action and bolted from the Airstream.

The group moved as a small herd toward the parking area. I jogged to catch them with the pistol held tightly against my thigh. The sound of a Harley bursting into life made me rush past them. Long Beard rocketed from the far side of Julio's trailer, already shifting to second when he turned onto the drive leading out. He was two hundred yards away when I broke into a sprint without a chance of an open shot. The booming laugh I heard over the loud exhaust was almost enough to make me fire anyway. Instead, I slipped the gun behind my belt and turned back, using my shirt to hide the butt.

My boss and her daughter were seated side-by-side on the front steps when I stalked past. "Hey, Cable," Caroline called. "Annie brought a couple chickens home for supper. How does fried sound?"

I shook my head and kept going until Annie opened her big mouth. "He's an asshole, Mom. I don't know why you ask his opinion about anything."

None of us were prepared for my reaction, including me. Frightened, frantic, and filled with memories of loved ones torn away, I turned on her in a rage. "I've gotten a bellyful of your loud mouth, you insufferable harpy." Both women shrank away as I stalked toward them. I wasn't aware of my tears until I got closer and their silhouettes wavered. Angered further by my emotional response, I ran a sleeve across my eyes and bulled forward. "You think you're the only one in this world who's lost someone?" I stopped at the sound of an oncoming Dodge pickup. Rather than continue with my outburst, I wheeled toward the machine shed and my trailer. "I quit," I hollered over my shoulder.

Both Caroline and Annie faced mortal danger if I stayed. As contradictory as it sounds, not only did I not want to expose them to needless peril, I wanted to die on my own terms, not at the hands of others. The sooner I could leave their ranch, the safer we'd all be. Once in my trailer, I searched for everything I owned and stowed it in my pack. With my gun holstered on one hip and two spare magazines sheathed on the opposite, I left my key on the table.

Voices stopped me as I neared the house. "Your balance is less than three hundred thousand," a male voice said. "I'll write a check for five times the amount right now if you'll sell."

"I've told you, Mr. Slater." I recognized Caroline's prim timbre. "We're not interested. Henry and I built this place with nothing but the sweat of our brows. It goes to Anastasia when I retire or die. Not to a man who tried to drive us off."

The Dodge obviously belonged to the fellow who attempted to take Caroline's spread. "You tried to steal it from us." Annie's voice was as pleasant as fingernails on a chalkboard.

"Ten times," the male said. "I'll give you three million if you'll meet me at the bank tomorrow."

I hoped both women kept their cool and didn't listen. Sixteen hundred acres—even in an isolated area of Colorado—was worth far more than Slater's highest offer. "It's not for sale at any price," Annie said.

Caroline was more pragmatic. "We've already signed papers with another lender. You can't force us off or buy us out, Mr. Slater. No matter who you know at the bank."

"We've filed an injunction to stop the financing," he said. "I'll tie it up in court until you're out of money. You'll wish you jumped at one point five."

Caroline answered his challenge. "You're wrong. We've been on the phone with the WCP Foundation twice today. Not only are they fighting you, but they assured us you don't have a leg to stand on. You're stalling us for a week, perhaps two at most."

"Let's go, Dee," a fourth voice pleaded. "They said no." It was one I'd heard before, and I stepped around the corner of the shed.

Leeann saw me first, as I stepped closer. For the first time since we met, she didn't smile. Her brother noticed me, too, and jerked in surprise. It suddenly made sense. When she spoke of her brother "Dee," it never entered my mind she could be Damien Slater's sister. In a way, I'd been spending time with the enemy.

"I don't believe it," I said. "Were you trying to learn what you could from a dumb cowboy? Information to help your brother fleece two women out of their home?"

My accusation staggered Leeann. "No," she said. "No, of course not. How could you even consider such a thing?"

My kneejerk reaction was obviously wrong—Leeann and I rarely talked about the guest ranch operation. No matter how hard I tried, I couldn't remember her pumping me for details.

Slater stared as if he saw a ghost, but Caroline didn't give him a chance to speak. "Cable, no. Will you please stay long enough to talk to me?"

I shook my head. "I have to get out of here. If I stay, you're in danger. The sooner I leave the safer you'll be."

Leeann's brother found his tongue. "Pearson? William Pearson?"

His naming me made it clear I was a day late in leaving the ranch and returning to my stump. Enough money was stored in my gun case to purchase a thousand bottles of the strongest alcohol money could buy. "You've got the wrong guy," I muttered.

He didn't buy it for an instant. "No, I don't," Slater said. "Three years ago, I stood closer to you at a financial conference in New York than I am now. You looked bored while your father spoke to Warren Buffet." Slater squinted. "You're older, grayer, and wearing a beard, but I could pick you out of a lineup any time." Caroline and Annie stared at him while they tried to make sense of what Leeann's brother said. "You didn't know, did you?" he asked my bosses. "This's William Cable Pearson IV. He and his family run the foundation who approved your loan."

Caroline switched her gaze to me, her brow deeply furrowed. "Cable? Is he telling the truth?"

Both camps—the Slaters along with Caroline and Annie—waited for my response. I took a different route by ignoring the man's charges. "Do you remember the dude who left today...the big man with a long beard? He rode a Harley." Caroline nodded, but I'm not sure she fully processed my question. "I don't know who he is, but I know what he does. The guy is deadly bad news, and you're looking at trouble merely by association. I have to go now."

Annie came to life. "Mr. Slater, I'd like you and your sister to leave. We aren't interested in your offer. Please drop your suit and don't come back." I liked this version of the woman, having steel and conviction in her tone rather than raw vindictiveness.

Leeann plucked at her brother's sleeve. "Let's go, Dee. We've been asked to leave."

I slung my pack over a shoulder while they retreated to their pickup. Slater's sister waved after they turned around—one I didn't return. She seemed like a nice woman, but it was before I knew more of her background. "In the house, Cable," Caroline said. "You're not leaving this place without a full belly."

It was a mistake, but at the time, complying seemed the easiest route, so I found myself sitting in the kitchen listening to the sizzle of frying chicken. Annie sat where I could see her tapping on an open laptop in the living room, while Caroline cooked supper. As usual, both Doug and Julio had returned to their families between groups of dudes. "You should call the police," I said. "As far as they're concerned, the people who hired the man on the Harley considers you fair game. You harbored an enemy of theirs. They'll send enough thugs back to burn your home to the ground if they find me here."

"Did I ever tell you what my nephews do for a living?" she asked. I shook my head. Hell, I didn't know she enjoyed an extended family. Nothing was ever mentioned. "My younger brother retired to Florida after serving six terms as our county sheriff. Two of his boys followed in his footsteps and still wear badges." Caroline stopped and turned the chicken before giving me her attention again.

"Then get on the horn and let them know you're in trouble. Bad things are about to happen, and they can't get here too soon. The more firepower they bring, the better off you'll all be."

"Who are they?" Caroline asked. "A better question might be who are you?"

"They're a biker gang known as the Brotherhood of Loki out of Sacramento. It's not a huge pack of vermin, but they're ruthless. They manufacture and peddle drugs, are heavy into prostitution, and murder for hire. All around bad guys. You'll need an army since I was recognized by a member." I wondered whether Long Beard happened along by chance or was he sent as a scout?

Annie came in the kitchen with her portable computer and sat across the table from me. "Why? What've you done?" she asked quietly.

"Why do you assume it was me who did something?"

She shrugged. "They're after you, not vice versa."

I bit a piece of skin on my lip and considered her question. "Some of them did bad things to my family. I retaliated. Now, they want to finish it."

"Mom?" Annie said. "Would you come over here?"

She turned her laptop to Caroline who squinted through the readers she wore, before gasping and covering her mouth with a palm. Her gaze flicked back and forth from me to the screen. "You're far more handsome with the beard and a touch of gray." She winked and went back to the stove.

Annie angled the screen so I could see it. I remembered the day well. "Where are you, and who's the man you're with?"

"He's my father," I said. "We were at News Corp headquarters in New York. I don't remember which floor. He was there to be interviewed by *Wall Street Journal* and *Fox Business.*"

"Holy shit." Caroline couldn't have sounded more surprised.

Annie'd been studying the photo. "You don't look happy."

"It was calving season. I was there only because my father demanded my presence."

"Do you always do what he demands?"

"We were...we'd recently reunited. It was my way to help mend broken fences."

"Ah...I see."

No, she didn't, but Annie'd never been pleasant to be around, and I wasn't going to rock the boat. I turned my attention to Caroline as she covered a platter in fried chicken and used the drippings left in the pan to make gravy. Best flavor in the world in my opinion. I could see why she did most of the cooking while Annie stayed out of the way. Caroline was constant motion until she finished.

The spread made my mouth water. Chicken, mashed spuds and gravy with roasted ears of corn. I was about to stab a couple drumsticks when Caroline stopped me. "I think we should say grace. Cable, will you do the honors?"

I shook my head. "Never been much of a church-goer, ma'am. Wedding and funerals have been about all." I'm a firm believer in God but figure I can pray and speak to the Lord wherever I am, whether in the saddle or seated on a commode.

"Very well," she proceeded to recite an obviously memorized benediction: "Bless, O Lord, this food we are about to eat; and we pray to You, O God, that it may be good for our bodies and souls; and if there be any poor wandering creature hungry or thirsty, send it unto us that we may share, just as You share Your gifts with us. Amen."

I could only grin back when I got a wink after she finished. No doubt who the poor, hungry, and thirsty creature was. When Annie chose a breast and Caroline speared a thigh, I made a pig of myself by taking all four legs. Drumsticks have been my favorite as far back as I can remember. I couldn't help but compliment Caroline. "Good. Really good," I said.

Annie'd been taking my measure between bites. "Where're you planning to go?"

I gave her my best disgusted look. "I wouldn't tell you even if I knew. If this gang gets their hands on you, you'll talk."

"No, we won't."

"Yes, you will. In fact, you'd damn well better tell them anything they want to know, even if you have to make it up. You hear me? Don't hold back and give them straight answers. You can't tell them anything that'll hurt me worse, so spill your guts." I stared hard at Caroline, too. "I guarantee they're already moving this way. Not all of them, but enough. Their organization used to be about two-hundred strong before their numbers got whittled down to under one-fifty. Expect no less than a couple dozen to pay the ranch a visit."

Caroline gave a pensive look. "So many. You're talking about a small army. What do I tell the police?"

"Tell your nephews the whole truth as you know it. Don't use my name unless you have to, but make them understand how critical a show of force by law enforcement is."

I stayed long into the evening at their table after the kitchen was clean while Caroline talked to one of her nephews. He promised to contact his brother and rally the cavalry. It sounded as if he would act immediately to head off the Brotherhood before they arrived at the ranch. When it came time to leave, I got hugs from both women and their agreement they'd be careful. Caroline promised me a big breakfast if I would stay the night and a ride to anywhere I wanted in the morning.

Knowing I left them unprotected bothered me, but they were better off with me gone as soon as possible. If my suspicions proved correct, once they learned I no longer resided on the ranch, they'd search north toward my old stomping grounds. I didn't think I'd need it, but remembered I'd forgotten the charging cord for my phone while we ate. Leaving my belongings at the corner of the house, I threaded my way between the garden and machine shed on the way to my trailer.

I'd barely reached it when something came out of the shadows and hit me across the upper back. Stunned with the wind knocked out of me, I went down hard to bang the side of my face against the trailer skin. The beating continued as someone pounded me while I covered my head. I felt my scalp spit and bleed when the weapon contacted an exposed part and stars exploded. I'd become too lazy and stupid from losing brain cells to booze while hiding from the Brotherhood. I fatally underestimated how fast the nasty bastards carried out their terror tactics, and no longer able to defend myself, I waited for the end.

A chuckle came out of the darkness, and a light flashed when my attacker lit a cigarette. Long Beard grinned in the dim illumination. "I ain't here to kill you, asshole, just soften you up for the boys. They got plans for you, Pearson. You're going to wish I beat your brains out instead of leaving you alive."

Chapter VII

I cursed the decision to leave my gun stowed in the pack while eating supper. Long Beard would look good with a half-dozen 10mm hollow points clustered around his belly button. He laughed again and speared the two-by-four at me from the shadows, the butt-end hitting me in the chest. I lay still and waited for what was to come. If he went into the farmhouse and missed where I left my knapsack, I'd arm myself and kill him inside. Long minutes of agony passed before I heard the distant roar of a Harley kicked into life.

After the beating, there was no way I could make the walk to my stump in the dark. My head spun while I tried to rise, losing my balance and falling a dozen times before I leaned upright against the trailer. Blood trickled from scalp and cheek to soak into my shirt. With the darkened horizon tilting crazily, I slid along the Airstream, leaving blood streaked along the side. I measured how far away my belongings lay, only to fall before I reached the corner of Caroline's house. Crawling about half the distance, I fumbled inside until finding the Kimber. I felt my way through threading its holster onto my belt while lying on my side. If Long Beard and any of his brethren returned while I was here, their times on earth terrorizing others were over.

My body worked on autopilot after I struggled to my feet again. The barn lay no farther than sixty or seventy paces, and I wobbled my way to it. The yard light came on at dusk and went to daylight, giving me plenty of illumination to get inside. Two dim bulbs were always shining, allowing me to locate Buster's stall.

He nickered when I fell against his gate. "Hey—" My mind thick with pain and confusion, I couldn't remember what I planned to say. "Easy, boy."

I took far too long getting him trail ready. I used the saddle fitting me best with an attached lariat, halter, an extra length of rope, and the biggest saddlebags I could find. Even a dusty oiled canvas tarp was thrown aboard. I hoped there weren't any holes in it. It lay folded on a workbench since I'd been hired. Buster was uncharacteristically calm until I wasted Caroline's dinner by leaning against the stall and vomiting. He side-stepped away to let me finish.

I located a three-legged stool for a step to mount. If Buster decided to challenge my authority, no way could I control him. He got restless after I moved it into place and stopped to lean against him for balance. "Easy, boy. I need your help."

I'll be damned if he didn't listen and stood until I was in my seat. Not sure where to go, I bumped his ribs with my bootheels. Rather than explode into a run, the appaloosa gelding walked into the darkness.

* * *

A gentle hand patted my shoulder. "Cable? Are you okay?"

My first realization I was alive was a familiar voice. Lying on my side, I rolled to my back. My lids fluttered before they opened and struggled to focus. "Leeann?"

"Oh, thank God! There's blood everywhere. For a few minutes, I thought you were dead."

"Lend me a hand to sit."

She struggled to get me into a seated position against scrub brush. I blinked hard until I could see only one of her. Even then, she floated back and forth, making me fall to my side. "Jesus, you need a doctor." Gentle fingers examined my head wound before straying lower to my cheek. "You're going to need stitches." My sometimes-riding partner pulled me upright again. "I've got water in my saddlebags. Are you thirsty?"

I moved my head slowly in a desperate effort to stop the world from spinning. My mouth was as dry as a popcorn fart. "Please."

She hurried back from her mount with a water bottle in each hand. She screwed the top from one and helped me tip it to my lips. "Go slow," she said. "Not too fast." Barely half went down before it came back up. I rolled to my side and heaved what little remained of my supper. "I need to get you to Caroline's or the emergency room. You've got a concussion or worse, and there's no cell service here. I'll have to ride home and use the landline."

"Huh uh. No doctors." I looked around. "Where's Buster?"

"He's tied in the trees behind you. Your horse is how I found you. I saw he was saddled and rode down from above to catch him. He was standing next to you."

I loved the animal more each day. "Can you get me into the saddle?"

Leeann knelt and then sat with her feet under her, the scarred side of her face toward me. "I'm not sure you know how badly you're injured. I can ride to Caroline's if you prefer."

I dared not shake my head lest the horizon go wild. "No. I quit last night."

Her brow furrowed. "Oh." Leeann's horse moved and got our attention. "What happened?" she asked and pointed to my injuries. "Did Buster throw you?"

"Nope. The biker I warned Caroline about waited in the dark. He got me good with a two-by-four."

"I don't understand. Why did he come back to hurt you?"

"You don't want to know." I glanced at her after she looked away. Even with her silhouette wavering, I could see the side of her face was swollen with her right eye closed. "What the hell?"

She knew what I noticed and a hand went to her injuries to probe tenderly around the orbital socket. "Dee didn't like hearing I'd spent time with one of Caroline's dude wranglers."

I leaned away and dry heaved again before wiping my mouth on my sleeve. I accepted the bottle she thrust out and rinsed my mouth. After finishing, I swallowed only two gulps. "Does he hit you often?"

"No, he's threatened and raised his hand more than once. He made up for lost time with one good punch."

"Find somewhere else to go, Lee. No sense in having it happen again. Next time, he might kill you. Go to Caroline and explain." I remembered her prayer. "It doesn't matter who your brother is. She and Annie will take you in."

Leeann studied me. "Where're you going?"

"I got a little place of my own where no one can find me." Except I was wrong. Both Annie and Caroline knew of my hideaway. Until my beating last night, I'd hoped to meet my maker there. Now, although always slow to anger, I grew more incensed each moment I thought of the sneak attack. "I need a boost to get aboard Buster."

She stood and brushed her rear end free of twigs and debris. "If you're refusing to see a doctor, at least let me run home and get a first aid kit." She handed me her second water. "Don't drink too fast, okay? I'll be back in an hour or so."

I sighed after she left on her horse at a dead run. Three women in my life, and I didn't want any of them near. I nursed on both bottles until the spinning landscape slowed to a wobble. With a half hour gone, it was time to find Buster.

Unable to take more than a couple steps before the world tilted, I dropped to my hands and knees and crawled, sometimes falling to my side. He waited where Leeann promised, stripping every bit of vegetation he could reach. I unfastened his bridle while kneeling, making him nervous. "Easy, man. I need your help again."

It took too many tries to pull myself up by the stirrup before I could drag myself into the saddle. I lost my equilibrium the first time and fell to my back. Lee would soon return, and I hoped to be long gone. Perhaps she would take my advice and speak with Caroline, whom I was sure would welcome her with open arms.

We didn't travel a quarter-mile before we reached the creek where I'd watched the turtle. I gripped the saddle horn while Buster drank his fill. Poor guy, he waited next to me without thinking of himself. I let him slake his thirst before his head came up, and he turned to look behind. I wheeled him so I could see without moving my head rather than risk losing my balance and falling from the saddle.

I cursed quietly to see Lee weave her way in my direction through dense brush. At less than a hundred yards, I could do nothing but wait.

She broke into the open fifty feet away before walking to me. Not only was her Tennessee walker piled high with gear, she led a small mare laden with panniers. "Were you hoping to leave me behind?"

"You shouldn't involve yourself with my problems. They'll get you killed. Stay with Caroline. She'll help get you on your feet." I turned Buster and thumped his ribs with my heels to cross the creek.

I waited until we were inside heavy timber before carefully glancing behind. Leeann trailed us by ten yards. She raised her chin defiantly when she caught me looking. "I'm not going back."

You'll change your mind when you see what's waiting. Judging by her brother's rambling house, she was used to an opulent lifestyle, and I was positive my stump would be her worst nightmare.

I took her on the scenic route before we reached my hideaway. We were less than a mile from the highway on the backside of the lake, but we traveled four when I brought Buster to a halt. I patted his neck before dismounting slowly, sliding down his side until my feet were on the ground. My head swam as I clung to the saddle in an effort to stay upright. Lee came from behind to put a hand on my shoulder. "Do you need to rest?"

"Nope. I'm home."

"Huh?" She glanced around, I'm sure searching for a cabin or at least a shack. "Where?"

I turned slowly with my weight against Buster and pointed to the giant stump. "There. Pull the limbs away."

She carefully threw branches aside used to disguise the entrance. "No way!" Lee sounded far more excited than I could have imagined. She pointed at the ragged cloth door. "There?"

I nodded carefully, so the horizon wouldn't go wonky on me again. "Go ahead. There's a candle stub and a lighter to your left when you get inside." Once she got a load of my place, there was plenty of time for her to return home or seek sanctuary with my old boss.

She used a stick to prop my door open and made her way in on hands and knees. I heard the flick of a thumb on flint before another exclamation. "No freaking way! This's incredible!" Her reaction was far from what I expected. "Did you find this or make it?"

"Found it. I spent a little time getting it more comfortable."

"I see stored gear. Is it yours?"

"Yeah. How much damage did rodents do?"

A garbage sack filled with my stuff got tossed from inside. Lee crawled out behind it. She loosened the knot I'd tied and dumped the contents to the ground. My sleeping bag and pad looked no worse for wear. She lifted the former until getting a whiff and tossing it away. "Holy hell, that stinks."

"I slept in it for over a year. It's never been washed."

"It's sure as heck going to be scrubbed now."

Buster shifting his weight was enough to send me tumbling. I rolled to my side, head wobbling, the whole world spinning around me. Vaguely aware of vomiting again, I gave in rather than continue fighting.

* * *

I woke to an absolute lack of light. Something pulled at my cheek, and I raised a hand to feel. A bandage covered the split skin. Checking my scalp cautiously, I found a portion above my left ear shaven and covered by gauze and tape. "Cable?" Lee whispered. "Are you awake?"

"Yeah. Where are we?"

"Your tree. I dragged you inside after you passed out."

"Where's Buster and your horses?"

"I used your rope and rigged a picket line. They seemed comfortable enough."

"Did you water him?"

The exasperation in her sigh was clear. "Of course, I did. They've got plenty of browse around them, too. Anymore silly questions?'

"Yeah. Can you light my candle? I've got to pee."

As it turned out, I was wrapped in a couple blankets, while Lee lay across the firepit from me snuggled in a mummy bag. My head swam, but I dragged myself outside and did my business from my knees. She was waiting when I returned and helped cover me. I was surprised we both rested our heads on small pillows, a camping luxury I appreciated like never before. "How're you doing?" she asked.

"My head's spinning, and I feel like crap. Hope like hell I'm better in the morning."

I wasn't. My stomach tightened not long after I opened my eyes to see light outside and moments later was retching again. My dry heaves woke Lee. "You need a doctor, Cable. Let me ride to Caroline's place and call."

Rolling to my back after I finished, I covered my face with an arm to block light. "A day or two and I'll be okay."

My campmate was far more prepared than I could have imagined. After she got me to keep water down, Lee lit a camp stove and opened a can of soup. I lay motionless on my side and watched her through the opening as she added extra water and a package of dried ramen noodles. She was stirring them when I nodded off.

Somehow, I made it through the day and slept all night, too. Although lightheaded when I woke again, I threw my covers aside and gingerly sat up. Cold, still, and gray outside, I crawled to where I could stand and braced my shoulder against the stump. Wandering a dozen yards from camp, I kept a sigh of relief to myself when I released my bladder. Locating the steel cup kept in my saddlebags, I squatted by the small spring where fresh water ran into the lake. A fish jumped no more than ten feet out while I drank and drank again.

I couldn't argue with the location Leeann picketed our horses. It was easy to see where she moved them throughout the day, making sure they stayed in fresh browse. Buster's head came up the moment he saw me. I hurried to him rather than have him nicker or whinny. He pushed his head against me when I got close, nearly knocking me from my feet. I hugged his neck and breathed in his wonderful scent. I would never forget what he did for me—possibly saving my life in his refusal to leave me behind. "You're a good man, Buster," I said. "We'll have to see if Caroline's willing to let you go when this's over." I led him to the spring to drink his fill before following suit with Leeann's walker and packhorse. Afterward, I moved their line to a neighboring location.

Lee continued to slumber when I reached inside and retrieved the fishing rod I'd left stashed. A hook and sinker were still attached to the aging line. Searching through grass on an open spit of land along the lakeshore, I located a handful of cold grasshoppers unable to escape me in the cool morning. Another fish jumped a moment after I cast, taking my bait with it. I set the hook, and the fight was on.

Movement near my stump caught my attention when Leeann crept out and stood. She glanced and spied me immediately, taking long steps as she hurried to me. "Are you better this morning?" She didn't wait for an answer and knelt to peer closely with her one eye still open. The other remained swollen closed and looked worse than when she found me. "Your pupils look good. They were different sizes yesterday. Are you still dizzy?"

"A little lightheaded, but I feel a thousand percent better."

She noticed the string of fish next to my feet. "You got lucky!"

"They've been hungry for sure," I said.

My gait was slow and steady when I followed her back. Not wanting to build a fire, I didn't complain when she offered her stove. "I brought soup, a sack of potatoes, and nearly anything I could clear from the panty in a few minutes. Most of my gear consists of things I bought to camp with someday."

A panful of fish, fried spuds, and freeze-dried eggs filled us both. She even thought to bring a coffee pot and a can of ground java. "I can't imagine you heard any activity yesterday, did you?" Other than the occasional powerboat, my camp was cut off from civilization. We sat on the bole outside where we could see across the lake.

Lee nodded. "I wanted to talk to you about it. A helicopter was in the air most of the day."

"Fly over us?"

She nodded. "Sometimes, but not low enough to scare the horses, so I can't imagine they were visible through the forest canopy."

I couldn't keep satisfaction from my tone. "Good. Caroline got reinforcements."

"For what?"

"It's a long and painful story. One I'm not willing to share."

She stared for a moment before looking away and coming back to me. "We've got nothing but time. When you're ready, I'll be here with a shoulder if you need it."

"Huh uh. What I need is for you to leave me behind sooner rather than later. My advice is to see if you can stay in the trailer Caroline provided for me."

"You worry about you," she said. "I'll take care of us both."

We spent the day napping, eating, and I caught another mess of trout. Without me living there over four months, the inlet I fished restocked itself. Lee washed my sleeping bag the previous day while I slept, and we made sure it dried in the warm sun. I got a good look in a hand mirror at Lee's surgical skills. She'd used a razor brought in her personal things to shave around the long split on my skull, and closed the wound with butterfly bandages. My cheek looked good held together the same way. We kept a wary eye for anyone who might creep up on us, and Lee kept her rifle close. She surprised me when I asked about her gun, explaining she carried a Winchester chambered in .32-20, an underpowered round primarily used on homesteads for small game a century ago. After seeing my astonishment at a caliber I knew well, she went on to explain it once belonged to her great grandparents and got passed down to her when her grandmother died.

I found she stripped the holstered Kimber from my belt before getting me situated in blankets. Lee left it with the spare magazines on a shelf I carved almost two years ago. She watched with interest as I ejected the magazine and checked the chamber to see if it was loaded. It was exactly as I left it. Nor did she miss my satisfaction when I handled it before holstering. "You love your gun, don't you?"

"Love? I'm not sure I'd put it that way. I'm attached to it and have a great deal of appreciation for what it can do and has done for me."

I glanced up to find her studying me. "Do you normally go by Cable, or do you prefer William or even Bill?"

Her brows went up when I glared. "William's my father," I said harshly. "My name is Cable." Only Z got a pass when calling me by my given name.

"Jeez, okay," she said raising a palm. "Don't bite my head off."

"I'm sorry. Didn't mean to snap."

She hazarded a lopsided grin. "Got a little baggage there?"

"Nothing you need concern yourself with."

We ate more fish for dinner. My head no longer pounded, and I could move it without getting lightheaded or feel the earth shift beneath my feet. We'd not heard aircraft nor sirens, making me feel more confident about Caroline's chances. As long as she or Annie didn't come looking, I felt comfortable Lee and I remained safely hidden. If no one...sudden fear struck. "Lee, do you have a phone with you?"

She fumbled for her back pocket. "Yeah, do you need it? There's no service here."

"Doesn't matter." I drew my jackknife after she handed it over to pry open. It didn't take but a moment to pop the battery out. "I hope like hell your brother doesn't have the cavalry out searching. They'll triangulate on your cell."

She accepted it back without complaining. "I doubt it. He and Alexandra left the same night he gave me this." Lee gestured to her black eye and swollen cheek. "I don't know where they were going, but don't think he's given up on Caroline's ranch. I love my brother, but he's been frantic since learning she secured financing. Unfortunately, I've been exposed to a side of him I didn't know existed. Threats yes, but following through on them is new."

My guess was he'd already sunk a fortune into financing a resort, certain he was soon be the proud owner of the dude ranch. Preliminary studies and conceptual engineering would be costly. Slater must've put his eggs into one basket he saw plummeting to earth. Many who lived a luxurious lifestyle were only a bad deal away from losing it all.

I located my saddlebags beneath the canvas tarp I brought. Lee watched with interest as I entered the code into my briefcase and then used my thumbprint to unlock. I unlatched and opened it to expose my own cell. I'd wondered how Long Beard located me. No more. The Brotherhood of Loki likely tapped Z's phone in hopes I'd someday contact her. They zeroed in on me the same way I feared Lee's brother would find his sister. If the Brotherhood did it once, they could do it again. I pried the phone open and removed the battery.

After taking care of the horses and moving them close to my stump, we left our gear outside, well-covered with my canvas weighed down with stones from the lakeshore. I could smell a late summer storm coming and wanted our things secured. The last thing we did before retiring inside was to speak softly to our horses. A strong thunderstorm would likely frighten them. I wasn't ready to lose Buster to weather.

With temperatures falling, I built a small fire contained by my inside pit. Not much larger than two hands combined, we kept feeding it twigs and knots to develop a bed of coals. Growing gusts blew the smoke around before the first drops of rain hit. "Keep your coat handy," I warned. "We'll be in the worst of it to calm the animals."

Rain nearly drowned the sound of approaching thunder. I glimpsed flashes when the bottom moorings of my cloth door tore away before the boom of clashing temperature differentials. A whinny of fear outside caught our attention. We stared at each other for only a moment before we crawled out to face the tempest. In the beam of Lee's flashlight, my horse reared and pulled at his picket line in fright. Buster's eyes rolled when I got close enough. "Easy, man. Easy!" I shouted over the storm and grabbed his lead rope when it slapped me in the dark. Lee's consoling cries continued from the dark after her flashlight went out. I wrenched Buster's head down with an iron fist to offer a hand of comfort. He pressed his forehead against my chest and pushed but allowed me to stroke from his poll to muzzle. Although I feared for Lee and especially her Tennessee walker, Buster was my first worry.

Her flashlight came on after thunderclaps faded in the distance. However, driving rain didn't abate. The soaked woman appeared at my elbow. "I think Winston's okay now. Purdy's so old and deaf she probably didn't notice much. How's Buster?"

"Better." As a four-year old, he likely endured the worst storm of his life. At ten, Lee's walker took it in stride almost as much as her packhorse. Rainwater splashed when I patted his cheek and gave him confidence by stroking his crest. "You okay, boy?" I asked. He responded by resting his chin groove on my shoulder. "Go on inside," I said to Lee. "I'll spend a little more time making sure he's settling down."

She refused and helped me calm Buster further. He enjoyed four hands on him as we stroked his coat. "I think he's okay," she said when he dropped his head to browse. "We'd better get undercover."

Our fire burned down to a hot bed of coals. They hissed and sizzled as I dripped on it while adding fuel. Flames flared as they bit into the dry twigs, providing enough light so Leeann could switch hers off. We both tossed on more as the fire grew, before I pointed out the obvious. "We're getting everything wet."

I turned my back while Lee changed into dry clothes. She'd brought a couple hand towels and washcloths, and I heard her dry herself—then, the crinkle of her sleeping bag before she said, "Okay, your turn."

I stripped buck-assed naked before using the extra towel. No sense in sleeping in my still smelly bag while I was damp. While rinsing it in the lake helped, nothing short of a hot fire to throw it on would absorb the stench. Leeann handed me a washcloth after I got situated. "I'm pretty dry. Save it for something else."

"Get your cheek, hair, and scalp," she said. "We need to bandage your wounds again if they're going to heal anytime soon."

We slept late after staying awake far into the night. I worried about Buster too much to sleep. Although water dripped steadily, I was heartened by the sight of a bright day. Dressing as quietly as possible, I slipped out to check on my horse. His head came up the moment he saw me, and I got a low nicker in greeting. I think he was becoming equally fond of me as I was of him.

Leeann checked on us as I was finishing dragging a curry brush through his coat. "I swear," she said with a giggle, "You baby that horse more than a mother with a new infant."

I chuckled because it was true. "I watered Winston and Purdy. If you want to brush them, why don't we move them to new browse first?"

Lee caught me hunkered over the frying pan nursing a cup of coffee when she returned. "Is there any left?"

"On the grate inside. I nursed a smudge back to life to make a pot."

She came out with a full cup and emptied the pot into mine before making herself comfortable on the log. We split a mess of fried spuds with onion and egg mixed in. Lee squatted at the water's edge when we finished to rinse our dishes. She seemed to be a stickler over a place for everything, and made sure camp was spotless.

I used brush as camouflage while I worked my way along the shore with my fishing rod. Two were on my stringer when Lee appeared. "What're you doing?"

"Trying to catch something for lunch or supper."

"A better question is what are you planning to do?"

"Fish." I held the pair of paltry trout high, neither more than nine inches. "Take a dozen more like this to fill our bellies."

"But...I...aren't you going to do something?" I threaded another grasshopper onto my hook. To miss catching it in a low branch overhead meant I needed to lean far to my right. My bait struck exactly where I aimed. "About Caroline and Annie. The guys you're afraid might hurt them."

"They're probably okay. She's got family in law enforcement."

Obviously, my answer wasn't what was expected, and she retreated in anger. Perhaps disgust. She was ready for me when I returned to camp, playing in a fire not bigger than her hand. "Check this out!" I held a stringer of fish as long as my forearm.

"I don't get it," she said ignoring our next meal. "Do you plan to live here indefinitely?"

I shrugged. "I was here almost two years before going to work at the guest ranch."

"What about me?"

My sigh didn't endear me. "I told you to go to Caroline's."

"You might have died if I did."

"I'm better now. You should consider either returning home or asking Caroline for help." Her blackened eye was beginning to open, and I hoped her brother might feel guilt over his handiwork.

"You're not who I thought you were."

I chuckled grimly. "You're more right than you know, sister."

"It might have been better if I left you where I found you."

Her indignant assertion didn't surprise me. "For both of us."

My agreement made her angrier. "I should just leave you here alone."

"See? We agree. I've been telling you the same thing since you started dogging my heels." I needed to drive her away before she got swept up in my problems.

Feeling a little lightheaded, I opted for a nap. Leeann stayed outside, and I hoped to wake and find her and her gear absent and only Buster and our tack left behind. No such luck. I smelled and heard fish sizzling before I opened my eyes. I closed them again, hoping to dream her away. "Might as well come out and fill your plate if you've finished snoring," she called.

I accepted my share of trout and sat against my saddle. "Figured you'd be gone by now."

"Well, I'm not."

"I can help you pack and show you a quicker way to the road."

"I'll leave when I damn well please unless you're kicking me out."

"Naw, you don't bother me when I'm fishing or napping." I pointed at her plate with my fork. "It's not like you eat a lot." Three fish were on her platter, while mine was loaded with eight.

"Then, I'll stay as long as I want."

Chapter VIII

Nearly two hours after dark, I left Lee sleeping soundly and crept from our stump. The waxing moon worried me with its brightness. I figured it would be full in two or three days, and I could already distinguish individual rocks on Caroline's drive.

Nothing looked out of kilter when I passed a dozen parked cars and trucks and approached the barn. I stopped in the shadow of the huge structure to watch for movement. Occasionally, dudes would stay out late, although Caroline frowned on it. More than once, she made sure her guests were exhausted at the end of the next day as gentle retribution. Doug and Julio took great joy in wearing them out after learning their boss wasn't happy.

Finding the barn unchanged since my departure, I eased through late-night gloom to the rear of the house and peered through the window. A range light shone in the kitchen and one brighter in the living room. Movement inside caused me to shrink back as Caroline brought in dishes. It seemed odd she'd work so late, but I usually beat everyone to bed while living on the ranch. Perhaps my one-time boss was more of a night owl than I knew. She emptied coffee grounds into a bucket kept under the counter and rinsed the strainer. "Bruce," she called. "I'm taking my kitchen refuse to the garden. Back in a minute."

My mind raced. Bruce? Was a male friend visiting or a guest swapping stories? "Make it quick," a male voice yelled. "Don't force me come looking for you again."

I stepped back to where she would have difficulty noticing me when she came outside and closed the door. Caroline stood still for a moment without looking my way. "Meet me next to the machine shed," she whispered. Christ, I made a piss-poor voyeur if she noticed me in seconds. Nevertheless, I crossed behind her and waited inside the shadow as she spread the contents of her bucket. Caroline finished and sauntered until she was out of the moonlight before hurrying to where I stood and throwing her arms around me. "You're alive! We found so much blood on your trailer we were sure you'd been killed and your body dragged away."

"Who the hell is Bruce, and what in the world is going on here?"

"The gang you warned us about came the next day. My nephews were here with a show of force and drove them off. A couple were thrown in jail. Two nights after the boys went back to their duties, Bruce...one of the guys staying in the house with us...kicked in the door. Annie and I were warned not to contact police or else." I felt her body shake against mine. "They're bad people, Cable. Exactly like you warned us."

"How many are here?"

"Eight. Three men and women in the house with Annie and me. Another guy and girl are in your trailer. Not even Julio or Doug know they're staying. None of them venture outside."

"Why? I don't understand why they're here."

"They want money from us because...as they say...we caused them to ride so far. We owe them is their argument."

I hated to ask. "How much are they extorting you for?"

"A hundred thousand."

"You don't have it even after the financing."

"Our terms of agreement haven't been submitted yet. Slater's got a legal team introducing legalese to block our loan. Your foundation hired lawyers to fight on our behalf, but we still have to go to court." It felt good to hear Z listened when I asked her to make sure our lawyers fight hard. "We've got one more party coming before the season's over, and we don't have enough to feed them. I don't know what we're going to do, Cable. We've ran out of nearly everything."

"You're short on food without cash?"

"Guests pay long before they arrive. The money's gone, used to pay our mortgage and bills. Our freezers are empty with nothing to fill them. I don't want to butcher my hens, but I don't know what to do."

"Can you drive to town and shop?"

"No, they won't let me or Annie leave, but I can get deliveries. We've done it many times in the past."

She needed to go. "Order what you need tomorrow, then find a reason for either you or Annie to check the stables after dark. Make any excuse. I'll leave money under the cinderblock next to the faucet on the north side. You remember the one I'm talking about?" I used it to set a bucket on to fill with water for stock stabled inside.

"Cable, you don't have to—"

I stopped her. "Yes, I do. Have faith in me, Caroline. I got you into this, so let me see if I can get you out."

"Do you have Buster? Tell me they didn't release or kill him."

She probably couldn't see my nod. "Yeah, he saved my life. You and I need to have a serious conversation about the horse...but not now." I paused for a moment before asking, "Caroline, have they touched you or Annie?"

"No, they made insinuations, but the women put an end to it. Not that it made us feel any better, because they don't mind when Annie or I catch the back of a hand."

"They've hit you both?"

"You know Annie's mouth. She's learned the hard way to keep it closed. These guys understand I have to interact and cook for our guests, so I haven't been roughed up much." I breathed a sigh of relief at the latter but felt terrible for Annie.

* * *

My stump loomed large at what I guessed was after four a.m. I slipped Leeann's flashlight under the edge of her pillow where she kept it after getting into my own bed. My head pounded with exhaustion after making the round trip on foot. I couldn't hear her light snore after getting situated and feared I woke her. Sleep caught me before I got a chance to worry.

I got up to find Leeann sitting on the shore holding my fishing rod. Two trout and a small catfish adorned her stringer. She didn't bother to look up when I stopped. "You got in pretty late," she said.

Lee glanced at me after I squatted. "I was afraid you heard me."

"Watched you leave, too. How're things at Caroline's? Or were you there to see Annie?"

"Annie can't stand me, and the feeling is mutual. She and Caroline are in a tough spot, though."

Lee abandoned fishing and swiveled to face me. "What's going on, Cable?"

"The guy I warned Caroline about returned with friends. They've set up in the house while they extort money from her."

"Oh, no!"

"Yeah, it's not good. Not only are Caroline and Annie in danger, but she considers their guests hostages, too. If we confront the crooks, they won't hesitate to hurt any dude they can get their hands on. Also, Caroline's got hungry mouths to feed and no money to buy vittles."

She frowned. "I don't get it. Weren't they approved by your foundation?"

"It's not mine," I said through clenched teeth. "It's my father's. He named me president, but I'm just a figurehead. Hell, I've never attended a meeting or got involved until I learned about Caroline's situation and made a couple calls. The foundation was an exercise of my dad's to take at least partial control of my life."

Leeann dropped the subject, and we returned to camp after I gutted her catch. She checked her watch when we reached the stump. "It's almost one. How does fried fish and soup sound?"

She cooked, and I washed dishes after we finished eating. I hoped Caroline made her food order—to be paid only if she got my cash. After I retrieved my case, Lee didn't hide her curiosity as I opened it. My almost indestructible attaché was an expensive gift I rarely let myself ponder because of painful memories about who gave it. Lifting one edge of the padded interior, I didn't realize I held my breath until the emergency money stowed away so long ago was visible. I retrieved it along with a debit card. A low whistle made me look up. "Caroline needs help," I said.

I counted a thousand in fifties before doubling it to two grand after eyeing what was left. "Do you always carry so much?" Lee asked.

I shook my head. "No, this's my mad money. If anything happened, I'd at least have a gun and enough to get by." It dawned on me she might think I was some rich man's kid, not knowing the value of a dollar. "I worked hard for every nickel of this," I said. Replacing what was left—eighteen thousand—I closed and locked the case.

"How're you getting it to her?"

"I told her where I'd leave it tonight after dark."

"You're not returning to the ranch, are you?"

"Of course, I am. I promised."

"Wouldn't they be safer if my brother bought them out? Dee offered three million, but I overheard him tell Alexandra he could get financing to pay eight." She felt around her damaged eye socket. "It was right about then when I stopped his knuckles with my face."

I stared at Leeann, deliberately taking her measure. "I'll give you a thousand dollars for your rifle. Right now, sight unseen." I hadn't yet handled the gun.

"No! It originally belonged to my great grandparents. Grandma asked that it go to me."

"Two thousand." She shook her head. "I'll give you five thousand, which is a few times what it's worth in what's called very good shape. Sell it to me. I've got the money right here."

"I can't. Dad told me the story of how they saved for a year before having enough to buy it. Great-Gram used it to keep the kids fed while great grandpa fought in World War Two. She killed deer and turkeys...and...and anything they could eat. I was born because she kept my grandpa from starving."

"You're telling me it means everything to you and selling would be too painful? Passing through generations makes it worth more, doesn't it? Sentimental value is far more important than a monetary equivalent."

"Of course. A precious family heirloom shouldn't be sold at any—" Her lids flared wide. "You're not asking to buy my gun. You're talking about the dude ranch."

I nodded. "She can't sell her property any more than you can let your family rifle go. Henry and Caroline built their place to pass down to their offspring. Annie's the only one left, so it goes to her. Not to someone who feels he needs it more. Caroline's got over forty years of sweat, heartbreak, and joy into it."

Lee sighed and made a face. "I know. Dee never let the news slip he hoped to purchase it until not long before I rode with him to their place."

"He didn't plan to pay three million or even half that much." I went on to explain her brother's meddling in Caroline's original loan, how the bank called it in, and made getting it refinanced elsewhere impossible. They'd be forced to sell for pennies on the dollar or let the bank take over. Her jaw grew slack and her eyes widened as I told what I knew of their story.

"What a bastard. If I ever thought of going back, it's over now. I don't want or need him to spend a damn dollar on me again."

"What'll you do? You need a job and place to live."

She shrugged. "I don't know and don't care. Guess I'll talk to Annie and see if she could hire me."

I winked. "I'll put in a good word for you. After Caroline is taken care of, as far as I'm concerned, you can have what remains in my case." I did a quick calculation. "Except for a hundred dollars or so."

"No! That's your money."

"I won't need it. If you change your mind, all you have to do is say the word, and it's yours." I left her behind with a funny look on her face as I wandered off to check on and curry Buster.

* * *

My anger grew as I stared up at Leeann already mounted. I'd saddled Buster and went inside the stump to retrieve the cash I'd fitted inside a Ziplock bag, along with two extra magazines for my Kimber. I wore Mom's .22 to access by cross draw just in case. Lee threw a leg over the walker's back as I crawled out. "You're not going," I said. "It'll be a quick in and out, and I'll be back before you know it. No sense in getting involved."

"You need me, and you know why," she said. I cocked my head impatiently. "No way can you walk Buster to the barn. He'll have to be left behind. Who knows what might befall him while you're gone?" Ah, she played on my heartstrings.

I mounted quickly. "Fine. It'll be your job to keep him still while I'm gone."

It wasn't quite dark when we got to the road, but it was black as the inside of an inkwell under the forest canopy, though I could see a mile down the gravel thoroughfare when we came out. While little traffic graced the course even in midday, it'd be my luck to get caught in the open where one of us could be recognized. We dismounted and waited inside the tree line until it was hard to see under a light cloud cover.

Neither of us spoke from the time we left camp until we stopped at the Hagseth driveway. I dismounted and passed my reins to Lee. "Might be a half hour, or it might take two. I'm not sure. Take Buster and ride like hell if anything happens. These guys don't play games." Standing inches from her thigh, I saw her nervous nod in the gloom. Good. Fear could very well keep her alive if events went south.

I crept forward in grass I'd mowed next to the drive. It took most of the thirty minutes I estimated to reach my goal. Although I could hear music, the barn felt still but for the occasional horse stirring inside its stall. No sense in getting in a hurry at the end, and I didn't move a muscle until finishing a slow count to a hundred. The cinder block I looked for lay within twenty feet. I glimpsed it twice when the moon gleamed through overcast. A side entrance through which I watered the stock beckoned.

I stepped inside the empty door casing leading into the interior between a stall and the tack room, basically, a fifteen-foot hallway partially open on one side. Listening carefully, I waited to get a mental snapshot of the ranch's heartbeat. Certain the time was now, I eased forward and slipped the Ziplock bag beneath the chunk of concrete before retreating to deeper shadows. Even if neither woman appeared, and Julio or Doug watered the horses the same way, the sealed plastic would keep the cash dry.

My move came none too soon. The farmhouse door flashed light and closed quickly, allowing loud music to escape for only a moment. Quick footwork as Annie ran down the steps made me groan. Why not Caroline? I kept out of sight inside the darkened hallway as she trotted closer.

The same door opened, this time slamming as another body followed her. "Get your ass back here, girl," a male voice yelled. I guess he didn't care how it sounded to guests who could hear.

She kept coming and called over a shoulder. "I've got to check the gate. Our stock will scatter across the county if it wasn't latched properly."

"Stop right there," the male shouted. I groaned to myself when Annie came to a halt within five feet of the faucet and twenty-five from me. He strode toward her with clenched fists. "You ask for permission to step outside, hear me?"

"I'm sorry. I'm sorry," she said, backing toward the barn with an outstretched palm. He didn't bother to offer warning before backhanding Annie across the cheek. She fell to her rear, barely missing the faucet while scrambling backward to escape his onslaught. Rather than punch her with a closed fist, the man pulled her up by the hair before battering her methodically with an open hand.

Another may have chosen a different method of handling the situation. The problem was I'd dealt with his people and knew what they were capable of. None of them played fair. He might beat Annie to death and never think about it again. I understood intimately the level of violence to which the Brotherhood of Loki was willing to stoop. He didn't stop his slow pummeling of her face until hearing four clicks when I thumbed back the hammer of my mom's .22.

Sights weren't needed to fire a gun I'd shot most of my life, and the bullet entered his brain a few inches above the bridge of his nose. He collapsed to land across Annie. I holstered the revolver as I hurried to her side and rolled him away. She took the hand I offered and rose, wobbling as she caught her balance. "You okay?"

Her arms went around me and she sobbed, "I thought he'd kill me this time."

"You need to call the police again," I said. "Stay here while I get Caroline out."

"No!" she whispered hysterically. "They promised if Mom and I ran off they'd kill our guests." She trembled violently in my arms. "Besides, they have our cellphones."

"Damn." I thought for a moment. Only one thing to do. Go through the front door and kill anything that moved except Caroline. "How many are inside?"

"Two men, now, and three women. Another couple in the Airstream."

Her news made me shudder. Thoughts of the lowest forms of life I could imagine sleeping in the same bed I once used twisted my mouth in disgust. "How soon before your dudes leave?"

"Tomorrow afternoon. Last group of the season will arrive Monday. They're here five nights and six days."

"What's today?" I tended to lose track when time was no longer important.

"Thursday."

I pushed her away. "You'd better get inside." I retrieved the hidden money and thrust it into her hands. "Tell them..." I thought a moment. "Tell them a horse was out, and it knocked you down because the gate was left open."

Annie pointed at the body. "What do I say about him?"

"Nothing. Don't let on you knew he was outside. You were busy corralling one of your guest's mount. I'll take care of him."

"Thank you," she said. "Cable, I'm sorry. So very sorry about the way I've treated you."

"No worries. Hustle inside before someone comes looking." I turned my back to face the job ahead.

Lifting a dead weight from the ground proved challenging. Annie was in the house before I stood with the dead gangster over one shoulder. The body slenderer and significantly shorter than me kept the job from being impossible. Yet I got the corpse only halfway down the drive before I could no longer carry it.

Leeann startled when I appeared. "Oh, God," she whispered. "You scared me."

I took the reins she held out. "Ride back to camp. I'll meet you there." I didn't look to see if she followed directions.

Buster refused to stand while I struggled to lift the body. I planned to fasten it across the saddle and lead my horse away. Lashed to the fence rail running from the road to stables, he danced and stymied my attempts.

My strength flagged. "Let me help." Shocked at the voice, I turned to make out Leeann dismounting in the gloom. "Winston doesn't mind packing. I'll hold him while you load."

"You know what this is?"

"I heard the shot," she said simply.

Like a scene in an old western movie, we tied him face down across her saddle. Lee was right. Winston didn't mind the dead weight or smell. "You okay riding double behind me?"

"Sure, but what's your plan?"

"Get the body away from here. Otherwise, we'll be looking at reinforcements being called. Refinancing will be the least of Caroline's problems."

I mounted Buster and took Winston's reins from Lee. Removing my foot from the stirrup, I braced myself to allow her to use it and swing behind. Buster humped a little after feeling the extra weight before settling down. Lee wrapped an arm around my waist after I handed the reins back.

We trotted in the grass to the road. "May I offer a suggestion?" Lee asked.

"I'm all ears."

"Ride east. We'll cut north through the area where I found Buster standing over you. From there, we can travel up the mountain past Leeann Lake to the ridge above. Beyond is a remote area with a deep canyon and dry creek bed. I think we can dispose of it there."

Christ, what she suggested would take four or five hours in the light of day. Besides, Lee would literally know where at least one of my skeletons was buried. I'd meant to dump it in the lake except I couldn't think of anything to weight it down. A floating corpse would draw unwanted attention to Caroline and Annie.

Using brief flashes of her mini mag, we passed her lake as the eastern sky brightened, and crested the ridge as the sun broke over the horizon. It took another hour before locating a way into the area she suggested. The terrain was far more rugged, causing me to fear for Buster. More than once, he sat on his haunches as we descended a steep slope. Winston fared better with half the weight lying low in the saddle.

The sun was high overhead when we located the perfect spot. An ancient creek eroded an overhang of dirt, rocks, and boulders. Lee helped untie the body and drag it into place. We put an hour into undermining the bank and burying the corpse under tons of debris. I stood back to gaze at our handiwork with a critical eye. To me, it looked no different than any other minor hillside collapse.

My throat was as dry as if I swallowed a handful of dust. Lee sat on a nearby boulder, looking as tired as I felt. Her dark hair hung wet and lifeless, while her cheeks were caked with a mixture of sweat and dirt.

I retrieved my canteen from a saddlebag and swished a mouthful before spitting, followed by two long pulls. "Thirsty?" I asked.

"Yeah." She caught the plastic container I tossed underhand. Lee mimicked me before screwing the top on and got ready to toss it back.

"It's going to be hot today. Drink all you need."

She underhanded it back to me anyway. "I'm good. What do we do now?"

"We don't have much water, but it's not safe to cross the hill again. I'd hate to be identified by the wrong eyes." I spoke while checking the seat jockey and fender of her saddle for blood after noticing the corpse didn't bleed. If any got left, I couldn't find it.

"Shall we spend the day on top and ride to your stump after dark?" She stood when I nodded—ready to ride.

"Let's go."

* * *

We found a cool spot out of the sun with plenty of graze for our mounts. Lee and I stretched out on our coats. She laughed at me when I took time to brush Buster, but relieved me of the comb when I finished and started on Winston. Both animals did yeoman work and deserved extra care. Each day Buster showed more he could eventually become a great horse. After finishing with her mount, Lee made herself comfortable on her coat again. "I'm hungry," she said.

Her announcement made me chuckle. "Makes two of us."

She sighed. "What I wouldn't give for a juicy steak right about now."

"Surf and turf," I suggested.

"Mm—"

We were silent a moment listening to our stock graze. "How're you doing?"

Her answer wasn't long in coming. "A little freaked out. I've never seen a dead body let alone help bury one."

"It was a first for me, too. The burying part, I mean."

"Am I going to prison for helping?"

"I won't tell if you don't."

Lee rolled to her side to peer directly in my eyes. "You owe me a story."

I made a face. "I stopped him from beating Annie. He might have killed her. She and Caroline are terrified."

"I'm sorry for her...for them both...but that's not the one I need to hear."

She watched without blinking as I took a deep breath and changed my focus to a point in the distance. "Trust me. You don't want to know."

"You owe me," she repeated.

"I grew up on a ranch not much different from Caroline's, except we raised beef instead of teaching dudes to ride. Mom and Dad divorced when I was five. I barely remember them together. She was the pretty young waitress in the middle of nowhere swept from her feet by the rich man who stopped where she worked."

"Why?"

"Why what?"

"What was the reason for their divorce?"

"Mom grew up on a farm wishing to own a ranch someday. She was a homebody, whereas my dad was seldom there. They couldn't live separate lives and make it work. Mom filed for divorce, and he fought her until finally understanding she didn't want his money. Only the ranch he'd purchased as her wedding gift. Then he couldn't sign papers fast enough from what I understand."

"Do you have any siblings?"

"Yeah—" Try as I might, I couldn't continue. Finally, I got up and walked to where I could better see Buster and Winston.

I heard her feet in the grass, so Lee's soft voice behind didn't startle me. "You don't have to finish. I can see it's something very private."

"I haven't told it before."

A gentle hand on my shoulder was almost enough to make me break down. It was reminiscent of one I'd felt most of my life. "Let's get some sleep," she said softly.

"I have an older sister," I told Lee after we sat. "Her name is Zoe, but I've always called her Z. We rarely saw each other after the divorce. She went with Dad to New York, while we stayed with Mom in southwest Montana."

"We?"

The pain struck me no differently than the impact of a locomotive. It crashed into me and ground my body into dust. I swear if Lee wasn't with me, I'd have eaten a bullet from my Kimber. "Jess. She was my twin sister named after Mom. Mom was Jessica, and my sister went by Jess."

"Was? Did you mean to say it that way?"

Lee watched as I slid my belt from my jeans loops and lay both guns aside. They weighed heavily on my waistband. "She was killed...murdered."

"Oh," she said in surprise. "I-I'm so, so sorry."

"We did everything together while growing up, the same as any other set of twins. I could start a sentence, and she would finish it. Jess was older by a few minutes and never let me forget I was the baby of two older sisters."

"What happened?"

Indeed. What did happen? "She wanted to see the world after we graduated from high school, where I wasn't interested in travel. Jess went to UTI-Sacramento, and I went across the mountains to Pocatello, Idaho. I earned a business degree in hopes of helping our ranch's financial viability. Mom scrimped where she could and saved every dollar of child support my dad provided. Jess and I both worked as much as we could to help pay the rest. She waited tables, while I stocked shelves and worked the counter in a sporting goods store."

"You didn't talk to your father about helping you with school?"

"Hell, no. Neither of us wanted anything to do with him. He left us and took Z away, although we talked to her on the phone. She came home during summer months until she was sixteen and boy crazy."

"I'm sorry. Divorce is difficult for children. They don't understand," Lee said.

"I got my bachelor of science in business admin and returned to the ranch when I was twenty-two. Jess stayed for a couple extra years and got her degree in veterinarian science. We always figured between the two of us we could turn the ranch into a money-maker. Problem was she came home with a big belly."

Lee's brow furrowed before she understood. "Pregnant?"

"Yeah, she didn't tell us, but Jess fell in love with a guy in Sacramento. She thought they would marry until he knocked her up. She came straight home after he booted her."

"How did your mom react?'

"She didn't. Mom died of ovarian cancer a few months after I returned from college. I didn't know she was even sick until I got home."

"Ohh—" Leeann whispered.

"Jess gave birth to a boy and named him Daniel after Mom's dad. Danny was almost six when it happened." I stopped shredding the grass stem I held while telling my sad story when Lee sniffed. Tears flowed steadily to drip from her chin.

"Turns out Danny's father was a member of a biker gang called The Brotherhood of Loki. Jess let me see plenty of photos she took in and around their clubhouse. It was during...as she called it...her rebellious years. She never confided in me or Mom about her personal life. I guess she considered herself a biker bitch and wore the tattoos to prove it. 'Tats' she called them."

"I'm sorry, but I'm not a fan of skin art," Lee said quietly. "A lot of my friends at school were covered."

"Me, neither." I made a personal exception to my rule in the case of service members who served in combat. Or the way Annie's husband's name was inked on the inside of her right wrist. "Dad came back into our lives not long after learning he was a grandfather. Neither of us trusted the old man, but it was his right to see his grandchild. He burrowed his way into our lives again over the next five years."

"What happened?"

"I've always guessed it was Jess's boyfriend who recognized her with dad. Probably on television. Like with me, the old man insisted she spend time with him in New York and meet the power players. I think Danny's father decided he could make real money by snatching and holding Jess and her boy for ransom. Took them off the streets of our hometown when they went shopping."

"No, not your nephew, too?"

"Police weren't to be notified, and the Brotherhood wanted millions for the return of my sister and nephew. I hoped I could mortgage the ranch and keep the old man out of it, but they insisted on too much."

"Couldn't your father pay?"

"He could've...but refused. Stingy old bastard insisted we could bargain to get Jess and Danny released if we reasoned with the gang and agreed not to press charges. Dad and I fought and argued for days, but he wouldn't give in. There was a live video feed where we could see them bound and gagged at a table. They eventually accepted dad's refusal of their terms and shot both in the backs of their heads while we watched." It happened exactly as Long Beard reenacted at Caroline's. I felt curiously empty rather than torn apart with the emotion I normally experienced when memories boiled to the surface. "Police located their bodies exactly where we were promised they'd be."

"My God," Lee whispered. "I can't imagine."

"I buried them and refused to let the old man come to the funeral, but Z insisted she be allowed to attend. Stayed at the ranch for a couple weeks afterward, too."

"Were the police able to gather evidence on the gang?"

I shook my head. "Nope. They may have gotten some leads, but nothing came of it."

Lee's tears finally slowed as she pulled herself together indignantly. "You mean to tell me no one caught their murderers?"

My heartrate increased as I remembered. "Yeah," I said. "I did."

Chapter IX

Exhausted by a lack of sleep, adrenaline rushes, and our long ride, I dropped the subject and made myself comfortable on my coat. Lee eventually realized I wasn't going to say any more, wiped her cheeks, and pulled herself together before settling in for a nap. Already tired before the emotional toll, I don't remember falling asleep. In it, I dreamed of better days when growing up with Jess.

I woke to a cool wind blowing inside my collar. Twilight took over as the sun dropped below the horizon. Down the mountain, the valley already lay shrouded in darkness. "Lee?" I reached and touched her shoulder. "Time to go."

She sat and pushed her hair back. "Ugh. I could've slept until daylight."

Her smile was crooked with the scar. It looked as if some of her facial muscles were severed in the accident, or she suffered a stroke. "We'd better find the horses, or your wish'll come true.

Buster heard my voice and already took hobbled steps in our direction. He pushed his long face against me when I draped a rope over his neck. The simple act was all he needed to follow me back to camp. Winston came willingly while Leeann trailed us. Although our water supply was low, both horses were thirsty. Lee and I barely wet our throats before I poured the remainder into my hat and split it between our mounts.

We rode fast and straight. Almost fully dark when we passed Leeann's Lake, Lee broke out her faithful mini mag flashlight for short bursts. Never stopping but once at what I called Turtle Creek Crossing to slake the horses' thirst, we hurried through the gloom until reaching my stump. Lee's packhorse nickered at our arrival. "I'll bet Purdy's thirsty, too," Lee said. She groaned after dismounting and catching her balance. It didn't take long before we got our stock taken care of and moved into new browse. We used our cups to drink from the spring until our stomachs sloshed. "Don't get me up in the morning if you wake first." It was more warning than idle comment.

"Same goes to you," I said. It felt good to slide into my sleeping bag no matter how it stank. My air mattress took away the uncomfortable debris I'd dealt with on the ridgetop. Leeann didn't bother to undress after kicking her boots off and falling face first onto her bed. Her snores began before I turned to my side and faced away.

Well after noon when we woke, Lee followed me out to a windy day. We lazed the rest of it away while napping and eating. Branches snapping and breaking kept us both on edge after what we'd done. To save an innocent life, I'd killed a man without hesitation. Curiously, I considered him more animal than human after suffering at the hands of his brothers. My sister and nephew were torn away from life with less thought than I offered him. Where they were innocent, the dead gang member's hands were as dirty as the killers of my family.

Leeann glanced at me while we were on our knees at the water's edge scrubbing dishes from supper. "You know what freaks me out?"

"Probably what you helped me do."

"Well...yeah...but not as bad as the other thing."

"What?"

"You don't seem bothered."

I couldn't help but glare. "How would you feel if someone kept your brother hostage before you watched him die?"

She nodded. "I get it, although I can't imagine."

"No. It's impossible unless you've suffered through it. Even then, it feels like a bad dream I'll wake from at any moment."

"What're your plans? Those remaining might be taking out their frustrations on Caroline or Annie, perhaps both."

Leeann gave words to my biggest fear. My former bosses faced a terrible future if I didn't do something. Unless Caroline or Annie got word out through a guest, they were without a way to contact help. "First, I need you to go home and make amends with your family." I didn't overlook her swollen cheek turning from black to blue and green. Although bloodshot, at least she could see from the once closed eye. Slater would pay for his misdeed if we met again. Lee proved herself as a great friend offering immeasurable aid, never shrinking in the face of life-altering danger. "You're dirty, sweaty, and I'm certain desperate for a shower. Think how good clean clothes and your own bed would feel."

We made ourselves comfortable on the log outside my stump with cups of fresh water. Lee obviously gave great thought to my suggestion while we sipped. "No, I don't think so," she finally said. "Damien isn't someone I want to see right now. You and I have food, water, shelter, and an inlet to wash in. I'll stay here, if you don't mind."

"If you haven't noticed, the nights are cooling. Won't be long before snow flies. Besides, we're not playing a game, Lee. I'm not going to lie. Bad things are gonna happen."

"Bad things are already happening," she said in a wry tone.

I could only nod. "Point taken. However, in this instance you could be killed. We're not playing a kids game of cops and robbers."

"Although distant, Caroline and Annie are neighbors of mine. I'd like to think they'd help me if I were in need."

"They would. You want to know what they'd do?" Lee shook her head. "They'd go home and call the sheriff's office to tell them you and your family were hostages. We've got a narrow window of opportunity. Caroline's group leaves today and the next doesn't arrive until Monday. There're no extra hostages for two full days. Now is the time."

Leeann didn't speak until she finished her coffee. "Okay," she finally agreed. "I'll do it. My gear and our provisions can stay here, and Purdy will go with me so I can resupply if it's possible. I plan to return either later tonight or in the morning."

We discussed her message to the authorities to keep my name out of the public. I waited until she mounted before handing Lee the lead rope to her packhorse. "Stay home if you can," I said. "Make peace with Dee. Next few days are going to get ugly if the law can't end this thing."

She put a hand on her thigh as she looked down at me. "You know, before all this started, I kinda liked you. Mainly as a great riding partner and conversationalist, although a good listener, too." She winked and gave me her lopsided smile. "Now? You're growing on me, Cable. Keep the candle burning until you hear my holler."

I didn't answer and stepped back as she turned Winston and clucked to start Purdy moving. My main job was to see Caroline and Annie safe before I could focus on myself again. I kept watch until she vanished into deeper forest.

Buster didn't bother to hump when my ass hit the saddle. It seemed he learned my moods and reacted to my needs. I turned his head toward the road where we could intersect Hagseth property, armed with both my Kimber and spare magazines, along with Mom's .22 revolver.

From my vantage looking down from the north on Caroline's ranch house less than half a mile away, I could discern no outside movement. Leeann left camp for home more than two hours ago. If deputies didn't arrive soon, I'd take the fight directly to those holding Caroline and Annie hostage. I wouldn't accept a surrender nor take prisoners.

An hour or less of light remained when the first flashing blue strobes appeared on the road. At least a dozen cruisers and SUVs were led by a heavy SWAT truck, and they turned onto Caroline's drive. Uniformed riflemen quickly took up positions in the barnyard facing the house. Officials weren't taking chances. Distant thumps got my attention as a state police helicopter arrived on the scene only minutes later.

I'm not sure if law enforcement contacted those inside. Someone didn't wait, exiting Caroline's kitchen and disappearing before heavily armed law enforcement moved around the house. Thing was, the bastard was running directly at me. The person vanished into the timber of the lightly forested slope. Dogs would likely be turned loose to locate the runner after officials got an accurate headcount. It was time to ride if I didn't want to get caught up in the excitement and ultimately handcuffed and fingerprinted.

Instead, I sat and watched from my high vantage. Spotlights from the circling helicopter switched on, illuminating Caroline's home in the gathering gloom. I suspected those in charge learned they were a head short when the beam widened its circles, moving slowly around the barnyard and adjacent buildings. Walking Buster through the trees to keep an eye on the sprinter, I got a good look at the ravine used as an escape route. The gully led away from my present position, but I knew approximately where it came out. Tickling Buster's ribs with my heels, I turned his head to reach it first.

The closer the runner got, the more I could see it was a man. Better yet, it was Long Beard, the one I surmised was named Bruce. He could have taken any other direction and climbed the far more open steep banks, but instead opted to take the route with more underbrush to where I waited next to the rootwad of a wind-toppled ponderosa. With Buster tied in thicker trees up the slope, I hefted a short length of busted pine bough the diameter of my forearm and three feet long.

I offered the bastard the same opportunity he afforded me when he broke through the brush to where I waited. Huffing and blowing, knowing he couldn't stop or risk capture, Long Beard didn't see me until I stepped forward in full swing. An arm coming up to block it snapped against the dense wood. Even partially cushioned, he didn't misdirect the blow meant to take his head off. Instead, the heavy branch impacted his teeth and nose. Long Beard's feet flew from beneath him, and he landed on his back without moving. Hunkering near the man to learn if he was dead or alive, I could only smile at his ruined features after I heard him breath. For a moment, I considered trussing him like a hog. In the end, I expected a K-9 and his deputy would locate the gangster quickly enough. With barely sufficient light remaining to find my way to Buster, I mounted and rode west in an attempt to avoid law enforcement.

* * *

Leeann hadn't returned when I got back to my stump. I breathed a sigh of relief. She needed to make up with her brother and pursue a life with a future. My watch read four-thirty after I got Buster situated. With daylight ninety minutes away, I didn't bother to leave the candle burning as she asked. Lee would be tucked safely in bed hoping her message to law enforcement got to the right people.

I woke early when Buster nickered. My watch let me know I got less than two hours of sleep. Dawn barely broken, I eased outside after peering around the cloth door with my Kimber in hand. "Cable?" No doubt it was a cry for help. I crawled out fearful of a trick.

Leeann stumbled and fell fifty yards away through the timber. "Lee?" I sprinted to reach her with the handgun in my fist. She waited on all fours with her head down. "Where's your horse? Were you thrown? How bad are you hurt?" She yelped in pain when I laid a palm on her back, and I jerked it away.

She dropped to her elbows and put her face in her hands. "He hurt me," she said with a whimper.

I took a knee next to her. "Who? Who hurt you?"

Leeann lifted her face. "Dee," she whispered through ballooned lips.

"What did he do?"

"He punched me again and whipped me with a belt."

A second black eye matched her first. "Is anything broken? Do your insides hurt?" I feared he may have used his fists where they'd cause life-threatening damage.

"No body blows this time...only to the face to knock me down."

"Let me get you to camp. You almost made it," I said. Best to keep my tone firm and steady to give her confidence.

She held out a hand so I could help her up, and I didn't miss lash marks on her forearm. "I'd almost given up finding you until Buster nickered."

"I'm going to kill your brother," I said under my breath.

Leeann heard my muttered threat. "No, you're not," she said as I carefully walked her to the stump.

"He's unhinged. I'm surprised he's never struck you before. He needs to pay."

Lee chuckled grimly before her breath caught, and she winced with each step when I steered her to the log out front. "Don't worry. He's going to pay."

I sat her carefully and grimaced when she flinched. Damien didn't miss her butt either. "Planning to press charges?"

"Worse," she said with determination. "I'll never speak to him again."

"Good for you, but I'm sorry for the friction I caused. This never would have happened if we didn't meet."

She shrugged gingerly. "Perhaps...perhaps not."

"What happened to set him off this time?"

"It started when I got back, and he accused me of stealing Winston and Purdy. Said I had no right to take them. He's wrong. I bought my horse with money I got from my high school graduation. Winston's mine."

"Purdy?"

Leeann's chuckle was devoid of humor. "I borrowed her."

"Your sister-in-law didn't help you?"

"She was in their bedroom and didn't come out. They got bad news today. He was already out of control when I walked into the house." When she didn't offer more, I decided it wasn't my place to ask.

Removing her jacket was difficult. She cried out in pain each time I tugged a sleeve. Finally, we got her hands overhead where I could slip it from both arms at the same time. "I need to lift the back of your blouse to see how bad it is."

"I know. I hope it hurts worse than it looks."

I cursed after tugging it upward and she helped by raising the front, too. "God damn it." Her skin looked more dreadful than I feared with welts dotting her back where the leather tip popped. Very little of what I could see wasn't black or blue. "You need to stand."

She asked me to give her a boost. "Is it bad?"

"Want me to lie or tell you the truth?" The bruising disappeared inside the waist of her jeans.

Leeann sighed. "Sugarcoat it a little."

"It's bad. Your skin didn't break open...but close. I see very little not bruised or welts. You should see a doctor." Some striping extended to her ribs and stomach with more on both arms. The bastard must have whaled the hell out of her.

"Not much we can do about it now," she said after a moment of considering. "I need sleep before anything."

"Actually, there is. Jess used to bruise easily. Mom used cold compresses on them to reduce swelling, then followed it with heat the next day."

"I'm tired, and we don't have ice nor a heat pad."

"We've got something close. Wait here." I hurried and soon returned with her larger coffee pot filled with cold spring water before ducking inside for a wash cloth. "Hold it on your face. Let's see if we can reduce the swelling."

While I saw no obvious change, I cooled her back and arms as best I could. Eventually, shaking from exhaustion and shivering with cold, Lee stretched out with my help to lie on her sleeping bag inside our humble home. Although equally tired, I left to water and move Buster to better browse.

My breath caught in my throat when I returned. She'd tossed her blouse aside and somehow skinned out of her jeans. The backs of her legs appeared almost as bad. "Are you awake?" I whispered.

Voice muffled by her pillow: "Yeah. How does it look?"

"Not good. I'd better get more water and work your hamstrings."

Cold as she was, Lee slept through my efforts. My hands ached from the freezing water. I rinsed the pot and cloth and left them outside. I needed sleep as badly as my injured campmate.

* * *

I left Leeann inside after I woke. She'd snuggled deep within her bag, and her slumber appeared peaceful. Memories of her striped back and legs made me shake my head. What sort of man could beat a family member—let alone a woman—and still be able to live with his actions? Feeling responsible for Leeann made me not only protective of her but angry. In trying to find my way out of this world, I'd allowed myself several emotional investments. Hoping to leave the Hagseth Guest Ranch in Caroline and Annie's hands invited attachments I hadn't foreseen. A once overpowering need to join Jess and Danny grew weaker by the day. Outrage now directed toward Damien Slater and the Brotherhood of Loki offered purpose and direction. Tossing my boots outside, I followed them on hands and knees mindful of waking Leeann.

Painful groans while I hunkered over a frying pan alerted me before hearing her stir inside. "Lee? You okay?"

"No, I'm not okay." Her grumpy tone made my brows go up. "I've been beaten within an inch of my life, and I'm pretty sure nothing remains untouched."

I grimaced at more grunts and moans. "Anything I can do to help?"

"No! I can't...damn it...can't get...my blasted jeans on."

Her panty-clad derriere in dim light hadn't gone unnoticed while I cooled her legs. Jeans thrown aside made me wonder how she got into them in the first place. Her rear end wasn't big, mind you, but the jeans she packed it into weren't overly large. Dee hadn't missed it either, but I deferred cooling her bottom. "Would larger pants be easier and less painful?"

"A larger...well...yeah."

"You'll find a couple extra pair of mine in my bag. Help yourself. There should be a set of suspenders, too."

I turned back to the meal I cooked on the stove. Our provisions grew meager. A couple cups of brown rice I'd boiled first were set aside while I fried chunks of onion, half a tin of Spam, and our last potato diced small. More groans from inside meant Lee located jeans even too big for me. I added the rice and put a lid on the frypan after stirring to let it simmer. "Something smells good."

Jesus, she looked far worse than before our long nap. More like a blind raccoon. I jumped to help her stand. "Wait here. Cold water should help with the swelling."

She didn't sit before I returned. I soaked the washcloth and handed it to her. Leeann folded and held it over her right eye. "Oh...that feels good."

My britches hung from her shoulders by the suspenders. "Hang on before you sit," I said. Inside my pack was a short length of quarter inch rope. Cutting what I guessed was right, I returned to thread it through the loops. Whatever I imagined her waist to be left me with almost a foot extra. Denim bunched at her belly button resembled a blooming flower.

She let me take the cloth and dip again before replacing it on her eye. "What's for breakfast? Or is it supper?"

"Probably the only meal of the day. It's pretty much the last of our vittles."

Leeann watched as I lifted the lid to stir our meal. "One of us needs to catch a mess of trout." I saw a flash of her pearly whites. "By one of us I mean you."

Some in the middle over direct heat scorched, but I made sure none of our meal stuck to the surface by adding a bit of water before replacing the lid. "Way I see it, we've got about four hours of light. Let's eat before I pack you out to Caroline's. I'll come back tomorrow for our gear. You need a doctor."

"I'd rather not if I don't have to. They'll report it as abuse, and I don't want to bring police into it."

She gave me the argument I expected. "Then, let's get you into a bed where you can have better care. Ice and a heating pad." I nodded toward her behind. "You could develop a clot. If it broke loose, you're looking at potentially life-ending repercussions." Mom took Jess to our local emergency room more than once if she couldn't get a bad bruise to show improvement.

"In the morning, okay? Let's give it tonight. I won't argue at all if it's not better."

Without seasoning but for salt and pepper, our meal was bland yet filling. Lee didn't bother to sit—I could see even shuffling around hurt. I ignored moans of discomfort floating back after she left camp with a roll of toilet paper. Her pain was something I didn't want to contemplate.

I landed three trout using a bobber before it got dark, then cast my bait long with only its weight to sink a baited hook. My rod got braced in case something big swallowed the grasshopper before daylight. With nights cooling, I lit a small fire inside my stump after we got situated in our sleeping bags. It produced enough light so I could snuff the candle. Lee faced me and the fire rather than away, covering one eye or the other with the compress. "Were you in the military?" Busy laying fuel on our smudge, her question surprised me.

"Huh uh. Mom and Jess relied on me to keep the ranch afloat. My life's been about horses, beef, and how to make them provide a living. Why?"

"Have you killed anyone before?"

"Again, why?" She trod dangerous ground.

"You shot that man once with a twenty-two. I've read it's the preferred caliber of assassins."

Her comment made me chuckle. "I don't know about that. Surely a killer for hire would use something substantially brawnier." Personally, I preferred far more power than a .22 long rifle from a revolver.

"Why are you here? In Colorado, I mean. Where's home?"

"Our...I mean my ranch is in southwest Montana." After so long together, it was difficult to think of the spread as anything but me and Jess's. We'd made so many plans, including someday marrying spouses and remaining on the place. Sweet little Danny would have made the perfect older brother and cousin. A gaping hole from the loss of my sister continued to yawn wide. Now, it seemed rather than the despair I'd suffered through since losing my twin, rough edges of the grievous wound showed the first signs of healing.

"How big is your place? How many acres?"

"A little over twenty-six thousand." I was happy to talk about anything but killing.

"Wow! I thought Dee's ranch was big...yours is over eight times larger."

"Mom grew up a few miles away and dreamed of owning it when she was a little girl. My father was the one who gave it to her."

Lee rinsed the cloth in cold water and switched to the other eye. "I get the feeling you don't care for your dad."

"He tore my family apart and took Z away. If not for him, Jess would still be alive. Even Mom might've survived cancer if she weren't left alone raising two kids and pinching pennies." For once, I wasn't overwhelmed with anger by thoughts of Dad. Bitter, yes, yet no longer enraged.

"What's your sister like? Zoe, I mean."

"She's a sweet lady. Fixated and relentless in her job, but Z's the kind of girl would stop traffic to save a kitten. She almost married twice, but the old man torpedoed two great relationships."

"You love her. I see it in your eyes when you say her name."

"Zoe's incredible. A little over five feet tall, she was the first of us kids but also the shortest. Wears her hair a couple inches long like a boy...barely enough to comb."

"What does she do for a living?"

"Same as the old man. Works on Wallstreet."

Wind swirled through the opening giving extra oxygen to our fire. A handful of branches broken into short pieces lay within reach. I stacked them on for both light and heat. "Did you ever find one?"

I glanced at Leeann in confusion. "Find one what?"

"A spouse."

Her question made me chuckle. "No, can't say I did. Not many women want to spend their lives on a relatively isolated ranch."

"Cable," Leeann said slowly. "If you're here, your mother and sister have passed, what happened to your place? Is Zoe taking care of it, or has it been sold?"

"Z isn't a part of the ranch. I signed papers for the family lawyer leaving my cow boss in charge of everything."

I loved Joe Hodges. Still do. I always thought he worked for Mom because he was smitten with her. He was somewhere between fifty and sixty and rough around the edges. First my mom and then Jess's death hit him as hard as me—he considered us his kids. My unexpected departure leaving him to make all the decisions probably enraged the coot. His idea of the perfect life was a .30-30 in his scabbard while riding the range. Made no difference the season—whether sweltering hot or fighting snow. Give him a horse, rifle, and cows to push, and Joe saw little reason to return to the bunkhouse. After Mom passed, he spent almost four months living with our cattle after we pushed them into government high country. He came down only when snow and the rest of us drifted the livestock onto WJP land again.

"You haven't really answered my question, Cable. Why're you living in a stump in nowhere Colorado when you have a ranch waiting?"

I shifted in my bag, making sure the fire was far enough away not to scorch my bed. "It's late. Want me to cool your back and legs before we call it a night?"

Leeann understood her question wasn't one I was willing to answer. "Sure." She unzipped the bag and threw the top aside. At least she didn't see my automatic wince. Tough to tell if it was any better or getting worse. I took the towel to slowly cool her skin from shoulders to heels. She jerked and hissed a sharp intake of breath the moment I rinsed and lay it on her upper back. The rag warmed quickly, causing me to dip it into the water again. Didn't take more than a few minutes before I ran to the spring for more and cursed Damien Slater's name each step of the way back. Leeann might think ignoring her brother was the best revenge—I wasn't so sure. My way would extract enough flesh to make sure his crime would be paid in full.

Chapter X

When we rode onto the Hagseth ranch in the light of day, nothing looked changed during my absence. Annie saw us from the veranda first and stuck her head inside the house to holler for her mom. Both women were standing at the edge of the porch to stare in consternation when I reined Buster to a halt. I kicked my left foot free of the stirrup and braced myself in the saddle. Leeann used my arm for support and the footrest to swing down. Our mount blew what I suspected was a sigh of relief. Although horses were strictly prohibited on the lawn, I dismounted next. "We could use your help, Caroline," I said. "I need you to take a look at Lee and see if you think she needs a doctor." I thought her backside—from heel to shoulder—looked worse than ever.

"She get thrown?" Caroline's guess after seeing two black eyes was reasonable. Although Leeann fretted, I refused to believe my former boss would deny help. She wasn't the type of lady who would judge a woman by the actions of her brother. I wasn't so sure about Annie.

"Nope." To her credit, Annie looked on with concern when I carefully helped Leeann up the steps. Soreness from the beating, bruising, and subsequent flight on foot left her almost incapacitated. "You've got to see for yourselves." We followed Caroline inside while Annie held the door. "Take her somewhere private and tell me what you think."

I waited on the couch with my hat in hand after the bathroom door closed. "Oh, my God!" The voice of surprise wasn't Caroline's, who appeared after a couple minutes.

"Looks bad," Caroline said. "Girl isn't talking, but do you know what happened?"

I nodded. "I do."

She waited a slow count to five. "Well? Are you going to tell me?"

"Of course not. It's her story to share if and when she's ready." Caroline crossed her arms and waited without comment. Annie and Leeann were still in the bathroom—I could hear voices but not make out words. "Let me put it this way...and this is just between us...if we're together, and you see Damien Slater first and don't tell me, I'll never speak to you again. I'm dead serious, Caroline."

"What are you trying to tell me?"

"I'm not telling you anything. It's Lee's story. Can you put her up for a while?"

"Lord, yes. She'll be a better guest than Bruce, his friends, and their bitches...as he liked to call the women."

"I can't apologize enough for bringing them into your life. Your nephews learned they were here?"

"Someone called it in. It wasn't you, was it?" she asked. I shook my head. "No matter. The Brotherhood gave up after an overwhelming show of force. State patrol even brought a helicopter! Can you believe it?"

"They're in jail?" I worried about the big one I clubbed and if he'd escaped after I left him behind.

Caroline nodded. "All of them are facing a lengthy list of charges. Bruce ran for it but didn't get far. Canine unit located him."

"Did they hurt you or Annie?"

She glanced around and lowered her voice. "Mike hurt Annie, but she said...she said you...well, you know."

"What happened after he disappeared?"

"Bruce threatened Annie and me...said he'd make us go away if we had anything to do with Mike vanishing. We reported him as missing to my nephews, too."

We stopped talking when the bathroom door opened and Annie appeared. We heard the shower start a moment before she closed it. "Don't mind me. I'm getting Leeann a bathrobe. Can she use one of yours, Mom? You're taller." Lee stood at least a head above her.

Annie disappeared after getting a nod. "There'll be a lengthy court case, I assume."

"We're expecting it. While we're on the subject, your foundation's lawyers cleared the way to finalize our loan."

"It's not mine," I said. "I simply stayed in contact with others who run it to make sure they fought for you."

"Your name was on every sheet of paper we signed."

"As a figurehead. I'm glad for you, though. Do you have enough cash to operate?"

Her eyes welled and threatened to spill over when she nodded. "We can't thank you enough for helping, Cable. If it wasn't for you, we'd be packing our things."

"I can't imagine anyone more deserving. The WCP Foundation was formed to help those in need. In your case, it was the perfect use."

"I'm curious," she said. "Do you know Olivia Justice, the woman who traveled here from New York and met with us about the loan?"

"Kind of. I've met her perhaps a half-dozen times. Talked to her on the phone or Skype a few others, too."

Buster's nicker was easy to hear through the screen door. "Oh, Lord!" Caroline exclaimed and stood. "I've still got lunch to prepare!"

"How many guests do you have?"

"Eighteen," she called over her shoulder.

I stepped onto the veranda as dudes passed in single file. The lawn was badly used where Buster waited. I mounted and turned him toward the barn, only to fall in step next to Doug. He nodded and didn't mention the Kimber and spare magazines on my belt, although he noticed. "Hey. You hear about Caroline and Annie held as hostages?"

"She was telling me some of the story. Frightening."

"Yeah, all along me and Julio was none the wiser. Not even our guests knew something was wrong." We drew our mounts to a halt at the corral. "Heard you quit."

"Got things straightened out," I said. "I'll give you a hand with the stock."

It felt as if nothing changed—I unsaddled and left the horses in the corral to slake their thirst. I noticed when I passed with Buster in tow, whoever took over my job did a piss poor job of cleaning stalls. No way could I finish today, but I got the first ten shoveled, swept, and covered in new straw.

Annie's the one who stopped me. She waited for me to return after dumping a load of manure into the spreader. I'd forgotten how far it was through the long stable. "You don't have to do this," she said.

I moved to the next stall. "Told Caroline I'd get her through the season. I plan to keep my word."

"Lunch is ready. Mom saved you a plate in the kitchen."

"Tell her I'll be right there." I needed to shovel at least one more load before I could sweep and have it ready.

"I'm sorry," she said quietly. "More than I can tell you."

"For what? It should be me apologizing."

"The way I've treated you."

I shrugged. "I was a drunk looking for a way out."

"It was still wrong. I almost killed you once. Yet you went ahead and saved my life anyway. Both of our lives."

She moved back when I loaded my shovel with horse droppings and tossed it into the wheelbarrow. I think she waited hoping I'd engage her. It was impossible for me to feel worse about the situation and what she and her mom went through. If I'd remained in my stump without taking work on the ranch, they'd have stayed safe, while I would have found a way to my earlier goal. Now they were worse for the experience, and I was ready to reenter the world again.

* * *

Guests spread across the veranda when I passed. Most were finished eating and simply traded stories of their day. I winked and nodded at both Doug and Julio as I walked by, getting surprised jerks of their chins in return.

Leeann still wore a robe while sitting at the table, nibbling on a toasted cheese sandwich with a bowl of tomato soup. I noted a cord traveling to a heating pad between her back and the upright, another under her legs. Caroline turned at my entrance and pointed a spoon. "Sit. I wasn't going to plate anything before you came through the door."

"If there's an extra horse available, I'll ride with you to move our gear," Lee said.

I appreciated her offer, but in no way should she be subjected to repeat the discomfort she endured on our ride in. "Thanks, but no thanks," I said, smiling to Caroline for the bowl of soup and three sandwiches she delivered. "If no one objects, I'll take a packhorse and bring your things after I finish eating." I caught my boss's eye. "I promised I'd get you through the season. If you don't mind, I'll stay at my stump and commute with Buster."

"You'll do no such thing," Caroline said primly. "The trailer you slept in before is open again. After I get things done here, I'll get Annie to help me clean it while you ferry your belongings."

The sandwich was good, and I saw why after the first bite. A thin piece of ham was added. Hungry as a bear from splitting the little food remaining to Leeann and me, I wolfed lunch and stood. "Be back as soon as I can."

Leann was grateful when I returned with her clothing but especially the rifle. She worried about it as much as I did Buster. The poor girl needed her things washed. Of course, I did, too. I liked how Caroline made Lee stay in her seat instead of helping. After getting my things in an empty communal washer, I returned to restoring the stalls to their former condition. Outside, Annie, Doug, and Julio gave basic roping lessons. Two dudes were lefties, and I wondered if the ranch kept any lariats with a wrong-hand twist. Probably not. I'd employed at least three cowboys I could think of who brought their own southpaw ropes twisted, tied, and coiled the wrong way.

It took two hard days of cleaning to whip the barn into shape. I complained to Caroline good naturedly, wondering who let things go. Turned out to be mere neglect while the Brotherhood kept Annie and Caroline indoors. Doug and Julio were kept busy wrangling guests, while my bosses were held against their will.

Eating alone in the trailer felt good again. While Annie got back to taking care of dudes, Leeann helped Caroline in the kitchen and served guests the third day. Although we didn't get the opportunity to speak, I saw her from afar. She appeared to move with little difficulty. What excuse she gave for two black eyes I could only guess. I reckoned she finally decided to face life head-on after recognizing how little her scar meant to others—something I barely noticed unless her smile was wide. Even then, I saw it as a part of her.

My accommodations were no different than before. I worried how much damage was done to the old trailer in my absence. Caroline made sure I knew she swapped out the previous pillow I used for one different. The thought of laying my head where a Brotherhood member slept gave me the heebie-jeebies.

Buster missed the hell out of me. He called with a whinny each time I was in the barn after smelling or hearing me. We didn't get a chance to explore more, but I brushed him each day without fail. I think he appreciated it as much as the oats he got from the feed bag. One truth I was certain of, he was ready for the trail.

Caroline caught me taking my time with lunch in Buster's stall. She'd fixed two plates stacked high with peanut butter and jelly sandwiches from which I snagged a brace. The day was cool with a pleasant breeze, and I enjoyed an insulated travel mug of coffee, too. "I thought I might find you here," Caroline said over the gate.

"Hey, Boss," I greeted. "Stables are looking better."

"They certainly do. Thank you." She rested arms on the top rail and smiled at Buster. "I thought he'd be sold and probably slaughtered. No way would he ever make it as a saddle horse. You've done an amazing job with him, young man."

I swallowed a bite of sandwich and washed it down with a sip. "He saved my life. When all the chips were pushed in, he made the right call and took care of me."

Caroline nodded. "Leeann told me she found you the next morning after that terrible night with Buster standing over you. Anyone else, and he'd have been nowhere near."

"I need you to sell him to me, you know."

My heart dropped at her quick response. "Can't. He's not for sale."

"Oh, hell." Her refusal hit me in the guts while Buster plucked at my collar with his bristly lips. Hot breath inside my shirt tickled.

"I'm not selling what's obviously yours. I'll write a bill of sale whenever you want."

"How much do you got to have for him?" Truth be told, I was willing to pay anything she asked, no matter how exorbitant.

She shook her head. "Nothing. He belongs to you."

"Are you certain? Name your price, and it's yours."

Caroline's eyes opened wide. "Watch what you say, Cable. I might take you up on it."

"I don't only want Buster...I need him. Sky's the limit."

She changed the subject. "Have you talked to Annie?"

"Not since the day Lee and I got here. Why?"

"My daughter feels terrible for the way she treated you. She barely sleeps. Especially after what you did for her that night."

"Water under the bridge. I told her not to give it a second thought. I should be apologizing for bringing my troubles to your door."

Caroline changed the subject again. "Have you spoken to Leeann?"

"No, I don't think so. We've been busy with your last group of the year." I gave her a sharp look. "You understand she's got nowhere to go, don't you?"

She nodded. "I do. Girl's been forthcoming about her life and what led her to our door. I made her understand she's welcome to stay unless a better opportunity rears its head."

"Very good. I appreciate it."

"I wish you'd take the time to talk to her. The girl's got it bad for you, Cable."

"Excuse me?"

Caroline frowned. "Just what I said. You're all she talks about. No matter the conversation, she twists it to include you. 'Cable thinks this'...'Cable says that,' is what we hear."

I shook my head. "I think you got it wrong. She's grateful I helped her out of a bad place, but she saved my butt, too. I'd say we're pretty much even."

"Speaking of even, color me curious, Cable. The night law enforcement took our captors into custody, one fled out the back and almost escaped. Bruce...you called him Long Beard...made a run for it. A canine unit located him on the hillside behind the house beat to hell. According to Jeremy, my nephew, they suspect someone waited and caught him by surprise. A bloody club was found next to him with a tooth from the bastard lodged in the wood. Whoever hit him broke his arm, knocked out most of his teeth, and left him with a shattered jaw. Even stranger is how they found shod tracks where a horse was tied in the brush. It made me think of how Bruce used a two by four on you. Is there anything you can add to the story?"

I almost wished Long Beard didn't have the opportunity to lift a hand and partially block my swing. I don't think he would have survived the blow. After giving it a moment of thought, I met Caroline's gaze while tamping down what threatened to bloom into a broad smile. "Seems to me a run of bad luck caught up with him. I think we can safely call it karma."

She stared for a long moment before grinning. "I don't think I want to be on your bad side, Karma. See you at supper."

Ahead of work needing done and nothing pressing, I decided to saddle Buster and stretch his legs. With few exceptions, most guests were following either Doug or Julio on trails. Tomorrow, they'd leave for the short cattle drive marking the end of their stay. My mount champed at the bit while he waited to be saddled. He didn't bother to puff his belly when I tightened the cinch and fastened the belly strap. Yet the moment I mounted and my ass hit the seat, he exploded into a dead run. Feeling his eagerness to burn off excess energy, I gave him his head until we reached the tree line. More than once I patted the Kimber to make sure it wasn't dislodged from the friction holster.

We got back a few minutes before my coworkers and our guests. Since my return, I felt more like a part of the employees and saw the ranch with different eyes. Where I once worked to help an old woman and earn enough to end my life, I now judged major deficiencies with a critical gaze and how to make them better. Caroline first needed a crew to shore up and repair the cavernous barn where she and Annie once left me drunk in the hay. It'd be costly, but more of the stables could be used better to winter horses rather than turn them free. A hundred tons of alfalfa could be stored in the old structure with room left over. I made my decision while finishing brushing Buster to touch on the subject with my boss.

Excited but tired dudes chattered over their meal on the veranda. I slowed when I passed, hoping to catch a glimpse of Leeann. It would be nice to see her and find whether her black eyes looked better. She didn't appear, but I got a friendly wave from Doug and Julio. I returned it to their obvious delight. Both men understood something changed and welcomed my return without reservation. After shoveling manure the first half of the day, I'd bathe before fetching my supper.

When I opened the door, Leeann already sat at the table with food-laden plates and bowls. A serving platter was pushed to the side. First, I noticed we were having spaghetti and garlic bread and a big bowl of roasted vegetables. It was my favorite. Second, it was impossible to miss her nice clothes and how well they fit. Third, her hair was put up with attractive ringlets in front of both ears. Her cheeks were a combination of fading black with patches of blue and green. "I hope you don't mind," she said. "I asked Caroline if I could eat with you, and she loaned me the key to your door. I didn't steal anything in case you're worried."

I liked her sense of humor and the way she occasionally teased and winked. "I'm not sure I own anything worth packing off."

Lee came right back. "I remember a hefty stack of cash stowed in your briefcase. All I have to do is push a few numbers, let it read my thumbprint, and I'm in."

"Hey, I was serious before when I offered it. If you need it, the money's yours."

"That's one of the reasons I'm here. I wanted to tell you Caroline and Annie offered me a job. I help Caroline in the kitchen and serve guests now. She plans to pay me a salary and provide room and board.

Pay won't be much over the winter, but she said summer will make up for it."

I tossed my hat past the bathroom to land on my mattress. "I told you! Really great news, Lee. Caroline can be trusted to keep her word. Even Annie's got a positive side."

"You were right. They're nicer than I imagined."

"Hey, I need to shower before eating. Mind giving me five minutes?" I hurried to find clean clothes after she nodded.

My empty belly pushed me faster. I barely hit the high spots with a soapy rag before a quick rinse, and opened the door already dressed at the three-minute mark. Although she ate slowly, Leeann waited for me like one pig waits for another. "That was pretty fast," she said. "I remember thinking a fifteen-minute shower was hurrying."

I scooted in across from her. "Live in my stump for a couple years and see how good even a short one feels." With a fork in one hand and a slice of bread in the other, I dove in to catch up to my guest.

"Caroline said you have milk. She left a half-gallon yesterday. Got glasses?"

I nodded and pointed with my fork. "To the left of the range vent."

She filled two glasses. It was impossible to miss the top three buttons open on her blouse, and how more of her natural charms were exposed once I wrestled my attention from her denim-clad derriere. Yet I made sure my gaze didn't drop lower than her nose when she was ready to eat again.

While Caroline was usually too busy to converse with, and Annie was still someone I avoided, Leeann was as easy to talk to as any cowboy I rode with. It didn't take long before we laughed over Buster taking my hat at the lake. Neither did she forget a big trout spitting the hook as I beached it, only to scramble for it on my hands and knees. We swapped stories of our upbringings, me telling of trouble Jess and I got into, whereas Lee told me of a younger brother doing the same with her. I learned Dee was substantially older, where Nickolas was three years behind. He was a submariner on deployment, but she hoped to see him soon.

"The season's almost over for Caroline," Lee said. "Got plans for after?"

"Make sure the place is ready for next year. Might have to paint and make repairs on the cabins. I've got a few ideas I hope will pique Caroline's interest, but that's about it."

"After that?"

Indeed, what about after I finished all I could find? I'd been giving it thought. "I've got a cattle operation to run." My general manager couldn't be expected to keep it afloat indefinitely. Joe probably looked forward to getting reinstated to his former title of cow boss.

"How long has it been since you left?"

"A couple years."

"Two years of living in your stump?"

I wasn't comfortable where our conversation led. "Not quite. Took a while to get here."

She obviously understood. "I know you never married. Does a girlfriend wait at home?"

Her question made me laugh. "No, no girlfriends. A couple at college didn't last when I saw none were interested in long term. Didn't I tell you how isolated my place is?"

"Figure you'll stick around a week? A month?"

"Oh, shoot." I did some mental calculations. "More than a week to finish repairs. Then I have to figure out how to break the news to Joe I'm still alive. Take him a bit to get used to the idea and make plans of how to get back at me, then drive south with a horse trailer for me and Buster. Might be close to a month."

"You're telling me I've got a chance?" She caught my gaze and held it.

I frowned. "A chance to what?"

"Show you my interest. Make my case. Whatever you want to call it."

"What're you interested in? Caroline already promised me Buster, and I'm not selling."

She rolled her eyes. "You, dummy! I'm trying to explain my attraction to you. I'd like to see if you've got the slightest bit to me."

"Oh!" Caroline tried to warn me. Unfortunately, I didn't take her seriously. I glanced around the trailer to formulate my thoughts.

"Well?" she said impatiently.

"Hang on. Cripes, I've never been in this situation before. You've got me flummoxed."

"Cripes? Flummoxed? Really? Are you from the nineteen fifties?"

I shrugged and made a face. "Feels like it sometimes."

"It's an easy question to answer, unless it's my scar. Do you prefer I slide a note across the table asking you to check yes or no?"

"Of course, it's not your injury. My answer is yes, but there's more to consider. Your home is Colorado. Mine is seven hundred miles...give or take...northwest of here."

Lee wound spaghetti around her fork and stared at me while chewing slowly. "Bridges ought to be crossed when we get to them, not dreaded because we know they're waiting."

"You're wise beyond your years, young lady," I said, before cramming bread into my mouth to help me regroup through the awkwardness.

It didn't take us long after the subject was tabled, before we relaxed and chatted like the good friends we are. Lee enjoyed the few days she worked with Caroline. Most of it was staying out of the way, yet not so far Leeann couldn't learn. She appreciated the opportunity afforded her. We parted after she administered a brief kiss to my cheek, stealing it when I loaded the kitchen platter with our dishware. Lee pulled back without embarrassment and grinned. "See you tomorrow, cowboy!"

* * *

The departure of our final group of guests was bittersweet. The successful season ended with Caroline and Annie in firm control of their ranch, but my time in Colorado drew to an end. An angry call from Caroline to Leeann's brother got her horse and tack delivered on the same day. I bided my time until the truck and trailer backed near the corral and opened the driver's door myself. Where I expected and relished a violent confrontation with Slater, he sent a ranch hand instead. To see Lee's reunion with Winston put a lump in my throat. She loved her horse as deeply as I cared for Buster.

Earlier, Z texted me to call, and I left the pair to bond with our bosses looking on to fulfill my sister's request. We hadn't spoken since she left Montana after Jess's funeral. Hundreds of texts if not more were exchanged, but neither of us took the time to engage verbally with the other. I pressed the call button after retreating inside Buster's stall. Her gentle answer shook me. "William?"

"Yeah, it's me, Z."

"Oh, I thought..." Her voice caught before she went on. "I was afraid I'd never hear your voice again. To lose Jess and then you was too much. Especially after Mom—" Her voice trailed away. With my throat closed off, I could do nothing but wait. "Are you still there?"

I choked on the word. "Yes."

"We thought...Dad and I were both afraid you died in the fire."

"I don't give a shit about him. What'd you find out?"

My sister is a professional and made the seamless switch with me. "You need to read the report to fully grasp it, William. Do you have access to a computer? I'll send you a PDF if possible."

"No. Just give me a summation."

She took me at my word. "Damien Slater's finances were stretched far too thin for what he planned. Desperation caused him—"

"Get to it, Z. Forget the highlights. All I need is the conclusion."

"Bottom line is he needed Mrs. Hagseth's ranch for the oil lying underneath. He paid dearly...far above the going rate...for satellite imagery and geological studies. I've analyzed available maps and discovered Slater detected a sizable puddle of crude beneath your feet. Several million barrels at least."

Oil. It made sense. If Slater could've driven Caroline and Annie from their home, he stood to become a far wealthier man. I no longer wondered about tire tracks leaving his property and crossing onto Hagseth ground—vehicles likely carried ground penetrating radar or similar technology. "What about Caroline? Does she own mineral rights and do they extend to oil?"

"I looked into it enough to find she does, and they do. Mineral rights normally...although not always...include oil and natural gas beneath the property. I suggest she contacts a lawyer familiar with oil and gas leasing and royalty information ASAP."

"I'll pass it on. Thanks, Z. You've been far more helpful than you know since I contacted you. You've dropped a lot of work to get my tail out of a jam."

"You're my little brother. It's just you and me now." I heard her sniff, then blow her nose. Her tone was far more congested when she continued. "I know your relationship with Jess ran far deeper than with me. It wouldn't have been any different if I'd stayed on the ranch. I can't make up for her loss, but I want to be a part of your life again. To be included. We both hurt from her passing, but I'll do anything if you'll let me in."

I fumbled at the knot holding my kerchief around my neck, then blew into it noisily before leaning my forehead against Buster's side. Wet cheeks were dried after I folded it. "I never loved you less than Jess, Z. It was...it was different with her."

"I know. The bond between twins can't be duplicated, but it's nice to hear you still love me."

"Toughest day of my life up to then was when you left us...when the old man took you away. Jess and I cried for weeks. Maybe longer."

Z was silent long enough to make me look at my phone to see if we lost our connection before hearing her voice. "Jess told me. We had a good talk when she and Danny spent a few weeks here before she...before they were taken."

"I...Z...I really don't want to talk about it, okay?"

"Sure. Hey, how surprised were you when you found your attaché? After you disappeared, leaving your truck behind, Joe called to let me know he was in possession. The moment I learned your whereabouts, I sent a woman from an agency we sometimes use to find and recover items to deliver it to you. I could do nothing less when your cow boss seemed to think it was important."

I wasn't going to tell her it was the stick that almost broke the mule's back and nearly sent me teetering over the edge. Seeing saved messages on my phone and knowing they were Jess's voice was too much. There was a good chance I could keep the madness at bay by never listening. "Thank you. It came in handy."

"What do you keep in that thing?" she teased. "A million dollars?"

She didn't need to know it was my failsafe holding a phone and gun. The cash and debit card meant nothing. What meant everything was who gave it to me. Jess saved for years to buy it for my last birthday she'd see. "Something with a whole lot less zeros."

"Be that as it may, you'd better think about girding thy loins when you contact Joe. He was certain you were dead."

"I was," I whispered.

"What? I didn't hear you, William."

"Nothing," I sighed. "And stop calling me William. My name is Cable."

"Okay...William," she teased.

I wiped my face again. "Listen, I need to go. We'll talk later, okay?"

"Can you call or take mine once each day?"

"Whenever we can."

We ended our phone conversation on the very best of terms. Z and I were never on the outs, but nor were we particularly close after she left. I wiped my face again and blew my nose before stuffing the wet rag into a back pocket. Footsteps neared, and I did my best to make myself presentable.

Chapter XI

Curry comb in hand, I turned to Buster and gave two long strokes from withers along his back before I heard my name. "So obvious how Leeann loves her horse as much as you do yours," Caroline said. "Annie's in tears just watching. I think my daughter forgot how to love for a while. Judging by her reaction out there, my girl's learning her heart is in working order."

"Winston's a good horse." Back to her, I chose neutral words, yet they were thick with emotion.

"Not you, too," she said.

I finally turned. "No, I've been talking to someone on the phone. Kind of tough hearing her voice. It's been a long time."

Caroline's features twisted with compassion. "Not bad news, I hope."

I shook my head. "Nothing but good."

"Cable, how're you doing? Be upfront with this old lady, because you seem to be in a better place now."

I switched my gaze from the toes of my boots to her. "I'm doing good."

"Are you sure? You don't seem to be as down, but I worry."

"If it makes you feel better, soon as I've finished getting you ready for next season, I'm returning home."

"Home?"

"I've got a ranch northeast of here in Montana."

She stared for a moment before a smile widened. "Makes sense. More than a few guests noticed the way you sit a saddle. Annie told me about a young couple wishing they could ride like you. Do you raise beef?"

I nodded. "Yeah. My place is big enough to cut costs by planting and baling our own hay and alfalfa."

"How many head do you raise?"

"Between thirty-five and forty-five hundred, depending on a host of factors."

"Holy shit!"

"No telling how many we've got now. My cow boss is in charge of the ranch while I've been..." I searched for the proper term. "...on hiatus."

"Is he who you were talking to?"

"No, my sister. I asked her to dig into Damien Slater's finances and see what she could find." I hesitated for a moment. "I probably should have told you this sooner, but while working Buster early on, I discovered tire tracks leading from what I now know is Slater's ranch onto yours. Deep marks made by something heavy. Zoe learned he needed your ranch for what lies beneath it." I held her gaze. "You're standing on a goldmine with a couple million barrels of crude oil under your feet."

Her eyes widened. "You're joking?"

"Nope. I'll give you my sister's number, and she can point you in the right direction in regards to your first steps."

Leeann rescued me from our shocked boss with Winston saddled. She wanted to ride after getting him back. Caroline left to pass on the good news to Annie, while I retreated to the tack room. It didn't take long before we rode from the stable with our noses pointed toward the lake my riding partner named after herself.

We didn't stop at the body of water and reached the ridgetop in late afternoon. Both horses seemed to remember where they were and didn't stop until they located their favorite browse. Neither Lee nor I spoke much, content to be with our favorite horses and riding partners. I didn't miss her thoughtful gaze in the direction of where we buried the body. When she dismounted, I followed suit.

A breeze blew hair hanging from beneath her Stetson, adding to Leeann's natural allure. "I love it up here," she said finally. "After Dee bought the ranch and his house was built, I used to make the trip a couple times each summer. It's been at least two years if not three since

I've made the pilgrimage, until you and I—" She stopped and left the rest unsaid.

"It's beautiful," I agreed. "I can darn near see my stump. Probably pick it out if I brought field glasses."

"What's the country like in your neck of Montana?" she asked.

"Lots of flat land where we winter the herd. Come summer, we move them into the higher country where we have a contract with Uncle Sam for grazing rights. We raise a couple thousand acres of hay and alfalfa and move a portion of the cattle onto the stubble after it's harvested."

"Is it in a pretty part of the state?

"Gorgeous in my biased estimation. WJP land butts up against national forest to the east. It's easy to fill my saddle bags, tie on a sleeping bag and tent, and gallop into the wilderness. Jess and I loved to ride the trails and..." My throat constricted. "...and fish the creeks and lakes," I said finally. "Mom used to go with us until she said it was too tiring. I guess it's when cancer started eating her."

Her gaze was direct. "You've went through a lot of heartbreak, Cable. I'm willing to take a chance if you are. Having me around might change your luck." She leaned forward, and when I didn't pull away, her lips touched mine. Our kiss deepened as our arms went around the other, and the world around us faded.

* * *

Without much to do in the kitchen with Caroline after the season wrapped up, Leeann helped me repair what I could on the ranch. Decayed boards around the stables got replaced where dry rot ate the wood. She wasn't shy about getting dirty or tearing out hard to repair walls. I found she could swing a hammer and handle a drill screwing in three-inch fasteners. There were also no complaints from carrying her end of a stack of two by sixes. As the weather cooled, I no longer got to admire the corded muscles of her forearms and biceps as she worked when we both donned coats. Her marred face healed until no evidence remained of the abuse her brother inflicted.

Z enjoyed me touching bases with her daily. More than once, she called me when I got too busy or forgot. Once I was in my trailer eating supper with Leeann, who showed an even more playful side by making faces and doing her best to make me crack up. Zoe eventually realized more went on beyond our conversation and left me to deal with my dining partner.

Leeann wasn't ready for our growing relationship to become more physical, and it didn't really matter to me—I was content with our quiet conversations and the soft warmth of her kisses. She told me of her formative years and drinking leading up to her accident. I learned her folks were still alive and retired on the gulf coast of Texas.

My time in Colorado was coming to a close. Although Caroline and even Annie searched for projects and tasks for me to tackle, nothing was left undone for the following season. My thoughts were turning toward home and dealing with what I knew would be a cross cow boss. The only thing to make me feel better—other than Lee's kisses—was the news from Z explaining the difficult position Slater found himself in. She was sure he was only months from bankruptcy without a way to pay his bills. He'd planned to already be drilling on Hagseth land. Couldn't happen to a nicer fellow if anyone asked me.

I rationalized putting off calls to Joe due to spending more time with Lee. Her, our bosses, along with Doug, Julio, and I were enjoying lunch on the veranda when a sheriff's cruiser idled in and stopped next to the lawn. I shifted to better disguise the Kimber on my hip—wearing it a habit easily formed. A uniformed deputy stepped out. "Hi, Auntie Caroline. Am I too late for lunch?"

She stood and waved him up. "Never for you, Jeremy. Let me get you a plate."

Her nephew was older than I initially surmised—at least in his forties. "Hey, cuz," he greeted Annie.

"Hey, yourself!" Her pleasure was evident.

He jerked his chin. "Doug, Julio...Auntie keeping you busy?"

Doug leaned across the table to offer his hand, and Julio did the same after. The three men seemed to be on friendly terms. "Sure is. She gave us fulltime positions again," Doug said.

His direct gaze swung to me as Caroline returned with a plate in hand. She saw where he was looking. "I don't think you've met Cable, have you?" She knew good and well the answer.

"I don't think so. A new hand?"

"We hired him as seasonal help. Cable, this's my nephew, Jeremy. I think I told you my brother's boys were deputies, didn't I?" I nodded. "Jeremy, I'd like you to meet Cable Pearson."

I saw no way out and stood to shake his hand. To step forward and reach across the table exposed the gun I wore, but I knew open carry was lawful. "Nice to meet you," I said. "Caroline's told me a little about her nephews."

Jeremy's gaze narrowed and his grip tightened. "She never mentioned your name. In fact, I don't remember seeing you during the excitement a few weeks back."

Caroline rescued me. "He was camping on the backside of the lake."

Leeann wasn't to be left out. "With me."

Jeremy released my hand when his attention turned to Lee. "Aren't you Damien Slater's sister?"

She nodded and held her palm out. "Leeann Slater. It's nice to meet you."

"Have a seat, cousin," Annie said. "Burgers are getting cold, and the potato salad warm."

Jeremy was nothing like the soft young man I initially envisioned. This deputy was a hardened and no-nonsense officer of the law—at least a decade or more older than me.

He finished a burger before redirecting his attention. "Where's home, Mr. Pearson? I don't recall seeing you around."

"Southwest of Ennis and Virginia City, Montana."

"Huh. Isn't the area famous for the Madison River and fly fishing?"

"Yes, sir."

His questions were meant to grill me for anything he could learn. No doubt he'd run a search to find more. "What is it you do in Montana?"

"I own a little ranch and run a few cows."

"How do you know Aunt Caroline?"

"She helped me out, and I was returning the fav-" I stopped at the sound of a truck barreling up the driveway, barely making the turn into the barnyard and sliding to a stop behind the deputy's cruiser.

Damien Slater threw open the door of his Dodge truck and stepped out with a rifle. "Where is he?" He shouted. "Pearson. Where is he?" he repeated. I heard the sound of the chamber being loaded when he worked the lever action. It appeared to be a model 94 Winchester, a standard rifle for any ranch.

Jeremy stood to face the irate man. "Lower the barrel of your weapon, Mr. Slater, so we can talk." One palm was outstretched, while the deputy's other hand rested on the butt of his service weapon.

"I'm going to lose everything," Lee's brother shook with rage and waved his long gun. "Pearson's to blame." He shifted his stance to get a good look at us seated at the table.

Leeann stood when I did and beat me to the porch edge. "This's nobody's fault but your own, Dee," she said. "Your choices brought you to where you are. Not Cable's."

I stepped near the bannister to keep her and the deputy on my left. "Your sister's right, Slater. Besides, no amount of money is worth getting killed over or spending your life in prison." The sounds of shifting and footsteps behind meant the other four were getting out of the line of fire.

"You bastard—" Slater snapped the rifle to his shoulder and fired before anyone could react, narrowly missing my head and hitting the post next to where I stood.

My draw was immediate as the stock left his shoulder to work the action rather than keep it tight against his cheek. The slowness of his method cost him. My Kimber leveled before Jeremy's left the holster, allowing me a quick but steady shot after acquiring my sight picture.

Rather than shoot to kill, I allowed myself a moment to target his rifle instead. At fifteen yards—should I have missed—a rapid follow up with the semi-automatic would have neutralized him instantly.

He bellowed and dropped the lever action, grabbing his forearm and sinking to the ground with his back against the Dodge.

"Dee!" Leeann flew down the steps and ran to her brother's side.

I holstered my handgun and raised my arms when the law officer turned to me. "Stay," he ordered.

A hand grasped my elbow, and I turned to see Caroline. "This's bad. I didn't want anything like this to happen," she said.

"It's not your fault. You and Annie are the victims here, not Slater."

I filled my coffee cup and watched from the veranda. EMTs appeared within fifteen minutes, during which Doug and Julio helped Jeremy and Lee administer first aid. After stabilizing the man, the ambulance left with his sister inside, too.

The deputy sheriff came to where I sipped java and waited. "It doesn't look good. Man's going to lose everything from the elbow down. Maybe more." He held a hand out. "Your sidearm, please."

I turned my back to allow him to disarm me. Zip ties fastened around my wrists weren't a great surprise because the deputy didn't know me and followed policy. The same when he recited my Miranda rights. "Caroline, would you please call Olivia Justice as soon as you can, and have her contact my sister? I'd like you to tell her what's happened. I'm going to need a lawyer or two. Let her know I'll pay my sister back." Her nod was all I needed before Jeremy led me away.

* * *

A mob of reporters waited outside the courthouse after my bail was posted. A shooting was big news in a rural county, made doubly exciting when the name William Cable Pearson was released to the public. Not so much my name as my father's. Journalists shouted questions I ignored while following two lawmen pushing the crowd back on the way to Caroline's truck. A gaggle tried to block our exit until they were forcibly moved aside.

I'd spent a night in lockup before three lawyers appeared with me in front of the judge. Z hired and flew the high-powered trio in from Denver to give me the best representation possible. I hated to think what they cost, but getting out of jail was imperative. Bail set at a half million dollars scared me. My team didn't miss a beat and informed me Miss Zoe Pearson of New York, New York, would cover all without a bondsman.

Caroline didn't hesitate when she saw the coast was clear. We left town driving fifty in a twenty-five. "My nephew shouldn't have arrested you," she said. "We all saw what happened. It was a clear-cut case of self-defense, but your lawyers assured us no witnesses would be necessary at a preliminary hearing."

I asked the question most important on my mind. "Have you talked to Leeann? Is she at the hospital or your place?"

"We haven't seen or had contact with her since she got in the ambulance." Caroline's quiet compassion was evident. "I heard at the courthouse they took his right arm below the shoulder. Jeremy told me the bullet appeared to have hit the receiver of Slater's rifle, then traveled the length of his forearm before exiting above the elbow. Initially, my nephew was sure there was no way it could be saved."

"Shit." I watched out the side window as we traveled. "I hated to see it happen, but he was going to kill me. What else could I do?"

"You're asking the same question I posed," she said. "Jeremy was of the opinion your rushed shot hitting his gun instead of Slater's chest was the best possible outcome." Caroline glanced over. "You didn't miss, did you?"

"No...I aimed at his rifle. Better than killing the man."

"You're one of the good guys, Cable. Most in your shoes would have drilled him."

We were quiet for the rest of the ride. Annie stood on the porch while we got out of the truck. "Did you hear?" she asked. "Slater lost his arm."

Caroline said, "We know. The press was all abuzz about it at the courthouse." Her attention turned to me. "Have you eaten yet?"

"Huh uh." After a shitty night of sleep in a holding cell, I contemplated crawling into my bunk.

"Can you eat if I fix something?"

"Just a sandwich, okay?"

Annie held the door while I traipsed behind Caroline and followed us in. "I made jalapeno jelly," Caroline said. "Interest in trying it on peanut butter?"

I dropped into a seat at the table. "Sure." I wasn't hungry and nothing sounded good, but it'd been almost twenty-four hours since I'd eaten.

A phone rang, and Annie checked the number. "Reporters have called all morning. I suppose this is another." She sighed and answered. "Hello? Yes, this is the Hagseth residence." She scowled. "No, there'll be no interviews..." Annie stopped and held the phone where she could look at it incredulously. We could all hear a voice on the other end. "Let me make this plain, dumbass," she said after putting it against her ear again. "You or nobody else will set foot on our property. If you do, I'll call the sheriff and have you arrested and sue you for trespassing. Although..." her eyes twinkled. "...I'm a pretty damned good shot, too." She ended the call and set her phone aside. "This's been going on since the Pearson name was released."

"I don't know what to say other than I'm sorry, ladies."

Caroline set two sandwiches in front of me, then both a glass of milk and cup of coffee. "Eat and drink. You'll feel better after."

As usual, Caroline was right. While sweet, the jalapeno jelly left a warm afterbite. I downed the milk first, then finished my meal with the coffee. Neither of the women offered more conversation, leaving me to yawn and finally excuse myself. I locked the door of the trailer behind, grateful to still have Mom's .22. Sleep, then I'd make decisions.

* * *

Where September arrived during a heatwave, October blew in with flakes of snow. Not able to leave with the shooting case still open, I poured my energy into helping a crew buttress the walls of Caroline's barn. Massive beams filled with dry rot were cut out, with solid replacements going in. After we finished with Doug and Julio's help, all of us stood back to admire our work. When a new roof was put on in the spring, the building constructed in the early nineteen hundreds was fit to endure another century.

Word came through the district attorney's office the first week of the month I wouldn't face charges, and my Kimber would be returned. With no word from Leeann—I could understand after almost losing her brother—a plan of action was clear in my mind. It was time to shake the dust of Colorado and return home.

With my phone at full charge, I made the call I most wished to avoid. It rang five times before a gruff voice answered. "WJP spread, Joe speaking."

"Hey, Joe, it's me."

I thought our connection was broken before he made sure I knew it wasn't. "Saw you on television, you goddamn good for nothing son of a bitch. I'm glad your mom ain't around to see the ass kicking I got planned for you. Might consider stayin' in Colorado if you wanna keep your health. Gonna take a doctor to pull my boot outa your ass."

Jesus, his voice sounded gravellier than I remembered. "I'm man enough to take my whoopin', Joe."

"What the hell you callin' me about?"

"I need a ride."

"You got yourself there...figure out how to get your ass home by yourself."

"Can't. I need you to bring the four-horse stock trailer."

Christ, it was no different than tossing a grasshopper into a lake filled with hungry fish. Joe's tone changed instantly as he snapped at the bait. "Oh, yeah? Whatcha got?"

"The best horse I've ridden in my life, bar none."

"Ah, bullshit. Ain't no horse better'n Midnight. You know it as well as me."

"Joe...he saved my life. We wouldn't be talking if it wasn't for him."

I definitely piqued his interest. "You don't say?"

"Wait until you meet my boy. You'll change your tune right off. About a hand...maybe two taller than Midnight."

Joe and I spent almost an hour talking about the ranch and how it fared during my absence. The first year I was gone, he sold seventeen hundred and nineteen calves with most weighing between five and six hundred. Going rate was a buck ten a pound, and the ranch banked over a million dollars. Responsibility for so much money scared my cow boss, and he filled my ear with more cussing. Joe and the boys finishing shipping our fall calves only a few days ago, and the market was good. He expected we'd see closer to a buck fifteen or even one-twenty for eighteen hundred and thirty-two calves. We might take in a couple hundred thousand dollars extra if Joe was right. Knowing he lived with a tally sheet and pencil stub in his pocket, I didn't doubt his numbers. Problem was the ranch employed seven plus me. Wages alone were over three hundred thousand each year. With equipment costs, breakdowns, irrigational lines, vet bills, insurance, utilities, and a remuda to be kept shod, profit margins were frighteningly thin. He held over enough heifers to replace aging stock and built the numbers to nearly forty-five hundred. As long as our hay and alfalfa fields produced, the ranch could hold a few thousand more. Mom would be proud after the way she slowly built our herd to over a thousand before she died.

Joe promised to be on the road after he got Odell to repack the wheel bearings of our smallest trailer and change oil in the truck. Rarely did we put a thousand miles on the twenty-year-old F350 ranch pickup in a year. He planned to leave a little after daybreak and sleep on the front seat at a truckstop before arriving at Caroline's place the next. If I wanted, we could share nonstop driving duties on the way home to save a few bucks. I bid him safe travel before we ended our call.

My last full day at the Hagseth Guest Ranch was spent in the big house enjoying time with Caroline and Annie. I got a chance to shake hands and say my goodbyes to Doug and Julio before they left for a couple well-earned days off with their families. "You sure Olivia provided enough working capital to get you through?"

Both Caroline and Annie were firm in their nods. "Enough to get us to the end of next season," Caroline said. "Besides, we don't make our first payment until after the first of the year."

"What of the oil Slater discovered? Got plans?"

Mother and daughter grinned at each other before turning their attention to me. "Our family attorney is setting us up with a group to walk us through the steps," Caroline said. "Neither of us want ranch life disrupted, so any wells will have to be out of sight. If oil actually flows, we plan to pay off your foundation and make much-needed upgrades. Should something come up to stop extraction, or there isn't enough to make it worthwhile, we'll still make our payments without fail."

No longer worried about losing their home, I barely recognized Annie. The spiteful harpy I'd grown used to avoiding disappeared, and in its place was a wonderful, relaxed young woman. She laughed and joked enough I wished I'd gotten the opportunity to know her. Crow's feet at the corner of her eyes were on full display.

Caroline slid a check and an envelope across the table after we sat for my favorite fried chicken supper. "It's not much, but I promised to pay you after the season ended. We reimbursed you the cash you loaned us, too."

I pushed the check back without looking. "Can't take it. You've given me more than you'll ever know. Besides, Buster is payment enough."

Tears welled, and one trickled to drip from her chin. She wouldn't accept it back and her voice cracked. "Keep it, please?"

Her face twisted more when I shook my head. "Other than to help you out, I was here to earn enough for one thing. Money was the next to last step. I think you understand what I'm saying."

She nodded. "What happened to drive a young healthy man like yourself to suicide?" she whispered. "It must've been terrible."

I stared at my plate. For once I could think of Jess and Danny without the madness creeping in. "I lost my twin and her boy."

"Her?"

"Jess was my older sister by a couple minutes, and Danny was her son...my nephew."

Annie'd stayed quiet until now. "I think I saw a picture of her with your father. Was she tall like you with dark hair bobbed short, and a tattoo on her neck?" I nodded. "She was very pretty."

I sniffed and swallowed hard. "A damn hard worker and a great rider, too. Got high marks in college and graduated in the top of her class."

Caroline bit her lip and waited to question me. "Dare I ask—" She left it unsaid.

"They were murdered by the same group who found me here."

Annie's spine stiffened at my explanation and her eyes narrowed. "That's why you didn't hesitate when he followed me to the stables that night. I couldn't help but wonder why you didn't take him prisoner."

My final day shouldn't be filled with sadness and I told them so. Caroline's crispy chicken was second only to memories of my mom's. We dug into our meal following a brief prayer, after which I marveled at the gravy. Our ranch cook, Davy, needed to take lessons from Caroline.

Breakfast was bittersweet. My belongings were packed and left behind on the veranda while we ate inside. Caroline sniffed and wiped her eyes with a dishtowel while she flipped hotcakes and eggs. Annie was quiet and glum while we ate, barely saying a word. Her mom brought up the topic I hoped we silently agreed to avoid. "What would you like us to tell Leeann?"

I shrugged. "Don't care. Turns out what I thought was growing between us was a figment of my imagination." For a few weeks, I thought she might be the girl I'd been looking for. We'd done nothing but kiss, hold hands a little, and talk, but Lee's the one who told me not to fear the future. She'd given me a reason to live, and for it, I'd never forget her.

The rattle of the F350 diesel came while I was washing breakfast down with coffee. Time to get Buster and face the music. I hoped my confrontation with Joe would take place after we left the ranch. He could be a bear anytime he felt wronged. I got a warm hug and a kiss to my cheek from Caroline, where Annie's soft lips landed on my mouth. Her warm embrace was one I could get used to.

Joe parked next to the corral. I gathered my gear and smiled at Caroline. "I put the bill of sale for Buster in your envelope," she said. "I know you'll take good care of him."

"I will," I promised. "He's the horse of a lifetime."

The slam of the truck door got my attention, and I turned to see Joe striding to the house. Rather than angry, his smile was meant to dazzle us. All five feet five inches of him stopped at the bottom step. I'd eat my hat if he weighed over a buck thirty. My cow boss swept his Stetson from a shock of kinky orange hair. I swear his ears could hold one three sizes bigger from sliding to his chin. He nodded. "Boss...ladies."

"Caroline...Annie, I'd like you to meet my mentor and best friend. Joe, Caroline and her daughter own and operate Hagseth Hills Guest Ranch."

"Pleased to meetcha," he said and climbed the steps to shake their hands. "Hope you put the boy to work."

Caroline smiled. "We certainly did. I'm not sure we've employed anyone who labored as hard."

He turned to me, the women forgotten. "Well? Show me this wonder horse." His eagerness was no different than a boy or girl looking forward to presents under the Christmas tree.

I tossed my gear onto the backseat of the Ford and led him inside the stables. I'd already watered and fed Buster. The big appaloosa nickered when he saw me. He reached over the gate and let me hug his neck. I hoped like hell I could feel as strongly about a woman someday. "Are you ready, boy? Your life is about to change in a big way."

"Damn, you sure as hell weren't joshin' about his height, were you?" Joe said.

After fitting his halter and snapping a lead rope on, I led Buster outside. He kept a sharp eye on Joe, curious about the man watching closely. With the rear ramp already down, he balked only a moment before following me inside. I fastened the divider into place after tying him in, leaving the horse with his feedbag filled with oats to put him at ease. Joe closed and locked the back when I walked out. Her eyes moist, Annie squeezed my elbow before retreating to the veranda. "Caroline..." I took her in my arms again. "...I'll never forget you and what you've done for me. If you're ever in southwest Montana, look me up. There'll always be a room for you."

She pushed away after a few moments. "Same with you, Cable. If you somehow find yourself in Colorado again...for any reason...stop in."

We didn't make it to the end of the driveway before Joe took stock of my general state of disrepair. "Seems those women appreciated you, boy."

He was hired by Mom when I was in grade school. He called me boy the first day, and it continued into manhood. It made no difference to me. He called Jess girl most of the time and Mom lady. "They're good people. The best."

Neither of us were big talkers, and we stayed silent until he got us up to speed on the highway. Joe fidgeted as he usually did while getting comfortable for a long drive. This time he seemed unable until turning his attention from the road to me. "Start talkin', boy. You've got a lot of explaining to do."

Chapter XII

Joe was more dad than my father ever was. I could no more avoid a subject he raised than Mom when she insisted. "There's no way to tell you how sorry I am," I said.

"You'd better figure out how in the next few miles. After you disappeared with blood in your eye, me and the boys watched the Brotherhood headquarters burn to the ground on television. You was gone a week...then the IDs of sixty outa sixty-three bodies was made public. Didn't take goddamned rocket science to figure yours was one they said got charred too bad. Boy, I can't tell you how torn up me and the crew was. Didn't invite anyone, but we put together a makeshift memorial for you back in the Snowcrest Range where you and Jess used to fish. Now, you show up alive and well without a hair outa place. Start talkin', asshole."

"When I saw wall tapestries on the videotape behind Jess and Danny, I recognized the Brotherhood of Loki clubhouse in Sacramento from pictures Jess once showed me. The moment I watched them die, I knew I was going to retaliate. Only thing is I got a third of the cockroaches, instead of just Danny's father."

"How'd you do it? All of the bodies was in the rubble."

If I closed my eyes, I could hear the screams. "There was a big meeting with drunken bikers stumbling in and out. I pulled a Raiders ball cap low, picked up a cup dropped on the ground, and walked in. Surprised I wasn't noticed. They have a firm rule against outsiders. No windows, though, with only two doors. Candles everywhere...must have been a thousand...meant no electricity, either."

Joe glanced from where he hunkered over the wheel. He always ran the split seat forward until it could go no farther. "No shit? You went inside? You got balls, boy. Big balls."

I shrugged. "I needed to see for myself."

"Well, what'd you find?"

"The tapestry. It still hung where we saw it in the video feed. Only thing I couldn't locate was the table. Too many people. I eased outside when they started some sort of ceremony. Two doors...one front and one rear, both opening outward with metal U brackets to pull. The back one wasn't accessible with boxed supplies stacked in front of it. Too big of a building for only one exit and no windows."

"Jesus." I barely heard his whisper over road noise. "Like shootin' fish in a barrel when they came running at you."

"My exact plan after I saw Danny's deadbeat dad take a seat at the far end. I knew him from Jess's photos even when ceiling fans flickered candles and twisted tapestries stenciled with deities and mythical beasts. It felt more occult than anything."

Joe repeated louder, "Jesus."

"No, their gods came from the other direction."

"What happened? How'd the place burn?"

"I gave them a few minutes to chant, then stepped back in. It was dark out, so they didn't see the door open. Thing is I didn't account for a guard moved into place just inside. I startled him as much as he did me. Big son of a bitch could've twisted my head off, but he drew a handgun instead."

"Ain't no one slicker with a short gun than you, boy."

"He was dead before he hit the floor, and the place went crazy. Got a good double-tap at Danny's father before candles were knocked over. Tapestries exploded into flame like they were soaked in diesel. I saw him go down hard, and I backed out when fire walled me off. Even kept the wherewithal about me to pick up my three empty brass before I shut the door and leaned a four-by-four against the metal pull."

"God, they burned to death. Must've been an awful way to go."

"Sure as hell hope so. Every one of the bastards participated in or condoned the murders. I imagine they're still on fire after getting to hell."

"Hey, I ain't complaining." He cleared his throat. "Zoe called and said you had a run-in with one of their members. She figured they somehow tracked you through her phone. How'n the hell did the assholes learn it was you?"

"I left a calling card."

He was obviously startled. "A WJP business card?"

"Nope. A picture of Jess and Danny I taped to the gas tank of a motorcycle parked outside. Must've been five dozen or more, so I chose one. Someone figured it out."

I sat forward to constantly watch the trailer in the rearview mirror. Buster was born on Caroline's ranch and was experiencing his first ride. If he fought his restraints, he could hurt himself badly. I hoped to spend the next twenty or twenty-five years riding the range with him.

We stopped for fuel and so I could check on Buster after crossing into Wyoming. He seemed happy to see me and hear my voice but wasn't interested in water. Joe offered to swap places with me, but without my wallet or even knowing whether my license was valid, I left driving up to him.

"How did you do it?" he asked. "The way you disappeared after leaving your Datsun and attaché at the ranch. None of the crew owned up to slappin' eyes on hide nor hair."

"I never expected to survive and wasn't sure what to do. I walked all night after parking it and eventually caught a ride with a trucker. He was on his way to Denver with a load of Kubota tractors. Got him to drop me off in southern Wyoming. I wandered from there."

I dozed a few hours and saw a sign for North Ogden when I woke. "Gonna stop in the next town to piss and fill my thermos," Joe said. "Got a cup in your gear?"

"Yes, sir."

Joe refused to eat at fast food joints and found a café with easy parking. While he used their facilities, I went inside the horse trailer to check on Buster. He seemed glad for human contact and the curry comb I brought along. My thought was to give him a memory of home. I was close to finished when Joe peered inside. "You might wanna hit the head before we pull out. Bought a couple hamburgers and got coffee to go."

He found a place to park along the Snake River north of Blackfoot, Idaho, as the sun set. It gave me time to walk Buster to the stream to slake his thirst. I secured his lead rope in browse close to the truck, while Joe and I laid out our sleeping bags. He took the front seat, and I got the back. Didn't take more than a couple minutes before he hollered to where I sat on the tailgate: "What in the hell stinks so bad?"

"I slept in my bag for two years. Needs a good washing."

"The hell it does!" He slid out of the truck in his long johns and cowboy boots to reach in the backseat and throw the filthy thing out. "I ain't puttin' up with no such stench. Got a couple blankets I stuffed behind the rear seat. Wrap yourself in 'em, boy." I moved Buster inside the trailer and locked the back. I'd hate like hell for thieves to hit us while we slept. The blankets were where he promised, and I made myself comfortable. The appaloosa banged around until he got comfortable and settled down. "I ain't layin' blame, Cable," Joe said. "No doubt losing Jess and Danny was gonna take its toll. Hell, their deaths 'bout killed me. Musta been worse for you." I rolled to my back and listened, unable to respond. "Lost my mind when your mother passed. I know it affected you kids, but to my eternal shame, I couldn't think past my own pain. Put the muzzle of my Winchester in my mouth a hundred times if I did it once, tryin' my best to pull the trigger. Stayed with the cattle all summer waitin' for the right time. Wasn't scared of doing it...I feared facing Jessica. Came close to the same thing with your sister till I learned I was responsible for the ranch, lowlife bastard y'are." He was quiet for a minute before deciding I wasn't talking. "It's why I would've bet money one of them missin' bodies was yours. Figured you went out in a blaze of gunfire."

I found my tongue. "My exit plan."

His grunt meant he appreciated my short, candid reply. "You wandered off to die?"

"Yes, sir."

"What stopped you?"

"A host of factors. Helping Caroline and Annie in their battle to keep their place was a part of it."

He chuckled. "The girl caught your fancy? She's a purdy one."

Yeah, but not her, I thought. "Huh uh. She was a bit too spiteful for my tastes. Liked to rip me a new one if I passed her."

"You still gave her a hand."

"Her mom," I corrected. Yet Annie wasn't entirely to blame for her hate and vitriol. Losing her husband followed by their neighbor trying to undermine their loan and steal their home was enough to drive anyone mad. Lord knows I suffered my own form of insanity. What else could I call a focused drive to kill myself slowly, while allowing pain and guilt to crush me first?

* * *

Joe idled forward on the driveway, avoiding potholes and rattling Buster. He got to where I could see the ranch house, barns, and outbuildings framed by the Snowcrest Range when I raised my hand. "Stop," I said. The tall mountains beyond my property line were painted with a fresh coating of early season snow.

He put the truck in park. "What's up?"

"Never thought I'd see it again." I ran my shirtsleeve across misty eyes.

Joe glanced at me to see what I meant and didn't miss my emotional response to home. "Oh." He looked back to the ranch. "It's a beautiful place. Your ma loved it. Hell, we all love it."

"Yeah, Jess used to have me drop her off about here. She'd walk the last leg home to enjoy it more." I got a wild idea and belted on the holstered Kimber and opened my door. "I'm going to unload Buster and ride him the rest of the way."

He was as eager as me to get out. I'd left Caroline's tack with her other than a halter and lead rope. At some point, I'd box up both and mail them back. At my urging, Joe left us behind to park our truck and stock trailer.

Buster's head was high as he absorbed his surroundings. Ears forward, he appeared as excited as I'd seen him. I stroked his neck and spoke softly. "Get used to it, man. This's your forever home." We watched and listened as Joe disappeared in the direction of the ranch. I led the horse to a high berm next to the road and used it to shorten the distance to his back. First tossing the lead rope over his withers, I jumped and threw my leg across to sit bareback. He seemed as surprised at my move as I was when he didn't pitch. I leaned forward to stroke his crest and neck. "It's just me and you now, man. I hope you're ready to explore."

He handled better than I hoped. Pointing his nose in the direction of home, I touched his ribs with my bootheels. Reaching a pleasing gallop instead of running flat-out, we closed the distance to the ranch headquarters quickly. I couldn't have been more pleased with his handling.

The boys were waiting with Joe and leaned against the pickup cab. I slowed Buster to a walk before stopping fifteen feet away and nodded at each one. "Davy . . . Odell . . . Lucky . . . Richie . . . Lynn . . . Gary . . . how're you boys holding up?"

Lucky was the youngest at twenty-one. "Holding up? Goddamn it, boss. We thought you were dead and held a funeral and everything for you." He stared a moment, more at Buster than me. "Shit," the kid said in disgust and slapped his wide-brimmed Resistol against a thigh, raising dust before stomping his way to the bunkhouse. The rest of my crew ignored his departure and stared silently.

"Is there an empty stall in the east barn?" I asked. It was closest to the house.

"First three," Odell said.

The second was blessed with a window a stallion broke out. Mom leased him as a stud to improve our lines. Midnight, once my favorite until Joe connected with him, was a direct descendant. The missing pane would make it breezier inside but provided fresh air and plenty of light. He would have line-of-sight to the ranch house to keep an eye out for me.

I blessed Lynn under my breath. He rarely said a word and let his work speak for itself. The clean stall needed nothing but an armload of straw, bucket of water, and a flake of alfalfa to make my horse comfortable. I curried Buster while he ate and drank to give him a semblance of home. "Make yourself comfortable, man. I'll see you in the morning."

The F350 was disconnected from the trailer and parked next to the machine shed when I closed the barn and saw my gear on the porch. My crew was nowhere to be seen as I started for the garage. My beat-up Datsun truck was parked inside as I'd done for years. The keys were still in the ignition, but I opened the glove box instead. My wallet was waiting there from two years prior.

Leaving the garage led me through the mudroom with the washer and dryer and into the kitchen, almost expecting to see Jess at the table or spatula in hand to turn a flapjack for Danny. I went through the living room to retrieve my gear from the front porch. The house was big, open, and silent, made worse by the lack of my nephew's squealing laughter as he ran from his mom. He may spring from the loins of a dirty son of a bitch, but no one could be around him for more than a few minutes before feeling his joy. His delight touched everyone he came in contact with until the Brotherhood.

I found a can of chili after a long shower. Felt good to wear my own duds instead of those I wore so long belonging to my former boss's dead husband. Field stripping the Kimber while I ate, I finished the meal when the gun was cleaned and reassembled. Caroline was never far from my mind, nor her good deeds in providing. I hoped she and Annie didn't think too badly of me after the misery I brought to their door.

The Kimber was purchased on a whim when extra money burned a hole in my pocket while perusing the local gun shop. My choices at home were standard ranch favorites, a .30-30 in a Winchester model 64, a scoped .30-06, scatterguns in several gauges, and a dozen thumb-busters chambering .22 long rifle to .44 Magnum. Grizzly sightings were common while riding the Snowcrest Range, necessitating the power of a rifle or heavy caliber handgun. The crew brought their own firearms, kept in a safe inside the bunkhouse until needed. Joe ran a tight ship, taking no nonsense from any employee.

If I wondered about someone coming into the house during my absence, it was abundantly clear no one did. Even the blankets on my bed were thrown back where I got up in a hurry the last morning. The same sheets with my pillow at the angle I always woke with. Although the hour was early, I sat on the edge of the bed and tugged my boots off. My clothes were left in a pile next to them while I got comfortable on the worn mattress. The years melted away as I relaxed. Perhaps the world would return to normal when I woke.

* * *

Asleep at seven, my eyes opened a few minutes after four. With at least three hours until daylight, I dressed in the same clothes and stumbled into the kitchen after a bathroom visit. I got out a metal pot to perk coffee in, rather than take a chance on something growing for two years inside my drip model. Although I was welcome to eat with the boys in the bunkhouse, I chose instead to dip inside an unopened box of Bisquick for hotcakes. Add a little water, and the result was filling if nothing else. I'd talk to Davy later about making a grocery run for me. Trading the Kimber and Kydex holster for an early model Ruger .44 and leather, I belted it on and dropped a handful of spare cartridges inside my wool coat pocket. It was nice to take my work Eddy Brothers down from its peg and fit it on my head.

Buster nickered at the sound of my step. I reached inside and flipped the light on, giving me illumination to prepare for an early ride. While the saddle I borrowed from Caroline fit me well enough, none was so comfortable as the heavy western model I'd used almost twenty years. A small set of saddle bags were enough to hold my thermos of coffee and a sandwich made of hotcakes, peanut butter, and jam. Leading my horse outside, enough dawn came from the east to make my escape into familiar high country.

Joe warned me we were less than a week from the opening of deer season. Afterward, hunters would be hiking and riding the mountains in search of wapiti. The Snowcrest Range is a small area, and many hunters chose to scour the Gravellies instead.

We climbed high in the mountains before I saw my first game. Instead of a herd of mule deer or elk, it was a huge boar grizzly. Ambling and checking beneath each rock, he finally tore into a stump and located something worth spending his time. I kept a wary eye on him while we circled wide to avoid the hungry bruin busy adding winter fat. Their populations were increasing each year. Seldom did I ride the high ridges without seeing one or an indication a bear traveled through. We lost a few cows to them each year, and I expected more would be turned into bear shit the next season.

Judging by his reaction to the mountains around us, Buster apparently enjoyed new country. I fed on his excitement as we traveled. Even at a walk, a tall horse with long legs covered ground at a prodigious rate. With the bear left far behind, we didn't stop until reaching my goal. Jess and I always took a break at what we named Big Buck Mountain. As children, we once watched a huge mule deer with massive antlers bedded where we eventually stopped to eat our lunches.

Buster and I spent the day high in patches of melting snow. Field glasses kept in my saddle bags came in handy when spotting deer and elk. For the first season in my life since I began hunting, I didn't plan to pursue furred or feathered game. Interestingly enough, I located seven of my cows and eight calves concealed in a deep swale. It looked like they'd hid out for quite some time. Too late in the day to move them, I planned to let Joe take a couple of cowboys to roundup and drive them home before deer season started. Fifteen cows and calves were worth over twenty thousand dollars. Too much to leave for critters capable of pulling them down.

We arrived at the ranch not long after dark. I gave Buster a feed bag of oats after watering and dropping a flake of hay rather than alfalfa in the manger. He enjoyed the time I spent with the curry comb brushing his coat and looking for gouges and scrapes. I wanted him to know nothing changed—although his home was different, it was still my job to take care of him.

A door slammed when I was halfway to the house. "Hold up, Cable," a voice called. Davy hurried to me with a plate in each hand. "I know you ain't got much in the house, so I brought you an extra steak I burned on the grill and some sides. You're welcome to join us in the morning."

Both plates were hot when I took them. "I appreciate it. Still five o'clock?"

"Yes, sir."

"Thanks, Davy. You're a good man."

He chuckled when I turned to the house. "Let's keep it between you and me."

The chunk of meat he sent could be considered a roast. It looked to be close to forty-eight ounces of medium rare beef. Slaw, beans, and a large square of pineapple upside down cake made up the rest of the meal. He even thought to add a thick dollop of horseradish. I hung my coat and hat after leaving dinner on the table, then swapped my boots for house slippers. The place was silent when I sat to eat, reminding me again of my loss.

My phone rang about the time I was ready to give up finishing supper. Wincing after checking the number, I answered. "Hey, Z. Sorry I haven't contacted you sooner."

Her relief was obvious. "Oh, William, I'm so relieved to hear your voice. I know the charges against you were dropped, but you haven't called nor taken mine."

"I'm sorry. It's...well...I really don't have a good excuse," I said.

"As long as you're safe. That's all I care about."

"Safe...and home."

"Home? The WJP?"

"Yeah. Joe and I got back yesterday."

She was silent a moment. "I'm glad. Is it hard?"

I glanced around the kitchen and into the living room. Danny should be fighting his momma over bedtime. The little guy never liked going to bed when others were still up. "Yeah, it's tough," I said. "Worse than I imagined."

"Can I go west? I'd love to spend time with you. See the ranch again."

"No, I'm not the best company right now. Besides, we've been sprinkled with our first dusting of snow. Temperatures are dropping."

My refusal didn't bother her. "Next spring, then?"

"Sure. Any time after the ground dries."

Z laughed. "Montana mud...is there anything worse?"

We talked another ten minutes before ending the call. My sister was right. We needed to build a stronger sibling bond. Talking regularly would go a long way unless the old man stepped in. He was always the wildcard when it came to Zoe.

* * *

Although I didn't hear voices when I stepped onto the bunkhouse porch, the smell of breakfast made my mouth water. I didn't bother to knock, and every head swiveled toward me when I entered. The boys sat at two tables waiting on me like one hog waits on another. Davy, Odell, and Joe sat at one, while my four cowboys took up the other. Davy pushed an empty plate in my direction. "Take all you want, Boss. We got plenty."

I made myself comfortable at their table. Bacon, eggs, waffles, and coffee hit the spot. I ignored the silence and dug in. Man, Davy could cook. Not like Caroline but better than a spread like mine deserved. He was originally hired as a part-time farrier until we learned he went to culinary school. While he still shoes the horses, his main job is keeping bellies fed no matter how many are hungry. Even Jess used to eat with the crew after Mom died until returning with Danny in her belly.

Joe wasn't surprised to learn over a dozen heifers and calves remained in the mountains. No matter how well the hills are scoured, a few turn up later each year. He promised to send Lynn and Gary to round them up when breakfast was over.

Joe waited until the tables were clean after the crew left for their daily duties. "Six slaughter trucks are comin' the first of next week. We've got orders for a hundred and fourteen beef. They're fenced on the north field where gettin' to 'em is easiest. Weather's supposed to hold, but all it takes is a little rain, and we're screwed."

"So many." I nodded to myself. "You've done a great job, Joe."

175

Selling beef to locals was Mom's idea. It didn't take long before word of mouth spread far and wide. We took orders and would kill and have their packaged beef ready at local butcher shops. The first year we sold only seven, but before losing Jess, we'd built to over sixty. Now, it seemed Joe almost doubled it. Profit margins were so thin every dollar and the way it got spent became important. I wasn't close to losing the place to creditors, simply because the old man bought and gave it to Mom as a wedding gift. Otherwise, we'd have struggled to make payments the same as every other rancher. Depending on hanging weight, we'd clear enough to pay at least four men's salary for the year.

Eating with the boys became routine. Davy replenished my kitchen, but I couldn't work up interest in cooking and eating alone in the big house when two ghosts wandered the rooms. Distant gunshots meaning hunters connected on game quieted after deer and then elk season were over. Never one for television, I spent my time in the office going over figures and paying bills. Gone two years and rarely spending money on myself before, combined with Joe's good management left our coffers in good shape. Odell did a respectable job of keeping our equipment in working order. Cutting and baling two thousand acres of hay and alfalfa meant keeping our machines in satisfactory condition.

I never felt lonelier than after I returned home. Caroline and Annie often occupied my thoughts. Leeann, too, although Z informed me Damien Slater was well enough to oversee the sale of his home. I'd never mentioned Lee and wasn't sure my sister knew of the young woman.

Our father tried to call me once. I recognized his number the moment it flashed across my screen. Rather than answer, I immediately dialed Zoe to voice my displeasure while staring outside at cascading snowflakes. "Tell the old man to leave me alone if he wants to stay healthy. Understand?"

"He wants to work toward bridging the gulf between you, William. Father plans to fly to Montana—"

I didn't let her finish. "Okay, then, tell him to come on out," I said. "I can dig a hole twelve feet deep with the backhoe. Cover him with a couple bags of lime, and one of my headaches is gone."

"William!" Z sounded shocked. "You wouldn't."

"Try me," I shouted. "Our sister and nephew are dead because the son of a bitch loved money more than his daughter and grandson."

We ended the call rather than cause more hurt feelings. Early in the day, I stomped around the house until making my decision. Hustling to the bunkhouse, I asked Davy to pack a big lunch before saddling Buster. The tall appaloosa felt my mood and shook with excitement while I threw a blanket and rig on him. A sleeping bag, tarp, and saddlebags were secured behind the cantle, along with my .30-30 in its scabbard under my leg and fender. Seconds after my ass touched the seat, Buster ran flat-out toward the distant mountains. Not only could he feel my frame of mind, he knew my salvation lay in the high ridges.

Chapter XIII

A heavy jacket and thermal underwear protected me from harsh conditions. Buster didn't balk nor slow when I turned his nose uphill. Sporadic snowfall and fog shrouded the ridges above as we traveled. *Who in the hell was the old man to think he could waltz into my life again after destroying it twice?* The bastard was used to setting conditions to favor himself. Air temperatures dipped as we pushed on, soon lost inside low clouds. It didn't matter to me. I'd ridden the slopes and ridgetops since given my first horse at seven.

A young spike bull elk still in his bed was surprised when I rode past only feet away. Somehow, he avoided hunters scouring the backcountry in search of their winter's meat. I silently wished him well without stopping and spooking him worse.

Tired from my ride, I reined Buster to a stop next to a stand of timber. It blew hard where I dismounted yet not enough to snap treetops. With an hour left until dark, I kicked through a couple inches of snow until I found what I looked for. An old firepit Jess and I used regularly. We'd brought Danny on our last trip together. Gusts blew hard enough to force me to string the tarp as a break and shelter. Buster looked on with interest as I used a wadded piece of waxed paper from my lunch held inside my coat to light a fire. Dead branches caught quickly to crackle and pop while they warmed enough to burn. A roaring jet stream overhead added to the magic of winter camping in the mountains.

I lay in my cold weather bag, eating one of the sandwiches Davy sent. Four in all—I planned to save three for breakfast and lunch. Thick tuna with cheese was enough to take the sharp edge off my hunger, and my small thermos was quickly drained rather than let hot coffee cool and go to waste. While Buster munched inside his feedbag, I poked at the fire with a stick and added more fuel. We were out of the worst of the storm and far more comfortable than I initially expected.

While my initial anger toward the old man cooled when in Colorado, it exploded into white-hot flame at the idea of seeing him again. I begged him repeatedly to either involve law enforcement during Jess and Danny's kidnapping or pay their ransom. Even a brief online foray into the Brotherhood of Loki's background assured me they played hardball. Our father was given options, and he chose the one with the greatest likelihood to kill our family. Although I recognized he'd most likely been devastated by their loss, I was unable to forgive or forget.

Buster didn't mind getting close and putting his head under the edge of my tarp. Strung perhaps six feet off the ground, there was plenty of room for his curiosity. He sniffed around and plucked at my collar with bristled lips. Damned horse—he acted more like a friend than a mount.

I kept the fire burning hot and bright, casting shadows to writhe through the trees. While the wind eased, falling snow made up for it. Using an oily rag kept in my saddlebags, I wiped the exterior of both my Winchester and Ruger. Mom scrimped and saved and bought the .30-30 for me on my fourteenth birthday. With a pistol grip stock and a half-magazine, the priceless rifle carried five rounds in the undertube— more than enough, although I kept an extra box of twenty in my saddlebags. A dozen mule deer bucks and almost as many bull elk fell to the receiver-sighted long gun over the years.

Mom worried about Jess and me while we both worked and explored the backcountry. She saw the magazines and articles I read without letting me know. I didn't ask, because I wasn't old enough, but she purchased a .44 handgun for my sixteenth birthday anyway. Joe helped me learn to control its recoil by starting me with lesser loads and working up to full magnums. Soon, it became an extension of my hand. I carried it every day until the Kimber followed me home. Returned to its holster, I kept the revolver close to hand. No telling what might go bump in the night at eight thousand feet.

I slept better than expected. Used to living in my stump, I woke twice to toss fuel onto the campfire. Finally, the gray edges of dawn filtered through fog thick enough to cut. Holding a hand over the ashes, I located a hot spot with glowing embers. Five minutes passed while I built it into a hot blaze. I enjoyed the heat while taking my time with a tuna sandwich breakfast.

The Brotherhood of Loki was never far from my thoughts. As long as I was alive, they'd never stop coming. At some point, they would show up at my door or on a street if I ventured to town. Like me, they'd never forgive nor forget and could make their appearance when I least expected. My cowboys were always unarmed and focused on work. If the Sacramento thugs planned well enough, they could infiltrate the ranch in the dead of night and stand a reasonable chance of killing all of us. I couldn't lose sight of the fact their members numbered at least a hundred fifty. Perhaps more joined in the two years I wasted.

Rather than pack and ride home, I moved Buster to a better spot for browse and to gather more combustibles. Not stopping until building a thick pile of branches and rotten stumps, I made myself comfortable on my sleeping bag with a bottle of water. Finding my way home in the blinding fog wasn't the problem—feeling a need to return to civilization was. Even from hundreds of miles away, the siren call of my stump was loud and persistent. It didn't care if I lived or died nor whether I was happy or sad. *Come live in me,* it whispered. *No consequences here. Come and stay until life no longer matters.*

The mountain remained socked in throughout the day. Without my wristwatch it would've been difficult to know what time it was. Flurries ended, but hard gusts blew the slope free of snow. I kept my fire going and an eye on Buster. He accepted our hiatus calmly as if spending time on the sides of tall mountains was common in bad weather.

Other than wipe my guns twice more during my stay, I hunkered next to the fire and let it roar against the elements. By nightfall, my stack of wood was piled high, and I ate my third sandwich slowly. Pain stemming from the empty big house couldn't touch me if I stayed away.

Ghostly calls for Uncle Cable couldn't reach where I hid from life. I dreaded returning and facing no future.

Morning was clear and cold when I woke. Temperatures were in the low teens or less judging by how deeply I burrowed inside my bag. Even Buster stood with his front end beneath my tarp. Hoping a warm spot existed, I searched for and found coals still alive. My last sandwich was left near the blaze to thaw enough to eat. Then, it was time to pack my gear and face the world.

I met Joe, Lynn, and Gary before traveling a half mile. All three carried rifles across their saddles. The trio drew to a halt with my cow boss standing in his stirrups for a better look. He wasn't happy. "What'n the hell's going on?" he asked. "Been laid up?"

"Needed time away."

"From what? Christ, you haven't been anywhere or seen anyone."

I clucked my tongue and touched my heels to Buster. He broke into a controlled lope when I urged him on while keeping the reins taut. I patted his neck to show my appreciation.

When we reached the flatlands, he shot forward when I gave him his head. Snow blew across the grassy range to pile against anything immovable, and he broke into a gallop until we reached the gate. Lucky beat me to it and held it open. I nodded my thanks and guided my horse into the barn, dismounted, and led him to his stall.

His head was in the manger when Joe rode past on Midnight. I reckon he gave his mount to one of the boys judging by how fast he appeared outside the stall. Buster earned his brushing and extra rations. Joe leaned against the gate. "You plannin' to let me in on what's goin' on, boy? Davy said you asked for a lunch before doin' your vanishin' act three days ago. Me'n the crew figured you was either down and hurt or turned into bear shit."

I shook my head. "I'm not ready."

Joe threw his hands up. "For what?"

"For any of this."

My mentor stared a moment before wetting his lips. "Talk to me, Cable. I ain't understanding."

Buster enjoyed long strokes from croup to gaskin. "I'm Rip Van Winkle waking from a sleep. Problem is it's two years ago for me." I ran a coat sleeve across my face.

"Two years..." Joe's lids opened wide the moment he understood. "Ah, hell, boy."

"The big house is as empty of life as a tomb," I said. "I can hardly stand it inside. Every second I expect to hear Danny running down the stairs with Jess giving chase, or his momma hollering at him to pick up his clothes."

"I get it," Joe said quietly. "I felt the same way about the place after Jessica died. Damn near quit. Didn't get any better when summer was over, and you and the weather chased me home. You and Jess was glued at the hip for the better part of your life. Hate to be the bearer of bad news, but you'll never get over what happened. Best you can hope for is to be able to control the pain." I didn't turn to face him or answer. I reckoned he said all he wanted when I heard the jingle of his spurs disappearing.

Davy normally doesn't serve lunch. Instead, he made hearty sandwiches and left a stack in the fridge in case hungry cowboys appeared midday. I smelled his cooking when I entered the bunkhouse and turned right into the kitchen. These quarters were one of three, but the only one with a kitchen. On the other end of the building were bathrooms and communal showers.

I dropped my duffle and leaned my rifle against the wall. Davy turned at the noise with a wooden spoon held high. "Get the hell...oh, sorry, boss. Figured you for one of the boys filching more oatmeal cookies." He frowned after noticing my gear and waited for an explanation.

I jerked my head toward the bunks. "Got room for an extra cowboy?"

"Sure. Got three open. Why, didja hire someone?"

A check of the fridge found me something to eat. A sandwich made thick with sliced roast beef and a hunk of cheese. I opened the cellophane and took a big bite while shaking my head. "No," I said after swallowing. "I'm moving in if you don't mind."

Davy tugged at his earlobe the same as any other time he got flustered. "Sure...I mean, there's plenty of space. Boss, you sure you want to sleep with the rest of these snoring varmints?"

A roll of my eyes would likely have drawn a swing with his spoon. No one snored worse than our cook. He'd put on at least a hundred pounds since accepting the position. At five eight, three hundred didn't look good on him. "Point one out so I can store my kit." I snagged a second sandwich before following him with my gear.

He suggested one in the corner. Both the bottom and top were open. I chose the lower, pushed my bag beneath, and left my rifle on the upper. Joe might not appreciate a gun outside of the safe, but I'll be damned if I was going to go unarmed.

* * *

Once my crew got over the shock of their boss living with them, it was Joe who privately suggested a multi-point driveway intrusion alarm. We could install each of the eight remote detection units where anyone approaching would trigger an alarm. He and I drew a map and then walked the areas of easiest and most likely ingress. I wanted Joe to understand my apprehension and worry after the Brotherhood discovered I was alive. Their attempt on my life wouldn't be the only time they'd try to kill me. Learning the hard way with Jess and Danny and again with Caroline and Annie, innocent lives meant nothing to the rogue cycle gang.

Joe and I set the boys down after supper to explain my growing concern over the Brotherhood. If any cowboy wanted out after learning of the danger we might face, I was willing to write a check for six months of severance pay and provide a letter of recommendation. "Are you telling us there's really a chance these Californian yahoos might want to take on the WJP?" Richie asked. He stood six inches above six feet and walked with a permanent limp after a horse rolled over him.

"It's a possibility," I said. "They want me, but I've seen firsthand they're willing to inflict collateral casualties."

Davy looked puzzled. "What's 'co-ladder-all' mean?"

"It means I want my rifle, Joe," Gary said. He was my oldest puncher at thirty-six. A couple inches shorter than me, the man was far stockier. All I knew was he was a marine after Jess asked him about a tattoo.

"I got no problem with it," Joe said. "Except it's either no guns or no booze. Not both on a spread I ramrod. You know they don't mix."

"I want my Colt, Boss," Odell's tone was firm. "Our livers could use a break."

Joe stood when they all agreed. "You know it's too damn cold for California bikers, don't you?"

"Don't care," Odell said. "Bastards show up, I'm not gonna get caught with my pants down."

"None of you are interested in my offer?" I asked. "I'll cut a check this minute to anyone who wants to step away. Even hire you back no questions asked after this's over."

Lucky seemed to speak for them all. "I'd as soon you shut the hell up. Ain't none of us gonna cut and run." He didn't appear over his snit from when I turned up alive.

I watched in surprise when Joe opened the safe and handed out long guns. My cowboys weren't like me with a hunting rifle. Davy accepted a heavy as hell Tommy gun with a drum magazine, while Richie, Odell, Lucky, and Lynn seemed to relish AR15s they were obviously familiar with. Gary, however, reached with eager hands for a rifle I'd read about in gun magazines—an M1A SOCOM in .308. It made me wonder if the best armed crew in Montana worked for the WJP.

* * *

After a long winter, Montana snow melted enough to see patches of bare ground in late April. We'd spent much of our time since late November transporting huge bales of alfalfa using two tractors with specialty forks. The cattle went through feed faster than I hoped, but we needed every one to live. We were down to a hundred wrapped bales left in the field, and the north barn held less than another fifty when temperatures increased enough to make me breathe easier. I'd hired extra hands between the end of January and April to help with calving, ear-tagging, dehorning, castration, branding, and vaccinations. Most cowboys did their work aboard 4-wheelers—including mine—except me and Buster who stayed in good riding shape. Most of the horses were fat and lazy and wouldn't be used much until we moved the herd into summer grass. Until then, we could only wait until fresh sprouts popped through the ground at higher elevations. Each day, I eyed our dwindling rolls of hay and judged them against the slow retreat of snow. Although I hated like hell to buy feed, the ranch account could afford what they needed.

Joe stopped me with a raised hand when I led Buster out of the barn to mount. "Where you headed?"

I put my foot in the stirrup and pulled myself up by the saddle horn onto the tall horse. It took me a second to get situated in the seat and bring him around. His eagerness to travel matched my own. "West field. Got sixteen calves grafted onto mothers who lost theirs. We may need to feed them milk replacer." We'd lost about two percent of the herd during calving season. Closest count we could get was almost twenty-six hundred newborns. Even a ten percent loss over the summer and into fall would provide the ranch its biggest sale. Prices wouldn't always be fair—we'd got paid even more than Joe hoped the previous season at a buck twenty-three per pound. Sell two thousand and we'd be left with three to five hundred for herd replacement.

"Cowboys are already there." He held his cell for me to see. "Lynn called with an update to say they found one dead. Looked like coyotes." I worried about wolves. They'd hit us once before we lost Jess and Danny, wiping out seventy of our young. My sister was incensed and spent her time on our range with a rifle across the front of her pommel. She damned near lived on horseback until certain the animals moved into the backcountry. I turned Buster to where I could see into the Snowcrest Range, but Joe read my mind. "Wastin' your time. Got a week, maybe two before you need to check on grass."

I glared at the short man. "Then I'm going for a damn ride. It's still a free country."

He chuckled rather than get mad. "I reckon." Joe gestured at the driveway. "You got about an hour of ridin' before I need you to pick up some parts for the John Deere. Pete called to say they're in, and Odell needs 'em by mornin'." A touch of my heels was all Buster needed, and Joe and Odell were the last thing on my mind as we sailed toward the pavement over a mile away.

Pete didn't say anything about the Ruger on my hip when I was inside. I'd planned to exchange it for the Kimber but hadn't made the switch. A small sack containing sensors and gizmos I didn't understand set the ranch back almost thirty-five hundred dollars. I didn't complain, knowing Odell wouldn't order parts we couldn't live without.

A pickup parked opposite of me after I stopped for fuel. I got the feeling someone was staring, and I fell into lash-shaded pools of blue above a beautiful smile. My jaw fell, and I stammered for a moment before her grin widened. "What in the hell brings you to my part of the country?" I asked.

"Shopping," Annie Compton said.

I barely recognized her with once prematurely gray hair colored strawberry blonde. "Groceries? Clothes? Dillon has good sales on boots this time of year," I teased.

"Mom and I are in the market for another horse or two. Plan to look at a half-dozen we found online while I'm here."

"Where's your trailer?"

"Parked it at a bed and breakfast where I'm staying. I plan to make the rounds come morning."

Christ, she was easy on the eyes, but I didn't remember her as quite so pretty. Probably because of the way her mouth usually twisted down when I was nearby. I checked my wristwatch before making a proposal. "Can I offer you supper? I saw thick packages of steak Davy planned for the evening meal. The ranch isn't far...less than forty-five minutes from here."

"A ranch filled with men, and just li'l ol' me tossed in the middle?" She attempted a southern accent and fanned herself with a hand. "Oh, my, a dinner date with Cable Pearson. Whatever shall I do?"

Damned if she didn't look good fluttering lashes longer than I remembered. "Say yes?"

She laughed out loud. "Mom's going to be so jealous. I got an invitation to the famous Pearson ranch!"

I nodded to her truck to change the subject. "I see you splurged. Did the bucket of bolts you were driving finally give up the ghost?"

She sobered. "Spun a crankshaft bearing not long after you left. It would have cost us more to have it repaired than the truck was worth. We shopped online for our best deal and found this one in Denver. She's got a lot of miles...almost two hundred thousand...but someone took good care."

"It's a diesel. You can put a lot more on it if you're cautious."

Annie glanced at her phone. "It's almost four. What time did you say supper is?"

* * *

A call to Joe warned him of incoming female company. He promised the boys would clean the bunkhouse, and Davy would put on another plate. I worried more about manners and something triggering Annie's volatile temper. She stayed close behind me, and I could see her speaking on her cell. It was only right she updated Caroline after I cheated and called Joe. I braked on the driveway where my cow boss once let me out to ride Buster to his new home. The way the mountains framed my ranch couldn't be beat.

I stopped the engine and got out. Annie followed suit without taking her eyes off the panorama. "Oh. My. God." she whispered. "Cable, it's so beautiful."

I stood beside her to admire the view. "Colorado and your ranch are pretty. Welcome to my place."

"I...I...it's spectacular."

"Most of my life has been spent here or back in the mountains," I said quietly.

She shook her head. "It's no wonder."

Joe and the boys waited outside in their best when she followed me the rest of the way. I parked in front of the big house, and she stopped next to me. Joe led the troops to us. "Ma'am," he said and shook her hand. "Nice seein' you again."

Annie spoke as if she'd always known him. "How are you, Joe?"

"Damn fine since I got my boy back. Lemme introduce you to our crew."

His declaration was surprising. Joe was everything to me, but he never spoke in endearing terms before. I'd always been fond of him and thought he felt warmly about me. We'd lain beneath the stars many nights telling stories and contemplating the universe. But never did we broach personal feelings about the other. It was more teacher/student than parent or guardian and boy.

The sides were already on the tables when we entered. Mounds of baked potatoes, beans, slaw, and rolls. The backdoor slammed, and Davy made his way in with heaping plates of steaks fresh from the barbeque. "You're in for a treat," I told Annie. "Davy's a master of burning meat over a fire."

Joe gave up his normal seat and pulled an extra chair to the table. It put Annie's back to the kitchen, and the boys got a better look. We loaded our plates after giving our guest the best cut of meat. "What brings you to our neck of the country, ma'am?" Joe asked. "Come to see Cable?"

Her immediate bray of laughter made red creep from beneath my shirt and work its way to my ears. "No, I've got different business. We're in the market for two or three horses. Mom's been talking to a ranch north of here with three they're willing to let me look at."

I enjoyed seeing and hearing from Annie. She let me know Slater's house sold, and she heard he moved south to be near his folks in Texas. When she didn't volunteer news of Leeann, I decided not to ask. I'd thought of the young woman constantly over the winter and hoped what she meant to me would eventually fade. Annie's gaze was frank and clear while speaking of her one-time nemesis, almost challenging me to broach the subject. Instead, I let Joe steer it away from the dude ranch to how our cows wintered.

She stayed another hour after Davy served hot apple pie for dessert. Although they were struck by her attractiveness, I steered her outside so the boys could shoot the shit before they rolled into their bunks. Joe followed us to her truck and stood next to me after I closed Annie's door. She licked her lips. "Cable, would you do me a favor? It's big, so feel free to decline."

"Can't hurt to ask. I probably won't say no after what you and Caroline did for me."

Her smile grew sad. "Not me and Mom. I was nothing more than an impediment. My mother deserves all the credit. I'm asking this favor for her, too."

I threw my hands up in surrender mode. "Then, it's yours no matter what."

She looked worried when she bit a lip and stared. "Could you take on someone who needs a job? A really hard worker?"

Joe didn't let me answer. "Got no need for one. Could've used another hand or two during calving season, but I'm not sure—"

I butted in. "Done. Let him know he's got a job and send him out. Does he have any ranching experience?"

She winced and dipped her head. "With horses mostly, but a great rider who's easy to teach and a quick learner."

"Never pushed cows?" Joe grumped his question.

"No, but—"

I raised a hand. "No buts. I'm here because you helped me when I needed it most. How old is this new hand?"

"Mid-twenties."

"Got a horse?"

She brightened. "Oh, yes!"

"Fix gates, dig post holes, and clean stalls?"

She grinned back, knowing I was talking of my job working for her and Caroline. "I guarantee it."

I shrugged. "He's hired. How soon can he be here?"

"In the morning," she said. "Is that too soon?"

"Nope. We've got a bunk ready if he doesn't mind the snoring."

Annie giggled. "You can work that out among all of you." She leaned out when I patted her forearm and pulled me to her, planting a wet kiss on my cheek. "I've got dibs if this doesn't work out," she said with a laugh. Rather than explain, Annie started the engine and left us standing in a cloud of dust.

Joe turned to me when she was out of sight. "Sure hope you know what you're doin'."

"Not a clue. Thing is Annie and her mom are why I'm alive. Otherwise..." I'd told him about my home along the lake. "...I'd be nothing more than a corpse lying in a stump. They asked a favor of me, Joe. I can't do anything less than help out."

He wasn't happy and didn't care if I knew. "You hired this cowboy. If he don't pan out, it's your job to let him go."

"We'll figure something out. I can't imagine Caroline and Annie sending us a dud." I pinned Joe with a stare. "On the other hand, if he does a good job, it's your place to teach him everything he needs to know." Joe didn't fight me on it and left to roll onto his own bunk after nodding.

* * *

The driveway sensor went off while the crew and I gathered around the breakfast tables. Two of Davy's big flapjacks were all I could put away in addition to hash browns and scrambled eggs. I worked on my third cup of coffee when it sounded. Clatters of silverware on platters stilled, and everyone looked to me. "It's probably just the new guy," I said. "In case it isn't, Joe, I'd like you behind the east barn. Gary? Are you any good with your M1?"

"Yes, sir. I can put five shots inside two inches at three hundred."

I nodded. "Take the north barn. Keep your head down until I say it's time, understand?" Gary bobbed his head with confidence. "Rest of you boys fan out and stay hid."

My .44 already belted on, I retrieved my Winchester from the top bunk and dropped a handful of .30-30 cartridges into my coat pocket. Joe and Lynn disappeared while Davy came out of the kitchen with his Tommy gun in hand. The man looked comfortable with the heavy .45

auto. Another sensor closer to the ranch house but still on the drive sounded. Too early for the UPS or FedEx guy, perhaps I was right and Annie was bringing our new cowboy.

I checked on Buster as I passed, hoping unwanted visitors weren't already in place. He nickered and tossed his head in greeting. Leaving the barn, I strode to where I could see past the house and fenced front yard. Something moved, but I was forced to squint. Soon enough I could make out a rider. I grumbled Annie's name, making the poor fellow face the music alone. Then again, she probably planned an early start on a quest for horses. Nothing to do but lean my back against the railing and wait, hooking a heel on the bottom board to get comfortable. Pulling the brim of my hat low, I used it to block out enough light to see better. A half-mile distant when I first made out the mounted figure, I straightened after realizing a second horse followed. Something in the gait of the lead animal caught my attention. I squinted, suddenly feeling like I'd been played for the fool. As it closed the distance, the coloring and running walk of the gelding was easily recognized.

I kept my head down with the hat shielding my face until our visitor drew her Tennessee walker to a halt. I knew the second animal well. Purdy was getting an opportunity to travel in her old age. Winston looked damned good, too. My gaze moved up until I met a pair of beautiful brown eyes peering back above a long scar reaching to the corner of her mouth. I reckon I glared more than stared, and Leeann appeared nervous. "How are you, Cable?"

"Joe?" I shouted. Not getting a response I hollered louder. "Joe?"

"I thought you might be angry. If you'll give me a chance to explain—"

"Joe! Get your ass over here."

My bellow elicited a response. "Goddamn it, give me a chance," my cow boss answered, panting and puffing as he closed. Too old for running, I'm surprised he didn't saddle Midnight or use a four-wheeler. He stopped beside me and looked where I did. "I thought we was gettin' a cowboy, but it's a damn girl! We can't have females around here, Boss. Where in the hell will we put her?"

I wasn't going to be the one to break our staring contest. "In the big house. Let her pick any room but Jess's or Danny's." When I mentioned the ranch headquarters, Leeann glanced at it, giving me the clear win. Purdy's panniers were loaded to overflowing with Lee's things. It looked as if she planned to stay a while.

We'd see about it.

Chapter XIV

Joe struggled to keep up with my long strides after I turned on my heel. Quick steps of Winston and Purdy followed. I pointed to the front door of the big house. "It's unlocked. Get her set up and comfortable. Then, she's yours to work into the ground. Understand?" My tone let him know of my unhappiness, although he didn't understand. I veered into the bunkhouse to let my cow man earn his money.

The boys appeared from nowhere, following me inside. "A damn girl? I thought we were getting another cowpuncher, Boss," Gary said, emptying the chamber and storing his rifle next to his bunk.

I faced my men, and they could see I was angry. "You'll treat her like any other employee. You will not make jokes, innuendos, poke fun, or lay a hand on her for any reason. Understood?"

"Boss—"

My voice rose. "Do you understand?"

I rarely if ever spoke harshly to anyone on the payroll, and their reactions showed it. "Yes, sir," six men said almost in unison.

I dug a small duffel from storage below my bunk. Most of my things were clean and stacked neatly. "Davy?"

Our cook peered from the kitchen. "Yeah, Boss?"

"I need you to put together a box of vittles for me. Enough for a week or two. I'll be back for it in ten minutes."

Buster was as ready as me for the trail. Winston and Purdy were still tied to the rear bumper of the F350 dually parked in front of the big house. I checked my knots a last time and mounted. It was best someone as levelheaded as Joe ran the ranch while my emotions were on a slow boil. I swung into the saddle and checked my revolver rode correctly and comfortably. I clucked and touched Buster's ribs at the same time, keeping the reins taut. We didn't need to run flat out into the mountains. I wanted to consider it a slow retreat.

Other than shaded areas and deep depressions, the snowline was higher than I imagined. Rather than flee into remote country, I chose instead to travel south to where I could see the ranch in the distance. Truthfully, I could keep a wary eye trained on far more acres than I could from the flatlands. Buster and I found a comfortable camping spot before the day was half over. A picket line kept my horse happy and gave me time to build the place into home base. A fresh spring lay within walking distance. A collapsible carrier would keep me in fresh water throughout my stay.

Only a few trees where I camped were large enough to store my rations out of the reach of grizzlies. It took me a couple throws with my lariat, but I eventually flipped the loop over a high limb and replaced it with a nylon variety. A black bear or griz cub might climb to get my food, but anything else would have to work.

Bugs were a problem. Included in my supplies was a facemask for Buster. No sense in flies driving him crazy. A smoky fire might help me but not my horse. The large footprint of an old nylon dome tent stored in an outbuilding gave me plenty of room. A mosquito net would keep the worst of them off me, while bug spray would help Buster.

It didn't take long to build a hot fire. Coals were pushed to where I could prop my frying pan and coffee pot above them. Davy chose well when he included four steaks, each one big enough to fill the skillet. They'd keep in the cool air above a snowy landscape. A couple pieces of thick cut bacon worked for grease before the chunk of beef went into the cooking vessel. Using my pocket knife and a whittled stick, I cut and ate rare chunks of meat while it still cooked.

Darkness comes late to high ridges, and I used it to my advantage. After cleaning camp and adding fuel to the fire, I used field glasses and a spotting scope to scan miles of ground below. Movement from a small herd of mule deer caught my attention. If I could see the distant animals so clearly, none of the Brotherhood could avoid my sharp eye. I liked the idea of using elevation to keep watch over my ranch and cowboys—now a cowgirl, too.

I was dimly aware how running away to be alone became my fallback reaction to any situation involving betrayal. It was either make a quick exit or lash out in hot, unreasoning anger like I did to the killers of my twin and her son. It was why I distanced myself from my father and probably even my older sister who still worked for him.

I didn't trust myself when I felt wronged, so I warned Z to keep the old man away from me for his safety. It might explain why I needed her to give me more time before a reunion.

For some reason along the same lines, Leeann using trickery to show up unannounced after long months of absolute silence felt like another painful double cross made worse by a brewing war with the Brotherhood. Once again, I found myself losing what little sanity and control I'd regained.

Ground fog shrouded my view after I got up and build my fire again. A cold wind made me shiver into a heavy coat before starting breakfast. Fried bread, bacon, and coffee filled me. Once the air cleared, I scanned the area below while munching an apple from a small bag Davy included.

Buster handled well in snow. Not deep, because I skirted the mountain in an effort to get behind the ridge and scout the high valley it hid. I touched the butt of my revolver and glanced at my rifle after crossing grizzly tracks. It didn't surprise me they were already out. The hungry bruins would look at my cattle the way I looked at a steak. This one I estimated to be young, perhaps two or three years old. Not huge, but big and aggressive enough I wanted to steer clear. My calves didn't stand a chance against a hungry bear. Perhaps like Joe before me, I'd spend my summer alone and guarding the herd while contemplating the future.

* * *

I made my supplies last a day past two weeks before a sea of bovines moved in my direction. Driving them were five cowboys with our smallest chuckwagon pulled by a 4-wheeler coming in last. Joe tended to keep the home fires burning while the crew pushed WJP beef onto new grass. Where snow once surrounded my camp, warm afternoons caused it to retreat to the highest slopes. Buster enjoyed better feed, and we searched for the best places. Although a mile or more away, I saddled and rode to meet the closest puncher.

Gary worked hard to keep the lead cow pointed in the right direction. I intercepted him when he drove a momma and calf escaping into brush back to the herd. Whistling, I waved my coiled lariat to catch his attention and pointed south. Far more plant growth awaited there than the direction he moved them. Buster seemed happy to help my cowboy and his horse. It took us a half-hour before the herd looped around. "Nice work, man," I greeted the stocky rider. "Didn't think she was going to make the turn."

He grinned and extended a hand. "How are you, Boss? You're right. I thought she was gonna fight us."

I nodded to the ocean of horns and tails. "How many you got here?"

"About twenty-eight hundred. We moved a little over a thousand to the west field and around seven hundred onto the Michaels place." Albert Michaels no longer ran cattle after his wife passed. I offered to pay grazing rights, but he swore my cows kept his fields in good condition and taxes lower. Joe or I always delivered fresh beef for his freezer each fall. "Any grizzly sightings?"

I nodded as we moved up the hill to avoid the east shoulder of the herd enveloping us. "Watched a boar three days ago on the backside of Big Buck Mountain. Found a sow with two cubs disappearing to the east, too. I hope like hell they don't stop until hitting the Gravellies." Chances were slim, but the male bear would kill her cubs if he got the chance to bring her back into heat. She might move into a new area than risk their lives.

We stopped driving them when the first cows reached green grass. Covering the mountainside like so many ants, they fanned out to graze. The boys riding drag were busy cutting off those wanting to return to the ranch. Gary and I waved to Davy when we passed the chuck wagon on our way to help.

Four cows and their calves bolted toward a brush-choked ravine. One of my cowboys missed cutting them off, only to have the livestock tear through it and out the other side. Cursing and putting my heels to Buster, we raced above them in an effort to get ahead. My cowboy stayed farther down the hill, leaning forward in the saddle to urge his mount on. We came together working as a pincer without allowing a single heifer to escape. My rider stayed between them and the hillside below, while I pressured them from the rear. Buster was blowing with excitement when we ran them into the main body of the herd.

I turned to my cowhand with a grin. "Damn fine riding, puncher," I praised until Leeann pushed her hat back and offered me a wide smile. Changing from compliments to shooting daggers in a heartbeat, I wheeled Buster to catch Davy and the chuckwagon.

"How you doin', Boss?" he greeted. "I bet you're ready for a thick sandwich or a steak about now. Am I right?"

"You did a great job of packing on short notice, man. I won't lie...I'm looking forward to supper."

His laugh boomed across the slope. "I'll fix extra tonight just for you."

Ignoring Leeann, I caught Gary tidying the higher elevations of the herd. A few with minds of their own seemed to think they should continue. He was there to drive them back and maintain cohesiveness. A large collective was far stronger against predators than a cow and her offspring on their own. "How many of you is Joe planning to leave with me?" I asked him. Since he helped form it, if anyone could read my mind it was my cow boss.

Gary urged his horse into a gallop and returned when he was satisfied another animal wouldn't bolt. "Two. We'll spent tonight and leave the day after tomorrow if the herd doesn't give us problems. We found over a mile of fencing down on the Michaels place. Gotta repair it before we can utilize the entire ranch."

A pair of riders to help me would work well until the critters settled down. I'd send one home once my cows were comfortable. A single hand and I could continue drifting them south while keeping an eye out for varmints. A pack of coyotes—let alone wolves—were capable of taking down an unsupervised calf. Technically, the herd could be left on its own and checked every few days unless we found dead animals.

We rode nonstop until dark. Lights burning from a generator brightened the area where the chuckwagon was parked. Gary and I were the last two in. The first four cowhands were already eating when we arrived. After dismounting, I unsaddled Buster and swapped his bridle for a halter. He was ready for water at the spring where Davy chose to set up. We'd used the place as a base since I could remember. I brushed my horse, while he made quick work of his feedbag. His needs came before mine after such a long day of hard work.

A folding chair awaited me after Davy loaded my plate with spaghetti. I dragged it away from Leeann, closer to a short cowboy who finally pushed her hat back and grinned. "You're looking good, little brother!"

I damned near dropped my supper. "Z! How are you, sis?" I set my food aside and welcomed her into my arms. Her crown barely reached my chest. "What in the hell are you doing here?"

"You said to come after the spring mud hardened. Here I am!"

I pushed her back to arm's length. "Christ, you look good. Why didn't you call first?"

She pushed me hard and sat with her food again. "I did. Problem is you didn't answer." Z made a face. "What was I supposed to do?"

"Let's talk about it later, okay?" I followed the example of my crew and dug into my meal. Davy filled my plate two more times before I stopped eating.

Gary, Lynn, and Richie traded grins without saying anything. I guess they knew a little of the story between Leeann and me, at least enough to find the uncomfortable atmosphere enjoyable. I took it while finishing a big slice of apple pie. Z stood and walked my empty plate and hers to Davy. She caught my eye and jerked her head toward the dark. I followed her past the remuda until we could see ranch light in the distance. "It's been too long, William."

I sighed. "Yeah, you're right. I should've invited you west to the ranch before now."

Her answer was quick and sharp. "No. Too long since our last phone conversation. You said you wouldn't shut me out, but here I am because you won't answer."

"It's been tough. The big house is like a tomb. Danny should be running the stairs with Jess scolding him every step. He loved splashing mud puddles in the yard and getting his feet wet. Jess ought to be helping with the herd right now, too, while Danny stays in the bunkhouse with Joe and Odell. I moved in with my cowboys because I couldn't stand it any longer."

Her arm went around my waist. "Your cow boss told me," she said quietly. "I never considered how awful it would be after you were gone two years and returned to an empty home you shared with our sister and nephew. I'm sorry. I wish I'd been here for you."

"Still feels like a nightmare I'll wake up from."

"Why didn't you tell me about Leeann?"

"Wasn't much to say. Even less than I thought."

"I've been here a week, you know."

"No kidding?" I thought back and remembered the F350 driving away and returning hours later. I'd assumed Odell needed more parts. "Why wait until now? You could have ridden up here alone or sent one of the boys to track me. I'd have pulled camp to see you." Z proved herself a natural on a horse once again by helping move the herd.

"I learned from Joe you hired a cowgirl and refused to talk to her or discuss the situation. She was a mystery who suddenly appeared, and you gave her the big house to stay in. The story piqued my interest, so I moved in with her until now."

"Shit."

Z chuckled. "You can say that again! Your girlfriend and I have talked and compared notes. William..." She laughed softly again. "...you were a bad boy not to share you finally fell for a girl."

"I didn't fall for anyone. We barely spent any time together."

"Not what I heard. From what I understand, you nursed her back to health...twice...and she did the same for you once. You rode together...

stayed together...worked together. Sounds like you were a regular couple."

"Did she mention she disappeared without so much as a see-you-later? Not a goddamn word from her until she rode in a couple weeks ago. Hell, Annie made it sound like I was doing her a favor by hiring a cowboy down on his luck. I'd have refused if I knew it was Leeann."

"Which explains their subterfuge. It was Caroline's idea, little brother. Don't blame Leeann for the deception."

"It's bullshit. All of it."

Z turned to face me in the dark. Something more than the chilly night wind made a shiver pass between us. "What's bull, little brother, is your bullheaded one-size-fits-all idea of treachery. Anyone can understand blazing hatred for that evil biker gang. I wish you didn't, but I can find empathy with your dislike of Dad."

"It's more than dislike—" I started, but she cut me off.

"Whatever! I'm not him, yet you treat me like I sold you out by working for his organization where I do a lot of good. An example is help for your friend Caroline. Now, you treat a girl like a leper who loves you and finds a way to be with you. I like her, William. I really, really like her. She's as open as any book. If I asked a question, she answered without hesitation. You need to talk and get her side of the story."

"We'd better get back to camp," I said. "You know as well as me daylight comes early up here. Still gotta put your tent up and make it livable." Cowboys and one cowgirl were busy setting up their shelters and rolling out sleeping bags. "Get yours, and I'll put it up for you."

My sister pointed to the one Leeann worked on. "That's where I'm staying tonight." She leaned close so only I could hear. "Your girlfriend and I plan to talk half the night away."

I groaned and kissed her forehead. "I'm out of here. See you in the morning."

She followed me to where Buster waited. "You going somewhere?" she asked when I tossed my saddle over my horse's back and tightened the cinch and belly strap.

Leeann didn't bother to hide when she watched and listened from beside their tent when I answered. "Yup. My camp is about a mile or two north." I slipped the bridle on Buster, buckled the chin strap, and mounted. "See you for breakfast, little sister." Although she was older, when we were kids, I soon outgrew my siblings and called both "little sister." Only a few minutes apart in age, Jess didn't seem to mind, but Zoe never liked it; consequently, I never missed a chance to rankle her with the nickname. Same reason she called me William rather than Cable.

My tent wasn't hard to find. I gave him his head after pointing Buster in the right direction. He didn't get a second brushing or a feedbag. Instead, I stripped the saddle and bridle before leaving him in decent browse and rolled into my bag. I had some things to think about, but my head barely touched the pillow before I was asleep.

* * *

Davy handed me dished victuals and coffee after I dismounted and tied Buster. The generator ran his kitchen and powered a couple bulbs. The sliver of light to the east didn't provide enough to see. This time the girls didn't conspire against me when an empty chair waited between Lynn and Gary. As the sun rose, I saw the herd bedded southward. At least they didn't bolt for home after dark. I made myself comfortable with breakfast balanced on my knees. Four hotcakes, three eggs, and a ham steak covered the plate. Hungry as a bear, I was no more talkative than my stoic crew. I dug in after covering it all with a healthy slug of maple syrup.

My meal almost finished, I looked up when a pair of feet approached. "May I have the syrup, please?" I'd forgotten how pleasant Leeann's voice was. I'd been too shocked with her unexpected appearance at the ranch to notice.

"Oh...yeah." I retrieved the bottle from where I set it next to my chair and offered it.

Leeann's chocolate eyes locked on mine when she accepted the container. They were wide and didn't blink. "Thank you," she said without moving. I nodded and glanced away.

Z broke the awkward silence. "Anyone need a refill on their coffee?" It worked to defuse the strained situation. Not even my cowboys smirked or snickered. Lee returned to her seat and held an empty cup for my sister to top up.

"What's the plan today?" I asked Gary after handing my plate to Davy on his way to the wagon. The hot cup in my hands felt good in the cool air.

He shrugged. "Not sure. Herd settled down overnight. If we keep the edges tight, there shouldn't be any stragglers as they graze. Give 'em a day or so, and they'll be fine. Won't take but a rider or two to babysit 'em all."

My cowboy was right. We worked the perimeter, but mostly, we tended the herd by relaxing on our horses and watching. Thick, lush grass gave them plenty of reason to move slowly.

It didn't take long before I saw Z dozing in the saddle. With the cattle complacent and the sun warming her, my sister slept like any other cowboy on the range. She might be a Wallstreet wonder worth millions, but after staying up too late enjoying gossip, even she needed to recharge her batteries. I wondered if her socialite friends and coworkers in New York could imagine her pushing cows. Ranch life in Montana was far removed from the cultured community she lived and worked in.

Leeann kept her distance. Zoe woke and glanced guiltily, grinning when she noticed me watching. I could only smile back and wave my hat. It didn't take long before she rode toward Lee almost a mile away. Their heads were together far too long for my comfort. I hoped they'd return to the ranch tomorrow with Davy and my cowboys, leaving me to tend the animals alone. As long as the Brotherhood stayed away, a summer of solitude isolated with lowing beasts and the occasional varmint was exactly what the doctor ordered.

The crew straggled into camp about midday getting a sandwich or two before returning to their posts. I figured I'd wait until they finished rather than risk a confrontation with Lee. Perhaps I could talk Z into moving her back to Colorado and leaving me alone. When they got a turn, the two girls rode in together and then split up, one walking her horse toward me. I cheated and used my field glasses. If Leeann thought she was going to run roughshod over me, Buster didn't mind exploring more wild country.

I stayed where I was after recognizing my sister. She was laughing when she reached me. "What's the matter, scaredy cat? Ready to cut and run?" Z reined in next to Buster and handed me a paper bag with two thick sandwiches of beef sliced paper thin. "I saw your binoculars!"

Her attitude grated. "I'm not scared, asshole."

My name calling didn't bother her. "Do you prefer big ol' baby?"

I waited to swallow the first bite before answering. "I prefer to be left alone."

Z stayed silent while I finished eating. She dug a small thermos from her saddle bags the ranch provided to all the cowboys. "Yours. I've got my own." I filled the lid and sipped coffee while keeping an eye on the herd. Most were bedded again, chewing their cuds. "Talk to her, would you? Please? There are two sides to every story. You've lived yours as you saw things...now it's time to hear hers."

My sister surprised me. She normally didn't involve herself in my love life. In fact, I couldn't remember her doing anything but laughing anytime Jess spilled the beans I was interested in a girl. I sighed. "I don't know."

Her voice raised. "Goddamn it!" Z didn't shout, but I looked around in case anyone was close. "The woman moved a thousand miles from everything she knows, working on a ranch to catch the eye of the man she's fallen in love with." Zoe lowered her voice. "Won't you at least hear her out?"

The word shook me last night in the dark, but Z saw it in the bright light of day. My sisters loved me—and my mom, too. But no other woman used the term of affection in relation to me. "I guess so," I mumbled before bumping Buster's ribs with my heels. I needed more time alone to gather my thoughts.

* * *

I didn't bother to dismount after returning to the chuckwagon at dark. The generator-driven lighting illuminated much of the slope. Davy saw me coming and left his plate to dish mine. He came out with a steak, potato, and the rest covered in beans. "Want me to take your horse, Boss?"

"No..." I balanced my food in one hand after he handed it to me. "...I'll be back in the morning."

I ate by flashlight, not bothering to build a fire. I watered Buster first, then brushed and staked him out to feed. Supper was cold when I got to it, but my belly was happy when I finished. I tossed the thick paper plate inside my ring of rocks before getting comfortable in my tent to keep mosquitos away. Tired as I was, sleep was a long time in coming.

* * *

Crackling wood and gleaming light woke me the following morning. I reached for my gun not sure who was outside. Unzipping my door a few inches, I peeked through the crack to see. Leeann hunkered next to my firepit, feeding wood into a growing blaze. Whether she noticed me or not, the young woman focused on building a bigger fire. She didn't seem surprised when I appeared in the doorway after taking time to fully dress except for my boots. I sat in the opening to tug my size thirteens on.

Lee didn't bother to look and kept her attention on her work. "Dee's my brother. The same blood courses through our veins. I couldn't leave him to die alone before our parents arrived." I poured a little water in my pot to swish the grounds and tossed them aside. The growing fire would soon produce enough coals. "He lost his arm halfway between his elbow and shoulder." Her scar stood out in the flickering firelight. She finally looked up to meet my gaze.

I shrugged. "A call. A text. You could've contacted Caroline or Annie. Instead, after all your talk about crossing bridges later, you went AWOL on me."

Tears wet her cheeks in the dim light. Lee nodded. "I know. Dee demanded my attention, and to be honest, I forgot about all else. I don't own a vehicle...never bought one after the accident. Rather than put Caroline out, I stayed at a local motel. By the time he and I...after he..." She bit her lip and looked away before her spine stiffened. "You were already gone when I contacted Caroline to see if my job was still available. She and Annie told me you were angry and didn't leave a forwarding address, nor would they give me your number." I scraped coals to where the coffee pot balanced best, while Lee broke more fuel and pushed it into the fire. "Either Dee or Alexandra stole my phone. I should have left then when they lied and swore neither were the culprit. By then, I was afraid you were angry or hurt." She snorted softly. "I was right."

"He hit you again?"

"Yeah, I caught the back of his hand after he was ready to go home. That's when I called Caroline about my job."

Leeann's news didn't surprise me, nor did breaking her declaration she would never speak to him again. Family bonds were difficult to severe. I couldn't blame her for attending to her brother after he was injured by a gunshot. For all she knew, he might die at any point. I understood what it was like to lose a sibling and wouldn't wish it on anyone.

I busied myself with keeping coals pushed under the coffee pot. Lee made herself comfortable on the ground and watched quietly. The slope where my camp lay slowly brightened as we waited to fill our cups. The moment I saw the first hint of a perk, I moved the pot to a cooler area. Her story made sense and wasn't far from what I imagined, except for the part where she was still interested.

Wiping the dirty rim of my cup on my grubby shirt, I filled Lee's first, then my own. Setting mine aside, I checked my frying pan for cleanliness and used my kerchief to give it a final scrub. Once it was ready after placed on hot coals, I mixed and cooked fry bread. Davy put together a large bag of flour, salt, and baking powder. All it needed was water for the simplest of meals. While Lee flipped them with a spatula I'd whittled, I opened a can of spam to slice and cook. We each made breakfast sandwiches to chase away our hunger.

She chuckled after I filled our cups again. "Seems like old times. How often have we eaten over a campfire exactly like this?"

Her reminiscing made me laugh. "The sheer volume of fish we put away was amazing."

"Neither of us with a license. Lucky we weren't checked by a game warden."

I sighed. "Life was pretty good in my stump." I wasn't going to tell her about the days without food, eating whatever I could scrounge, while sometimes shitting my guts out. Nor the days running together when I purchased enough booze to make me black out.

"It was. Will it ever be so simple again? Sitting together around a campfire and enjoying an uncomplicated life?"

"I hope so," I said quietly.

Lee stiffened. "You hope what?" Her eyes were wide and unblinking.

"I hope we have the opportunity to spend a lot of time hunkered over a fire together."

"Are you...I mean...are you saying—?"

I grinned and offered my hand. "Something tells me there's a lot of camping in our future."

Tossing her cup aside, Lee ignored my hand and launched herself. Knocking me to my back, she straddled my body and pinned my shoulders to the ground with her palms. I loved her lopsided grin before she lowered soft lips to mine.

She pulled away and said, "Always bet on me, Cable. You'll never regret it."

Chapter XV

One tent and a pile of gear awaited us after we eventually returned to main camp. A lone rider far to the south caught my attention. I stopped Buster where the chuckwagon was parked last night and pointed. "You know anything about this?"

Leeann nodded. "Gary and Davy made plans before bed. They opined one or two riders could handle the herd after they settled down so well. Gary asked for volunteers, and Zoe suggested she and I stay with you."

"Joe didn't plan to keep you working around the ranch?" My cow boss was strict when he came to a decision or was given an order. I'd left him with instructions to work Lee into the ground. Perhaps Z overruled my plans.

She seemed surprised. "No, not that he told me. I was supposed to pack my gear in the chuckwagon, help move the herd, and stay out of trouble."

I wasn't sure she understood Joe's definition of the word. Trouble while moving a herd meant avoiding death by stampede or a myriad of other ways a rider fought to stay alive.

We split up after making sandwiches, filling our saddle bags, and each taking a topped thermos Davey left behind. Lee was to stay in sight and keep an eye out for varmints. Her .32-20 got left on the pile, and she fastened the scabbard under the fender after an okay from me. Other than giving her word she knew how to shoot, I wouldn't be confident until I saw it for myself. Except for normal wear, her carefully maintained Winchester in almost pristine condition spoke volumes.

Z was off her horse when I caught her. Sunday—a palomino— was her favorite mare when she spent time on the ranch, and it bothered me when I saw her mount standing riderless. Instead of being thrown, she was on her knees deep in a watering hole, digging out the clogged spring. Water didn't always turn on by itself after winter ravaged the soil. She heard Buster and turned, shivering with cold. I grinned back when she leaned on a folding shovel and smiled. "C'mon in...the water's fine!"

Good thing her boots were set aside. Once she had the flow going, it inundated her to the waist. Retrieving a sandwich from my saddlebag, I slid my right foot from the stirrup and wrapped my leg around the saddle horn. Buster didn't seem to mind, so I unfolded the waxed paper from my meal. "Nope," I said. "Seems to me you've got it handled."

My sister reached her hand deep to assure water flowed freely before standing and wading to dry ground. What'd been an empty natural trough already filled. Once finished, it'd measure almost twenty feet long, eight wide, and about three deep. "Look the other way," she said. I heard sounds of her skinning out of her jeans and wringing them out. Taking my time with the sandwich, I munched slowly until given the all-clear. "Okay, you can turn back." Zoe was already sitting and tugging her boots on. She stood and seated them with a stomp before putting hands on her hips and grinning again. "You rode back together. That's a good sign."

"Did Joe know you planned to play matchmaker?"

"Huh uh. He was against her going. Said he was under strict orders to make her life miserable."

"Was he doing a good job of it?"

Zoe laughed. "He tried. Unfortunately for both of you, Leeann worked hard and refused to complain. From washing dishes to tightening every gate on the north road, she took everything he saddled her with and asked for more. Joe even went so far as to make her dig out the ditches with a spade where culverts got plugged."

I chuckled to myself. Good old Joe. It was my job each spring using the ranch backhoe. I'd asked him to work her into the dirt, and he took me at my word. "How'd you get her off his shitlist and a part of moving the herd?"

"Said I'd report him for sexism to Labors & Industry," she said with twinkling eyes. "He startled and backed away and said Leeann was my problem and I'd answer to you. Kind of wished I hadn't signed my third of the ranch back to you after Mom and Jess died. The fun I could have with Joe!"

I didn't laugh with my sister. She probably scared the hell out of my cow boss. No way could I replace him after his twenty-five odd years working on the WJP. Chances were he'd never heard of the governmental agency, but understood getting the state involved with our ranch was bad. "You scared him, Z. Don't do it again...please. The place needs his guiding hand. Losing him could be a stake through our collective heart."

She couldn't mistake my sincerity. Stopping laughing immediately, Zoe nodded. "I'm sorry if I overstepped, little brother."

"Joe's an integral part of making this place pay for itself. Hell, I don't remember when we were this far in the black. A couple good winters made a difference for sure, but I can't help but think my absence didn't contribute. No doubt he knows what he's doing. I haven't told him, but I plan to give Joe a substantial raise and a stake in the ranch. I'm thinking five percent."

The businesswoman made her presence known. "If you think his decision making is that important, I don't see how you can do any less. Giving him a stake in profits if the ranch does well is smart thinking."

Davy left us three coolers filled with provisions, along with two crates of dry goods. I waited until late afternoon to wave the ladies back to camp. They beat me in by a couple minutes and were already stripping their horses. "I'll be back in an hour or so," I said. "Gotta tear down my camp and move it here."

They hadn't talked since Lee and I reconnected, and I guessed the girls made up for lost time while I was gone. Both beamed when I returned with my gear. Not smiling, but grinning like Cheshire cats. A folding table held a camp stove, small propane barbeque, and cooking implements. I dismounted and put Buster on a picket line to browse after I stripped him. "Hamburgers and baked beans sound okay, little brother?" Z asked.

"Sure. Anything is fine. Give me a few minutes while I erect my tent, and I'll give you a hand."

"Put mine up, and you can throw your sleeping bag in with Leeann's." Zoe grinned after her offer and waggled her eyebrows at Lee. "Check to see if they'll zip together!"

"Zoe!" Leeann sounded appropriately shocked, but I wasn't so sure.

"Hey, neither of you are getting any younger..." my sister started.

"...said the spinster to her brother," I finished.

"That's enough," Lee said. "Cable and I have a lot of catching up to do after my stupidity."

"Nope. No stupidity except mine. Family is everything."

"Yes, it is," Zoe said. Her eyes quickly brimmed with emotion when she glanced at me. "I've neglected ours far too long. As much as I'd like to, I can't go back in time to make things right."

"How long do you plan to stay?" I wanted the subject changed. "You pissed away a week before letting me know you were in Montana. On the ranch, no less."

She sniffed and ran a sleeve under her nose. "I told Dad to expect me about the time we moved the herd. Looks like I'm a little late for work."

We made thick hamburgers—a trio for me and the girls split three. With all of us pitching in to help, cleanup was nothing with plastic silverware and paper plates. Buster tried to get to me long enough I remembered what he expected. A feedbag of oats and the curry brush. I used long strokes while I checked him for injuries and set him at ease. If he'd been a dog, he would've been curled up on my lap. I spoiled him in Colorado and saw no reason to change.

Z strolled nearer sipping from a cup. I guessed Lee stayed at the table and tidied to give us privacy. "I was told you pampered your horse," my sister said. "You were always one for taking good care of animals."

I didn't take my attention away from what I was doing. "He saved my life at a time I was still breaking him," I said quietly. "Any other horse would have thrown and injured me worse. Not Buster. He waited until I mounted and walked...Z...he walked where he normally bucked and bolted. I needed him and he came through for me. More than once I might add. When the chips were down, I could always rely on Buster to save my bacon."

She ran a hand down his side. "You bought him from Mrs. Hagseth?"

"Traded about five months work."

"Leeann told me a little about him. She warned me not to get between my brother and his horse. If you were forced to choose between us, she wasn't sure I'd like the answer." Buster turned his head and gave her a frank appraisal, making Zoe chuckle and stretch to stroke his ears. With my horse over seventeen hands, and Z barely five feet, she couldn't have reached his nose if he lifted his head.

"He's special," I agreed. She lifted her cup and sipped before I got a whiff. My sister enjoyed an occasional shot of whiskey. Mouth watering, I focused on the effort of finishing the job of brushing, before leading Buster to water and back to his picket line.

She saw me glance at the bottle of one-oh-one proofed Wild Turkey whiskey on the table. Z squinted before making eye contact with Leeann. When the latter shook her head almost imperceptibly, I guessed either Caroline or Annie shared my story with her. Perhaps even my sister learned of my slow-motion attempted suicide. Thoughts of alcohol never entered my mind until smelling the strong drink. No matter, I'd never touch it again.

* * *

Zoe enjoyed her time in the high country on the back of Sunday. The subject of the Brotherhood reared its ugly head one night around the campfire. "We thought you were dead, you know," she said. "Dad was as sure as Joe one of the unidentified bodies was yours. I was the only one holding out hope."

"Cable?"

Leeann sat next to me with my hand in hers. I smiled to myself at her clean fingers and nails after she worked hard scrubbing them in a bowl of water before handling food. "What would you think of flying to New York and spending time with Zoe?" I said.

Her brow furrowed as she glanced between my sister and me. "I'm sure it'd be fun, but I need the work here." Although she hoped to reconnect with me, a job was important without Dee to fall back on.

"It'd be paid leave."

She dropped my hand and twisted in her seat to see me better. "What? No. I don't have even a month's pay coming."

"What's going on, William," my sister asked.

"The weather's warming, and you know as well as me the Brotherhood is coming since learning I'm alive. I need you both out of here and safe somewhere. I can't think of a better place than Z's."

"You come, too," Zoe said. "They can't kill what they can't find. I've got plenty of room."

"I can't hide forever. They'll locate me sooner or later."

She sat forward in her seat and pointed a poking stick for the fire at me. "I'm not losing my last sibling and only brother to them. We can't forget they took little Danny from us, either."

Leeann was still in the dark. "I don't understand. Why would everyone think you were dead?"

Zoe stared at me while she explained to Lee. "William disappeared not long after we buried our sister and nephew. A week later, the clubhouse outside of Sacramento owned by the Brotherhood caught fire. At least two died from bullet wounds, but another sixty or so burned to death. Against all fire codes and common sense, both exits were blocked when panic caused a crush and piled bodies. Some were charred so badly that an overworked forensic crew didn't take special pains to make all identifications. We all feared William was a victim after he disappeared without a trace."

Leeann absorbed the abbreviated story and then nodded. "That's when you appeared in Colorado at Caroline's place, and why we buried the man you killed instead of calling police."

Z was clearly shocked. "What?"

"One of the Brotherhood decided to beat Annie a few feet from me," I said. "I didn't know if he was going to kill her, but all I did was put down a sick dog."

"Jesus," she whispered. "You can't go around killing people, William."

I pinned her with an angry glare. "You never saw the video feed when Jess and Danny were murdered, did you?" Zoe shook her head. "I've got it saved. One more word out of you about who I can and can't take care of, and I'll make damn certain you watch. We'll see how fast you change your tune."

Leaving them at the fire, I retreated to first check on Buster and the remuda before seeking my bed. The mattress needed more air before making myself comfortable. It wasn't long before I heard whispering and rustling inside the ladies' tent fifty feet away. Rolling to put my back to the screened door, I punched my pillow into shape for extra comfort.

The sounds of light feet, canvas, and nylon stopped outside. The opening to my shelter unzipped, and I heard a whisper. "Move over."

I shifted away not a moment too soon. Another mattress was stuffed inside and positioned, before a sleeping bag was tossed in. Rolling to my back, I saw Leeann crawl inside and quickly close the entrance to keep mosquitos out. "What's going on?" I whispered.

She set her boots at the bottom of her bed before worming out of her jeans. "My place is here with you," Lee whispered back. I didn't look away in the gloom when she removed her blouse and replaced it with a sleeveless shirt before unfastening her bra and pulling it from an armhole. It went into the same pile with her Tecovas footwear. She made herself comfortable facing me. Reaching out, she ran light fingers across my features before stroking my jawline. "Seems like old times, except we don't have a fire between us."

I chuckled. "It does, doesn't it? At least we don't have to contend with the stinking bag I slept in."

Her teeth gleamed in the gathering darkness. "I never minded. When I smelled it and the fire, I knew we were safe."

Soft fingertips continued their motion, touching my lids, nose, and lips. I waited until they moved to my scalp before answering. "I miss my stump," I said quietly. "It meant a simple existence and few worries."

"It also signified no family or friends. No relationships. No future."

I found her face with my hand and enjoyed the delicate and smooth features. "You're right. Nothing waited but death."

"Zoe's hurting," Lee said. "You were rough on her tonight and owe her an apology in the morning."

I turned my head and raised my voice. "Z?"

"Yeah?"

"I'm sorry."

"I never doubted it, little brother. I'm sorry, too."

"I know. Talk tomorrow?"

"Sounds good. Night."

"Good night."

"Did you mean it?" Leeann asked.

"With all my heart," I promised.

"That's the man I knew you could be, Cable," she whispered. "Once you work through the pain, your heart will soften again. It's going to take time."

I considered the enormity of her broad statement. "I don't know if I'll ever...ever..." I stopped to gather my thoughts. "Can you help me?"

"Can I hel...oh, God, yes, Cable! It's why I'm here. I'll do anything in my power to lend a hand and give you my heart." She shuffled and moved her sleeping pad and bag closer. My arm went around her, while she pulled my mouth to hers.

Lee was my future—as long as I could leave the past in my rearview mirror where it belonged.

* * *

I woke well past daybreak. Leeann and I talked long into the night, where I bared my soul and released emotions I didn't know I harbored. She held me at times and prodded me to continue when I struggled.

214

I'm not sure but toward the end, I thought I heard a sob and retreating footsteps outside. It didn't matter—a lot of apologizing lay in my immediate future. Lee's tousled head lay on her pillow facing away, and I rolled to my side. I guess she felt my movements when she turned to her back. "Hey," she said.

I used a finger to move hair covering a part of her features. "Hey, yourself."

Leeann smiled when I stroked her cheek. "I could get used to this."

"If you don't, I'm not doing it right." Our faces were separated by less than twelve inches, eyes locked on the other's.

Her blinks were slow. "How are you this morning?"

"Better." My hand went behind her to where I could stroke the back of her neck. "A little embarrassed."

Her hand found my cheek. "There's no reason to be self-conscious. I know you better, and last night you released an extraordinary amount of pain and anger."

I sighed and moved to my back, putting an arm behind my head. "Can't blame it on booze lowering my inhibitions."

"It was good for you, Cable. I think you'll approach life differently, now. At least you'll be able to move forward without the past to hold you back."

Closing footsteps outside caught my attention. "Cable? Best you get up," Z said. "The herd has grazed south far enough I can only see a few stragglers."

Leeann and I dressed without a thought of shyness. I was pulling my boots on when she was already crawling out the tent flap. Zoe stood nearby with my field glasses, keeping tabs on the vanishing cattle. I took a brief look after she offered the binoculars. "Saddle up. I think the main bunch is turning west. We need them moving south or even southeast. There's a good-looking canyon about a mile east of them. I planned to push around the mountain in a couple days."

We ate breakfast sandwiches in the saddle. My sister was kind enough to make one each for her and Lee and two for me. She remembered my appetite and didn't forget thermoses. Where the wayward cows would take us was anyone's guess. I hoped like hell the culprit wasn't a marauding bear or wolves. Plant growth as we galloped was almost nonexistent, so their bellies could be the problem.

The herd travelled farther than I imagined—at least three miles as the crow flies. I took lead along the western edge, while Leeann trailed by a couple hundred yards and Z farther back. We walked and trotted rather than gallop and spook the plodding mass. My cowgirls were under strict orders to turn with the herd if they stampeded, work their way to the edge, and let them go. No amount of beef was worth anyone's life.

I found the lead cow with an idea firmly planted inside her hard head. No telling where she planned to go. Leaving Lee and Z on the west edge, I turned Buster into the mass and guided him to her. They were leaving green grass behind, so I turned her east and then back into the body of the herd. She fought me, along with fifty others, but hollering and swinging my lariat did the trick. I was pleased to see how well my plan worked, only to find Lee not far away and helping by swinging her own rope. She rode Teton, one of my quarter horse geldings proven on the ranch rather than Winston.

We rode hard until late afternoon. Even Buster showed the effects of our nonstop efforts. Only when fifty percent of the herd was bedded down did I wave my cowgirls closer. "Do you remember the spring running from the galvanized pipe below Blackbird Knob?" I asked Z. She squinted before shaking her head. "It's below the brush growing under the rock outcropping." I pointed at the hillside a mile or less away but farther up the slope. "It's rusted and about two inches in diameter."

She looked surprised. "I remember drinking directly from the pipe years ago." Z shaded her eyes with a hand. "Yeah, I see about where it is."

"I'll take Lee to help move camp. She's packed up with me before, so I'm counting on you to choose a level spot and gather firewood. You're not armed, are you?" My sister shook her head. "Here." I drew my rifle from its scabbard. "You've got five in the magazine. If you see an aggressive bear or wolves, don't hesitate to run like hell on Sunday if you can, okay? Shoot only if there's no other way."

Our remuda waited near camp. Six horses in all, three were trained to pack. Panniers got filled, but packing and moving took time. Almost dark when we left our old camp, only a fire burning high on the next ridge pointed the way.

Although hungry, we erected tents and put up our kitchen by flashlight and the glowing blaze. It wasn't until I got the horses picketed with Buster curried when it dawned on me the girls were already in bed. Z heard me picking through bags and raised her voice. "There's a tuna sandwich waiting on the table."

"Thanks, sis."

I squatted near the spring and enjoyed my meal along with a half dozen cups of sweet spring water. Returning by firelight, I unzipped my tent and crawled inside. The night would be short, but I looked forward to my pillow and uninterrupted sleep. Setting my boots outside and tossing my shirt toward the end of the tent, I zipped open my jeans and awkwardly pushed them down, until rolling to my left and touching something unexpected and yelped. "What the hell?"

My heart slowed when I heard the low chuckle. "Surprise!" Lee whispered.

"Holy crap," I mumbled. "You took a decade off my life." I finished what I was doing and tossed my pants before getting in my bag. "I thought you'd be sleeping with Z."

She chuckled again. "Why?"

"Why? Well...shoot...I don't know, I just thought you would."

"Would you rather I sleep in hers...or put up my own tent?" Her warm hand stroked my jawline again.

"Whatever you prefer, I guess."

"Jesus, William," Z hollered. "Tell the woman you want her with you, so I can get some damned sleep!"

* * *

I woke before light worried about the cattle. Tossing my clothes outside, I slowly tugged the door zipper closed and dressed. Five minutes later, I walked Buster south in search of my cattle. Topping a hillock with a hint of sunrise to the east, I stopped to wait for better light. For each minute I dawdled, the landscape beyond came alive.

Metal on stone behind alerted me to a visitor. I turned in my saddle to find Leeann within fifty yards. She looked cold with her heavy coat closed to the top, her collar up, and hat pulled low. Lee reined Teton after reaching us. "Holy crap," she whispered. "Is Montana always cold as a witches you-know-what in the morning...and hot as hell in the afternoon?"

She looked so uncomfortable I couldn't help but grin. "Nope. Pretty soon it's going to stay hot. In six, maybe seven months, you're in for a real treat when it comes to cold. Won't be fit for man nor beast."

Her teeth chattered. "I c-can't wait."

My cows became visible as light chased shadows across the landscape. Most were bedded while others grazed contently. I clucked my tongue and touched Buster's ribs with my heels. No sense in turning—I heard Leeann urging Teton to follow. We kept our horses to a slow walk while we stayed west of the herd. Few paid any attention to us and even less stood. They were comfortable to lie and chew their cuds in grass six inches deep.

Leeann and I stopped to admire the countryside as the sun burst over the ridge. She shook her head. "Fantastic. An absolutely incredible part of the world. I thought I could see most of America on the ridge above Leeann's Lake, but from here I can almost see both oceans!"

Her hyperbole made me smile. "I occasionally see friends in town who wonder where I've been. It's hard to explain how I'd rather be here than anywhere else. I've got everything as far as I'm concerned. From a working ranch to watching deer, elk, bear, cats, wolves, along with nearly every other critter you can imagine this ground holding." No matter how many sunrises I enjoyed, watching the land come to life each morning was something I never tired of.

"I understand." Her tone made me glance to see her wandering gaze and nod. She turned to me and grinned, the skin around her scar pulling while only part of her face responded. "You've been lucky to have grown up here. I can't imagine how amazing your early life must have been."

We walked our horses east and left the herd behind. A long slope brought us to a summit above my cows. A herd of mule deer scattered when we started down the back side. One, a mature buck, caught my attention. I pointed him out to Leeann after I motioned her closer. "If I'm lucky, I'll bring him home for the freezer in the fall," I whispered.

Her eyes grew large. "He's huge!"

We scouted until the sun hovered high overhead. Lee's coat was tied behind her saddle long before the day warmed. I needed to see what direction to push the herd as they grazed. A natural swale would welcome them eastward if nothing spooked them away. Riding in a wide loop, we stopped to see our new camp below. Leeann nodded when she realized where we were. "I thought so. The last ridge we crossed threw me for a bit. Wasn't sure if we'd be closer to where Davy parked the chuckwagon or more toward your beef."

I used my field glasses to locate Z. She was far enough away I wasn't sure if her horse was moving. Then, she disappeared into a ravine to reappear and skirt a thicket of brush I remembered well. Giving Buster his head, we traveled down a steep slope in the direction of our tents.

Zoe walked Sunday into camp after Buster and Teton were stripped and staked out to feed. "Cows are settling down," she said. "They've sprawled out from last night but seem happy enough."

I glanced up from where I cooked Brats and sliced onions on the barbeque, a pan of chili heating on the stove. "Thanks for checking. Lee and I were sitting on them as day broke to make sure they hadn't moved." I followed her to the picket line where I slid the saddle off, and Z exchanged a halter for her horse's bridle.

"Where did you and Leeann disappear to?" She waggled her brows and added a lecherous grin. "Or dare I ask?"

I groaned. "Damn it, Z."

Lee spoke from where she made herself comfortable on a camp chair and nursed what I thought was her third cup of water. "We rode east from the herd and into some rough places. He showed me some of the most beautiful country I've ever seen." Zoe listened, hands on her hips, with obvious disappointment.

She dropped onto the chair beside Lee—across the table from where I cooked. "Jeez, not exactly the scandal I hoped to hear."

Leeann was the face of innocence when she deadpanned while looking straight at me. "I left out the part where your brother tore me from the saddle and ravaged me in a meadow filled with beautiful flowers."

I straightened in embarrassed surprise. "I did no such..."

They didn't give me a chance to finish before both girls broke into laughter, cementing their joke with a high-five. Although their hoots continued at my expense, I ignored them and finished cooking our lunch. Rather than tell them when our meal was ready, I loaded my plate and sat, leaving them to figure it out. Neither seemed bothered while they chattered and filled their own paper dishes. Their heads were far closer together than I would have liked, especially when one or the other would glance at me with a wicked smile. I could only shake my head and ignore them both.

My belly finally filled, I stood and stretched, walking to where I could see better. Farther down the slope, movement caught my eye. "Ladies? Finish your meal." I turned and sprinted for my field glasses. Both women were standing when I passed them a second time.

"William?"

Although far off, I adjusted the binoculars to see clearly. A horseman pushed his steed far too hard as they raced in our direction. The small rider and black mount told me everything I needed to know. "Saddle your horses," I told my cowgirls. "Now."

We were ready when Joe located us and reined Midnight to a halt, lather and foam streaking them both. I caught the horse's bridle to hold him. "Goddamn it, Joe. Are you trying to kill him?" The big horse blew like a freight train and tried to throw his head.

"I'll kill him and every other horse to save family and hands, boy. We've got bigger problems than our animals." I waited, my guts twisting as I absorbed Joe's distress. "I was on the phone with Pete from the

John Deere dealership when he mentioned a couple hundred bikers rode through town." He leaned on the saddle horn while fixing me with a stare. "It's the Brotherhood, Cable. They're here."

Chapter XVI

If the bikers weren't a large group simply passing through, my worst fears were confirmed. "You call the boys in?" I asked Joe.

"Yep. Lucky's on the ridge overlookin' ranch headquarters with a two-way. Rest of 'em are loadin' magazines and shovelin' food into their bellies." He snorted. "Act like it's the last vittles they'll get."

"Reckon I'd better figure a way to get the girls off the ranch before any shooting starts," I said. "Any sign of them moving closer to the WJP?"

"Nope. Davy called the Clines and old man Bridges and asked if motorcycles passed their places. Neither noticed anything."

Both homes were between us and Dillon. My guess was the gang wouldn't cut fences and leave the highway on their low-riders and heavy road bikes. The easiest point of entry to the ranch was down our long driveway, each side lined with five strands of tightly strung twelve and a half gauge four-point barbed wire. Outside of a frontal attack, the only way I could imagine their success was catching me between home and town.

While Joe awaited orders, I took time to gauge Z's and Leeann's reactions to the news. My sister kept to the side—her features drained by alarm. Lee, however, stood relaxed with thumbs hooked in the pockets of her jeans, as if listening to an interesting story. "Saddle and mount up, girls. We leave everything here but personal possessions."

Zoe touched my sleeve. "What about the cattle?"

"They're on their own," I said grimly.

Lee was the last rider mounted. Before she did, she dug through her things to locate two boxes of ammunition. One went into a saddle bag, the other she opened and dumped a number of cartridges into her palm. Checking her rifle first, she expertly thumbed them through the loading gate and into the tubular magazine. Where my .30-30 held only five rounds, I guessed her rifle took twelve or more. She thrust it into the scabbard again before noticing my interest and grinning. "I normally keep it loaded with five. Figured this was the time to fill 'er up."

Buster didn't like Midnight leading our group. He fought the bit and my grip on the reins and threw his head. I loosened my hold and allowed him to gallop past to spearhead our group. The older Morgan was too tired to answer his challenge.

Gary saw us coming and held the gate. I reined my horse to a stop. "Any news?"

"Not a damn thing, Boss," he said.

"Where're the boys?"

"Davy thinks he's cooking for an army, Lucky's still on the ridge, Odell's working on the Allis-Chalmers, and the rest are inside eating or sleeping."

"How long's Lucky been up there?"

"Since about nine this morning."

Leeann and Z weren't far behind Joe and me when we entered the bunkhouse. My tone was brusque. "Lynn, I'd like you to spell Lucky. I'll send a replacement before sundown. We can take turns as lookouts around the clock."

Joe's raspy voice broke the silence. "You were pretty quiet on the ride home, boy. Got a plan?"

I did, but not one I was willing to share. The idea didn't make me happy, but if the Brotherhood wanted me, I was going to make their mistake far more costly than they could imagine. "For now, we keep watch. Get on the phone and put out feelers. See if anyone's laid eyes on them since you talked to Pete. If we're lucky, perhaps it's a bike club getting an early jump on Sturgis." Joe's cold stare meant he didn't believe my optimistic hypothesis any more than I did. "Davy?"

Listening from the kitchen, our cook strolled out with a mixing bowl in hand and a spoon in the other. "Yeah, Boss?"

"Buster's got a loose shoe. I need it tightened."

Our resident farrier as well as kitchen manager, the rotund man frowned. "Don't have time now, but I might be able to get to him tomorrow or the day after."

I checked my watch. Four-thirty. "How long until supper?"

"Fifteen minutes or less."

"Okay. Let's make it quick. Zoe and Leeann can clean up once we're done, while you and I take care of my horse's shoe. I want it done tonight, Davy." My tone let him know my resolve.

"Yes, sir."

After our meal, I left the table first. "Meet you in front of the barn when you're finished eating," I told our cook.

He didn't disappoint. The man understood horses' hooves. Davy took one look and stood. "I need to pull all his iron, then trim and fit new shoes. Should've done it before you took out this last time and ran into the hills."

"Whatever you think is best," I said.

He was trimming a toe when I hear a voice behind me. "If it's not too much trouble," Leeann said sweetly, "could you take a look at Winston's shoes? Tell me if he needs work?"

Davy didn't bother to look up. "Find a halter and get him out here." He was tacking the first shoe on Buster when Lee appeared with her horse. I loved watching the man work. He understood hoof anatomy. Sweat ran profusely long before he finished. "Let me see you walk him," he said.

Winston was next after Davy pronounced Buster trail-worthy. Not having taken care of him when we returned to the ranch earlier, I brushed him while he got a helping of oats. Although fit and in riding shape, my horse needed rest. Unfortunately, I planned to ask even more of him. He got part of a flake of alfalfa in his manger as a reward for his hard work. I was almost finished currying my mount when a voice surprised me. "Busy spoiling your boy?" Leeann asked. She leaned on the gate and watched me work.

"Thanking him for a job well done. He's got the makings of a once in a lifetime horse. Did Winston need much?"

"Huh uh. Feet needed cleaned and shoes tightened, then Davy used a rasp to shave his hooves back. Didn't take long."

"I need him to check Sunday and Teton next, along with the remuda. We didn't use them much, but it's time for an inspection." I'd found a small gouge on Buster's chest I covered with Bag Balm after cleaning the wound. Unless a mount falters, its rider rarely knows when a stick might jab them. Lee opened the gate and let me through. She closed it while I hung the brush and feed bag in their places on the wall.

"You've been quieter than normal," she said. "What're you planning?"

"Deciding how to evacuate you and Z. No sense in either of you getting hurt or killed."

Her head came up, and Leeann appeared to swell twice her size. "Like hell you'll send me away. Not only am I a hired hand no different from the others, but my place is here with you. Get Zoe out if you want, but she might have something to say about it, too."

I used a stare causing her to squirm. "If I find a way for you girls to leave, you'll go. Understand?"

She stood her ground. "No." she shook her head. "Seems you're going to learn the hard way I don't back down."

"You're fired. Pack your shit." I left her fuming and returned to the bunkhouse.

Joe waved his cell. "Heard back from Pete. He put out feelers and found out the gang stopped south of Dillon along the Beaverhead."

"Where?"

"The cable hole."

I knew the area well. Mom used to take Jess and me swimming there when we were young. A single cable remained of an old swinging bridge. My sister loved to say how it was my spot to swim, because it was named after me. "Odell? I'd like you to go over my Datsun. See if it runs and the battery can hold a charge."

"Yes, sir," my mechanic said.

"Boss," Joe said, "you ain't thinkin' of goin' after 'em, are you?"

My answer was harsh. "It's in case we need extra wheels. I want the Brotherhood to come to us so we call law enforcement. Then, we're the aggrieved party. We take the fight to them, and we're the attackers. For now, we play defense."

Neither Zoe nor Leeann were anywhere to be seen. I suspected they were in the big house. I didn't like the idea, but I was going to have to call my father and arrange an evacuation. Preferably by helicopter. First, I needed a nap. Kicking my boots off, I let the boys decide how they would divvy the watchman's job overnight.

I woke after sundown to other cowhands snoring. Checking my watch, I saw I'd slept three hours. After disabling the north road sensor, I eased outside in my stocking feet with a light coat, my boots, handgun, and rifle. It didn't take two minutes before I was at Buster's stall. "Hey, man. You up for another adventure?" I whispered while switching my headlamp on low.

He was, and I walked him until out of hearing distance of my cowhands and Richie perched on the hill above. He couldn't see the corner of the barn and the north road from where he watched. My light shined enough to see the road in front of us but little more. Having walked Buster to the first gate before mounting, we galloped to the second before I stepped down to open it. I led my horse through and stopped before latching it, swearing at an approaching light from the ranch. If he discovered what I was about, Joe wasn't going to be a happy cow boss.

The clink of iron on rock let me know it was a mounted rider. I waited, ready to give whomever it was a piece of my mind. Leeann reined in Winston. "What the hell are you doing?" I said. "Go back to the big house."

"I can go wherever the heck I want. You aren't my boss anymore, remember?"

"Then, you're trespassing. Get the hell off my property."

She used her horse's shoulder to push past me through the gate. "We're wasting time."

"Goddamn it," I said under my breath and mounted after locking the way behind us. There wasn't much I could do except put my heels to Buster's ribs. I didn't look behind, knowing I couldn't shake her.

I made a call to my neighbor, Albert Michaels. Although I got him out of bed, he was up and waiting when we rode into his yard. A light was on when I stepped from the saddle and knocked. I heard shuffling inside and remembered his age. He opened the door. "That you, Cable?"

"Yes, sir."

He handed me a key. "It's parked along the machine shed. Try to keep it in one piece, okay?"

"Is there a place I can put my horse?"

"My horse, too," Leeann called from where she waited.

"Put 'em in the corral. There's fresh water in the trough and hay in the barn."

"I'll be back as soon as I can." I hesitated before lowering my voice. "I might need the same favor tomorrow."

"Leave the key in the ignition and park it where you found it," he said.

I hesitated. "You haven't seen me, okay?"

Albert squinted over his spectacles. "Seen who?"

We shook again. "Thank you."

My headlamp led the way to the corral. We stripped both horses and turned them out before I located a bale of hay and tossed them a flake. Leeann followed silently after we left them behind. Exactly as Michaels said, his '74 Ford pickup was parked next to the shed. My plan to ditch my uninvited guest went awry when I used the key to unlock the driver's door. Instead of waiting on the passenger side for me to reach across and unlock it, Lee pushed past me with her rifle to slide in and across the seat. I didn't miss her look of smugness when I closed the door and started the engine.

The dirt roads I took were familiar. It'd been years, but to drive cross country in order to reach blacktop took a little more than two hours. We crossed I-15 and took Highway 278 for a couple hundred feet before turning onto another dirt thoroughfare.

We saw the bonfire long before reaching my objective. I switched off our lights and maneuvered the pickup's nose toward the highway. If I was forced to run, I didn't want anything slowing my escape.

Leeann opened her door when I did. "Nope, you're staying," I said. "It might get hairy from here on."

She nodded. "Okay, I'll wait here quietly and work on what I'm going to tell Joe and Zoe."

"Goddamn it. You're going to get me killed, Leeann."

She closed the door quietly and circled to my side with her long gun. "Huh uh. I'm along to keep you alive."

I worked the lever of my rifle to chamber one, eased the hammer down to quarter-cock, and slid an extra into the magazine. Six rounds weren't much, but I could feed more quickly if needed. The Ruger on my belt was backup.

We hiked upstream across from the bustling camp. The Beaverhead River was low, and I considered wading it. Getting close enough to hear and judge who these people were was imperative. Screams of excitement and shouts were clear, but conversation was impossible to discern.

Leeann followed suit when I sat and tugged my boots off. It was tough to see much of the water except by what light the fire produced. Leaving our footwear and hats behind, I led by feeling my way across in stocking feet. My partner in crime pulled at my sleeve when we reached the other side. "We aren't running off and leaving my shitkickers," she murmured. "They cost too much."

"Should've thought about it when you wouldn't take no for an answer," I whispered back.

Tents were set up with no thought to organization. My faintly glowing Timex let me know it was a half past midnight, yet campers showed no signs of wearing down. Music blared while men and women danced and writhed in the firelight. "What's your plan?"

"Recon, only. Assess the enemy to learn their strengths and weaknesses. Make sure we're not jumping the gun." I estimated fifty feet lay between the river bar and a haphazard wall of tents. Most were small dome varieties, but a number were far larger. A series of picnic tables were covered with food, drink, and lanterns. Most campers sat, lounged, or milled around the fire smoking, drinking beer, or both. We were closer than I anticipated when I was struck by an epiphany and motioned to Lee. "We should blend in," I breathed in her ear. "Make anyone who looks twice think we're together." I got a stiff nod. Even in near darkness I could sense her terror, made worse by standing in their camp. There was every right to be petrified. I wouldn't have long to live—Leeann either—if our identities were discovered.

A nearby tent moved while we waited, watched, and listened. I drew Lee close, keeping our rifles sandwiched between our bodies. A zipper sounded, and I felt her tremble. A man stood first, then a woman, before stretching and looking in our direction. My arms went around Leeann and drew her close. "Kiss me," I whispered.

Her lips parted when she felt the touch of mine. Originally for show, I didn't have to sell my passion for her as our smooch deepened. Two chuckles let us know we were watched. "Get a room," the female called. "At least find a tent!" I waved a hand to let them know we heard, but we didn't stop our kiss. Glancing after chuckles from both, I watched from the corner of my eye as they wound their way to the refreshments. I kept an arm around Lee's shoulder and guided her beneath a huge oak. Far more shrouded in darker shadows from curious eyes, I pulled her closer and leaned against the tree.

An hour passed as I waited for the unknown, and hoped I'd recognized whatever it was when I heard it. We didn't have long to wait when three painfully thin young men materialized next to tents I guessed were their own. "...ready to get it over with," one said in a low tone. "Lacie's called three times in the last hour. She's ready for me to be home."

"Best you remind the bitch who the boss is," another said. "Besides, gotta finish recon. Way I hear it, ain't more than a half dozen on the ranch. Klein's not willing to commit before we know more."

"It's hot as hell. I'd as soon be home as baking my ass off here," added an unhappy third voice. "No telling how long it'll take to get the drone airborne again."

A light flared, and I saw a man draw deeply on a pipe before the lighter sputtered and went out. A handful of tries before it burst into life again. The pipe got passed between the trio, each hacking as their lungs tried to expel the smoke. "The old man was promised repairs would be finished day after tomorrow," one of the voices rasped before more violent coughing. "A last day of watching before we move on Pearson's ranch is my guess. Bet it's over in an hour or less. No way can they stop over a hundred of us storming their house. Klein's gonna burn the place to the ground with everyone inside. His idea of payback."

"Good," the first answered. "I can give Lacie a better idea of when I'll roll home. Her old man ain't happy I'm two payments behind on my bike he cosigned." All three laughed and strolled toward the bonfire, taking turns with the pipe.

I stood tall and stepped away from Leeann, committing the layout of their encampment into my memory bank. Ready to leave, I put my mouth within a few inches of her ear. "Let's go. Easy...we don't need to draw attention now."

We sat to wring the water from our socks and stuff wet feet into boots after crossing back. Although we didn't run, Mr. Michaels' truck loomed quickly. Neither of us said anything until after east of the freeway. I searched for the dirt road we needed to return my neighbor's truck. Leeann expelled a shaky breath. "Oh! My! God!" she said. "I can't believe what we did."

I wrenched myself back from plans already forming in my mind. "It was definitely a nice kiss."

She backhanded my shoulder. "You know what I mean. Standing inside the enemy's camp was more than dangerous!" I loved her low chuckle. "The kiss *was* nice."

Our way back took longer than I hoped. We parked the truck where Mr. Michaels asked and saddled our horses. "Are you going to be okay?" I asked Leeann. A glance at my watch showed the sun would rise in two hours. We'd been going hard for almost twenty-four hours.

She blinked hard and rolled her eyes. "If you're okay, I'm okay."

I mounted, and she followed suit. "Let's hustle."

* * *

Clattering plates and silverware woke me. The clock on the wall indicated fifteen past five. Less than an hour of sleep was afforded me after collapsing on my bunk. My crew stirred inside their blankets. I rolled to my back ready to go over my plan again. It depended on both stealth and luck to not only succeed but let me emerge alive and preferably unscathed—perhaps end the attack before it began. The worst-case scenario would certainly end my life, but perhaps my cowboys, cowgirl, and Z would be spared.

I sat up and rubbed my face and gritty eyes. "Come and get it, you damn pigs," Davy called.

The smell and sound of coffee poured is what it took to make me move. It felt good to slip into clean socks, jeans, and a dark shirt. My .44 got traded for the 10mm Kimber along with two extra mags in their sheath and a spare slipped into a pocket. A razor-sharp belt knife with a stout blade got threaded on, too.

Joe beat me to the table. I slid in across from him as Davy brought platters of hotcakes, sausages, bacon, scrambled eggs, and hash browns. "You look like hell, boy," Joe said.

I blew across my cup before sipping the robust brew and glared. The door opening behind me kept any sharp responses to myself. Z sat to my right with an open place left between us. "Be a few minutes before Leeann gets here. She growled like a bear when I woke her."

The table behind me sounded as if a pack of wolves attacked breakfast. "Won't be nothing left if she doesn't hustle," Odell said.

Leeann straggled in as I was pouring syrup over pancakes and sausage. Not a word to anyone, she plopped beside me and almost lunged for her coffee cup. "Mm...good," she said, hunkering over the cup between her hands. I didn't bother to look—she probably resembled how I felt. My thoughts were slow, and my ears rang from lack of sleep.

"Need someone to spell Lynn," I said. "He'll want breakfast and some shuteye."

"I'll take the next shift," Gary said. "Lucky can take over about noon."

"Got your truck running, Boss," Odell said. "Probably should replace the battery. She doesn't have much cranking amperage."

"Thanks. I appreciate it."

Joe hadn't stopped looking. "Ain't you a pair to draw to?" he asked, looking from Leeann to me.

"I need more sleep," Lee muttered under her breath.

"Well, you ain't gettin' none. Got horses to feed and water, along with stalls to clean. Didn't think I forgot, did you?"

"Don't have to," she said. "I got fired yesterday."

The bunkhouse quieted. "She's tellin' the truth?" Joe asked.

I swallowed my food before answering. "Yep. Insubordination."

"William!" Z sounded shocked. "You really let her go?"

My answer was cryptic. "I didn't want her to go, so I fired her."

Lee picked at hash browns and scrambled eggs after downing three cups of coffee. "Now, you know why I'm going back to bed."

I shook my head. "Huh uh. No can do. I'm reinstating you with back wages included." I checked my watch dramatically. "Looks like about eight hours or so. Joe's my cow boss and your boss. He says clean stalls and take care of the stock, you do it." She'd be too tired at day's end to blow my plans wide open.

"We should explain to Joe why you canned my ass," Leeann said.

"He gets any pertinent information from yours truly. If you've got something he needs to know, you go through me. I suggest you finish breakfast and find your gloves."

Rather than angry, the look Leeann sent my way was one of respect. She even gave me a brief nod. I feared whatever it was she considered, and worried she was a couple steps ahead of me. No matter, too many chores needed accomplished before darkness fell.

My cow boss caught me after I backed my Datsun from the garage. The truck was forty years old but ran strong. It was the only vehicle I'd purchased with my own money at the tender age of sixteen. Odell was right about battery strength. It turned the engine over and started it but without any real cranking power. I'd have to be careful to make sure it was parked where I could use compression to get it to run. "You ain't leavin' on your own, are you, boy?"

"Checking the north road. Make sure it's passable by truck if we have to retreat. Gotta figure a way to get the women out if we face an actual attack."

He nodded. "Makes sense, but I've spent plenty of time between our place and the Michaels ranch these last few months. Road's in good shape."

"I believe you, Joe. This's to set my mind at ease. Zoe's everything to me."

He winked. "To say nothing of your cowgirl."

"She's special for sure. Take care with her and don't push too hard, okay?"

"Nothing tough. My plan is for her to learn the ins and outs of the ranch. Reckon she might be my boss one of these days."

* * *

I was thinking of Joe's parting smirk when I parked at the line between Albert Michaels' ranch and mine. It seemed my cow boss read through my plan of treating Leeann no differently than any other hand. Until circumstances between us were more permanent, we'd ignore our affections toward the other until we were in private. My cowboys were probably aware of our budding relationship, but I wasn't ready to bring it into the open until the Brotherhood issue was resolved.

Hiking the last half mile, I saw Albert's wave before I went through his gate. His short steps were painful to watch. Once tall and powerful, my ancient neighbor stooped more each year since losing his wife.

"Wasn't sure when to expect you if at all," he said. "Where's your lady friend?"

"Getting her chores done like any good cowgirl," I said. "Mind if I borrow your truck again?"

"Nope. All I ask is you take care of her."

"Mind if I use it a third time...probably tomorrow night? Also, I need a crowbar and a maul if you got them."

"Hell, no, I don't mind. You, Jess, and your mom helped me and the old woman more times than I can repay. You're welcome to anything I got. Tools you're looking for are in the barn."

His heartfelt words choked me for a few seconds. "Thank you, sir." I took a few steps before stopping. "Mr. Michaels, same thing as before. You didn't see me."

"See who?" he repeated.

I got back in early afternoon. Just as my neighbor asked, I left his Ford parked where I found it with the keys still in the ignition. Tired from little sleep in the past forty-eight hours, I stumbled and almost fell on my return to the Datsun. The idea of a quick nap crossed my mind. The danger was I'd likely not wake until tomorrow. Best to hit the sack early and be ready for the following day.

Lee struggled with a bale of straw in a wheelbarrow when I got back to the ranch house. Although not heavy, the load was large and cumbersome. I hustled into the stables where she disappeared. While I didn't own the number of horses of Caroline and Annie did, cleaning the stalls of eighteen took time and energy. Winston, Purdy, and Buster brought the total to twenty-one, but no one was to touch my horse or enter his stall.

I found her spreading a part of her load on what looked to be a spotless floor. The stables were connected to the north barn, making a short pack for hay and straw. "You do good work," I said quietly.

Not caught by surprise, Leeann glanced from under the brim of her hat. "For a bunch of yahoos, your boys have done a good job keeping up on the place." She leaned over the wood gate. "Come here." Her lopsided smile made my heart jump. The kiss we shared kept it beating fast. "What's your plan?" she asked after pulling back.

Nothing to do but shrug. I wasn't going to give it away to anyone—no matter how stupid—especially to the woman in possession of my heart. "Keep a sharp lookout and hope for the best. They might realize by now how tough an assault on the ranch would be."

She snorted. I didn't have to hear her opinion after seeing her look of disgust, but she let me have it anyway. "I was there, remember? I know what they're intending. They won't take prisoners. If I were in your place—"

"You aren't."

"I'd have every law enforcement agency in western Montana in position around us."

"A civilized way doesn't work on the totally uncivilized." I steered the conversation elsewhere. "Let me fly you out with Z. If you agree, my sister will go, too. Otherwise, she won't leave, either."

The ringing of the supper bell stopped our conversation. Lee turned her back to finish spreading straw before leading one of our quarter horses inside and latching the gate. "I don't know about you," she said. "I'm hungry."

I watched her go, vaguely admiring her denim-clad rear end, wondering if I was making the right decision.

Chapter XVII

After supper, I listened to our end of Joe's phone conversations with every neighbor he could contact before I rolled into the covers on my bunk. Near as my cow boss could figure, our enemies still camped on the banks of the Beaverhead. I was running on less than an hour of sleep with my battery drained. I'm not sure when the boys joined me—not waking until dawn the following day.

Turning to my back, I lay quietly while planning the next twenty-four hours. My chances of surviving were fifty-fifty at best. I considered watching the execution of my sister and nephew again to remind myself of who I fought against. The memory of their deaths was enough to make my blood run hot. Throwing the covers back, I dressed in clean clothes, choosing a black pair of Wrangler jeans and a matching long-sleeved shirt I rarely wore. The belt knife and Kimber were strapped to my waist along with extra magazines. After moving it into the correct position, I made firm contact with the butt before drawing slowly and thrusting the muzzle forward. My offhand wrapped around the other fist as the sights lined up. I repeated the process twenty-five times before satisfied with how smoothly I could clear leather. If events were to my satisfaction, I'd never fire a shot. If forced, I was confident of ability to draw and fire a double tap in a quarter of a second.

I holstered a final time before noticing a pair of watching eyes. Gary lay still, but nothing missed his sharp gaze. We made eye contact for a moment before he dipped his chin. The fight was brought closer with each passing moment. Time to face it head on.

Other than Richie, the lot of us were gathered around the tables when Z and Leeann appeared. Our breakfast was hearty with thick steaks, eggs, and toast, along with slices of cantaloupe and watermelon.

Lee broke protocol by kissing my cheek as she sat. Other than a wink, she ignored me when I lifted an eyebrow. Nothing alike in looks, she and Z could be sisters by the way they filled their cups and sipped coffee before thinking of food. Both spooned fruit and scrambled eggs on their plates while ignoring the cuts of beef. I suspected Davy included fresh fruit for the ladies—he'd seldom offered it to my cowboys.

Joe checked his phone a last time before sliding it into a pocket. "No word about the Brotherhood. What's the plan for today, Boss?"

I remembered what Lee and I heard in their camp. "Need everyone on the lookout for drones. Might be one...could be more. We need to bring it down if it's within range. Ought to have a man with a shotgun while the rest of us use rifles."

"You privy to somethin' I ain't been told about?" Joe asked.

"It's the twenty-first century. Kids fly the damned things, so what better method of recon? Seems easy enough to me." I didn't dare glance at Leeann in case we gave something away to my cow man. "Lucky? I'd like you to spell Richie after you've finished breakfast. I'll send someone for you around noon or a bit after. Keep your eyes peeled and radio Joe even if you think you hear a motor."

I took my time in the bathroom in hopes my cow boss would be gone when I finished. Gary wiped his M1A with an oiled rag with what appeared to be a dozen loaded magazines lying within reach, while the rest of the crew found work close to the ranch. Hustling to the east barn, I passed Buster on my way to the back without a thought. A lock on a heavy door opened to my key, and I switched the light on. It took me a bit to find what I was looking for in a box high on an upper shelf. Two caps and a length of fuse. A crimper went into my back pocket.

Most of us found something to do. I watered, fed, and brushed Buster, while Odell changed oil in the Allis Chalmers and greased every fitting. Not even usual good smells from the kitchen could mask the reek of fresh-forked manure and straw I wheelbarrowed past the bunkhouse. Time crawled with everyone on edge.

Shouts made me run for the front of the barn. Joe, Lynn, Gary, and Richie were outside peering skyward, while Leeann and Z rushed from the big house. Lynn pointed. "There it is!" His long arm stretched high overhead. With my back to the sun, I saw a drone far bigger than I envisioned. With it out of shotgun range, I drew my Kimber as I heard an action levered over the sound of buzzing rotor blades. I glanced across the yard to see Lee taking careful aim with her Winchester.

She missed her first shot but tagged it with a hasty follow-up. With four propellers keeping it upright, she needed to hit only one to bring it down. I guessed the range at least five hundred feet, but in a clear blue sky, it was impossible to be sure. It fell quickly to crash on the steep north barn roof, slide off, and fall to the ground. All of us sprinted to stop its escape in the unlikely event it could get airborne again.

Leeann levered the empty out and a fresh cartridge into the chamber and pointed the muzzle. "What do you think?" she asked without taking her eye away from the sights.

"Kill the camera," I said. Her rifle report was sharp, and parts flew. "Great. No more eye-in-the-sky for those bastards."

Joe squatted and lifted the craft before turning to me. "You were right, boy."

I shrugged. "Good thing someone spotted it." I looked around. "Who?"

"Lucky," Joe said. "He radioed earlier he was good until this evening and saw it from his position."

I put a hand on Lee's shoulder and squeezed affectionately. "My Lee-Annie Oakley." She flashed me her lopsided grin, one to make my heart race. I couldn't help but put my arm around her shoulders and squeeze. Each day it seemed I saw another side of the woman I fell in love with. If only...no, it wouldn't do to think past the Brotherhood, lest it get one of us killed. Best to focus on the here and now.

* * *

I led Buster to the first gate on the north road an hour after dark before mounting. We galloped to the second gate before running hard toward the third. It took us less than twenty minutes to cross onto Albert Michaels' property. He knew to expect me, just not when. Pulling the saddle and pad from Buster, I led him into the corral before cursing when Winston appeared from a dark corner next to the barn. "Goddamn it," I whispered to myself.

Leeann waited in the truck. I strode to the passenger side to drag her out, but she anticipated me and locked it. Circling the pickup, I opened the driver's door. "Out, now," I whispered. "Get your ass back to the ranch."

She kept her voice low. "I don't know what you have planned, but you can't do it without me."

"Yes, I can. What I'm going to do won't take but a minute."

"Then, my riding along won't hurt anything."

"Lee..." I stopped myself from raging at her and took a deep breath. "It's going to be dangerous, and I don't want you hurt."

She patted her rifle. "All the more reason for me to go and keep the boogeymen off your back."

I slapped the cab above the door. "Damn it! Are you ever going to listen to me?"

Leeann grinned in the low light. "Sure! When you aren't going out to do something stupid." The muzzle of her rifle moved in my direction when I reached across the seat. "I wouldn't if I were you," she said.

With each tick of the clock working against me, I gave up and slid in. Moments later, we idled from the barnyard and onto the dirt road leading west. "How can I keep you safe if you won't let me?" I asked.

She didn't answer long enough I thought she decided against it. Finally, she said, "I've been in this since I helped you pack and bury the man you killed on Caroline's ranch." Lee reached across to put a hand on my forearm. "We're a team now. Your problems are mine. Would you do any less for me if circumstances were reversed?"

"No—" I trailed off as the lights of Dillon came into view.

We were almost to blacktop when she asked another question. "What's this roll of tubing on the floorboard?"

"It's called detcord . . . normally to detonate high explosives, but it can damage and set off stuff you wind it around."

I heard a sharp intake of breath in the darkness. "Oh, no."

"See why I wanted you to stay home?"

She lifted the inert roll to the seat. "Where did you find explosives like this?"

"A quarry north of Dillon. Busted the lock on their powder shack and liberated what you see here."

I parked in a wide spot off the secondary road, on the same side of the river as the huge encampment. During our earlier reconnaissance I'd noticed where and how the Brotherhood parked their bikes, a pickup, and two cars. One long line of mostly Harleys were bracketed by the cars on one end and the truck on the other. The only hiccup in my plan was the possibility of a posted guard, but I hoped they were comfortable enough after a week in the area. No people in their right minds wanted to mess with an enormous motorcycle gang, except me, but perhaps I wasn't entirely sane when it came to those I considered evil.

Stopping with the truck pointed the way we came for a quick getaway, I shut the motor off. "Stay here. I'll be right back. If I haven't returned in an hour, drive Albert's truck to the ranch and tell Joe what's happened, okay?"

"No, I'm here to help. Tell me how."

I was tired of arguing. "By staying in the truck. By staying alive."

She wore me down in the end. Running out of time, I didn't fight her when she followed me in the direction of the camp. The group wasn't nearly as rowdy with perhaps a dozen bikers seated around a fire. Both of us bent at the waist until reaching their truck, I squatted to peer around. No guards were visible, and the men and women gathered near the flames didn't bother to look in our direction, some hundred yards from the camp. "What do you want me to do?" Leeann whispered in my ear.

"Hold the spool and let me pull the cord. Keep a little tension as I go and don't let it uncoil when you feel me stop, okay?"

I crawled beneath the truck and worked my way down the line of bikes, many worth tens of thousands of dollars. I threaded my line over the twin cylinder engines and beneath their fuel tanks. Footsteps came near as I moved from the fifth or sixth bike to the next. Crouching beside a Fat Bob, it provided enough cover so a huge bearded man with an enormous belly didn't notice me in the shadows. He went through saddle bags of a full-dressed hog cursing quietly as he searched. "Got it!" The biker held a semi-auto overhead as he called out. I didn't move until he was seated at the fire again, showing off the gun.

My count stopped at one hundred nineteen motorcycles. The final Harley got the tank wrapped three times before I looped the plastic cord as best I could. More bikers gathered around the growing fire as I crawled back.

Leeann's eyes were big when I returned. "Oh, you scared me! What now?"

I used a big rock to secure the cord on our end after I cut it. "You step back while I crimp this into place." Fishing a blasting cap stowed separately up front and the crimping tool from a hip pocket, I motioned her farther away. Crimping the cap too close to the explosive cord meant possibly setting it off. Using it to crimp the plastic cord and cannon fuse together, I measured the latter by how far I could reach. Uncoiling three times my arm's length, I cut it at what I estimated to be eighteen feet. Each foot bought us one minute. Eighteen minutes burn time would have us safely away. Glancing a final time at the camp, I turned my back to act as a shield and used a Bic lighter to ignite the fuse. I dropped it to the ground and waited a moment to assure myself it still burned before making our escape.

"What if..." Leeann pointed to the revelers. "What if someone checks on their bike?"

She got a shrug from me. "It's too bad." I only needed to conjure the memory of my sister's murder to feel no compassion.

We didn't run. Instead, we walked briskly using the Brotherhood truck to mask our withdrawal. Four minutes by my watch before we were driving away gave us at least thirteen or fourteen more to make our escape.

I didn't stop on a low ridge the dirt road crossed a moment too soon. I turned us in the general direction we needed to watch, and barely a half-minute passed before an enormous explosion lit the darkness. A fireball rose high into the night sky. I could only wonder what casualties the camp took. The more taken out of the fight the better. Perhaps my attack could be the catalyst to hasten an end to hostilities. Satisfied my plan worked and not needing to see more, we continued our trip home. Leeann and I got away with a successful preemptive attack.

* * *

We arrived at the ranch with plenty of time to spare. I returned the tools I borrowed from Albert to liberate the roll of cord from a local gravel company to his barn. We stopped along the way to bury the remaining detcord, blasting cap, and cannon fuse in three separate locations. The explosives couldn't be traced to me, nor by the cap and fuse most ranchers and farmers kept on hand. Only those who suffered my assault would know in their hearts. If gang members were smart, they'd find a way home and never return. I kissed Leeann good night before we split up to stable our horses, but I waited until I saw her enter the big house. Creeping through the backdoor and into the kitchen of the bunkhouse, I rearmed the north gate alarm before slipping between the sheets.

* * *

Sounds of Davy setting the tables woke me. Three hours in the sack wasn't nearly enough, yet two wins in one day made me smile. A downed drone and over a million dollars of motorcycles destroyed in less than twenty-four hours was a victory by any measure.

I beat everyone to the table. No way did I want to give away to Joe or the boys my exhaustion a second time. As usual, Leeann and Zoe were the last two to drag their butts in to eat. I felt Lee's familiar touch across my upper back and neck before she bent close to kiss my cheek.

Our meal was hotcakes, scrambled eggs, and patty sausage. I noted a platter of fruit likely placed on the table for the girls but speared a couple slices of apples and cantaloupe for me. Hardly a sound was made but the clinking of forks and knives on stoneware. Joe pushed back first. "What's the plan for today, Boss?"

"I want everyone ready for war. No one goes unarmed, understand? My guess is the Brotherhood got a good look at our layout before Leanne took down their spying eyes. Who's on the ridge?"

"Gary," Joe said.

"It's time I take a turn. All of you stay close to positions you can fall back to in the unlikely event they somehow take us by surprise or try to overwhelm us. Z, I want you and Leeann in the bunkhouse near to Davy and the boys."

"Okay if I give you an extra pair of eyes as a lookout on the ridge?" Lee asked.

"I don't mind. We've got another set of field glasses you can use." I got up to stand behind Davy where I could see the room. "Don't do anything foolish, all right? We defend the ranch and nothing else. Shoot only if you have to. We're in the right as long as they bring the fight to us. All of you but Leeann knew Jess and Danny and understand the evil we face. These bastards are the animals who took two sweet souls from us. I don't want to lose anyone else. Understand?" I waited until getting a nod from everyone, including Z.

Davy made a lunch for Leeann and me to take. I brought a knapsack along, tossing in extra ammunition for both my .30-30 and 10mm. Lee returned from the big house with her rifle and loose .32-20 rounds to resupply her tube magazine. The Brotherhood might overrun us, but it wasn't going to be without a massive loss of life on their side, too.

The hike wasn't long, but we didn't get there any too soon. Gary looked dead on his feet, his eyes bleary with exhaustion. "Outside of mule deer and a coyote, no sign of life, Boss."

I shook his hand. "Thanks, man. Get yourself to the bunkhouse and fill your belly with breakfast before hitting the sack, all right?"

"Yes, sir." He gathered his things and rifle, too.

"Oh...Gary?" My cowboy stopped. "Keep your gun handy. Sleep with it if you want. Don't let it get more than an arm's length from you."

I liked what the boys did. With so much time on their hands, they piled rocks into a horseshoe shaped redoubt perhaps four feet high and just as thick. An ancient wooden fencepost spanned from a cradle of rocks on each side for a comfortable place to sit but not fall asleep. I set the wicker basket with our midday meal in the shade.

Lee and I scanned the horizon with our binoculars, each pointing out deer we thought the other might have missed. An enormous forked horn buck caught my attention. His antlers appeared heavy at even a mile. I estimated they were over twenty inches long past the fork and perhaps thirty wide. Not able to stop watching, I breathed a sigh of relief after he eventually fed out of sight. Leeann chuckled. "Couldn't take your eyes off the deer, could you?"

"Good Lord, no. To think a mature buck like him has lived on the ranch, and I never set eyes on him until now. Shows exactly how much we don't see."

Lee lowered her field glasses. "Cable—" She stopped as if unsure. "How...I mean, how do you see this ending? Is it over now?"

"Huh. Good question. I'd love to call it even. I can never replace Jess and Danny, but I took a pretty good swing at them in California. I think my sis would be happy knowing she and her boy were worth sixty to two."

"Think any were killed last night?"

"Hard to say. I've never used so much detonation cord before. Bet the explosion knocked out a few windows toward Dillon. I'd guess quite a few campers are temporarily deafened. Might be a few more serious injuries, too."

"Will the police know it was us?"

"They shouldn't. It's why I stole the cord from a local gravel company. They have no way of pointing the finger at me. Caps and cannon fuse can be bought anywhere...especially the internet...so no way of backtracking to me. If I did this right, only you and I know the truth. Speaking of the truth—" I stopped searching the horizon and turned to Leeann. "Can you handle it?"

She cocked her head. "Handle what? I don't understand."

"Can you not blame yourself for whatever happened last night? If the carnage is worse than I suspect, can you handle being a part of it?"

244

Lee sighed. "I thought about it a lot while I sat in Mr. Michaels' truck and waited for you. You'd been quiet about what you planned, if anything. After our scouting trip I knew you had an idea. Wish you would have done it the night before."

"The night before last? Why?"

"Because I waited halfway until morning in our borrowed pickup. When you didn't show by midnight, I saddled Winston and rode home in hopes of meeting you along the way. Wasted a good night of sleep."

I couldn't help but laugh. "What if I didn't show last night?"

She laughed, too. "I would've needed to nap in the barn when Joe thought I was busy. Whatever you planned was going to start at the Michaels ranch, so that's where I waited." What a fearless woman. Not only did she plan to help me but thought nothing of riding an hour alone in pitch darkness. I didn't hide my frank appraisal, and she finally turned her head. "What?"

"I love you. God, I love you." I could only stare, her eyes pooling with moisture. "Pretty much figured I'd be a confirmed bachelor, and it'd be up to Jess and Z to have families." A tear escaped to make its way down her cheek, which I caught above her scar and wiped away with my thumb. "Yet here you are."

Her face twisted and chin trembled. "I've waited for you my whole life," she said between sobs. "Then, I saw a man searching for Caroline's horses and wondered if you were him. The way you sat on Buster made me go weak in the knees, but you couldn't see me."

Lee was right. "I was searching for a way out. So much pain and heartache...I was filled with despair. It was impossible to think past it."

She twisted next to me and took my hands. Her eyes searched mine. "No more?"

"No, no more. Oh, I'll always feel the acute loss of Jess and Danny, but I don't need to be with them any longer. They—" I thought back to my brush with death after Annie provided the bottle of Everclear. "They made it plain it wasn't my time."

Leeann frowned. I'd never explained how close I'd come to joining them both and their obvious displeasure. She started to say something before movement caught our attention, and I keyed the mike on the radio. "Lookout to Joe."

He answered quicker than I expected. "Go, lookout."

"Got a rig on the road coming toward the ranch house."

"Got an ID on it?"

"Negative...hold it." I set the two-way aside and used both hands to hold my binoculars steady before readjusting the focus. "I think it's the law. Looks like county."

"Roger."

"Joe, send Lucky up now. Tell him to sprint. The rest are to pull back and don't let the law see we're armed."

We met him hustling up slope with a rifle in one hand. He barely nodded as I handed him the handset when we passed. Lee and I reached the east barn as the county SUV drove in and parked in front of the big house. A giant of a man I knew well stepped from the driver's side—another I wasn't familiar with on the passenger. The corners of the former's eyes crinkled when he grinned. "Been a long time, Cable."

"It has. How are you, Ace?" I hurried across the packed dirt and gravel to shake his hand.

"Ha! Long time since I heard that nickname."

I chuckled. "Well, you did score one!"

Andy Norton was a fearsome lineman on our high school football team. A couple years older than me, he played two sports, football and baseball. The basketball team was short players his senior year, and he was talked into turning out. Problem was he couldn't play a lick. Not only did he make passing the ball look awkward, he never made a single layup. Consequently, our team went winless until the final game of the year. We were playing a local team with a record of 15-4. Cleaning our clocks wouldn't move them up in the state rankings, but it would give our school a skunk for the year.

Both teams went at it hard with Andy hurting us as well as helping our adversaries. Throwing his big body around on the court didn't make him friends, and we were tied with three seconds left when he came open under the bucket. He looked surprised when the ball was passed to him for an easy layup. We all think he would have hit it, except one of the other team's forwards fouled Andy hard. The score was 49-49 when he stepped to the free throw line for two with one-point-one seconds left. The opposing side went wild when Andy missed everything on his first attempt. The bucket, net, even the backboard. Our crowd was silent with dejection. You could've heard a pin drop while he prepared for his last attempt, everyone knowing we'd probably lose in overtime.

Except Andy was the hero. His shot was flat and far too hard, but the ball somehow rattled around and dropped through the hoop. The crowd on both sides went wild, and for a few minutes, it felt like we won the state championship instead of our only win of the season. I gave him the nickname of Ace, and it stuck until he went off to study criminal justice. His grin grew. "Only time I was ever the hero."

I slung my rifle and offered a hand. Mine disappeared in his when we shook. "You deserved every bit of it."

His eyes shifted. "Who's this?

Leeann stepped forward. "Andy, I'd like you to meet my newest hire, Leeann Slater. Lee, this's Andrew Norton. We went to school together."

She offered her palm. "It's nice to meet you, Deputy Norton."

"Likewise. You taking over Davy's job?"

Lee grinned. "Nope, I get paid to put my butt in the saddle."

He turned to me in mock surprise. "Say it ain't so, Pearson. Hiring cowgirls, now?"

"Got no problem with it if they work as hard as this one." I didn't miss his roving eyes. "You got business with one of my hands?"

Andy shook his head. "I'm not sure. Is there a place we can talk privately?" His partner waited at the corner of their SUV until then. I reckoned their business was serious. "This's Sal Hewitt. We're investigating an explosion last night."

I did my best to look surprised. "Natural gas line?"

"No, a motorcycle club got blown sky-high about midnight. Know anything about it?"

"Andy, I'm grazing five thousand head of beef. Part are here on the ranch, while the biggest percentage is up in the Snowcrest. Why in the hell would I know about a bike gang?"

The big man shifted his feet uneasily. "Because yours is the only name to come up when we questioned the survivors."

Chapter XVIII

My heart skipped a beat, but I didn't let my return gaze falter. "Mine? How in the heck would any of them know it? Are they looking to cash in on my family's name?"

He gave Leeann a sharp look and came back to me. "Mind if we take this inside?"

"No, come on in." I hated to go into our headquarters, but the bunkhouse was filled with cowboys bristling with long guns.

Lee tugged at my sleeve. "Cable?"

Although she looked cool on the outside, I could almost smell her fear. "You should come along." No sense in her fretting until the meeting was over.

I led our group into the kitchen where we took seats at the table. Z probably heard the door judging by how quickly she made an appearance. Dressed as any other cowhand, my sister didn't seem put off by law enforcement. I saw the recognition in her face when she read Andy's nametag. "Officer Norton. I know you by reputation and from years ago," Z said.

Andy was clearly surprised. He'd grown up with Jess, the same as everyone at our local school, but our older sister moved away with Dad while still very young, although she attended primary in Dillon. "Zoe?"

She grinned and held out a hand. "Still chasing girls around the playground?"

His booming laugh filled the house as they shook. "No, I finally caught one. Now, we've got our own little ones in school. You?"

"I never found the right guy."

"Ain't surprised. You probably won't in New York. Come back to Montana and find a man who can rope a steer and handle a six-shooter."

She nodded, her expression serious. "You're probably right." Whereas I sat across from our visitors with Lee at my side, Z took her place at the head of the table. She was well versed as a power player and used it to her advantage. "Are you here for business or pleasure?"

"Business. I'm investigating an explosion in the camp of a biker club staying along the Beaverhead at the City Park south of town."

"Oh? Anyone hurt?" Z asked.

"No one killed, but there were a number of casualties."

"What does this have to do with the WJP?"

"We've been questioning the survivors. Your family name comes up repeatedly. These folks seem to think Cable is behind it."

Z should have pursued acting. "I returned to the ranch because of how shorthanded it's been." She nodded at Leeann. "We've resorted to hiring women able to ride and handle a rope. I can assure you that Cable and the rest of us are far too busy to harass a biker club passing through."

"It's why we're here, Miss Pearson. Just wanted to clear things up." He turned his attention to me. "Where were you around midnight last night?"

"The WJP is running more cattle than ever before, Andy. We're grazing the largest portion back in the Snowcrest. All of us are either pushing cows to fresh pasture or sleeping. Does that answer your question?" Outright lying bothered me, but skirting the truth wasn't as repugnant.

A knock at the door stopped our conversation. Joe clomped across the hardwood floor of the living room and stopped when he saw us. "Everything all right, Boss?"

"I reckon. You want to come on in?" I nodded at our company. "Officer Norton may have some questions for you."

Joe hustled to the table and sat at the opposite end from Zoe. "How are you, Andy? Ain't seen you in a month of Sundays."

"Pretty good, Joe. These folks keeping you working?"

"We're either in the saddle or in our bunks," my cow man said. "Who's your partner in crime?"

"This here's Deputy Sal Hewitt. We've been partners almost three years now."

"Where're you from, son?" Joe asked.

"Helena, sir." Hewitt said.

"I ain't no sir. Joe'll do. Now, can someone tell me what in the hell we're doin' here?"

"There was a big damn explosion outside of Dillon last night," Andy said. "Happened next to a group of bikers camped along the Beaverhead south of town. None dead, but a good portion of those able to talk are pointing their finger at your boss."

Joe stared incredulously before breaking into raucous laughter. "Cable? Christ, Andy, he's been busier than the rest of us, and most of the crew are dead on their feet on account no one gets enough sleep."

"Where were you around midnight last night?" Andy asked me again.

My cow boss didn't let me answer. "Goddamn it, Deputy. I just told you every last one of us were in bed."

Andy didn't look away from me. "Cable?"

I guess I took too long, and Leeann butted in before I could answer. "He was with me."

My old school chum never took his eyes from mine, and I didn't allow him to see my surprise and smirked instead, then winked and shrugged. Let him think of me as a Lothario. His eyes flicked to Z. "Is she telling the truth, Miss Pearson?"

"She moved here from Colorado after meeting and falling in love with my brother. Cable hired her because he felt the same way. Their attraction for one another hasn't been a well-kept secret."

"You know about this, too, Joe?"

"Me and the boys knew somethin' was goin' on between 'em. Constant bickerin' and fightin' like cats and dogs."

"Last question is for Cable," Andy said. "Were you with Leeann last night?"

I didn't blink and nodded without hesitation. "Yes, sir, I was."

He stood and deputy Hewitt followed suit. "I guess we're through here."

We followed them to their patrol car. Andy lowered his window after belting in. "I might have more questions after the investigation moves along."

He grinned when I said, "No problem, Ace. I'd like you to keep me in the loop as much as you can." I didn't, but there was no need for him to think I was hiding something. All of us breathed a sigh of relief when our company left.

"Son of a bitch." I turned at Joe's strong language. "Seems the Brotherhood got a taste of their own medicine. Whatcha think, Boss? A bomb intended for us accidently exploded in camp?"

"I think that's as good of an explanation as anything else," Z said. "Andy promised he'll keep us updated. I'm sure we'll eventually learn the cause. Couldn't happen to a nicer bunch in my opinion."

"You ain't made me particularly happy by sneakin' around in the middle of the night, boy," Joe said. His tone made it clear he was miffed. "You could've got yourself killed."

"No need to be concerned, Joe," Z said. "It never happened."

Leeann turned in surprise. "How do you know?"

"Because I'm a light sleeper. Believe me, if anyone came into the house, I'd be aware of them before the door..." She winked at me. "...or window closed."

"You lied to the cops?" Joe asked Lee.

She ducked her head in embarrassment. "Yes, sir. Suspicion would always be on Cable unless an alibi were offered. I couldn't think of a better one. A bunch of sleeping cowboys wasn't quite as helpful."

My cow boss grinned. "Damn, girl. I knew there was a reason I liked you."

Zoe spoke up: "Leeann's fairly safe. If those were federal boys, she might face felony charges, but for Montana law enforcement, the offense is a seldom-enforced misdemeanor. Almost expected from girlfriends. Anyway, her maximum fine could only run five-hundred dollars. The alibi she provided is cheap at twice the price."

I turned at Joe's words and hurried inside the east barn. Buster nickered the moment he heard my footsteps and met me at the gate. I buried my face in his mane and stroked his neck with what Joe said echoing in my ears. "Cable?" Leeann's hand startled me when it touched my shoulder. Threatening tears spilled over at the contact. "Did I do or say something wrong?'

"No." I shook my head against Buster's neck.

Her insistent hand tugged me to face her before taking me into her arms. "Then what? What's wrong?" she whispered.

I hiccupped a couple times before I could get it out. "Joe...Joe used to say to Jess what he told you. It was one of his favorite things to tell her when he was happy with something she did."

"About liking me?"

"Yeah. It was their thing. He never said it to anyone I know of other than Jess. Now you."

"You're saying it was a great compliment?"

"The best. It took me right back to hearing him say it to my sister. His praise would make her so happy she'd beam."

Lee sniffed. "I'm glad, if you don't mind."

"Oh, God, no. It means he's accepted you into the family. You're one of us now. A part of the ranch."

She pushed back, and her eyes searched mine before a I saw a smile attempting escape. "Does that mean you can't fire me again?"

I ran my sleeve across wet cheeks and laughed. "It means I'd have to fight Joe if I did. Probably duke it out with my sister who's now your lawyer, too."

Her arms went around me again, pressing her cheek against my chest. "I'm happy. It seems I've won at least half the battle."

I hugged her tightly. "No, I think you won the war."

* * *

Andy provided regular updates. Many of the Brotherhood casualties were airlifted to larger hospitals in Missoula. None were expected to lose their life, but eleven were in poor condition. I suspected those gathered around the fire nearest Leeann and me were those most gravely injured. Andy called to let me know three days later. "It was definitely an attack." I'd let the boys check on the cows kept on our land and Albert's, but only in groups of three. "Forensics suggest the explosion was triggered by detonation cord. Gas tanks worked as extra incendiary devices. It's a miracle no one died."

"Could it have been a rival motorcycle group?" I asked.

"Hard to say. At this point, the investigation is wide open. No telling what direction it may lead us."

"Learned any clues as to why my name was mentioned?"

"No, but they use it like a curse word."

"Andy, could they have the wrong Pearson or messed up on the name?"

"How many other Pearsons run cattle in our neck of the woods? The fellow who appears to be the leader was insistent before clamming up. Can't get anything from him now."

"Okay. Let me know if I can help in any way."

I got an update on beef while we ate supper. "Cows on the ranch and over on the Michaels place look good, Boss," Joe reported. "Can't find where we've lost even a single head. Got fence to repair...near a hundred feet is about to fall over. Lucky, Lynn, and Richie plan to replace rotten fence posts with steel and tighten the wire."

"Whatever you think best. I'll take Buster and check on the herd in the Snowcrest. Plan to leave at first light. Gotta locate 'em and check on the gear left behind."

"I'm not sure your plan is a good idea, Boss?" he said. "No tellin' what the sons of bitches still got in mind."

Joe voiced my biggest worry. What if it wasn't over? I reckoned Lee and I destroyed every bike and probably the truck and cars, too. Those not injured lacked a way home. Still, Andy and local law enforcement were aware of my enemies and unresolved motive for their hatred. With their every move scrutinized, the Brotherhood wouldn't likely have an opportunity to follow through with their wicked plans. Joe and Zoe agreed after I expressed my initial thoughts.

Leeann and I'd spent the last few evenings on the front porch swing at the big house. Our conversations were of the ranch and its potential, along with stories of growing up when Z sat with us for an hour or so each evening. Three was a crowd, she declared, and left Lee and I alone to discuss the future. When I asked my sister about her job and tardiness in returning, I learned she used her computer and worked from the ranch office. Our father wasn't happy and expected her eventual return. I hadn't spoken to Lee about my plans, and she set her fork aside at my revelation. "Mind if I ride along?"

"Can if you want. We'll be gone two...maybe three nights."

"Perfect. I'll pack my gear after supper."

"You're welcome to tag along, too," I told my sister. "We could use another horse to push cows."

Lee and I left the ranch after breakfast as morning dawned. Z refused my offer with a smile. Buster was raring to go enough he hopped a couple times after I mounted. I checked to make sure my rifle scabbard and saddlebags didn't loosen during his bucking before riding through the gate Joe held for us. "Take care up there, boy. Don't let any bear chew on our cowgirl."

We reached the first of our two campsites in early afternoon only to find our goods and gear torn apart. Easy to see by toothmarks which critter helped itself. I could only hope any grizzly satisfied its curiosity and hunger and left my cows alone. Leeann dismounted immediately with an unladylike curse. "Damn it!" She hurried past where I still sat on Buster. "My clothes. This's most of what I own. Using the washer and dryer in the big house every night is the only way I've been able to wear clean duds. What am I gonna do?"

I stepped down to help look through her ruined things. Some were salvageable, although most weren't. "The ranch will reimburse you," I said. "I'll ask Z to take you shopping after we get back. Deal?"

She gave me a glum look. "You're looking at the only female in the world who doesn't enjoy buying clothes."

"Then, I suggest you take full advantage of online shopping with the WJP debit card. Squeeze it until it's years before you need to update your wardrobe."

We stacked anything salvageable. A couple tins of pork and beans, one of Spam, and a can of chili. Our pots and pans were badly bent but still usable. Not so for the dual burner cook stove. Lee located an unopened box of Bisquick missed by our nocturnal visitor. "Looks like we can eat breakfast tomorrow."

After finding a couple bikini panties under what remained of our table, I twirled them on an index finger. "Is this what you consider daily cowgirl wear? Haven't you read the mandate concerning ranch uniforms?"

"Throw 'em here. It'll be nice to have underwear again." My brows went up while my eyes dropped to her hips, unconsciously searching for lines beneath her jeans. She shifted her stance while I stared before my gaze rose. A broad smile awaited to let me know I was caught before she laughed. "Gotcha!"

I grinned back with only a hint of embarrassment. "You know, I'm starting to like you. Might keep you around now, so we'd better check our camping spot and gear."

We filled our water bottles and let the horses drink after reaching our camp. Surprisingly, nothing seemed to have been touched. Zoe's tent and sleeping bag were exactly as she left them. The same for my shelter and both Leeann's and my gear. Even bugs couldn't find their way in with the zippers snugged tight.

We dismounted to let the horses rest while Leeann and I tore into our sandwiches. Not a cow was in sight from where we lunched quietly. We'd conversed little on our ride into the backcountry. "What's the plan?" Lee asked.

"Pack our belongings and load it as best as we can behind our saddles. I'd like to think we can locate the main herd before nightfall."

We left Z's gear behind and loaded my tent, our sleeping bags, and mattresses. It wasn't easy to throw my leg over the bulk of our gear lashed atop my saddlebags. Once comfortable, I found Lee didn't wait. Buster was impatient to overtake Winston, and I gave him his head.

We discovered what I hoped was the western edge of the herd at nightfall. Lee was the eagle eye to spot a cow far to the east at the edge of a high ridgetop. It fed around and out of sight before I could raise my binoculars. I shrugged while we rode toward an area I hoped was a flat smooth place to pitch our tent. "At least we know where to start looking in the morning."

We erected our camp as light retreated and shadows grew to eventually be swallowed by approaching darkness. It didn't take long before the horses were picketed in grass already grazed down. Lee and I each saved a sandwich sent along by Davy, and we made ourselves comfortable to watch the western gleam disappear. Other than the occasional bird preparing itself for bed, the lack of sound gave rise to the feeling we were all that remained of life on earth. "So incredibly beautiful," Leeann spoke in a hushed tone after she snuggled into my side with a bottle of water.

Like her, I couldn't bring myself to speak in a normal tone. "I don't get tired of this." My whisper matched hers. "I've watched hundreds if not a thousand sunrises and sunsets from these mountaintops since getting my first horse. It was as important to...to Jess as it was to me to put the sun to bed at night and get it up in the morning."

An arm snaked around my back to squeeze. "If you don't mind, I'd like to fill her spot and enjoy them with you from now on."

I pulled Lee close and kissed her forehead. "I can't imagine anything better. She would've loved you."

"She was a part of you, and I can't envision not loving her back," Leeann said. "I feel I almost know her from the stories you and Zoe have told. Even Joe talked about her after you left me alone on the ranch. How much she was adored by not only you but the hands, too."

"We can't forget Danny, either. He was named after Mom's dad. I barely remember Grandpa since he and Grandma died when I was very young."

"So much pain and heartache for such a small family," Lee said. "You deserved none of it. If you'll let me, I'd like to make up for as much of it as I can."

I took a deep breath as the last sliver of red was consumed behind the horizon. "Will you marry me?"

She didn't hesitate. "Yes," Leeann answered quietly. "A thousand times yes."

* * *

Lee's tousled head appeared from within the tent as I filled my cup with hot coffee. A can of the pork and beans already warmed over a low flame on the stove. I loved how the first thing she did was step out and pull her Stetson on and then boots. "Something smells good," she said without taking her eyes from my cup.

"C'mon, I'll share with you."

She took her turn warming digits around the hot cup, while I dug to the bottom and stirred the beans with a steel spoon. It wasn't a lot to be split between us, but I wasn't particularly hungry. Java would go a long way in arresting my appetite. She got my attention when she giggled quietly. I looked to see her chocolate eyes dancing while sipping the hot jo. Her mouth widened into as much of a smile as her scar would allow. "Feels good to wear panties again."

Spit went down the wrong pipe when I swallowed during her declaration making me choke and cough, much to her delight. "You weren't kidding?" I sputtered.

Lee laughed out loud. "Nope! All of my underwear was abandoned when we left for the ranch."

I grimaced. "Must've been uncomfortable."

She wrinkled her nose and continued to grin and held the cup out to be filled again. "Not really. I was wearing boy's underwear. Well...men's." Her admission took me a moment to process before I caught on. She didn't miss my recognition. "Yep! I've been wearing your shorts. A little baggy in some places and too tight in others, but I've made them work."

"Jesus." I stirred the beans a last time and turned the stove off. "You never cease to surprise me."

"Hey, I'm pragmatic and make do where I have to. I sure as heck wasn't going to complain on a ranch filled with cowboys about not having underwear."

My turn to laugh. "Good call!" I handed her the warm can wrapped in a kerchief along with the spoon, while taking the coffee cup for myself. "Be sure to save some for me."

One thing I learned about Leeann: she approaches circumstances head on. Her gaze was direct and frank after swallowing a healthy bite. "Do you have a date in mind?"

I knew what she was asking. "Whenever you're ready and not a day sooner."

"I'm not a big fan of long engagements. A girl I know from high school has been living with her boyfriend over seven years. I hope you don't think you can string me along like that, mister."

Pulling her close by her lapels, I kissed her lips and tasted pork and beans. "Whenever you're ready. I don't care if it's the day after we get back to the ranch, next week, next month, or next year. Whatever you're most comfortable with."

"We've known each other for over a year. If we wait until next summer, people could say you're stringing me along. On the other hand, if we married before September, others might think we're too hasty."

I blew over my cup before sipping. "Since when did you worry about what other people think?"

Leeann grinned with a mouthful of beans and then swallowed. "Never! How does the second Saturday in September sound?"

"Too soon."

"What?" she yelped and slapped my shoulder. "Why?"

"I've got my reasons, and you'd know if you thought about it. How about a month later? Second Saturday in October."

We left camp where it was while saddling to check on the beef. Buster rolled his eyes in excitement when he felt my weight in the stirrup before I got seated. He humped a couple times—I think to let me appreciate his enthusiasm. I leaned forward to pat his neck and show my affection.

I knew what to expect but Leeann didn't. We crested the far ridge only to rein in. A shallow valley filled with cows lay below. As best as I could measure using Google Earth, it was roughly four miles long and almost two wide. With running water available, my beef would make themselves at home for an extended period. "Wow!" she exclaimed quietly. "They knew where they were going."

"The older ones remember. It's the young ones who concern me. Our lead cow is worth her weight in gold. She hasn't calved in two years but knows where the feed is. Must be...nine or ten years old. Cross referencing her ear tag would tell me for sure."

We rode the perimeter in a wide circle. A few strayed too far for my tastes. If trouble arose, they wouldn't stand a chance to reach the main body for protection. Lee and I pushed them closer as we went. Those bedded watched carefully as we passed, some rising to show aggressiveness and prove their calves wouldn't easily be taken by predators.

It required a significant portion of the day to work our way to the southern edge. Odd shapes ahead caught my attention, and I lifted my rifle clear of the scabbard. First, one animal rose warily to its feet, followed by six more. I levered the action of my .30-30 to load the chamber and glanced grimly to Leeann. If I wasn't angry, I might've smiled at the way she already gripped her .32-20. "C'mon." I'm not sure if I was talking to her or Buster, but we broke into a gallop to rush the pack of wolves, their muzzles slick with blood. "Hah!" I shouted. "Get the hell out of here!" Rather than show fear as he barreled toward the huge brutes, Buster's ears were laid back in our charge. Instead of weathering our onslaught, the beasts turned tail only to stop on a rise. I dismounted before Buster fully stopped and threw the reins to Lee. "Hold tight." Between Winston's reins, those I threw to her, and the rifle she held, her hands were full as I ran at the canines levering and shooting with each long step. They were gone before I fired my last cartridge in the direction of where they disappeared. I climbed the rise as I thumbed shells through the side port and loaded the chamber again. As I hoped, they were a half mile away and running hard. I shot into the air twice more as incentive against their return.

Leeann stood next to calf remains after I hiked back. Little was left of the poor animal once weighing over two hundred pounds. No doubt which cow was its mother. One stood closer than the rest as she watched with anxiety. "Did you hit any?" Lee asked.

"I wasn't trying. All we're allowed is to chase them away. Ranchers are given a green light only if it's a slaughter, or they're aggressive to people."

"Whew...glad I didn't shoot! I might've killed them all or at least most."

"Only if one of us carried a wolf tag, and I haven't purchased one this year." I thrust my loaded rifle into the scabbard again and mounted. "You know, I've seen your handiwork, and you're awfully confident of your shooting."

She slid her long gun into her own case. "I was first taught to use it when I was a little girl. Only gun I own or even shot."

We walked our horses toward the last few stragglers and pushed them closer to safety in numbers. "There's an old saying. 'Beware the man with one gun because he probably knows how to use it.' I think in this case we can safely say beware the woman with one gun."

Lee and I spent a last night in the rugged backcountry where we came together as one. Our loving was passionate, intense, and emotional. Finally, with half the night gone and our energy expended, she fell asleep in my arms as I considered the past and future. When I least expected or deserved it, love found and rescued a beaten and lost man who only wanted to move on to the next plane. Now, a woman I only dreamed of lay in my arms with the promise to take my name and build a life with me. The easy part was over. Time to get on with whatever destiny awaited.

* * *

We loaded our horses with what gear we could. I planned to send a couple cowboys back with packhorses to retrieve what got left behind. Our packing took longer than it should have—neither of us could pass the other without a caress or kiss. Love and affection pushed aside while I focused on an enemy who wanted to destroy me surged to the fore. Knowing we would build our life and family together overwhelmed me. Fiercely protective one moment, the next filled my heart with pride as I took time to watch Leeann work. She refused to shirk responsibility and wait for me. I loved how she jumped in to do her best without direction where possible.

Although we started our day at sunup, noon was an hour gone before we mounted. My goal was to reach ranch headquarters by supper. I didn't mind added gear slowing our trek home. Each moment I spent alone with Leeann was one I cherished. She was quiet and introspective, sometimes meeting my gaze with a shy smile. I suppose I wasn't any different. Our newfound intimacy was still in its infancy. I looked forward to our shared love growing and blossoming throughout our lives together.

Knowing Davy served supper at six sharp, a hasty glance at my watch worried me. Almost five when the ranch came into view, at least an hour of riding confronted us. My belly rumbled loud enough it caught Lee's attention. The shared breakfast was long gone.

Leeann reined in Winston and pointed. "Uh, Cable?"

I stopped Buster. "What do you see?"

"Am I looking at Deputy Norton's SUV or one like it?"

Retrieving field glasses from the saddlebags, I trained them on the headquarters. "Yeah. We've got company." Too many bodies made me nervous. My attack using detonation cord was a federal crime—one which could put me behind bars for decades. While I was no criminal mastermind, my actions were considered long and hard before I acted. I quietly feared the unknown and what I may have missed. A tire or foot track, perhaps even a camera I wasn't aware of was enough to make authorities sniff in my direction.

I pointed. "Why don't we cut toward the Michaels place and catch the north road back to the ranch? We can ease in without anyone the wiser."

Winston fell in next to Buster. "Do you think...I mean...could they have discovered something we missed?" she asked.

A deep breath calmed me. "I don't know. Best we're ready." I gave her a sharp look. "If Andy or any of law enforcement have evidence linking me to what happened, I want you to move back to Caroline's place, okay? No need for you to go down with me. Only you and me know what happened."

"No!" she replied indignantly. "I was a part of it, too."

It shames me, but I jerked Buster to a halt. He champed at the bit I hurt him with while I made myself clear. "We gain nothing if you spend the next twenty or more years in prison, Leeann. I'll pay the penalty while you live your life for both of us, understand?" She shook her head with her jaw set. "I'm serious, woman. Don't think I won't rope and leave you hogtied if I'm forced to." I used Buster's bulk to crowd Winston. "I'm not making an empty threat."

Chapter XIX

I left Leeann responsible for both horses on the far side of the barn north of the big house. Voices were plainly heard, but I couldn't make out their words. Angry tones and occasional shouts were easy to decipher as I worked my way behind first the bunkhouse and then the east barn. A little-used door opened after putting extra effort into it. Passing the room where we kept blasting caps and cannon fuse, I eased by Buster's empty stall to the front where I could see better.

My heart jumped when I realized the extreme seriousness of the situation. Deputies Norton and Hewitt were cuffed with their hands behind, and both were spread-eagled against the front fender and hood of their SUV. Four men and one woman I didn't recognize kept the cops, Z, Joe, and my cowboys under their guns. It didn't take a genius to see the Brotherhood somehow slipped past our defenses and caught us unprepared. With Andy and Hewitt under lock and key, I didn't doubt my enemies planned to leave everyone dead. While I'd taken deer out to a hundred yards with my Kimber, the kill zone was a foot square. With the Brotherhood in such close proximity to my family and friends, I wasn't comfortable taking headshots at half the distance. Not against five—not even two. I cursed myself for leaving my Winchester on Buster.

Zoe saw me first, and her wide eyes got bigger. Nothing to do but take the fight to them, and I strode from the barn with long deliberate steps to close the distance. My right arm swung lazily against my side to conceal my handgun for as long as possible. I was sure they would open fire immediately if I advanced with it in my hand. Fifty yards, forty, thirty, then twenty before a barked command: "Stop right there, Pearson. Not another step." A shotgun held by the woman was trained on my chest—one I guessed was Andy's riot pump. The man speaking wasn't whom I initially thought led the group. Instead of an unkempt long-bearded biker in leathers, he'd be far more comfortable in a three-piece suit. Hair cut in a flattop, his face was clean shaven. He gestured to his companions and spoke in a casual tone. "On their knees. I want them all on their knees."

I left my right thumb hooked in the top of my jeans pocket and gestured with the other. "Why? Can you tell me what you hope to gain from this?"

"Gain? You killed over sixty of my best friends and family. They burned to death." He paced, words growing to shouts before he stopped behind Zoe.

"What happened to bring me to California?" I asked.

"You were too cheap to buy your sister's and her rug rat's release. What's a few million to a family like yours? It would've been a tax write-off."

"A helluva lot to a rancher like me. I couldn't've raised fifty grand after beef prices cratered back then. You murdered my sister and nephew before my father could agree. Another day...two at most, and you'd have gotten your money. Goddamned money." I hawked and spat a goober. "There's what I think about grubbers like you."

Even from sixty feet, I could see maniacal light in his eyes. The guy wasn't all there. He suddenly raised a handgun and pointed it at the back of Z's skull. For a moment...a fleeting instant...I thought I'd faint. First Jess and Danny—now Zoe? It couldn't happen. I wouldn't allow it. "I'm going to end the Pearson lineage," he said.

Certain he'd kill without qualms, I needed to divert his attention. "Why?" I asked again. A second man stepped behind Joe, and a third in back of Davy. The woman with the shotgun shifted to cover Andy and Hewitt. "Damn it, answer me." When the leader of the Brotherhood grinned and made eye contact with me, I knew he was going to shoot and needed to make sure I watched.

Zoe stared at me, her features drained of color by both fear and shock. I'm sure she was certain her life was about to end and mouthed, *I love you.* Not ready to accept the end, time slowed as my body reacted. One moment my thumb was tucked in a pocket, the next my hand flashed for my Kimber. Years of repetition flooded back as it slid cleanly from the Kydex friction holster. My hand made solid contact, fingers wrapping into a tight grip, flicking the safety off with my thumb as the muzzle rose. With much of their bodies exposed behind kneeling victims, my targets seemed as big as barrels. Thrusting my gun forward, I squeezed the trigger the moment my eye looked over the sights. One to center mass, a second higher as the leader collapsed before I shifted the barrel minutely. Joe's anticipated executioner dropped at the sound of my gun, as did the next behind Davy without getting off a shot. Turning my 10mm toward the two remaining, I found only the woman standing—to collapse at the crack of a rifle to my rear. I spun and knelt, ready to return fire. Instead, Leeann sighted grimly down the barrel of her .32-20 as she searched for more targets.

Sprinting toward my sister and cowhands, I looked for signs of life from the brotherhood—not to render first aid but to finish the job. After kicking guns away from their inert bodies, I gave Z and my men help to stand on their feet. Davy was toughest because of his bodyweight, causing me to first cut his bindings with my jackknife. "Any others?" I asked.

Joe answered while he waited for me to sever the zip ties around his wrists. "No, this's it."

I turned to Z and took her in my arms. "You okay, sis?"

"They said they were going to kill us. All of us," she cried against my chest.

"You're not hurt, are you?" I watched over her head as Joe unlocked first Andy's, then Hewitt's handcuffs.

Zoe shook and clung desperately. She would never come closer to death, and I perceived the shock she endured. "No, scared is all."

I looked for Lee, only to find her watching from where she leaned against the barn with a hand in her pocket and her rifle hanging loosely from the other. Prying myself from Z's grip, I led her to the barn with an arm around her shoulder. My fiancée's mouth twisted with emotion to mirror my sister's when they embraced.

"Great shooting, Leeann," I said quietly. "Couldn't've done it without you."

Her face swollen with grief, Lee pulled away from Zoe to face me and took my hands in hers She smiled through tears. "What did I pledge to you not long ago? I meant every word when I made the promise."

I frowned while trying to remember. "I...I'm not sure."

"I said always bet on me, Cable. You'll never regret it."

Her vow after we made peace between us flooded back. "You certainly did. I apologize for my faulty memory."

She hugged me, then included Z in our embrace. We were allowed only seconds before Sheriff Norton interrupted. "Cable? Could I have a few words with you?"

Both Lee and my sister followed me to where he waited at the open door of his cruiser. "Is this where you read my rights and cuff me, Andy?" The two officers were now privy to much of the story between my family and the Brotherhood.

"We've got state patrol, county, and medics headed this way. Can we talk in the big house?"

"Joe?" I waved him to us. "You might want to come along. Z and Leeann, too."

Andy spoke low to his partner. "Don't let anyone touch or move the bodies. Make sure the WJP cowboys stay here. No one talks before I'm back, okay? I mean you, too." Deputy Hewitt frowned before nodding.

Zoe made coffee while the rest of us got comfortable around the table. Leeann sat close enough our shoulders touched and her palm rested on my thigh. "Don't string me along," I said to Andy. "How bad does it look?"

"I've got a question first," he said. "How in the hell did you do it? I shoot regularly, not just to qualify, but with men and women who're at the top of our field. What you did out there defies physics. His gun was aimed with his finger on the trigger. It's impossible to beat."

I shook my head. "Not impossible, my friend. Reaction time is everything. My hand was moving before his brain could perceive motion. Then, his choice was to follow through shooting Zoe, or save his life by turning his gun on me. I didn't give him time to make a decision. My hand rested next to my pistol, and I made the first move. The others took their cues from him and he was dead. My biggest worry was missing the kill zone."

"Makes sense, but I've never watched a fast gun work." Andy redirected his sharp gaze to Leeann. "Great shooting. The woman was ordered to use my shotgun to kill Sal and me." His brows went up before turning his attention back to me and nodding at Lee.

She wept silently when I turned to her, a steady cascade of tears already dripped from her chin. I pulled her to me and held her close. "It's okay," I whispered.

"N-n-no i-it isn't. I-I've n-never shot anyone before. I've never killed anything."

"You saved our lives," Andy said quietly. "Most or all of us would be dead if you weren't willing."

"It's a bitter pill to swallow, but it gets better," I crooned in her ear. "I promise." Rubbing her back seemed to help with her sobs. She didn't answer but held on for dear life instead. Other than her, the room was silent but for the loud clearing of Joe's throat and Z who'd started hiccupping.

"I couldn't be prouder if you were my own flesh and blood, girl," Joe said. "You, too, boy."

Leeann knew the story of Joe's decades old habit of calling me boy and Jess girl, and her weeping intensified at his praise. If our freedom was about to be snatched away, at least she got the opportunity to become an important part of our family, including the protection coming with it. Z came around the table to offer her support. "You both saved me...saved all of us. Anyone could have stayed hidden but not you. Instead, you appeared from the corner of the barn as if an avenging angel and gave us a new lease on life. Don't cry, Leeann. Be proud. Be as proud as I am to call you sister."

Andy, Joe, and I sipped our coffee quietly and allowed their already strong bond to grow tighter. Finally, Lee blurted our secret. "Cable asked me to marry him!"

"He did?" Zoe said, and pushed back holding Lee's hands. "I hoped he was smart enough! Let me be the first to formally welcome you into the Pearson family."

* * *

With Hewitt's help, Andy saved my bacon by purposely overlooking the short conversation concerning the Brotherhood's murder of my sister and nephew along with my swift retaliation. The deputies were taken hostage during an interrogation at the park where those bikers remaining in Montana were again camped outside of town. Neither officer was given an opportunity to radio for help due to handguns pressed against their heads. Once on the ranch with my cowboys caught by surprise, the gang prepared for the executions of all they could find. Only Leeann and I returning stopped what was sure to be a bloodbath.

Z found Leeann and me on the porch swing after law enforcement departed. She sat across from us in a wicker chair. "I've been on the phone with Olivia Justice. Her team is going to investigate the Brotherhood since the head has been cut off. She plans to hire more investigators and field at least two dozen on the case."

I whistled. "Gonna be expensive."

Zoe stared, lips a flat line crossing her face. "By all rights I should be dead. All of us should be at the morgue. Money means nothing at this point. I want to know what they plan if and when the remaining gang reconstitutes." I could see her anger when we made eye contact. "Dad agrees. Sky's the limit."

"He knows what happened?" I asked.

She nodded. "We spoke for over an hour. Putting Olivia on the case was his idea."

"What else did you tell him?"

Zoe squinted and made a face. "He knows everything, William. From the time you resurfaced after shooting Leeann's brother to now."

Her smile was tight without mirth. "We have these new technological doodads called cellphones. He and I talk regularly."

I was in no mood. "Funny."

"Funny or not, we've stayed in constant contact since I'd been here, except while I rode and camped with you."

"How much longer do you plan to stay?"

"Have you decided on a wedding date?"

Leeann answered for us. "The second Saturday in October."

"This year?" Z asked.

"Yes."

"I'd like to stay until after. Help in any way I can with your plans if you'll let me."

Her revelation excited Leeann. "Oh, yes, I'd love it!"

My sister turned her attention to me, suddenly serious. "Dad'll want to come, you know."

I sighed. "I know."

"You have to let him, Cable," Lee said. "You have to. I'm sure my parents will be here, too."

"Have you spoken to them since what happened to your brother?"

She nodded. "They were angry with you...and me by default because I defended what you did. We didn't speak again after I provided testimony in your favor, but Damien was being released and Caroline offered me a chance to stay at their ranch again. So much happened in only a few hours. We didn't talk again until a few weeks later."

I nodded to Z. "He can come if he wants. I suppose you'll return to New York with him?"

"Only for a while. I need time to sell my apartment and move my things to Montana."

I welcomed her news. I needed family again. "Move back? To the ranch?"

She nodded. "If you'll have me. Otherwise, I can find a place in Butte, Bozeman, or Missoula. Don't want to crimp your style."

"You're welcome to stay here. I don't know about Lee, but I'd prefer it."

Leeann nodded. "I'd love it!"

Z jerked her chin toward the house. "All of us one happy family?"

I laughed and gave voice to a thought. "No, you can take the big house. Too many ghosts for me. If she doesn't mind, I thought Lee and I could break ground and start building our own place in the spring." A kiss on my cheek was answer enough. Time to begin a new chapter in our lives.

* * *

Our grand jury didn't indict us, so by the end of August, Andy informed Leeann and me the county attorney dropped all charges against those involved at the ranch. Although the girls spent hours each day planning our upcoming nuptials, neither missed a day in the saddle. Sweltering conditions meant making sure pumps kept water flowing to cattle on the ranch without fail. Lynn and Gary stayed with the herd in the Snowcrest Range to keep springs open and the cows safe and happy. Joe and I rode together and helped anywhere extra hands were needed. He'd been uncharacteristically quiet since we learned Leeann and I avoided court.

We were tightening fencing on the Michaels place with a come-a-long. He took a last staple held between his lips and pounded it tight before tossing the hammer into the bed of the truck. "She doesn't take Jess's place, y'know."

"Huh?" I'd been thinking about an evening ride on Buster.

"Leeann. It's nice to have a woman on the ranch again, but she doesn't take Jess's place," he repeated.

I could see my sister in my mind's eye, hair flowing behind as we raced our horses down the driveway. She loved to win, and I didn't mind when she did. Her laughter at crossing the finish line first made losing worthwhile. Our Jess, always smiling, laughing, and spontaneous, her eyes flashing with undisguised joy. "No, she certainly doesn't," I said quietly. "Lee's different. Quieter and more deliberate, I guess."

"Don't get me wrong, boy. Your girl's a wonderful woman. I can't imagine a better match for you. The way she looks at you when you don't know it..." He stopped and whistled. "You're a lucky man."

I tossed Joe a bottle of cold water from the cooler and made myself comfortable on the tailgate. "She saved my life."

He cracked the top and took a long pull, almost finishing the container. "Jess would've loved her. Jessica...your mom...would've been right proud. She lived for you kids."

"I wish...I wish they both could have met her."

"Zoe needs her as much as you. Don't reckon your sister understood it until they linked up. I wish you could have seen your sister's shock when I introduced 'em. Didn't take but a day or two before their heads were together plannin' and plottin' against you. It's why I let the pair of 'em help push the cattle into the Snowcrest. Why put off the inevitable? You didn't stand a chance, boy."

"You were supposed to work her hard enough to run her back to Colorado," I reminded.

He laughed. "I tried! Thing is she took everything I dished out and asked for more. You know I put her to cleanin' ditches and diggin' out culverts with a spade? Even set her up to fill potholes in the driveway. Never complained, not once. Sometimes, she could barely drag her ass to the supper table. I felt guilty as hell, but you're the boss."

"Something I've been wanting to bring up. You did a great job running the ranch while I was in Colorado. We're further into the black than ever before. I need to show my appreciation."

"I can't take all the credit," Joe said. "Cattle prices have been good."

"It's easy to run an operation into the dirt. You know it better than me."

"You got a good place here, boy. Jessica knew what she was doin' when she talked your old man into buyin' the ranch for her."

"I've already spoken to Zoe and my lawyer. Papers are being drawn up giving you five percent of the ranch. A fifty percent bump in your salary goes with it."

My cow boss jerked back and stared in surprise. "Boy—" Unable to respond, he turned away.

"You've earned every bit of it, Joe. Mom always said hiring you was her best decision. She'd be proud knowing what you've helped build."

I gave him privacy by loading our tools and spools of barbed wire. Sounded like he put his kerchief to good use with all the sniffing and honking. I leaned against the cab and waited. His nose was still running and eyes red-rimmed when he turned. "Can't thank you enough, Cable. Truly I can't. Ain't never owned nothin' before in my life. Not in my wildest dreams did I imagine this."

"You deserve it. Remember," I joked. "Five percent isn't worth much if the ranch doesn't make money. Then, there's wages to come out of it, insurance and maintenance take a big bite..."

"Christ," Joe interrupted with a groan and wink. "Is it too late to give it all back?"

* * *

Lee and I married in the orchard behind the big house on a beautiful October afternoon. It frosted overnight but warmed into the mid sixties by the time her father walked her from the house to where I waited with friends and family and a preacher from Dillon I'd never met. While not overtly hostile, Mr. and Mrs. Slater weren't friendly. I got the feeling they attended our wedding out of duty rather than love. Damien stayed away, but both Lee and I were overjoyed to welcome her younger brother's arrival. Home on leave from the Navy, Nicholas ran to his sister, swept her from the ground, and administered a warm kiss. I was happy for my bride-to-be. In the weeks leading up to our planned nuptials, she worried none of her family would attend.

Nicky, as Lee called him, greeted me with a strong grip and piercing gaze. "I wanted to meet the man who won my sister's heart," he said. "It needed to be someone who could see the person she is within, rather than her outside beauty."

She backhanded her brother's shoulder. "Nicky," she admonished.

"He's right," I told her before directing my answer to him. "It was her toughness and willingness to fight for what she knew was good. Not once did she attempt to take the easy way. Your sister is one of the toughest people I've met in my life."

Lee left her brother's side, took my arm, and leaned her head against my shoulder. He squinted and then smiled before nodding.

"You've grown, Leeann. You're far surer of yourself." He didn't mention the altercation between Damien and me, although Leeann assured me he knew.

We got visitors Friday afternoon before our big day. A pickup I saw only once made its way up our dusty drive as I rode in on Buster. We'd spent much of the day on the Michaels place where I could check fences after selling and shipping 2241 head of beef. Prices were down, but Joe and I shook hands with the buyer after agreeing at $1.06 per pound. After running them across the scales, the average cow loaded on the truck weighed 550. Alfalfa and hayfields were cut and rolled bales, much of it left in the field, although a portion was stacked in the east barn.

I walked Buster out of the way to let the truck park. The passenger side burst open as I stepped from the saddle. "Cable!" Although stove-up from sitting, Caroline hobbled her way to meet me as the driver's door opened. She didn't hesitate in wrapping her arms around me. "I've missed you. God, I've missed and thought about you every day. We both have." Her shoulders shook while I held her.

Annie waited her turn with a grin after seeing my surprise. I barely recognized her with hair dyed blue. Obviously, she was going to have a different color each time we met. "I've missed you, too, Caroline. Whenever I walk to the barn and hear Buster's nicker, I'm taken back to Colorado."

She pulled away. "Oh, Buster," she said and rubbed his forehead. "I hope you're being treated like you deserve."

Zoe and Leeann came from the big house to stand next to Annie in time to hear Caroline. "I'll never ask him to choose between his horse and me, Caroline," Lee said. "You'd think Buster was his lapdog to be petted and spoiled."

Caroline turned in surprise. "Leeann!"

Zoe stood to the side and watched our reunion. More than a few tears were shed by the ladies while we reconnected. I finally motioned my sister to join us. "Caroline, I'd like you to meet my sister. Zoe, this's Caroline and her daughter Annie."

"I've wanted to meet after hearing so much about you," Caroline said. "It was Cable with your help who saved our ranch. We couldn't have done it alone."

My sister didn't hesitate to embrace them both. "Thank Cable. He made us aware, and I did what I could on my end."

"Oh, we have," Caroline said. "Many, many times."

Driving the same truck as I'd seen Annie in earlier in the year made me curious. "Were you able to tap into the oil reserves found under your land?"

Both ladies grinned. "Drilling began last month," Annie said. "Too soon to say how much can be pumped, but we're told it won't be long until it's coming up."

"I'm glad," I said. "After what you were put through, no one deserves it more than you gals."

Zoe and Leeann took Annie and their suitcases into the big house where they'd be staying. Caroline pointed into the Snowcrest Range behind the ranch. "It's beautiful, Cable. We hated to see you leave, but now I see one of the reasons. I'll bet Buster is well acquainted with the high country now, isn't he?"

As if he knew he was being talked about, Buster nosed me from behind to make me lurch forward, then rested his chin on my shoulder. Bristles posing as whiskers poked and tickled my neck. "He knows every inch. We explored and then stayed with the cattle for weeks this summer. I can never thank you enough for allowing him and me to bond. He's the horse of a lifetime, Caroline."

She wrapped her arms around my midsection and squeezed. "To know your life is squared away is thanks enough," she said. "I never worried and prayed over someone as much as I did with you. The Lord answered."

"It seems you wield powerful invocations. I'm glad you were on my side."

Caroline looked up. "I saw something the first time we met. Even as awful as Annie was to you, the moment you found our mare in distress and what needed done, I knew you were a good man. There was no hesitation in you until the job was done."

"How is little Stranger?" I asked.

She pulled back to stroke Buster's neck. "Not so little anymore. He's gentle and should make a wonderful addition to our remuda in a couple years. You know why I called him Stranger, don't you?"

I'd never given it any thought. "No, ma'am."

"After you."

"Me?"

"I didn't know you at the time...not even your name, and thought Stranger appropriate. I think of you each time I call him." Her simple logic made me chuckle, although after getting to know her, Caroline's reasoning was sound. Our future together was one neither of us could have anticipated and for sure not something I desired at the time. Yet we came together as employer and employee to look after one another and set a course for futures free of strife, and our lives were better for knowing the other.

Chapter XX

Leann reined in Winston when I stopped Buster and turned him to see where we'd started. The ranch was long out of sight, but I wanted to look west. Already early afternoon, daylight faded quickly in mid-October. Purdy and two of my packhorses seemed grateful for the rest. The sky was clear, and temperatures in the high country dipped precariously. I didn't think our chances of missing the season's first snowfall was good. A two-week honeymoon in a wall tent took us into early November. With the ranch doing well, I offered to fly my bride anywhere in the world to celebrate our nuptials. She flat turned me down and confided her dream was to spend our first weeks alone in the mountains. "Almost there." I nodded my head to the ridge above. "Big Buck Mountain is what Jess and I called it."

Lee knew the story and gauged the steep and partially timbered slope above. "Will we have time to erect the wall tent before dark? Get the stove set up inside and gather enough wood for a fire?" Temperatures would be uncomfortable without a hot blaze.

"Only if we keep moving." I touched Buster's ribs with my heels to urge him on.

Z questioned my choice of camping sites after I let her and Joe know where I planned to set up base. "Are you sure, William?"

She gave voice to a concern plaguing me. It was the last location Jess, Danny, and I camped before they were taken and ultimately lost their lives, and other than the big house, where I felt their presence strongest. "I have to. I need them to meet Leeann and let them know I'm carrying on with my life again."

"You seem awful sure they keep watch."

I closed my lids at her comment, remembering both Jess and Danny in my mind's eye as I last saw them. Both were unhappy and urged me to stay within the land of the living. "Trust me on this," I said seriously. "They are."

Two and a half hours of light remained when we reached our destination. A high lake lay a half mile farther up the mountain and provided a bubbly spring fifty feet from where we'd camp. I brought fishing rods and a can filled with worms dug from the ranch manure pile. The trout were small in size but in plentiful numbers. Thoughts of a crispy panful made my mouth water.

We worked fast after dismounting and unloading our supplies. I cut poles for our wall tent, while Lee unfolded the canvas where I showed her. Although late in the season, enough browse for our mounts remained. I planned to bring them in close at night—easier to keep them safe from predators strong enough to take down a twelve-hundred pound horse. They would alert us to both marauding wolf packs and hungry grizzly.

At least a half hour of light remained when our home away from home was ready. A smudge built in the stove already warmed the interior. Another outside in the firepit grew in size as we both fed it limbs and knots. We'd spoken little, except with our actions. A touch or a kiss as we passed showed how much we cared. Lee squatted across the growing blaze from me, her elbows braced on her knees. "Thank you for speaking to your father and introducing us. Zoe appreciated your efforts, too."

"Was he what you expected?"

"I didn't have expectations," she said. "He's the father of my husband, and I wanted to meet him, warts and all."

Perhaps Zoe warned him, but my dad limited his time near me. We spoke briefly and shook hands when he arrived and again before his car returned to drive him and Z to the airport. Leeann seemed to captivate his attention during his brief stay, and I left them to converse without me. According to my sister, he remained aware I continued to hold him responsible a notch below the Brotherhood for the deaths of my sister and nephew. "What'd you learn?"

She gnawed at a lip and pushed more fuel into the fire. "He loves you and Zoe with all his heart. You're all he could talk about, other than the terrible mistake he made that cost Jess and Danny their lives."

Zoe told me much the same. It would take time before I could let go of my bitter hostility, although it seemed to recede as time passed. "What about your folks? Did you reconnect?"

Leeann thought a moment before nodding. "I think so. It helped when they got to meet and realize you didn't breathe fire."

"I miss Caroline already," I said. "We need to visit often."

"We do," Lee said seriously before I saw a twinkle. "What about Annie? Don't you miss her, too?"

I gave a mock shudder. "It's hard to think of her as anyone but the woman who made my life miserable. Been nice since she's come around."

"She feels terrible about how she treated you. Not only her, but Caroline talked about it while I stayed with them." Lee grinned. "Once you were sober, clean, and working hard, she kind of fell for you. Did you know that?"

I couldn't hide my horror. "Annie? My next shudder was real. "She might be pretty, but you never know the form she'll take the next time."

Leeann laughed out loud. "That's what she told me you'd say. You may also be interested in a thank-you she asked me to relay. I hope you understand better than me. Something about thanks for saving her bacon behind the machine shed when you punched someone in the dark?"

Somehow, Annie knew it was me. Either by my walk, or she caught a glimpse in the low light. Apparently, she didn't tell Caroline. To learn she always knew made me chuckle. "I wondered if she recognized me. A dude pinned her against a wall in an attempt to show how much he admired her. It was after dark, and the barnyard floodlight didn't reach. With no way for her to escape, I clobbered him on my way to the trailer without slowing." I tossed a couple bigger pieces on the fire and stood, brushing my knees free of twigs and dirt. Feeling my breast pocket I knew it was time or I'd lose my courage. "There's something I've got to do. Mind tagging along?"

Lee didn't hesitate and stood quickly, not voicing the question in her eyes. Already she knew me well enough to feel the powerful emotions washing over me. "Anything," she said.

After lighting a lantern to hang from a tree and another to go inside the tent, I took her hand as we climbed to a knoll. A ring of rocks within a wide flat area signified an old campfire, one I cooked over many times. A pine on the backside was my objective. I knelt and fumbled inside my pocket, withdrawing a photo I'd laminated. Using two thumb tacks, I pressed them deeply to secure the picture against the trunk. Leaning back on my heels, I couldn't help but remember the day. Jess held Danny in her arms as I snapped a selfie of us all. My nephew grinned for the camera while my sister's lips were pressed against his cheek. Her eyes were closed, and it was impossible not to feel her love. My cheesy grin would be wiped away within weeks. The image was taken almost exactly where I knelt. Leeann made herself comfortable next to me. "You were beautiful," she said. "All three of you. So happy—" My wife trailed off while she looked closer. "It was here. You took it with your backs to the pine!"

"Jess...Danny...I—" My voice cracked, and it took a minute to regain my composure. "I did what you asked and didn't follow. Can't lie...I really wanted to. You were right in telling me I needed to stay. It's safe to say we can thank the woman next to me for giving me a reason to live."

Leeann scooted closer until we touched and her arm went around my shoulders. "I married her yesterday, sis. You'd both love her—" My voice broke again, and I took the time to wipe my face with a kerchief. Two deep breaths allowed me to continue. "Anyway, I thought it was time for you to meet. Jess, Danny, I'd like to introduce you to my wife, Leann. Lee, my sister and nephew."

Leann kissed two fingers and pressed them against the photo. "I wish we could have met," she said. "We'd have been sisters. Please don't worry. I'll do everything in my power to keep Cable safe and make your brother and uncle happy."

I stood and drew Lee up with me. "Don't concern yourself about the ranch, Jess. It's doing fine. Old Joe turned into a helluva businessman. We're keeping the wolves at bay, too, so you wouldn't have needed to ride the range. Oh, and Z's coming home. She'll be in the big house if either of you feel the need to check on her."

It was tough to see the picture any longer without a flashlight. "We'll look in on you from time to time," I whispered into the darkness. Life is for the living, and I was done wasting it.

A gentle breeze raised, caressing our cheeks and reaching inside my collar. If I didn't know any better, I might suppose it resulted from Jess and Danny waving goodbye. I could only marvel as we gazed down the slope at our lighted camp, my arm around my new wife. While an important part of my life was ripped away, it was filled again with the mate of a lifetime. I took Leann's hand, kissed the back of it, and we hiked carefully until reaching our tent. I lifted the canvas to let her inside first and enjoyed a familiar nicker before following.

Our lives lay ahead, and I looked forward to the challenge of meeting it head-on with my wife at my side.